THE STEPS TO THE EMPTY THRONE

Robert the Bruce, both Norman lord and Celtic earl, is one of the great heroic figures of all time. But he was not always a hero—as he was not always a king. He grew towards both under the shadow of a still greater hero—William Wallace—in that terrible forcing-ground of heroism and treachery alike, the Wars of Independence which, from 1296 to 1314, hammered Scotland into the very dust until only the enduring idea of freedom remained to her.

Edward Longshanks, King of England, was the Hammer of the Scots, a great man gone wrong, a magnificent soldier flawed by consuming hatred and lust for power.

These two fought out their desperate, appalling duel, with Scotland as prize—should any of Scotland survive.

Not only these. To John Comyn, Lord of Badenoch, head of the most powerful house in Scotland and nephew of the deposed and discredited King John Baliol, Bruce was as spark to tinder. Their friction blazed to flame that shocking day when blood soaked the high altar at Dumfries, and a new Bruce was born. But this tremendous story is not all blood and fire. Elizabeth de Burgh saw to that. Humour and laughter are here too, colour and beauty, faith and love.

This enormous and ambitious theme of Bruce the hero king is no light challenge for a writer. Nigel Tranter has waited through nearly thirty years of novel-writing to tackle it. In this, the first of a trilogy, he ends that long apprenticeship and takes up the challenge.

Robert The Bruce

The Steps to the Empty Throne

The First of a Trilogy of Novels

Nigel Tranter

CORONET BOOKS
Hodder and Stoughton

Copyright © 1969 by Nigel Tranter

First published 1969 by Hodder & Stoughton Ltd.

Coronet edition 1971
Twelfth impression 1984

Printed and bound in Great Britain for
Hodder and Stoughton Paperbacks, a
division of Hodder and Stoughton Ltd.,
Mill Road, Dunton Green, Sevenoaks,
Kent (Editorial Office: 47 Bedford
Square, London, WC1 3DP) by
Cox & Wyman Ltd., Reading

ISBN 0 340 15098 X

When, in 1286, the well-beloved Alexander the Third, King of Scots, fell over a Fife cliff to his untimely death, he left utter disaster behind him for his country. His only surviving heir was an infant grandchild, a girl—and a foreign girl at that, and sickly, Margaret the Maid of Norway, daughter of his own daughter who had married the King of Norway and died leaving only this baby. There could have been no less suitable monarch for turbulent Scotland—and almost immediately the dynastic feuding and designing began.

There were innumerable far-out claimants to the throne, mainly descendants of the three daughters of David, Earl of Huntingdon, younger brother of King William the Lion. Of all these, the two with undoubtedly the most valid claims to be next in line to the little Maid of Norway were Robert Bruce, 5th Lord of Annandale, and John Baliol. The former was the son of Earl David's daughter Isabel; the latter the grandson of her elder sister Margaret. Baliol's father was an English lord, his mother the famous Devorgilla, Lady of Galloway, founder of Baliol College, Oxford.

Robert Bruce lost no time in making his position clear. With his son, the sixth Robert, who had married the Celtic Countess of Carrick in her own right, another Galloway heiress, he invaded that wild and beautiful province of South-West Scotland against the Baliol interests now established there. And with success. In the civil war old Bruce—he was then seventy-six—won most of the province, including the royal castles of Wigtown and Dumfries (then considered part of Galloway) and the Baliol seat of Buittle, former headquarters of the ancient Lords of Galloway. He was now well placed to exert suitable influence on the child monarch when she should appear; and meantime to dominate Scotland.

Two events conspired to confound his plans. Edward the First, puissant warrior King of England, perceived a notable opportunity to take over Scotland as a vassal kingdom, by marrying his young son to the infant Maid—who was indeed his own grandniece—and moved to that effect, at the Treaty of Birgham. Then, the same year, 1290, the said Maid died at Orkney, on her pathetic way to her new kingdom.

All was changed. Edward had placed himself in a position of political and military power, on the Border. Scotland was leaderless and disunited, the competitors for the empty throne balanced between civil war ind invasion.

Edward acted shrewdly. Dissimulating his own ambitions, he offered to preserve the peace by acting as honest broker. If the claimants to the Scots crown would submit their cases to him, he would act fair arbiter and so save strife.

It must be remembered that at this stage Scotland and England were good friends. The long centuries of warring had not yet started. Most of the Scots nobles owned lands in England, and *vice versa*—indeed they were nearly all equally Norman-French in origin. Edward was the foremost prince of Christendom, renowned, admired. His offer was accepted.

The Plantagenet, for his own purposes, in 1292 chose John Baliol as King of Scots. And, as an afterthought to the judgement, announced that he himself was Lord Paramount of Scotland.

Thereafter, for four inglorious years, the weak Baliol attempted to rule a restive Scotland whilst suffering Edward's dominance. This was no theoretical overlordship. Grimly, saxagely, Edward rubbed his puppet's nose in the dirt. He summoned him to London to give accounts of his stewardship; even had him arraigned before the King's Bench of England for judgement, like any criminal. At length, in 1296, even Baliol revolted, and taking to arms, made a mutual support treaty with France, also suffering from Edward's oppression. The English invaded Scotland in overwhelming strength. The Bruces, and many like them, did not support Baliol – they never had done. The puppet-king fell, and Edward Longshanks was master of Scotland, at last.

Old Bruce, the Competitor, was now dead, and his son the sixth Lord of Annandale no warrior, though proud enough to have resigned his earldom of Carrick to his own eldest son, another Robert, aged twenty-two, rather than make fealty for it to Baliol.

The new Earl of Carrick was a very different character. Robert the Bruce is one of the great heroic figures of all time. But he was not always a hero—just as he was not always a king. He grew towards both, indeed, under the shadow of a still greater hero—William Wallace—in the terrible forcing-ground of heroism and treacher alike, the Wars of Independence which, thereafter until 1314, hammered and ground Scotland into the very dust, until only the faintest flicker of stubborn hope and the enduring idea of freedom remained to her. But hammered her into one equally enduring and undivided nation, nevertheless. Edward, King of England, was the Hammer of the Scots indeed, a great man gone wrong, a magnificent soldier flawed by a consuming hatred and a lust for power. Against this backcloth, young Robert Bruce and Edward Plantagenet, linked most strangely by a sort of mutual understanding and reluctant admiration, played out their desperate, appalling game, with Scotland as the prize—if there was to be any Scotland left at the end of it.

But not only these two. Almost as important was Sir John Comyn the Red, Lord of Badenoch, head of the most powerful house in Scotland and nephew of the fallen and discredited King John Baliol. To him Robert Bruce was as a spark to tinder—and well Edward knew it, and shrewdly blew on that spark until it should be a flame that should burn more fiercely than all the other fires he lit to turn Scotland to ashes; a dire conflagration that burned on in Bruce's heart long after the shocking day when blood soaked the high altar at Dumfries and a new Bruce was born.

But this tremendous story is not all blood and fire, battle and treachery. There is humour and laughter too, colour and beauty, faith and love—love of men and of women, beyond all telling. And pride—pride and a great ideal, when all else was gone.

PRINCIPAL CHARACTERS

In Order of Appearance

KING EDWARD THE FIRST: King of England; Hammer of the Scots.

ANTHONY BECK, BISHOP OF DURHAM: Capt. General of St. Cuthbert.

ROBERT BRUCE, EARL OF CARRICK: eldest son of Lord of Annandale.

JOHN BALIOL, KING OF SCOTS.

JOHN COMYN, EARL OF BUCHAN: High Constable of Scotland.

ROBERT BRUCE, LORD OF ANNANDALE AND CLEVELAND: son of the "Competitor".

LORD NIGEL BRUCE: third son of above

LADY ELIZABETH DE BURGH: daughter of the Earl of Ulster.

RICHARD DE BURGH, EARL OF ULSTER: friend and companion of Edward.

GARTNAIT, EARL OF MAR: brother-in-law of Bruce.

GILBERT DE CLARE, EARL OF GLOUCESTER: son-in-law of Edward and kinsman of Bruce.

SIR JOHN COMYN, LORD OF BADENOCH: head of the great Comyn family, and kinsman of Buchan.

SIR NICHOLAS SEGRAVE: an English knight and captain.

MASTER JOHN BENSTEAD: Clerk, and Keeper of King Edward's Pantry.

ELEANOR DE LOUVAIN, LADY DOUGLAS: second wife of Sir William Douglas.

JAMES DOUGLAS: heir of Sir William, later "The Good Sir James".

SIR WILLIAM DOUGLAS: 5th lord thereof.

LORD JAMES STEWART: High Steward of Scotland.

MASTER ROBERT WISHART, BISHOP OF GLASGOW: patriot.

SIR ALEXANDER LINDSAY, LORD OF CRAWFORD.

SIR JOHN DE GRAHAM OF DUNDAFF: one of the few noblemen who supported Wallace.

SIR ANDREW DE MORAY, LORD OF BOTHWELL: heir of Moravia.

WILLIAM WALLACE: second son of Sir Malcolm Wallace of Elderslie, a small laird and vassal of the Steward.

ALEXANDER SCRYMGEOUR: one of Wallace's band. Later Standard-Bearer.

SIR HENRY PERCY, LORD OF NORTHUMBERLAND: nephew of Surrey the English commander.

SIR ROBERT CLIFFORD, LORD OF BROUGHAM: an English baron.

LORD EDWARD BRUCE: second son of Annandale. Later King of Ireland.

MASTER WILLIAM COMYN: Provost of the Chapel-Royal. Brother of Buchan.

MASTER WILLIAM LAMBERTON: Chancellor of Glasgow Cathedral. Later Bishop of St. Andrews and Primate.

LADY MARJORY BRUCE: child daughter of Bruce.

LADY CHRISTIAN BRUCE, COUNTESS OF MAR: second daughter of Annandale. Later wife of Sir Christopher Seton.

MARGARET OF FRANCE, QUEEN: second wife of King Edward.

SIR JOHN DE BOTETOURT: bastard son of Edward. Warden of the West March.

JOHN OF BRITTANY, EARL OF RICHMOND: nephew of Edward and Lieutenant of Scotland.

SIR JOHN STEWART OF MENTEITH: second son of Earl of Menteith and Governor of Dumbarton Castle.

SIR CHRISTOPHER SETON: a Yorkshire knight married to Lady Christian Bruce.

SIR ROGER KIRKPATRICK OF CLOSEBURN: a Bruce vassal.

ABBOT HENRY OF SCONE: custodian of the Stone of Destiny.

ISABEL, COUNTESS OF BUCHAN: daughter of MacDuff, Earl of Fife, and wife of the High Constable.

AYMER DE VALENCE, EARL OF PEMBROKE: English commander.

THE DEWAR OF THE COIGREACH: hereditary custodian of St. Fillan's crozier, in Glendochart.

THE HOUSE OF BRUCE

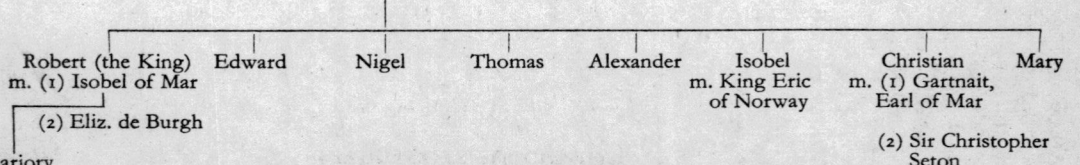

Robert de Brus or Brux, Lord of Cleveland 1st Lord of Annandale c. 1124

Robert 2nd Lord (fought at Battle of Standard 1138)

Robert 3rd Lord m. illeg. d. King William the Lion

Robert 4th Lord m. Isabel d. of David, Earl of Huntingdon, b. of William the Lion

Robert 5th Lord ("The Competitor") m. Isabel de Clare, d. Earl of Gloucester

Robert 6th Lord m. Marjory, Countess of Carrick

Robert (the King) Edward Nigel Thomas Alexander Isobel Christian Mary
m. (1) Isobel of Mar   m. King Eric m. (1) Gartnait,
    (2) Eliz. de Burgh   of Norway   Earl of Mar
Marjory   (2) Sir Christopher
                                                                          Seton

THE SCOTS SUCCESSION

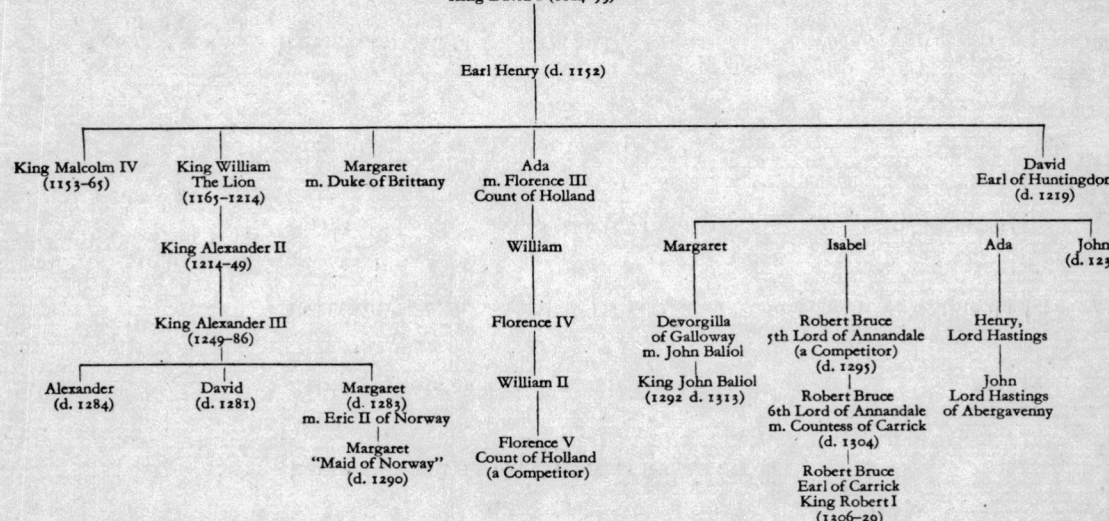

King David I (1124–53)
│
Earl Henry (d. 1152)

- King Malcolm IV (1153–65)
- King William The Lion (1165–1214)
  - King Alexander II (1214–49)
    - King Alexander III (1249–86)
      - Alexander (d. 1284)
      - David (d. 1281)
      - Margaret (d. 1283) m. Eric II of Norway
        - Margaret "Maid of Norway" (d. 1290)
- Margaret m. Duke of Brittany
- Ada m. Florence III Count of Holland
  - William
    - Florence IV
      - William II
        - Florence V Count of Holland (a Competitor)
- David Earl of Huntingdon (d. 1219)
  - Margaret
    - Devorgilla of Galloway m. John Baliol
      - King John Baliol (1292 d. 1313)
  - Isabel
    - Robert Bruce 5th Lord of Annandale (a Competitor) (d. 1295)
      - Robert Bruce 6th Lord of Annandale m. Countess of Carrick (d. 1304)
        - Robert Bruce Earl of Carrick King Robert I (1306–29)
  - Ada
    - Henry, Lord Hastings
      - John Lord Hastings of Abergavenny
  - John (d. 1237)

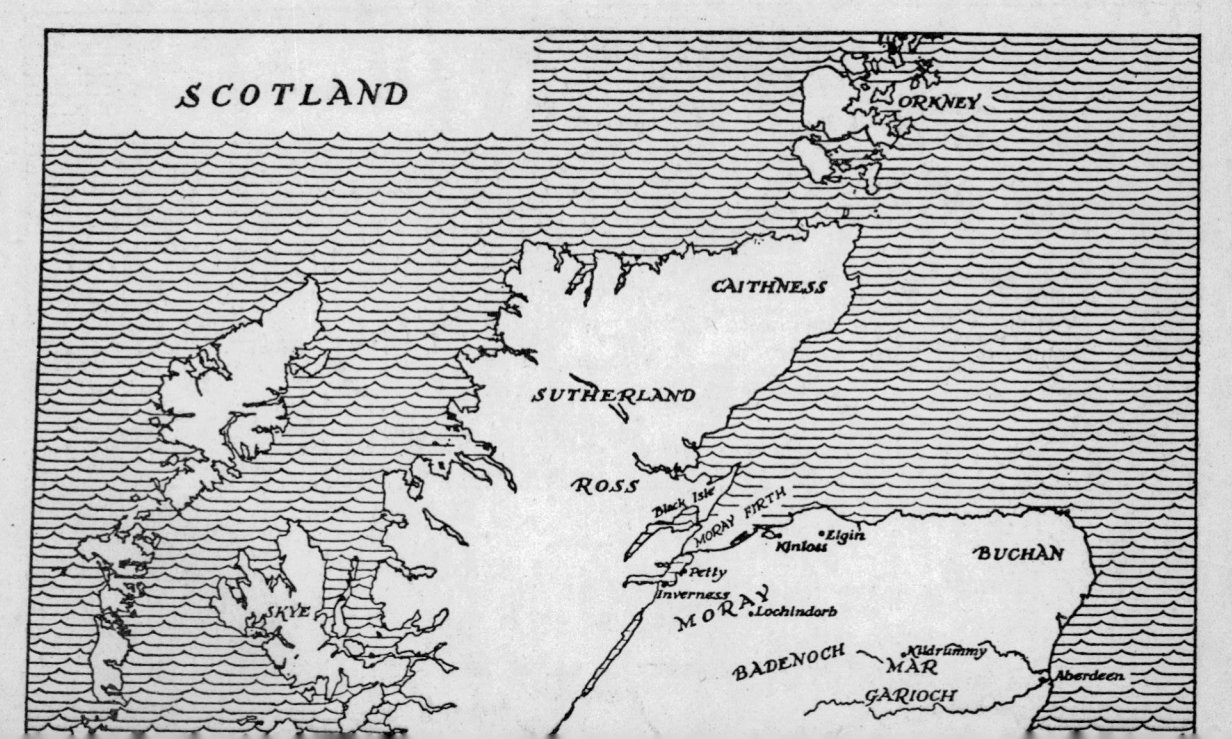

PART ONE

CHAPTER ONE

EVEN strong men, hard-bitten, grim-faced men winced as the horseman rode right into the church, iron-shod hooves striking sparks from the flagstones, their noisy clatter stilling all talk and reverberating hollowly under the hammer-beam roof. Stracathro was no mighty church, merely a prebend of the nearby Cathedral of Brechin, and horse and rider seemed enormous in its narrow echoing constriction.

Both mount and man were indeed large, the former a great and ponderous war-horse, massive of build, thick of leg, shaggy of fetlock, such as was necessary to carry the burly, weighty man with the extraordinary length of leg, clad in half a hundred-weight of steel armour richly engraved with gold. Right up to the altar steps, the length of the church, the horseman rode, with behind him other striding armoured figures led by one notably broad, squat, pugnacious of jaw, with a tonsured bullet head, who bore a mitre painted on his dented black steel breastplate. The waiting, watching men, as of one accord, drew further back against the bare stone walls of the little church.

Up the steps into the chancel itself the rider urged his cumbersome steed, there to pull it round in a lumbering half-circle, its great hooves scoring and slithering on the polished granite. Turned to face the nave and all the waiting throng the big man remained seated in the saddle, grinning. The thick-set individual with the underhung jaw took up his position at the other's right-hand stirrup, and the remainder, who had followed him up, ranged themselves on either side. The long shoulder-slung sword of one of them knocked over a tall brass candle-stick flanking the altar, with a crash, spattering hot wax. There was a curse. Somebody laughed loudly.

The man on the horse raised his hand. He was handsome, in a heavy-jowled, fleshy, empurpled way, in his late fifties but with strangely youthful-seeming hot blue eyes and a leonine head of greying hair, bare now, with the great crested war-helm banded with the gold circlet hanging at his saddle bow.

"Have him in, then," he cried. "God's blood—must I sit waiting here?" There was just the slightest impediment in the man's speech, but it lost nothing in forcefulness thereby.

As men at the door hurried out, a voice spoke up, old, quavering, but tense. "Highness—I do protest! To use God's house so! It is ill done . . ."

The speaker was a frail and elderly man, not in armour like most of those present but wearing the robes of an ecclesiastic, sorely stained and patched—William Comyn, Bishop of Brechin. This was one of his churches.

"Silence, knave!" A knight nearby raised a mailed gauntlet and struck the Bishop, a blow that sent the old man reeling. A second buffet was descending, when the steel-clad arm was grasped and held.

"Enough, Despenser! Let him be."

The English knight found himself staring into the grey eyes of a young man, richly dressed in only half-armour over velvet tunic and hose, worn with long soft doeskin thigh-boots and a short satin-lined heraldic riding-cloak slung from one shoulder. The velvet-clad arm that restrained the steel gauntlet was steady, strong, despite its soft covering.

"Curse you—unhand me! Unhand me, I say!" the Englishman shouted. "No man mishandles Despenser so. Even you, my lord Earl!"

"Then let Despenser not mishandle an old done man, see you. And a churchman, at that," the young man returned, though he released the other's arm.

"A traitorous clerk! Raising his voice . . . !"

"In this place, might he not have some right?"

The two stared at each other in very different kinds of anger, the one hot, the other cold. Sir Hugh le Despenser was a noted commander, veteran of much warfare; Robert de Bruce, twenty-two-year-old Earl of Carrick, was a scarcely-blooded warrior, his campaigning spurs still to win, a sprig of nobility, merely the son of his father—or more significantly, the grandson of his grandfather, the old Competitor, barely a year dead. All around men held their breaths, their glances more apt to dart up towards the figure that sat his saddle in front of the altar than towards either of the protagonists, or even old Bishop Comyn, who shaken, leaned against the wall.

The long-legged horseman was no longer grinning. His heavily good-looking features were dark, thunderous, a mailed hand tap-

tapping at that gold-circled helmet at his saddle-bow. Then abruptly he laughed, head thrown up, laughed heartily – and men breathed again. The hand rose, to point down the church.

"Whelps snapping!" he shouted, chuckling. "I'll not have it. Before the old dog! Enough, I say. If my friends must bicker, let them choose better cause than a broken-down old Scots clerk! A mouse squeaking in its barn! Shake hands, fools!"

The two down near the door eyed each other doubtfully; neither would be the first to reach out his hand.

"Robert, my young friend—your hand. Sir Hugh—yours." That was genial. Then, in one of the man's lightning changes of front, as hands only faltered, the big man roared. "Christ God! You hear me? Do as I command, or by the Mass, I'll have both your hands off at the wrist, here and now! I swear it!" And the speaker's own hand fell to the pommel of the great two-handed sword that hung at his side.

Hastily knight and earl gripped hands, bowing towards the altar.

As still the roof-timbers seemed to quiver with the sudden storm of fury, a clanking sound turned all eyes towards the door. The clanking was not all made by armour-clad men; some of it was made by chains.

Strangely, the new advent was brilliant, splendid, colourful, compared with all that was already in the church—where, apart from a few handsomely dressed individuals such as the young Earl of Carrick, most men were in the habiliments of war, not the vivid panoply of the tourney but the more sober and often battered practicalities of stern campaigning. Eight men came in. The first admittedly was an ordinary English knight, less well turned out indeed than many present, a mere captain of cavalry. But he carried one end of a rope. Behind him came a breathtaking figure, magnificently arrayed, a tall, slender man of middle years and great dignity, despite his hobbling gait, who walked with a slight stoop, head bent. Bareheaded, he wore no armour but clothes of cloth-of-gold and worked silver filigree with jewelled scintillating ornamentation, and over all a most gorgeous tabard or loose sleeveless tunic, heraldically embroidered in blazing colours, picked out in gold and rubies, depicting, back and front, the red Rampant Lion of Scotland on a tressured field of yellow, a coat of such striking pride, brilliance and vigour as to challenge the eye and seem to irradiate the somewhat sombre stone interior of the little church. In his hand he carried a flat velvet bonnet rimmed with pearls, to which was clasped with an enormous ruby, large as a pigeon's egg, a noble curling ostrich-feather that tinkled with seed pearls. On either side this splendid personage was flanked by an ordinary man-at-arms, each of whom kept a clenched hand on the bejewelled and bowed shoulders. The man was limping slightly, and being tall, had obvious difficulty in adjusting his stride to the short chain of the leg-irons which clamped his ankles. The rope from the knight in front was tied to his golden girdle.

Behind, between another couple of soldiers, came a burly man with a bandaged head, dressed in the finest armour in all that building, gleaming black and gold, but also with his legs shackled. He made a less careful business of the difficult walking, and in fact stumbled and tripped constantly, scowling and cursing, to the imminent danger of the handsome crimson cushion which he carried before him and on which precariously rested in sparkling, coruscating splendour the Crown of Scotland and the Sceptre of the Realm. A heavy portly figure, older-looking than his forty years, he kept his choleric head high and glowered all around him — John Comyn, Earl of Buchan, Constable of Scotland, the proudest and most powerful noble in a land whose nobles were proud above all else. Another rope was tied around his middle, and trailed behind to be held by the aproned grinning scullion from Montrose Castle's kitchens, who brought up the rear of the little procession, a white painted rod in his hand.

Some few of the watching throng bowed as the first chained man hobbled past, but most certainly did not. Many indeed laughed, some hooted, one spat. Robert Bruce of Carrick stared expressionless. Or nearly so, for his lip curled just a little; his was an expressive face, and it was schooled less perfectly than was intended.

The knight-led, scullion-finished group clanked and shuffled its way up to the chancel steps, and it was strange how, despite all the humiliation, the light seemed to go with it, drawn to and beamed forth by all the colour, the jewels and gems and gleaming gold. At the steps they were halted, with exaggerated abruptness, by the knight. At last the gorgeously-apparelled man looked up — and he had to raise his head high indeed to seek the face of him who sat the great war-horse that champed and sidled there.

"My lord King," he said, quietly, uncertainly. He had sensitive, finely-wrought features and deep, dark eyes under a lofty brow—but there was a slackness of the mouth and delicacy of the chin which spoke worlds.

The big man on the horse looked down at him, and in the silence of the moment all could hear that he was humming some tune to himself—and doing it flatly, for he had no music in him. He did not speak, or in any way acknowledge the other's greeting as the moments passed. Then he glanced up, to consider all in that church, unhurriedly, and yawned hugely, before his gaze returned to travel indifferently over the man waiting before him and to settle on the stocky, pugnacious-jawed individual with the tonsured head who stood at his stirrup.

"My lord Bishop of Durham—see you to it," he said shortly. "Do what is necessary." He snorted. "And in God's name be not long about it, Tony!"

Something like a corporate sigh went up from all who watched and waited and listened.

Anthony Beck, Prince-Bishop of Durham and captain-general of Saint Cuthbert's Host, perhaps the toughest unit of all Edward's army, stepped forward. "Sire," he said, bowing. "As you will." Then he turned to the shackled man, and thrust the round bullet-head forward, jaw leading. "John de Baliol, traitor!" he rasped. "Miscreant! Fool! Hear this. I charge you, in the name of the high and mighty Prince Edward, King of England and of France, of Wales and Ireland, Duke of Normandy and of Guyenne, and suzerain and Lord Paramount of this Scotland. I charge that you are forsworn and utterly condemned. You have shamefully renounced your allegiance to your liege lord Edward and risen against him in arms. You have betrayed your solemn vows. You have treated with His Majesty's enemies, and sought the aid and counsel of wicked men. You have in all things failed and rent your realm of Scotland. Have you any word to say why you should not forthwith be removed from being its king?"

The other drew a long quivering breath, straightening up, to gaze over the Bishop's head. He did not speak.

"You hear me? Have you nothing to say?"

"Nothing that I could say would serve now," the King of Scots muttered, low-voiced, husky.

"You will speak, nevertheless, I promise you!" Anthony Beck looked up at his master.

Edward Plantagenet did not so much as glance at either of them.

"What would you have me to say, Sire?" King John asked.

The other monarch patted his charger's neck.

Angrily Bishop Beck thrust out a thick forefinger at his victim. "You will speak. You will repeat these words. Before all. After me. By the King's royal command . . ."

He was interrupted. "If His Grace will not speak, I will!" It was John Comyn, Earl of Buchan, from behind. "Neither you, sir, nor your king, have any authority so to command him. His Grace is King of Scots, duly crowned and consecrated. He owes allegiance to no man. Only to God Himself!"

Frowning, Edward flicked a hand at the Bishop, who strode forward, past the Scots monarch and the escort who still clasped his shoulders, and raising a mailed arm, smote Buchan viciously across the face. "Silence, fool!" he cried. "How dare you raise your voice in the presence of the King's Majesty!"

Blood running from his mouth, the bandaged Earl answered back "Base-born clerk! I am Constable of Scotland, and have fullest right to speak in this realm, in any man's presence."

A second and still more savage blow sent the older man reeling, and shackled as he was, he would have fallen had his guards not held him up. As it was, the crown and sceptre were flung from the cushion he held before him, and fell with a clatter to the floor.

Cursing, Beck was stooping to pick them up, difficult for a man in full armour. He thought better of it, and was ordering the guards to do so, when Edward Longshanks spoke.

"Let them lie," he said briefly. "His Grace of Scotland will pick them up!"

The unsteady Buchan made choking exclamation, and sought to bend down for the fallen regalia, but his guards jerked him back. King John turned to sign to him, with a shake of the head and a sigh. Stooping, he recovered the symbols of his kingship. He stood, holding the crown in his right hand, the sceptre in his left.

At a nod from Edward, Bishop Beck went on. "You will speak now, sirrah. Say after me these words. Before His Majesty, and all these witnesses. Say 'I, John de Baliol, King of Scots by the grace, permission and appointment of my liege lord Edward of England . . .' "

For long moments there was silence broken only by the stirring of the horse. Then, head bent again, and in a voice that was scarcely to be heard, the other repeated.

"I, John de Baliol, King of Scots, by grace, permission, appointment of my liege lord Edward . . ."

"Speak up, man! We'll have no craven mumbling. Say 'I do hereby and before all men, admit my grievous fault and my shameful treasons.'"

". . . admit my grievous fault. And . . . and my shameful treasons."

"'Do renounce and reject the treaty I made against my said Lord Edward, with his enemy the King of France.'"

". . . renounce and reject . . . the treaty with France."

"'And do renounce and reject, and yield again to my Lord Edward, my kingdom and crown.'"

A choking sob, and then the broken words, ". . . renounce my kingdom. My crown."

"'And do throw myself and my whole realm humbly at the feet of and upon the mercy of the said noble Prince Edward, King of England and Lord Paramount of Scotland.'"

"No! Never that!" a voice cried, from the back of the church. Other voices rose also, to be overwhelmed in the roars of anger and the clash of steel and the thuds of blows, as James Stewart, fifth High Steward of Scotland, and others near him, were rushed and bundled out of the building by ungentle men-at-arms.

Scowling, though King Edward appeared faintly amused, the Prince-Bishop waited until approximate quiet was restored. "More of such insolence, folly and disrespect, and heads will fall!" he shouted. "You have my oath on it!" He jerked that thick finger again at John Baliol. "I am waiting. My lord the King waits. Speak, man."

"Do not say it, Sire," Buchan burst out from behind him. "Not this. Of the realm. Not Lord Paramount. There is none such. Save you, Sire. It is a lie . . . !"

He got no further. This time the guards, even the scullion at his back, did not wait for Beck. With one accord they set upon the Earl and beat him down under a hail of blows. He fell to the stone floor, there at the chancel steps, and so lay.

High above, Edward Plantagenet watched from hooded eyes, a smile about his lips.

King John repeated the required words, falteringly.

The Bishop leaned forward, and snatched the Crown of Scotland from its owner's hand. "By His Majesty's royal command, you are no longer King of Scots," he cried. "The kingdom reverts to him who gave it to you. To do with as he will. You, John de Baliol, together with your son, heirs and all posterity, are hereby deprived of all office, rank, title, property and lands. You and yours are the King's prisoners; your lives, as traitors and felons, are his to take and do with as he will. In the name of Edward, King of England." He turned, and handed up the crown to his master.

Edward seemed almost as though he would reject it. Then, shrugging great shoulders, he took it, turned it this way and that in his hands, casually inspecting it. But he seemed little interested. Without warning, he tossed the glittering thing down to the knight in charge of the prisoners' escort—who only just managed to catch it. "Here—take it, Sir Piers," he said, with a laugh. "It is yours. Perhaps it will serve to pay your good fellows. The Jews may give you something for it!"

Something between a sob and a groan arose in that church—to be swiftly lost in a menacing growl.

The Bishop of Durham, when he had assured that King Edward did not intend to say more, resumed—not at first with words. Stepping close to the taller prisoner, he reached out and took hold of the splendid jewelled and embroidered tabard with the proud red Lion Rampant, grabbing it at the neck. With savage jerks of a short but powerful arm he wrenched and tore at it. To the sound of rending fabric, its wearer staggered, and as the glorious garment fell in ruin to the floor, something of the light and colour seemed to go out of that place.

The Bishop now took the sceptre away, and handed it to the scullion, who stood grinning astride the prostrate person of Buchan the Constable. He took in return the white rod of penitence and humiliation this man had carried, and thrust it at Baliol.

"This is yours, now," he said. "All you have, or will get! Save perhaps the rope! Now—down on your knees."

The other took the rod, head shaking. But he remained standing.

"Fool! Are you deaf? You heard me—kneel. Or do you not value your wretched life? Your traitor's skin?"

"I no longer value my life, my lord. Or I would not have come to submit to His Majesty. But how could I be traitor? How could the King of Scots be traitor to the King of England? I submit me —but I do not . . ."

John Baliol was too late by far with any such reasoning. Fierce and vehement hands forced him to his knees, beside the groaning figure of the Constable.

"Speak—for your life," the Bishop commanded. "You are now nothing, man. Not even a man. Dirt beneath His Majesty's feet, no more! He could, and should, take you out and hang you. Draw, quarter and disembowel you. As you deserve. And not only you. All your treacherous, beggarly Scots lords. Rebels against his peace. All should die. As the scurvy rebels of Berwick town died, who also spurned King Edward's peace." Only a month or so before, after the frontier town of Berwick-on-Tweed had resisted the English advance, Edward had ordered the slaughter of no fewer than 17,000 men, women and children in the streets, and the burning of every house, in this the richest town and seaport of Scotland. The Bishop's threats were scarcely idle, therefore.

Baliol sank his greying head. "So be it," he said. "I seek His Majesty's clemency. For the lives of all who have followed and supported me. Mistakenly. I humbly seek mercy."

"And for your own life also?"

The kneeling man looked up, from Bishop to King, and for a moment a sort of nobility showed strongly in the weak and unhappy features. "Very well," he acceded. "If that is necessary. If that is your requirement. I ask for your mercy on myself and mine, also." He paused. "That the cup be filled."

Beck looked a little put out. He frowned, then shrugged mail-clad shoulders. He turned to the Plantagenet. "Sire," he said. "All is done. In your royal hands is placed this felon's life. And the lives of all his people. Of his own will. To do with according to your mighty pleasure. There is no longer a King of Scots. Nor a realm of Scotland. All is yours." Bowing, he stepped back, duty done.

Edward even now seemed the bored and disinterested onlooker. He glanced round all the waiting company, as though, like them, he had been a mere spectator of a mildly distasteful scene. He appeared to shake himself out of a brown study.

"My lords," he said. "My noble friends. And . . . others. Have you had enough? I vow that I have. Let us be out of here. This place stinks in my nostrils. Come, Tony." And without so much as a look at the figure still kneeling there, he urged his heavy destrier forward.

Almost he rode down both Baliol and Buchan, even their escort; only the slow cumbersome movement of the war-horse permitted all to get out of the way of its great hooves. And everywhere the cream of two nations bowed low, as Edward of England passed on.

Or not perhaps quite the cream of two nations. For practically everyone in the church of Stracathro that July day of 1296, save some of the humble men-at-arms, was of one stock—Norman-French. Edward himself might be an Angevin, Baliol a Picard, Beck, or de Bec, and Comyn were Flemings and Bruce sprung from the Cotentin; but all were basically Normans. Of the true English stock there were none present, though there had of course been some intermarriage. Of the indigenous Celtic Scots, none likewise. Possibly the young Robert Bruce was the nearest to a Scot, for his mother had been the daughter and heiress of the last Celtic Earl of Carrick, of the old stock, whose earldom he had inherited. A Norman-French military aristocracy had for two centuries been taking over both kingdoms, indeed much of northern Europe—but only at the great land-owning and government level. Every word spoken in that church had been in French.

The cream of this aristocracy, therefore, both victors and vanquished, bowed as their master rode down towards the door—leaving a somewhat doubtful soldier-knight distinctly uncertain what to do with his utterly ignored and rejected prisoners. A round dozen earls were there, and more than a score of great lords—and some of those with Scots titles bowed lower than the English, not in abject vanquishment but in loyal fealty, for many of them, in unhappy and divided Scotland, considered that they had borne no allegiance to King John, looking on him as usurper, and worse, nonentity, not a few holding almost as large lands in England as here. For such men loyalty and patriotic duty were hypothetical and variable terms.

Edward was half way to the door when a man stepped forward, one of those not in armour. "Sire," he said. "A petition. Hear me, I pray you."

Across the church, the young Earl of Carrick, frowning suddenly, made as though to move, to speak, but thought better of it. His hand gestured towards the petitioner, however, eloquently. But ineffectually.

The King pulled up. "My lord of Annandale," he said, blank-faced. "I conceived you to be in Carlisle."

"You summoned all 'leal Scots to attend you here, Sire."

"Your lealty I do not doubt, man. But I appointed you governor of Carlisle. To keep the West Border. And Galloway. Here is a strange way of keeping it!"

The other bowed. He was a handsome man, of Edward's own age, quietly but tastefully dressed, with the long face of a scholar or pedant rather than that of a warrior, despite his governor's position. It might have been a noble face, the noblest in all that company, save for a certain petulant stubbornness.

"The West March is safe, Sire. I have three strong sons holding it secure for Your Majesty. With Galloway. I came to see this good day's work."

"Aye—you never loved Baliol, my lord! Nor loved *me* the more that I made him King of Scots, hey?" That was cracked out like a whip-lash. "So you came to see me eat my choice? To crow, Bruce? To crow!"

"Not so, Sire. I am your true man. And have proved it. From the first." That was true, at least. For this man, who bore the lesser title of Lord of Annandale, should have been the Earl of Carrick since he it was who had married the heiress-Countess; but he had deliberately resigned the earldom three years before, to his eldest son there across the church, rather than have to kneel and take the oath of homage for it to John Baliol as King. Robert Bruce, the father, was that sort of man. "I came to see Your Majesty's justice done on this empty vessel! A good day's work, as I said. But it could be bettered."

"You say so, my lord?" Edward looked at him, sharply.

"Aye, Sire. You have undone what you did three years ago. Unchosen your choice. You can make good now what was wrong done then. There was another choice. That you, in your wisdom rejected—for this! The Bruce claim. You can make *me* King of Scots, Sire. And complete your work."

Edward Plantagenet's florid face had been growing purple. Now he burst out. "Lord God in His Heaven! *You* tell me what I should do! Me, Edward. You! You came from Carlisle, a hundred leagues, to tell me this! Make you king? By the Blood of Christ—have I nothing else to do but win kingdoms for such as you! Out of my way, sirrah!"

Expressionless, Bruce inclined his grey head, as the furious monarch kicked huge jagged spurs into his charger's flanks.

But Edward reined up again in only a few yards, and turned in his saddle to look back over his heavy shoulder. "Mind this," he shouted, as everywhere men cringed. "You, Bruce. All of you. Scots curs. There is no King of Scots. Nor will be again. There is no kingdom of Scotland. It is now and henceforth part of my realm of England. A wretched, discredited province—but part! Your king I have deposed. Your Great Seal I have broken in four pieces. Your charters and records I have commanded to be sent from Edinburgh to London. Your Black Rood of St. Margaret is sent to my Archbishop. Your Stone of Scotland I shall take from Scone to Westminster. Your crown and sceptre are there—playthings for my men. There is nothing—nothing left for any man to play king over. And hereafter, all men shall take the oath of fealty to me, as King, for every inch of land in this Scotland. For every office. On bended knee. On pain of treason. Hear—and heed well."

He moved on.

But at the very door, again he drew up, and turned his head once more, this time over his other, his left shoulder—and his manner had undergone one of its drastic transformations. "Where is the whelp?" he demanded, almost jovially. "My friend the younger Robert? Ha, yes—there you are, my lordling of Carrick! See you, I counsel you, my young friend, to look to your father. If you would *remain* my friend! Look well. Your old grandsire, The Competitor, was trouble enough. He is well dead. I am a peaceable man, God knows—and want no more trouble. With Bruce. Or other. See you to it, boy—if you would have me to pay any more of your debts! Pay for all the fine velvet you are wearing! See that my lord of Annandale, your father, is escorted back to his charge at Carlisle—henceforth not to leave it lacking my express command. And you, then, join me at Berwick town, where we will consider your latest list of creditors!" Edward hooted a laugh. "Would I had had so lenient a liege lord!" He faced front again. "Come, my lords. Surrey—muster the guard."

Robert Bruce the younger stared across at Robert Bruce the elder, and his brow was black. Apart from that he offered no other recognition of his father, or indeed of anybody else, as he pushed out of the church. Few indeed now so much as glanced up towards the chancel steps, where the lawful King of Scots stood, forgotten as he was rejected.

Chapter Two

IMPATIENTLY the hard-riding little group pulled off the Tweedside roadway, splattered through the flooded water-meadows to the side, and the horses had to clamber, hooves slipping, up the raw red earth and outcrops of the broom-clad knowe beyond, to win back to the road again, in front of the slow-moving throng that blocked it. Young Robert Bruce cursed, in the lead. It was not that he was in any particular hurry; just that when he moved, he liked to move fast. And patience was not outstanding amongst his virtues. But it had been like this almost all the way from Galloway. All the world seemed to be heading for Berwick-on-Tweed—and all the world, on the move, tends to be a slow process. Seldom had Bruce made a more frustrating journey. It was as though everyone was on holiday, making for some great fair, important enough to pull them right across Scotland.

Not quite everyone, perhaps, and not quite in the fair-going spirit. It was the pride and circumstance, the substance of the land, that took its way by every road and highway, to Berwick, that August day, nobles, knights, lairds, landowners great and small, prelates and clerics, sheriffs, justices, officers of the higher degrees. And none looked in festive mood, or really anxious to reach their destination. Few, of course, by the very nature of things, were youthful, like the Earl of Carrick and his little troop of Annandale mosstroopers, who esteemed hurry for the sake of haste. For, in fact, Bruce himself was not especially eager to reach Berwick. His urgent mode of travel was merely habitual. Moreover, he had his nineteen-year-old brother at his side, and young brothers of that age needed to be left in no doubt as to what was what, and as to how to behave in a chivalric society.

Robert's snort of disgust was eloquent indeed as they spurred round the bend of the broomy knowe and there saw the road blocked once more, immediately ahead, and by a larger, slower and more ponderous company than heretofore.

"Save us—more of them!" he complained. "And crawling. Cumbering all the road. More fat clerks, for a wager—churchmen! Look at that horse-litter. Only some prideful, arrogant prelate would ride in such a thing. Filling all the highway . . ."

"Let us give him a fright, then!" his brother Nigel cried, laughing. "Shake up his holy litter and liver, in one! His bowels of compassion . . .!"

Nothing loth the other dug in his spurs, and neck and neck the two young men raced onwards, their grinning men-at-arms a solid pack close behind.

They were very obviously brothers, these two, and close friends. Robert had the stronger face—though the years might alter that —the slightly more rugged features. Nigel was the more nearly handsome. But both were of arresting looks, medium of height, slender but with good wide shoulders, fresh-complexioned, grey-eyed and with wavy auburn hair—the touch of red in it no doubt inherited from the Celtic mother. They had keen-cut almost bony features, vivid, mobile and expressionful, with something of their father's stubbornness of chin without the petulance of mouth. They looked a pair who would burst into laughter or sudden rage with equal readiness; yet there was a sensitiveness about their faces, especially Nigel's, which warred with the rest.

As they thundered down on the company ahead, the younger shouted. "A banner. Forward. See it? A bishop, at least!"

"Our own colours—red and gold! Can you see the device...?"

"A cross, I think. Not a saltire and a chief, like Bruce. A red cross on gold. We'll make it flap...!"

The other looked just a little doubtful now—but here was no occasion for hesitation. No man of spirit could pull up now, and have his followers cannoning into his rear while he mouthed excuses for a change of mind. A man must never look a fool before his men—especially if they were Border mosstroopers. Moreover, churchmen were all insufferably pompous and requiring of diminishing. They hurtled on.

Horsemen at the rear of the leisurely cavalcade were now looking back, at the urgent drumming of hooves. There was a certain amount of alarmed reining to this side or that. The riverside road was not only fairly narrow, but here, near Paxton, cut its way along a steep braeside of whins and bracken and thorn trees, with the ground rising sharply at one side and dropping steeply at the other. There was little room for manoeuvre—although if the company ahead had ridden less than four abreast, there would have been room for a single file to pass.

If there was some last-moment drawing aside towards the rear of the column, it did not extend to the middle, where an elaborate and richly-canopied litter in red and gold was slung between a pair of pacing white jennets, something between a hammock and a palanquin, curtained and upholstered. This swaying equipage, with its two horses, took up almost the full width of the track. Perhaps a score of men rode behind it, and another score in front.

With cheerful shouts of "Way for the Bruce! Way for the Bruce!" the laughing young men bore down on this dignified procession—and very quickly its dignity was dispersed in chaos as the tight-knit, hard-riding group drove in on it without slackening of pace. Like a spear-head the Bruces bored on and through the ruck of swearing, shouting men and rearing, plunging, stumbling horses. Low over their own beasts' necks the Bruces crouched, hands flailing at heaving flanks. Everywhere riders were forced off the track, mainly down the steep bank towards the river, in a bedlam of protest, malediction, neighings and mocking laughter.

The jennets with the litter were led on a golden cord by an elderly liveried horse-master on a substantial cob. He, like the escort, wore the red cross on gold on breast and back. At the uproar behind he turned and hurriedly raised a protesting hand. Quickly perceiving that nothing of the sort would halt or even slow down the oncoming group, he agitatedly sought to drag off some little way to the right, the river-side, the two litter-horses. But there was nothing effective that he could do, without the near-side beast going right over the lip of the bank, which would eventually have tipped up the litter and probably thrown out its occupant. Such conveyances, though an enormous aid to comfortable travel, were awkward indeed to handle in an emergency.

The Bruces came pounding on. There was obviously no space for them to pass the litter two abreast without headlong collision, and at the last moment Nigel, to the left, wrenched round his mount to force it up on the climbing bank a little way. Even so his brother's powerful stallion jostled and all but overthrew the gentle left-side jennet, causing it to stagger over, white legs sprawling wide. In its turn this pushed the other jennet over the edge, and the litter, slung between them, canted up at an alarming angle, leaning over to the right precariously, front high.

As he swept past, Robert Bruce's grin went from his face like sun behind a scudding storm-cloud. It was no proud priest who clutched the lurching sides of the curtained brancard but a young woman. And even in the hectic moment of passing, he recognised that she was a beauty.

Bruce seldom, by his very nature, did anything by half-measures. No sooner had the perception of error penetrated his consciousness than he was reining up in savage and utterly abrupt decision, with no least heed for the immediate consequences, his stallion neighing in shocked protest, rearing high on its hindquarters, hooves slithering and scoring the dirt surface of the roadway in a cloud of dust and sparks, forelegs pawing the air. Almost it toppled over backwards, and only superb horsemanship kept its rider in the saddle.

Complete chaos ensued, as the following men-at-arms piled up in a pandemonium of agonised horseflesh, lashing hooves and flailing limbs. Fortunately all these mosstroopers were practically born to the saddle, and their mounts, unlike their masters' thoroughbreds, shaggy nimble-footed garrons bred to the hills and the hazards of the chase in roughest territory; otherwise there would have been disaster. As it was, two men were unhorsed, one garron went down—but struggled to its feet again—and the left-hand jennet was cannoned into again and knocked down on its knees.

Oddly enough, this last casualty had the effect of momentarily levelling the litter considerably, both sideways and fore and aft. Even as the cause of all this upheaval dragged his mount's head round to face the rear, with the brute still high on its hind legs, the young woman leapt nimbly out of her tossing equipage in a flurry of skirts and long silk-clad legs—no easy task from a re-clining position and an unsteady base—to land directly in front of the rearing stallion and its appalled rider. She stood, apparently unconcerned at the danger from those wicked waving hooves, glaring up at the young man in proud and pale anger.

Mortified, Bruce sought to quieten his horse, bring its feet down clear of the girl and the other milling brutes, doff his velvet bonnet and stammer apologies, all at the same time. His code of chivalry, which could accept as no more than a mere under-standable prank the riding down of an elderly churchman or a fat merchant, was outraged by any such insult to a young and attractive female—so long as she was a lady. Careless of all the commotion around him, save for this aspect of it, he shook his auburn head and sought for words of excuse, of explanation.

Words came rather more swiftly to the young woman. "Fool!" she cried. "Witless, mannerless dolt! How dare you, sirrah? How dare you?" Despite her choler and fright, her blazing blue eyes and quivering lips, she had a notably musical and softly accented voice, with cadences in it such as the Islesmen used.

Some part of Bruce's mind recognised and placed those cadences. But that was at the back of a mind at present fully occupied frontally.

"Pardon, lady!" he gasped. "I beseech you—pardon! My pro-found regrets. Of a mercy, forgive. I had no notion . . . a woman . . . a mistake, I promise you. We thought . . . we thought . . ."

"You thought to play the ape! The masterful ape, sirrah! By riding down peaceable folk. Driving them off your king's high-way, in your arrogant folly. Using the weight of your prancing horseflesh in lieu of wits and manners! You need not ask pardon of me, sir." She raised her head the higher.

The girl had a high head anyway, on a notably long and grace-ful column of neck, a proud fair head held proudly on a tall and slender fair body. She was young for so much hauteur and autho-ritative vehemence, no more than eighteen probably, of a delicate yet vigorously-moulded beauty of feature. She had a wealth of heavy corn-coloured hair piled up high above lofty brows, from beneath which flashed those alive blue eyes. Despite her long slenderness she had handsome breasts, high and proud as the rest of her. She wore a travelling-gown of dark blue velvet, the swell-ing bodice patterned with silver and edged at neck and sleeves with fur.

"All day we have been held back by slow-moving folk, cumber-ing the road, lady." That was Nigel, rallying to his brother's aid.

"Quiet!" Robert's barked command was less than appreciative. "You have my regrets, madam. I will make any amends suitable." He said that stiffly. He would not grovel to any man, or woman either.

"Others have ridden all day. Without becoming boors!" she returned. "Your regrets are over-late. And your best amends, sir, will be to remove yourselves as quickly as you may."

"You are scarcely generous . . ." Bruce was protesting, when another voice broke in.

"What a fiend's name goes on? Elizabeth—what's to do?" A stern-looking thick-set man in early middle age, splendidly attired and clothed with most evident authority, had ridden back from the front of the ambling column. He would have been handsome had it not been for the great scar which disfigured his features from brow to chin.

"It is nothing, Father," the girl said. "You need not concern yourself. Travellers with more haste than manners—that is all. There is no hurt done."

"There had better not be, by God!" The newcomer glared around at all and sundry, as men and horses sorted themselves. "You were not upset? Outed? From your litter?"

"No. I . . . stepped down." The young woman raised an eye-brow at Bruce. "There is no profit in further talk. Nor in further delay of these so hasty young men."

"No? Yet you are in a rage, girl! I know that face on you!" the man declared. "If these have occasioned my daughter offence . . . !"

"Scarce that, my lord," she returned, with a flash of scorn. "Their offence will be if they linger further!"

Bruce cleared his throat. "I have apologised, sir," he said. "It was a mishap. We had no notion that there was a lady in it. I would not offer offence to any lady. Especially such as . . . such as . . ." His words tailed away—which, in that young man, was unusual.

"No doubt. You would needs be bold indeed to choose to offend Richard de Burgh's daughter!" the older man said grimly.

"De Burgh? You . . . *you* are de Burgh?"

"I am. Richard de Burgh, Earl of Ulster. And you, sir? Have you a name?"

The younger man drew himself up in his saddle. "Some, I think, would call it a name, my lord of Ulster, I am Carrick. Robert Bruce, Earl of Carrick."

"Ha! Bruce? A sprig of that tree! Carrick, eh? Then I went crusading with your father, my lord. And found your grandsire a sore man to agree with!"

"Many, I fear, so found!" Robert Bruce risked a smile. He actually bowed a little. "Myself he could see no good in. Nor my brother here, either."

The Lord Nigel grinned, and sketched a comprehensive flourish rather than a salute, less awed perhaps than he should have been. He knew the name, of course—who did not? Richard de Burgh, Lord of Connaught and Earl of Ulster, was the greatest Norman name in Ireland, one of the most noted warriors of the age—and, more important, King Edward of England's most trusted crony, adherent and companion-in-arms.

"It may be that the old devil had the makings of sense in him, then!" That comment was accompanied by a distinct twinkle of the eye, strange in so ravaged and stern a face. It was strange, too, how the Norman-French de Burgh voice had, in only three generations, acquired so liltingly Irish an intonation and character. "Your father, the Lord of Annandale—is he in health? And in the King's peace? Or out of it!"

"I scarce know, my lord. From day to day!" That was bold, in the circumstances.

The older man grimaced fierce appreciation of the fact. "Aye. No doubt. His Majesty's peace is not always easy to keep. But, as I mind it, your father was always a fool where his own good was concerned!"

"In that you have the rights of it," Bruce acknowledged. "I swear he . . ."

It was the Lady Elizabeth de Burgh's turn to clear her throat—

and she did it in no tentative or apologetic fashion. "These young lords travel in great haste, Father," she interrupted loftily. "That, they made all too clear! It is not for us to hold them back. Moreover, I would not choose this place and company to stand and talk!" Most evidently she disapproved of her righteous indignation being submerged under a masking tide of masculine camaraderie. She turned to her litter again.

Her father grinned, and nodded. He reined round his horse to ride back to his place at the head of his company.

The elderly horse-master, from gentling and soothing the jennets, was moving forward to aid his mistress into her equipage when he was roughly thrust aside. Young Nigel Bruce had leapt from the saddle, and in a stride or two was seeking to hoist up the Lady Elizabeth, with laughing gallantry. She did not reject his help, but, settling herself unhurriedly on to her couch, eyed him up and down coolly.

"What do I thank for this?" she asked. "My father's name? Or King Edward's?"

Abashed, the young man drew back. "I but . . . would serve you," he said. "A lady. And fair . . ."

"Was I not that when you tipped me out? A good day to you, sir."

The other returned to his horse, wordless, and with his brother, bowed, and rode on. It was no mean feat to have silenced the young Bruces. It was perhaps a pity that in their stiff constraint, however, they did not, could not, look back—or they might have perceived a notably different expression on the young woman's face.

They rode soberly now, in single file, past the remainder of the Ulster entourage, respectfully saluted de Burgh at the front, and then, once well past, spurred ahead, with one accord anxious to put distance between them and their humiliation.

"A hussy! A shrew! A very wild-cat!" Nigel exclaimed, as he drew up level with his brother. "Have you ever seen the like!"

"No. Nor wish to."

"So much to-do over so little a thing! Women are the devil! And yet . . . she is bonny!"

"So, perhaps, is the devil! Who knows?"

Their brooding over their wrongs did not last long—only as far as the outskirts of Berwick town. Thereafter where the broad silver river reached the azure plain of the sea, sparkling, clean, infinite, even the young Bruces, used as they were to the detritus of invasion and civil war, became increasingly preoccupied with other matters. Never had either of them seen the like of this. Here was offence of a different sort, on a different scale, offence to every sense—but especially, perhaps, to their noses. Everywhere they looked, in the narrow fire-blackened streets, were bodies—bodies in heaps and piles, bodies that hung and swung, bodies crucified, disembowelled, decapitated, mutilated and made mock of, bodies untidily asprawl or neatly laid out, bodies of all sizes, ages, and of both sexes, naked, clothed, half-burned. Every ruined house was full of them, every gaping window festooned, every street and alley lined with them, only sufficient of the causeways cleared to give meagre passage through the main thoroughfares. And all this vast dead populace of Berwick-on-Tweed was in an advanced state of putrefaction, for all had been slain weeks before. It was now August, high summer. The stench was utterly appalling, suffocating. The throbbing hum of the flies was like a constant moaning of this host of departed souls in their anguish, and the clouds of them like a black miasma over all.

Coughing, choking, next to vomiting with the stink of it, Nigel gasped. "What folly is this? Have they taken leave of their wits? The English. Letting all these lie? Should have been buried weeks ago."

"Left of a purpose. Edward overlooks nothing," his brother answered grimly. "This will be on his orders. A lesson. To all."

"But . . . to hold a parliament here! Amidst this."

"The more telling a lesson. The parliament's but a show, anyway. This, to point it!"

"God—it is not to be endured!"

"It will be endured. Because it must."

"It could raise revolt."

"More like to raise the plague!"

"Aye. In this heat. Is your King Edward mad?"

Even in the company of their own mosstroopers, Bruce glanced round and behind him quickly, frowning. "Watch your tongue!" he jerked, low-voiced. "I counsel you—save your breath!"

It was good advice. Seeking to breathe as little and as shallowly as they might, the brothers trotted through those terrible, silent streets of Scotland's greatest seaport and trading centre, the customs of which were said to have been worth a quarter of those of all England. They were climbing, by steep cobbled alleys and wynds still black with the blood that had cascaded down them to stain the very estuary, up from the wharves and piers and warehouses of the once-crowded lower town towards the lofty proud castle which crowned its soaring cliff-top promontory, high and serene above river and town and horror, the great banner of England streaming splendidly from its topmost tower. Up there, at least, the air would be pure.

Many travellers were climbing that long hill, and few there were whose faces were other than pale, eyes averted, lips tight. The Bruces pushed past none now. Haste was no longer valid, even to escape the smell.

At the gatehouse to the outer bailey of the castle they must perforce join a queue, inconceivable as this would have been in any other circumstances. All men-at-arms and retinues were being detached, irrespective of whose, and ordered peremptorily off to right and left, to wait and camp as best they might in the crowded tourney-ground and archery-butts which flanked the final steep and rocky knoll which the castle crowned. Only the quality travellers themselves, bearers of the royal summons, were being admitted over the drawbridge and into the castle precincts. But of these there was no lack, this August day; for never in Scotland's history had so many been required, commanded, to forgather in one place at one time. Patiently as they might, if less than humbly, and dismounted necessarily, the Bruce brothers took their places in the long shuffling column that only slowly worked its submissive way forward.

Over the hollow-sounding timbers of the bridge that spanned the dry ditch surrounding the towering ramparts, they reached, at length the arched stone pend that thrust beneath the gatehouse itself. Here a burly perspiring master-at-arms, supported by halberd-bearing minions in dented jacks and morions, scrutinised each arrival, and roughly separated sheep from goats, his rich Dorset voice hoarse with much shouting. As the Bruces drew close, awaiting their turn, Robert sought to occupy himself and his sorely-tried temper by considering the present state of the handsome flourish of heraldry carved above the archway. It represented the Douglas coat-of-arms, of a blue chief with stars on a silver field; but it was now hacked and defaced, spattered with dried thrown horse-dung, with hung over it a derisory bull's testicles and prickle, shrivelled in the sun. The veteran Sir William *le hardi* Douglas had commanded here, and had held out in this castle throughout the Sack of Berwick, surrendering to Edward only when water and food had run out. The surrender had been on honourable terms; but Douglas was said to be still in chains, and walking all the way to London Tower, like a performing bear, for his pains.

When they reached the master-at-arms, the fellow hardly so much as glanced at them.

"English? Or Scots?" he demanded unceremoniously.

Bruce threw up his head. "I am the Earl of Carrick," he said shortly.

"English or Scots, I said, man. Did you not hear?" That was weary but curt.

"Fool! Did *you* not hear?" Nigel cried. "Bruce! Earl of Carrick. We are Scots, yes—since our father should be King of Scots. But we have great English manors. In Durham, Yorkshire, Sussex and Essex. And our father is Keeper of Carlisle for King Edward . . ."

"I care not, cockerel, which dunghill your sire keeps! You are dirty Scots, curse you—so to the left you go, wi' the rest. Off wi' you. Next . . ."

When the Bruces would have protested, their arms were seized by the supporting guards, and they were ungently pushed and hurried through the pend.

Fiercely Robert broke free. "Hands off Bruce, cur!" he exclaimed, and at the sudden sheer blaze of fury in those steel-grey eyes, even the rough soldier blinked and released the arm, dropping his hand to his sword-hilt instead. Utterly ignoring him thereafter, the other stalked on, to turn left inside the outer bailey, his brother hurrying after him.

"Edward shall hear of this!" he grated—and then all but snapped off Nigel's head as he began to deliver himself of his own opinions.

It appeared after a few moments however, that King Edward might be some little time in hearing of the offence offered to his illustrious friends and supporters. For the Bruces found themselves joining another and still longer queue that wound its sluggish way round this side of the outer bailey, through a side postern door in the next tall parapeted rampart, and into the inner bailey, there to cross the cobbled courtyard to the kitchen entrance to the castle proper. This slow-moving column was strictly hemmed in and controlled by a double rank of armed guards, shoulder to shoulder—and when the Bruces perceived their lowly scullions' destination and tried to break away, in righteous wrath, they were savagely restrained and manhandled.

Nor were they permitted to turn back, as they would have done. Jabbing dirks and halberd-points left them little scope for argument or manoeuvre. Along with more amenable visitors, they were herded will-nilly along towards the kitchens.

It took a long time to reach that lowly doorway and the dark sweating-stone, food-smelling passages beyond, where the cream of Scotland's quality edged forward, pushed and jostled by cooks, servitors and menials carrying haunches of beef, trussed fowls, fish and the like. Climbing the narrow corkscrew stairways beyond, step by slow step, in the choking reek of pitch-pine torches, and making room for the impatient flunkeys and domestics with their trays and flagons, seemed to take an eternity—and even here the restricted space was much taken up with a lining of stationary scowling guards. It was the best part of an hour after reaching the outer gatehouse before the Bruce brothers stepped, by the service entrance, into the Great Hall of Berwick Castle, Robert at least seething with a cold rage such as he had never known, nor had cause to know, hitherto.

The Hall was a vast apartment, full of noise, colour and activity, heartening at first sight after all the weary trailing—although not all would confirm that impression after a second glance. Up one side of the great chamber were set long tables, groaning with good cheer, served by the busy menials, at which sat or lounged or sprawled drunk a gay and well-dressed company of laughing, talking or snoring men and women. At the head of the room was a raised dais, and on this was set a much smaller table, at one end of which sat King Edward in a throne-like chair, with Bishop Beck, the Earls of Surrey and Hereford, his commanders, and Master Hugh de Cressingham, a Justiciar of England. Nearby, and being used as an additional side-table for bottles, flagons and goblets, was a curious lump of red sandstone, flat and roughly oblong. High above, half way to the vaulted ceiling, in a little gallery, minstrels played soft music.

So much for the first glance. The second revealed a different aspect of the scene. The long queue of Scots notables still maintained its formation and patient shuffling progress. It was strictly confined to the other and right-hand side of the Hall, all but pressed against the stone walling indeed by drawn up ranks of guards—though all others ignored it. Right up to the steps of the dais area it went, to another table at which clerks sat, a table on which were no viands and which was placed directly behind the King's back, though at the lower level. And here, as each Scots landholder reached it, his name was called out, ticked off a list, and he was required to kneel on the floor and thus take an oath of homage to Edward of England for every inch of land he held. Here was no taking of the monarch's hand between his own, as homage was normally done, the oath not administered by any prelate; the monarch indeed never so much as glanced round from his eating and talk, and the clerks it was who demanded the oath, gabbling out its terms and ordering its repetition. Thereafter, homage done, the ignored suppliants were allowed to rise, bow low, and then sign their names or make their crosses on one of a great pile of sheepskins, each already lettered with the wording of the oath of fealty, sign or mark for each holding of land in each county or sheriffdom of Scotland, for each office or position held. Whereafter, the signatory was hustled away by men-at-arms to a side door, and out. They were being put through two at once, and as quickly as possible, but even so it took a deal of time. Hence the queue's lack of momentum.

"Dear God — see this!" Nigel Bruce cried. "See what they do! Look — there is Mar kneeling now. Gartnait, Earl of Mar, your own wife's brother. With that bishop. Save us — is it possible?"

His brother did not answer. Pale, set-faced, he was eyeing all that scene, noting all. He noted that it was only the English who sat at the long tables — all who ate and drank were Norman-English, or perhaps Norman-Irish or Norman-Welsh or Norman-French. He noted that none save the clerks at the signing table paid the least attention to the oath-taking, least of all those at the King's high table. He noted that none of the Scots, however illustrious, were being permitted to remain in the Hall after signing.

His wrath rose to choke him. Suddenly he strode out, bursting from the painful procession, pushing through the steel barrier of the guards.

"My lord King!" he shouted. "My liege lord Edward! I protest! It is I — Robert Bruce of Carrick. Majesty — I crave your heed."

There was much noise in that place, but even so his outcry must have been heard by most. Certain faces at the long table did turn towards him — but none up on the royal dais.

The guards were not slow to react. At first hesitating, in their surprise, they swiftly perceived that no sign came from the King, and a number hurled themselves upon the protester. He did not resist, knowing well that it could be accounted treason to brawl or engage in physical violence in the presence of the monarch. But he did raise his voice again. And this time it was directed not at Edward but at one of those who sat quite nearby at the long table.

"Cousin—my lord of Gloucester!" he called. "Your aid, I pray you." The guards were pushing him towards a door, not back to his place in the queue, as he said it.

A tall, thin, grave-faced man rose at the table—Gilbert de Clare, Earl of Gloucester, son-in-law of King Edward and cousin of the Bruces' father. He did not speak nor make any gesture towards his young relative, but after a moment, unhurriedly went stalking in stiff crane-like fashion up towards the dais table. At sight of this the guards halted in the pushing of their prisoner, and waited.

Gloucester bowed before the King, and said something low-voiced, turning to point back down the Hall. Edward glanced thitherwards, shrugged wide shoulders, and made a remark that ended in a hoot of laughter. He waved a careless hand. At the other end of the room, Bruce's pale face flushed scarlet. Gloucester came pacing back.

"Permit my lord of Carrick to return to his place in the file," he told the guards curtly, and without a word to his cousin, went back to his chair at the table.

Further humiliated, almost beyond all bearing, Robert Bruce was pushed back in the queue beside his brother. On the face of it no further attention was paid to him, any more than to the others. Nigel's muttered sympathy was received in stiff-lipped silence.

The Bruces' creeping progress towards the signing-table proceeded frozen-faced thereafter—until perhaps, half-way there, exclamation was in fact wrung from both brothers by the elaborate arrival of newcomers on the scene—not by any humble servitors' entrance these, but by the main Hall door. It was thrown open by a bowing chamberlain, and in strode Richard de Burgh, Earl of Ulster, followed by his daughter. A buzz of interest ran round the great chamber—to be lost in the louder noise of rising and pushing back of chairs, as Edward himself rose and turned to greet these honoured guests warmly, and perforce all others awake and sufficiently sober must rise also.

When they mounted the dais, the King slapped his old comrade on the back heartily, and raising the curtsying Lady Elizabeth, kissed her cheek with a smack, at the same time managing to nudge her father in the ribs in jocular fashion, obviously paying masculine tribute to her appearance. And admittedly she was very lovely, changed from her travelling dress into a magnificent shaped gown of pale blue satin, high-throated and edged with pearls, which highly effectively set off her fair beauty and splendid figure. She wore her plentiful ripe-corn-coloured hair looped with a simple circlet of blue cornflowers instead of the more usual elaborate headdress with net and horns. No large number of women were present, for the English were not apt to take their ladies campaigning with them, and the Scots summoned to the signing were all men; but such as there were shone but dully beside Elizabeth de Burgh, and by their expressions, knew it.

Little of admiration was reflected on the face of the Bruce brothers either. Indeed Robert's carefully maintained and haughty lack of expression was now cracked into something like a glower.

"A plague on them! This is beyond all!" Nigel growled. "Must we suffer this too? She will, she must see us here. Crawling like, like worms! Vanquished."

The man immediately before them in the column turned. "We *are* vanquished men, my lords," he said simply. It was Sir Richard Lundin, a middle-aged Fife knight known slightly to both.

"You may be. But we are not, sir," Bruce declared heatedly. "We ever fought on Edward's side. Opposed the usurper Baliol. And now—this!"

"My heart bleeds for you, my lords!" A young man looked back from further up the queue, speaking mockingly. "To have betrayed your own crowned liege lord and realm, and to have received *this* in reward!" That was Sir John Comyn, younger of Badenoch, nephew of King John Baliol and kinsman of the Constable, Buchan.

"Comyn! *You* to speak! You, who stole my lands. Bruce has never acknowledged any king save Edward, since Alexander died. Comyn swore fealty to Edward likewise. Can you deny it? And then turned rebel. Jackal to Baliol! For which treachery you were given *my* lands. And you talk of betrayal!" During John Baliol's three-year reign, he had forfeited the Bruces and divided their Carrick lands in Ayrshire amongst the Comyns, his sister's family.

"John Baliol was, and is, King of Scots. Nothing that you, or that tyrant there, can say or do can uncrown him. Crowned at Scone, on the Stone of Destiny. You it is, Bruce, that is rebel . . ."

"My lords, my young lords!" In between them the old Abbot of Melrose raised imploring hands. "Peace, peace, I pray you. This can serve no good. For any of us. Of a mercy, watch your words. Already they look at us . . ."

That was true. Despite the general noise and the evident policy of ignoring the Scots, the young men's upraised voices had attracted some attention, the fact that it was the Earl of Carrick again no doubt contributing. Edward himself had not glanced in their direction, but Surrey, his chief commander, now looked round and down. And sitting at the King's table now likewise, Elizabeth de Burgh was also considering them thoughtfully.

Perceiving the fact, Robert Bruce cursed below his breath, and looked determinedly elsewhere. Never had he felt so helpless, in so intolerable a position—he who should be Prince of Scotland if he had his rights. And to have that chit of a girl sitting there looking down on his ignominy . . . !

His brother was also looking carefully anywhere but at the dais table. To change the dangerous subject was as essential as was not meeting the young woman's interested gaze. He tapped Robert's arm.

"That piece of stone? With the flagons on it. What is it?" he asked. "How comes it here?"

His brother shook his head.

"They say that it is the Coronation Stone, my lord," Lundin informed. "The same that the young Lord of Badenoch spoke of —the Stone of Destiny. King Edward took it from Scone Abbey, and carries it south with him. To London. As symbol that there is no longer any king to be crowned in Scotland. So he misuses it thus—as stool for his viands . . ."

"God's curse on him!" somebody snarled, though low-voiced.

"I' faith—you say so?" Robert Bruce was interested now. "That ugly lump of red rock the famous Stone of Destiny? The Palladium of Scotland? Who would have thought it?"

"Only fools would think it!" That was Sir John Comyn again, scornfully. "This is not the Stone of Scone. It is some quarryman's block!"

"Then why is it here, at the King's side?"

"Edward Plantagenet says it is the Coronation Stone. And whatever else he is, he is no fool!"

"Nevertheless, that is not the true Stone, I tell you," Comyn insisted. "I know. I have seen it. At King John's coronation, at Scone. My kinsman Buchan placed him on the Stone, and put the crown on his head. I stood close by, holding the sword of state for him. Think you I would not know the Stone again if I saw it?"

"Hush, man—hush!" The Abbot of Melrose sounded agitated.

"Then what is this?" Lundin demanded.

"God knows! Some borestone for a standard, perhaps. But it looks to me new-quarried. Fresh. Sandstone. The true Stone is quite other. It is higher—to be sat upon. Dark, almost black. Harder stone. Polished. And carved. Carved with figures and designs. Erse designs. Not a dull lump of soft sandstone, like that . . ."

"Of a mercy, my lord—hold your tongue!" the old Abbot exclaimed, tugging at Comyn's sleeve. "They will hear . . ."

"What of it?" Comyn, known as the Red—although that was a family appellation and not descriptive of his colouring—was a fiery hawk-faced character, about Robert Bruce's own age, lean, vigorous, contentious. His father had been one of the Guardians of Scotland during the interregnum that ended with Baliol's enthronement, and had married Baliol's sister. The son, as heir of the Red branch of the most powerful family in all Scotland, a family that boasted three earls and no fewer than thirty-two knights, was a man whom few would wish to counter.

Nevertheless, even this proud and passionate individual must now bow the knee to English Edward—and bow it, mortifyingly to Edward's uncaring back—or be forfeited, dispossessed of his wide lands, and imprisoned as rebel. Owing to the fact that the three men in front of him were churchmen, and there appeared to be some dispute as to the lands they were to do homage for, Comyn was beckoned forward, there and then, and ordered to kneel. With ill grace and muttering, he obeyed.

The form of words, which all had heard *ad nauseam*, mumbled or chanted monotonously from the moment of entering that Hall, was once again read out. It committed the taker to fullest and sole obedience, worship and fealty to his liege lord Edward, by the grace of God King of England, Lord of Ireland and Duke of Guyenne, and to him only, his heirs and successors, to the swearer's life's end, on pain of death in this world and damnation in the next. It was noteworthy that Edward was not now calling himself sovereign of Scotland, Lord Paramount or other title which could imply that there was in fact any kingdom of Scotland at all. After the oath followed the list of lands, baronies and offices, in each county, for which the homage was being done, as feudal duty. In Comyn's case this extensive list, however rapidly gabbled through, took a deal longer than the oath itself to enunciate. Sir John, features twisted in sourest mockery, went through the required procedure, deliberately malforming the words from stiff lips. Then he rose, took the proffered quill, and signed the sheepskin with a contemptuous flourish, made the three required valedictory bows to the royal back at speed, and flung out of the chamber while his cleric neighbour was still on his knees.

Quickly it was Robert Bruce's turn. As he stepped to the table and one of the attendants demanded his name, rank and lands, he raised his voice loudly, addressing not the clerks but the dais-table.

"Here is error," he called. "I, Robert Bruce, Earl of Carrick, have already done homage to my liege lord Edward. At Wark, in England. In the month of March. His Majesty, that day, gave me this ring." He held up a hand on which a ruby gleamed warmly. "I call as witnesses to that homage Anthony Beck, Bishop of Durham; John de Warenne, Earl of Surrey; Humphrey de Bohun, Earl of Hereford. All here present, and at the King's table!"

There was a momentary hush in that room. Even Edward Plantagenet paused in his talk for a second or two. Then he resumed his converse with Richard de Burgh, without a glance round, as though nothing had happened, raising a goblet to his lips. A sigh seemed to ripple over the company. Bishop Beck gestured down peremptorily to the clerks.

"Kneel, my lord," the chief clerk said, agitatedly. "The oath. All must swear it. His Majesty's command."

"If my previous oath, willing, is considered of no worth, shall this, constrained, be the better?" Bruce cried hotly.

Furiously Beck rose at the dais-table. "Guard!" he roared. "Your duty, fools!"

Edward chatted on to Ulster—though that man looked less than comfortable. The Lady Elizabeth, at his side, was now considering not the line of Scots but her fingernails, head lowered.

Mail-clad guards stepped forward to grasp the Bruce's arms and shoulders. Perceiving that further resistance not only would avail nothing but would probably result in his Carrick lands not being restored to him but given to another, he dropped to the floor—but on one knee only. There he muttered the terms of the oath, after the clerk—and on this occasion this minion was so relieved that he did not issue the usual warnings to speak clear. Rising, Bruce took the quill, signed with barely a glance at the sheepskin, bowed briefly and only once, and stalked to the door. None sought to bring him back to complete the triple obeisance.

He was striding in black rage down the slantwise castle court-yard towards the outer bailey, to be off, when his brother caught up with him. And not only Nigel—an officer of the guard.

"My lord of Carrick," this individual said stiffly. "A command. A royal command. His Highness the King commands that you attend him at the banquet and entertainment he holds tonight. In this castle at eight of the clock. You understand, my lord? It is the King's pleasure and command that you attend tonight."

"God in His heaven!" Robert Bruce exploded. "Who is crazed —he or I?"

.   .   .

It was the same Great Hall, crowded still, and with minstrels playing—but with an atmosphere that could hardly have been more different. All now was colour and ease and laughter—King Edward's the heartiest of all. When the Bruces arrived, deliber-ately late, four dwarfs were entertaining the company with a tumbling act, aided by a tame bear, which seemed to amuse the warrior-king immoderately. Indeed he was pelting them with cates and sweetmeats from the tables, in high good humour, and even roared with mirth when the chief dwarf actually threw one back approximately in the royal direction. The brilliant company, taking its cue from its master, was in the best of spirits, with wine flowing freely. No least emanation from the dead, corpse-filled town below penetrated here.

Looking round on all that glittering and animated throng, the newcomers could see no other Scots. They knew a great many of those present, of course, for Robert in particular had been around the English Court, off and on, for years, holding almost as great lands in England as in his own country. But the constraint of the afternoon's proceedings was very much with them still—and obviously with others also, for such glances as came their way were all very quickly directed elsewhere, and none of the other guests came to speak to them. Not even Gloucester, or any other of their English kinsmen, came near their corner.

The dwarfs' act over, the King called for dancing. The floor was cleared and the musicians reinforced. Now the notable shortage of women was emphasised, and comparatively few of the men could take the floor for lack of partners. Edward headed up a lively *pas de deux*, with jovial gallantry choosing Elizabeth de Burgh as partner, her father following on with the Countess of Gloucester.

All others must press back to give the dancers space, so that the young Bruces, though hemmed in, were no longer lost behind a crowd. And when the heavily playful monarch and the graceful young woman glided past, both undoubtedly noticed the brothers standing there. Indeed Edward obviously made some comment, with a smile, to his partner. She did not smile, however. Nor did Robert Bruce.

The dance over, and a soulful lute-player taking over the entertainment while the guests refreshed themselves at the laden tables, a page brought a summons for the Earl of Carrick to attend on His Majesty. Set-faced, wary, Robert moved after the youth. Everywhere men and women watched, even though they pretended not to.

Edward was up at the dais end of the Hall again, selecting sweetmeats for Elizabeth de Burgh from dishes lying on the lump of red sandstone, which had not been moved since the afternoon. He turned, as Bruce came up and paused some distance off, bowing.

"Ha, Robert my friend!" he cried, in most genial welcome, holding out his hand. "Come, lad. Here is a lady to turn all hearts and heads! Even yours, I vow! The Lady Elizabeth of Ulster has made thrall of me quite. Let us see what she can do with you. Since someone must needs do so, it seems, on my behalf and service!"

Bruce inclined his head, but came only a little nearer that outstretched hand. "The Lady Elizabeth and I have met, Sire. This afternoon. Before . . . before what was done here," he said stiffly. "And her undoubted charms are not necessary. To win my loyal devotion to your service."

"No? Is he being ungallant, my dear? Or just plain Scots? For they are a stubborn and stiff-necked crew, God knows! What think you?"

She looked at the young man levelly, gravely. "I think that perhaps he conceives Your Majesty to have mistreated him. And sees not what any woman has to do with it!"

"Mistreated? I, Edward, mistreated him? No, no—the boot is on the other leg, I swear. Have I mistreated you, Robert?"

Bruce swallowed, but raised his head a degree higher. "I say so, Sire."

"Damme—you do?" The King looked incredulous, sorrowful and amused in one. "You, that I have nurtured! Lavished gifts upon. Paid your duns and creditors. By the Mass—here's ingratitude!"

"No, Sire. Not so. For what you have done for me, in the past, I am grateful. But, if I needed aid, debts paid, was it not because I had lost all in Your Majesty's service? My lands of Carrick, Cunninghame and Kyle, taken from me by Baliol for supporting your cause. I became a pauper, Sire . . ."

"Ha! A pauper, you say—for Edward! Behold the pauper!" The King gestured mockingly at Bruce's rich velvets, jewellery, gold earl's belt. "Would you say, my dear, that my lord of Carrick starves on Edward's bounty?"

The girl shook her head, wordless, obviously reluctant to be involved in this clash. Indeed, she was sketching an incipient curtsy, preparatory to moving away, when Edward reached out and held her arm.

"I humbly suggest that Your Majesty has had good value for the moneys you have disbursed on my behalf," the younger man declared carefully, picking his words. "You have had the use of a thousand Bruce swords and lances. Of our great castle of Lochmaben. We have kept Galloway in your peace . . ."

"All of which it was your simple duty to render, I'd mind you, Robert," the monarch interrupted. But he said it conversationally, almost sadly. "Else what for was your oath of fealty?"

"That I wondered, Sire. This afternoon! When you forced me to a second and shameful oath-taking. Abasing me before all, as though I were some defeated rebel!"

"Forced, boy? Needs must I *force* you to show your lealty to me?" Edward shook his leonine head, and turned to Elizabeth. "You see the stubborn pride of this young man? What am I to do with him? The signing of today's Roll, this Ragman's Roll, was too much for him. All others who hold land in Scotland must do new homage for it—as is only right and proper, since there is no longer any King of Scots. But not our Robert! I wonder why— on my soul I do? Could it be . . .? Could it be he has high tastes, the lad? In more than clothes and horses and the like—as my purse knows full well! Could it be that he sees himself, perhaps, as one day sitting in John Baliol's throne?" That was still directed at the young woman—indeed the King still held her arm. But the mock-sorrowful voice had suddenly gone steely. "His father, see you, had such notions. And his grandsire before him. How think you, my dear?"

"I do not know, Your Majesty. These are matters quite beyond my ken."

"But not beyond mine, Sire!" Bruce said, "And I say that you misjudge if you so think. No such notion is in my mind. My grandfather claimed the throne, yes. And Your Majesty chose Baliol rather than he. To the hurt of all, as it has transpired. But that is an old story. If my father still hankers after an empty crown, I do not."

"As well, lad—as well!" Sibilant, soft, there was nevertheless something almost terrifying in the older man's voice, despite the smile. "For that folly is done with. You hear? Done with. As Almighty God is my witness, there shall be no King of Scots again. No realm of Scotland. Mark it, Robert Bruce. Mark it, I say." He jerked his head. "Why, think you, that Stone lies there? On its way to Westminster. Why?"

"That I wondered," the girl said. "So strange and rude a thing. So, so lacking in any grace . . ."

"Graceless, aye! Like the people who cherished it. Rude and hard—but none so hard to break! I take it to London because, from time beyond mind, the ancients have declared that where that Stone lies, from there will Scotland be governed. Every petty king of this unhappy land has been crowned thereon. But none shall sit on it again. The Kings of England hereafter shall use it as their footstool! In token that the realm of Scotland is dissolved. Gone. For all time to come. I say mark it well, Robert."

"I mark it, Sire. I mark also that it is not as described by those who have seen the Stone of Scone! It is different. Not carven. Bare a foot high. Soft sandstone, rough-hewn. It is said that the true Coronation Stone is otherwise . . ."

"Dolt! Numskull! Insolent puppy!" Suddenly Edward Plantagenet was blazing-eyed, in quivering rage. "How dare you raise your ignorant voice in my presence! That is the Stone of Destiny. I, Edward, say it. I took it from Scone. I burned its abbey. I cast down its custodians. That it should be so ill-seeming a thing is but to be expected of this barbarous, damnable country! That is Scotland's uncouth talisman!" He leaned forward abruptly, snatched up a flagon, and smashed it down in fierce violence on the top of the sandstone block, with a crash. Wine and fragments splashed over all three of them. "And that is its worth and honour, by the Mass!"

At the noise the lutist faltered to a halt, and everywhere men and women fell silent gazing alarmed up towards the trio at the dais.

Edward raised a jabbing hand, to point at the musician. "Sing, fool! Did I command you to desist?" He glared round at all the company. "What ails you? What ails you, I say?"

Hastily all turned away, began urgently to talk with each other, to resume their eating and drinking.

Bruce wiped with his velvet sleeve some of the wine which had splashed up in his face. "Have I your permission to retire, Sire?" he asked.

"No, you have not!" The King swung on him, fierce eyes narrowed. "That Stone. Do you still, in your impertinence, say that it is not the Stone of Destiny?"

"No, Sire."

"As well!" He took a pace or two away, and then back. "Why in God's good name are you such a fool, Robert?" he demanded, but in a different voice. "Fools I cannot abide." He turned on the young woman—whose fine gown was now sadly stained with wine. "What think you? Is his folly beyond redemption? Could *you* redeem it, girl?"

She shook her head. "I myself am but a foolish woman, Your Majesty. If my lord of Carrick is indeed so foolish, then other than I must deal with him."

"Ha! Is that the way of it? You see—she does not want you, man! And I cannot say that I blame her."

The young man looked quickly from one to the other. "*I* cannot say that I understand you, Sire. In . . . in anything."

"Because you are a fool, as I say. You lack understanding. Let us hope that is all you lack! Think on that! I had plans for you. Other than just the payment of your debts. But I swear I must needs think again." Edward tapped Elizabeth's shoulder. "My dear, I fear the matter is beyond redemption. But see if a woman may instil a modicum of sense, if not wisdom, into that stubborn head. For I confess I have lost all patience with it."

Without a further glance at either of them, majesty stalked off, beckoning to the ever-watchful Bishop of Durham.

Mystified, Bruce stared at the young woman. "Of a mercy— what means all that?" he demanded. "Has he taken leave of his wits? Or is he drunken? What does he mean? What has he conceived against me? And how come *you* into it?"

Troubled, she bit her lip. "He is strange, yes. But you know him better than do I. Before today, I had not seen him since I was a child."

"I thought that I knew him passing well. Always he was passionate. Changeable. A man of moods. But he has ever seemed to esteem me well enough. To trust me. What have I done that he should treat me like this?"

"I do not know. But from what he has said, I think that he questions your loyalty. You have come from Galloway, have you not? Perhaps what you were doing in Galloway aroused his suspicions?"

"I was in Galloway, yes, when he summoned me here. Baliol was Lord of Galloway, before Edward named him king. Owned great lands there, heired from his mother, Devorgilla of the old race. Bruce also held Galloway lands, which Baliol took when we clove to Edward. Since Baliol's fall, I have been visiting these . . ."

"And the former King's lands also?"

"I could scarce help pass through some. And why not? He seized all my Carrick lands, and gave them to Comyn . . ."

"No doubt, my lord. But perhaps tales have reached King Edward. From Galloway. Perhaps he believes that, now that King John Baliol is gone, *you* are seeking his great Galloway lands. And more than his lands. My father says that Galloway, properly mustered, could raise ten thousand men. Perhaps, my lord, His Majesty would prefer that the son of the man who now claims that he should be King of Scots should not control those thousands?"

He frowned at her. Chit of a girl as she was, she talked now like Richard de Burgh's daughter.

"There is no truth in that," he said. "I have no thought to raise men. Against Edward. I have ever been loyal. I have raised men *for* him . . ."

"Loyal, my lord? Loyal to Edward of England? But not to Scotland, it seems. There are loyalties and loyalties!"

He stared at her. "What do you mean? Baliol was ever the enemy of our house. When he became King, we fought against him. What else? Would you have had us lick his boots?"

"You put Bruce before your Scotland?"

"Would you not put de Burgh before Ireland?"

"No. *I* would not."

He shrugged. "What is Scotland? A rabble of hungry, quarrelling lords. A land rent in pieces. A pawn in this game of kings."

"Then is not here, perhaps, your answer, sir? If Bruce will put Bruce before Scotland, may he not put Bruce before Edward also? And when his father claims the Scots throne, Edward must needs look at Bruce with new eyes. And listen to the tales that men tell."

"You think that is it? But there is no truth in it, I tell you. My father is something of a fool. Weak. But stiff-necked. Perhaps he is, indeed, what Edward calls *me*! He will talk, but not act. He is a man of books and parchments, not the sword. Edward need not fear him."

"It is you he fears, I swear—not your father. And thinks to change his plans for you . . ."

"Aye—plans. What plans? What was he talking of, that he needs now to think again?"

"You do not know?"

"No. How should I know? He has told me nothing. Summoned me here, and then insulted me! Told me nothing, save that I am a fool. And, perhaps, traitor . . . !"

Elizabeth de Burgh looked away. "You had a wife, my lord?"

He nodded. "Aye. Isobel. Daughter to the Earl of Mar. We were wed young. She died. Two years ago. Giving birth to our daughter Marjory."

"I am sorry." She drew a deep breath. "I have learned, since I came to Berwick, *why* my father brought me from Ireland. To this Scotland. It was King Edward's command. He thought to marry me. To you!"

"Lord God!"

She raised her head, in a quick gesture. "Well may you say so, my lord! Such match would have been as unwelcome to me as to yourself, I assure you. More so. So, I give thanks for the King's change of mind!"

"But . . . but this is crazy-mad. Why? Why should he have had us to wed? Unknown to each other. How would such a match serve Edward?"

"That he did not reveal to me. But he is my god-sire. My father has long been his close companion. Perhaps he thought to bind you closer to him, thus. Make you more his man . . ."

"I' faith—by foisting a wife on me! My father chose my first wife—a mere child. My next I shall choose for myself ..."

"And welcome, sir—so long as you do not choose Elizabeth de Burgh!"

"H'rr'mm. I am sorry. I but mean that ..."

"Your meaning is very clear, my lord. But no clearer than mine, I hope. Let us both thank God for His Majesty's doubts! It has saved me the distress of refusing him. And you! I bid you a good night, sir." With the merest nod she turned and swept away, making for a door.

It did not take long for Robert Bruce to seek escape also, though by a different door. Nigel could look after himself.

But, as in the afternoon, King Edward proved that he had keen eyes. A messenger again came hurrying after the truant.

"His Majesty regrets that you saw fit to leave without his express permission, my lord," he was told, expressionlessly. "His Highness, however, will overlook the omission. But he commands that you attend the parliament he holds here at noon tomorrow. On pain of treason. You have it, my lord of Carrick ...?"

.　　.　　.

Scotland, in 1296, was not notably advanced in parliamentary procedure; but the parliament held at Berwick that 28th of August was by any standard the most extraordinary the ancient kingdom had ever seen. For one thing, although it was held on Scottish soil and to deal with the affairs of Scotland, it was purely an English occasion; only English commissioners had power to vote, although the summoned Scots representatives were there, under threat of treason, in greater numbers than ever before. No Scot might even speak, unless he was specifically invited to do so. Even the Englishmen, indeed, did little speaking, save for Bishop Beck, who stage-managed all. And his clerks. It was, in fact, no parliament at all, but a great public meeting for the announcement of the details by which Edward Plantagenet's dominion over conquered Scotland would be implemented. Although the King left most of the actual talking to Beck and his henchmen, his opening remarks made very clear what was required of the assembly, and what would result from any failure to achieve it, or the least questioning of the programme—as witness to which he there and then announced orders for the arrest and imprisonment of any who had failed to obey the summons to attend, including even an illustrious prelate, the Bishop of Sodor and Man. Thereafter, Edward's interventions were infrequent, but as telling as they were brief.

The main business was to announce the machinery by which Scotland would hereafter be governed. John de Warenne, Earl of Surrey, would be Viceroy; William de Amersham, Chancellor; Hugo de Cressingham, Treasurer; William de Ormesby, Justiciar. The clerks Henry of Rye and Peter of Dunwich were appointed Escheators, officials with general supervision over all revenues north and south of Forth respectively. Another clerk, William Dru, would be Bishop of St. Andrews, and therefore Primate, since Bishop Fraser had fled; and would administer also the earldom of Fife and the customs of Dundee. The royal servants John Droxford, wardrobe-keeper, Philip Willoughby, cofferer and Ralph Manton, tailor, with others, would have oversight over all other earldoms and baronies as King's Procurators. Every Scots stone castle would be garrisoned by English soldiers, and every wooden one burned, without exception. All Scots official records were to be sent to London. Heavy taxation was necessary to pay for the recent campaign, the administration, and the army of occupation; this would be enforced on all classes, and the Church in especial, with the utmost rigour. And so on.

In the quite prominent position to which he had been conducted, Robert Bruce listened to all this, features controlled, and wondering why he had been required to attend. It was not until late in the proceedings that he learned. The clerk at Beck's left hand, reading out a list of minor enactments and edicts, found another paper passed to him. He read it out in the same monotonous gabble.

"It is hereby commanded that the Lord Robert Bruce, sometime Earl of Carrick, shall forthwith proceed to the lands of Annandale formerly held by his father, and there receive into the King's peace, with all necessary persuasion, all occupiers of land, all arms-bearing men, and all lieges fit of body and mind. These he shall cause to take oath of allegiance to King Edward, all under the supervision of Master John Benstead, clerk of the King's pantry. Thereafter the said Lord Robert shall muster these said men of Annandale in arms and proceed to the contiguous lands of the traitor William, Lord of Douglas, formerly keeper of this castle, where the wife of the same, who has already incurred the King's displeasure, is wickedly and treasonably holding out against the King's peace in the Castle of Douglas. There he shall destroy the said castle, waste the said lands, and bring captive the said Lady of Douglas to the King's appointed officers here at Berwick for due trial and punishment. All this the said Lord Robert shall perform, and such else as may be directed by the said Master Benstead of His Majesty's pantry, it being expressly forbidden that he proceed into the lands and territory of Galloway. By the King's royal command."

As the clerk continued with the next edict, Bruce sat as though turned to stone, though the knuckles of his clenched fists gleamed white. A man, he knew, could accept only so much and remain a man. Edward was testing him, but beyond acceptance. On Edward Plantagenet's head be it, then . . .

Chapter Three

ANOTHER Great Hall in another castle, another oath-taking and roll-signing—though few here could do more than make their rude marks against their names and holdings, and fewer still knew what they were signing for before their lord's son and the Englishmen. The farmers, shepherds, drovers, horse-dealers, millers, smiths, packmen and the like, of Annandale, one hundred and fifty square miles of the best land on the West March of the Border, were not knowledgeable or greatly interested in the political situation or in who occupied thrones or made laws. They followed their lord, paid their rents, gave of their service—and hoped, this done, to be left in approximate peace to lead their own lives. If their lord—or, at least, their lord's son, young Robert—summoned them to the Castle of Lochmaben in their hundreds, and required them to utter some rigmarole of words, and scratch crosses and marks on papers, they were perfectly willing to humour him, however much of a waste of time it might be. If, thereafter, they were to go riding, armed, in the tail of the same Lord Robert, as was rumoured, then few would find this any great trial, since such ploys usually resulted in sundry pleasurable excitements and sports, cattle and plenishings cheaply won, new women to be sampled. The Annandale men had had little enough of this sort of thing these last years, with the Bruces dispossessed temporarily, and the absentee Comyn Earl of Buchan getting the rents; and latterly the English captain and small garrison established in the castle, though arrogant and objectionable, had not greatly troubled the local folk. Some little friction there had been earlier on, mainly over their attitude to the women, but the independent, hard-riding Border mosstrooping population was not one to offend lightly, and the Englishmen numbered no more than four score, a mere token garrison. So a sort of mutual live-and-let-live had developed. But now, with the Bruces back, more than this could be looked for.

Robert Bruce lounged in a high chair at the dais end of the Hall, looking bored and restless; but at least he did not turn his back on the queue of oath-takers, nor eat and drink while they made their patient way through the prescribed procedure.

Indeed, sometimes he nodded, raised a hand, or called a greeting to this man or that, whom he recognised, and even occasionally came down to speak with old acquaintances amongst the tenantry—for here it was that he had spent much of his childhood, although Turnberry, up in Ayrshire, was the principal seat of the Carrick earldom.

Nearby, also on the dais, another man sat throughout the prolonged business, though he gave no appearance of boredom or restlessness; he was in fact sound asleep—Sir Nicholas Segrave, captain of the castle's garrison, a grizzled veteran of the wars, grey-headed, inclining to stoutness, still a good man in a fight but grown appreciative also of the benefits of quiet inaction.

But if these two on the dais seemed to lack interest in the proceedings, there was one who could not be so accused. The man who sat behind the signing table, with the Lochmaben steward and his minions, watched all with a keen and careful glance. He was a small, misshapen man, almost an incipient hunchback, discreetly dressed all in black, thin, with a darting beady eye, and lank black hair that fell over his chalk-white face. Efficient, industrious, shrewd, Master John Benstead, clerk to the royal pantry, was a man of swift wits, sarcastic tongue and some learning—indeed an unfrocked priest it was said, and always knew just what he was doing. In these last winter months he had lived closer to Robert Bruce than any of his brothers—and that young man had come to loathe the very sight of him. He was now snapping questions of Dod Johnstone, the steward, about almost every man who came up to the table, and taking quick notes of his own on a sheaf of papers—for what reason, none could tell. But if none liked it, since it made all uncomfortable, none questioned it either—even Bruce himself, who had not been long in recognising that though *he* was the earl and men took this oath of allegiance to Edward through him as feudal superior, it was this deformed clerk who was, in all that counted, the master. One was the all-powerful King of England's trusted servant, with unspecified but comprehensive authority; and the other, whatever else, was not. Even Sir Nicholas, up there on the dais, though he got on passing well with the young lord, now took his orders from this base-born clerk, however reluctantly.

The interminable process at the table—which was clearly much more concerned with the new and damnable notion of tax-assessment than with the ostensible allegiance-giving—was nearing an end for this grey March day, and Benstead was closely cross-questioning an impassive upland farmer as to his stocks of wool—for by a new edict all Scots wool was to be confiscated and sent to the nearest port for shipment to London for the King's use—when there was an interruption. A booted and spurred courier came hurrying in. It was noticeable that though the man bowed perfunctorily towards the pair on the dais, it was to Master Benstead that he made his way, to speak low-voiced, urgently.

Sir Nicholas, with an old campaigner's ability to waken at need and completely, bestirred himself and stumped down to see what was to do. After a moment or two, Bruce swallowed his pride and did the same.

The messenger, an Englishman, had come from Lanark, from Edward's newly-created Earl of Clydesdale and Sheriff of Lanark and Ayr, William de Hazelrig. His tidings were dramatic. Sir William Douglas had escaped from his bonds in the south, and was believed to be heading for Scotland again, if he was not already over the Border. Moreover, open revolt had broken out in Galloway, where James Stewart, the High Steward of Scotland, and Bishop Robert Wishart of Glasgow, had risen in arms against the English garrisons. It was thought that Douglas would make for Galloway to join these traitors, since he had married the Steward's sister. But before that he might well seek to collect a force of men on his own estates in Douglasdale. The Earl of Carrick, at Lochmaben, had been charged with the duty of dealing suitably with the Douglas lands. He must see to it without delay that this renegade gained no men there, that he was apprehended if he came thither, and that the territory of Douglasdale was left in no condition ever again to be a danger to the King's peace.

"You hear, my good young lord?" Benstead asked, pointing a

long, ink-stained finger at Bruce. He infuriated the latter in innumerable ways, but in none more effectively than this deplorable habit of referring to him as his good young lord. "Your delays stand revealed. Indicted. If this Douglas reaches his lands before you do, and gathers men there to aid these rebels in Galloway, then *you* will be held responsible. I have told you."

"And I have told you, sir, that in winter months there can be no campaigning in these hills. You are not in your Lincolnshire now! To take a large force over into Douglas Water means the covering of forty miles of savage hills, choked passes, flooded valleys, rivers in spate, no bridges. It could not be done, these past months. But nor was there any danger from there, since no more could the Douglases have moved in force. Sir Nicholas knows that, if you do not, Master Pantler!" To term the man this was Bruce's retort to the good young lord phrase.

"I know that you could have raided Douglasdale before the winter closed in—and did not, my lord. Despite my advice. I know likewise, even though I *am* no soldier, that it is no longer winter, and men determined in the King's service might have been amove ere this! As have these rebels in your Galloway, it seems! Perhaps it is as well that His Majesty forbade that you go into Galloway, when he did!"

"What do you mean by that? I do not take you, sir. Perhaps you will explain?"

The other looked quickly from Bruce to Sir Nicholas Segrave and the courier, and shrugged his twisted shoulders. "I would not wish to see a loyal and noble servant of the King's Highness endangered amongst rebels, that is all," he answered smoothly.

Sir Nicholas intervened. "This rising? In Galloway. How large a matter? You say the High Steward, and one of their bishops . . .?"

"It is serious, I fear. Now that King Edward has gone campaigning in Flanders, these treacherous Scots think that they may safely rebel. They must be taught otherwise. Eh, my good lord? There have been a number of petty revolts, all easily put down. But this is more dangerous. The Steward, despite his strange title, is an important lord. And the rascal Bishop of Glasgow, this Wishart, is the most potent of their prelates. I would have thought that the man Baliol's fate would have taught them their lesson!"

"Galloway was Baliol's country, and these have risen in Baliol's name," the courier amplified. "They declare that he is still their king, the fools. But neither the Steward nor the Bishop are soldiers—whereas this Douglas is. Therefore my lord of Clydesdale says that it is of the utmost importance that he does not join them. He says that my lord of Carrick must act without delay. In the King's name."

"As he shall. Eh, my lord?"

Bruce inclined his head. He had put off the unsavoury business of harrying his neighbour's lands for as long as he could. Not that he had too nice a stomach for raiding and feud, in the time-honoured fashion; but Douglas was an old friend of his father's, distantly related indeed, and it went against the grain to attack his wife and family during his absence in captivity. It seemed, however, that he could procrastinate no longer. Better that he should do it, perhaps, than Hazelrig from Lanark, a man renowned as a butcher.

"It will take a little time to muster sufficient men," he said.

"Two days, no more," Benstead asserted. "We have planned it all, times without number these last months. You agree, Sir Nicholas? Two days." He turned to the courier. "My salutations to your lord, at Lanark. Tell him that my lord of Carrick will be hammering at the gates of Douglas Castle three days from now. And that every effort will be made to lay hands on its master. But once we have his lady and children, we shall have the means to halt his treasons, heh? Through them we will bring the cur to heel very promptly—or my name is not John Benstead! Tell my lord of Clydesdale that it is as good as done."

Bruce turned away and left them there, the clerk's mocking laughter following him.

.   .   .

So, a few days later, a mounted host of some six hundred men wound its way through the green Lowther Hills, forded the waters of Daer, Potrail, Elvan and Snar, feeders of Clyde, crossed the high peat-pocked moors beyond, and over the lonely pass of Glentaggart where the snow still lingered in the north-facing corries, rode down the Glespin Burn into the fair wide valley of the Douglas Water. Bruce and Sir Nicholas Segrave led, with a contingent of half the English garrison; the rest were all Annandale men, irregulars, tenantry rendering their feudal service. Their stocky, short-legged shaggy garrons, used to the hills, made a notably better job of the difficult terrain than did the English regulars' cavalry horses. To the satisfaction of all concerned, Master Benstead had elected to remain behind, allegedly on account of pressure of paper work, but, Bruce was pretty sure, actually to conduct a great search for hidden wool, while most of the able-bodied men and heads of households were away with their lord.

But there was some cause for dissatisfaction also. Hitherto, ostensibly in the interests of secrecy, so that they might descend upon the Douglases unawares, there had been none of the looked-for and prescribed harrying and laying waste of the land. These barren uplands, of course, were scant of people and houses, and admittedly this was not the best time to encumber themselves with flocks and herds. But it made dull riding for so puissant a force.

In the early afternoon of the second day, with the richer broad bottomlands of Douglasdale opening before them, the temptations became much greater. There were still some four miles of populous country to cover before Douglas Castle, when Bruce halted his force and ordered all to gather round and attend well to what he said. Clad in a handsome suit of chain-mail under a heraldic surcoat of red and gold, girdled with a golden earl's belt, a plumed helmet on his head, he caused his horse to mount a little knoll, and spoke from that.

"My friends—we are here, not for our own advantage but to bring this Douglasdale into the King's peace. Remember it. There may well be pickings for one or two, when our work is done. But not until then, I say. You hear me? Our task is to reach Douglas Castle quickly, before the Lady of Douglas and her folk have time or opportunity to put it in state of readiness against us. For we are not prepared or equipped for a seige, as you must know. It is a strong house, and we have no engines to reduce it. So we hasten. It is understood?"

Men murmured or growled, but made no more specific protest at such a poor programme for Border mosstroopers.

"I do not think to see much fighting," Bruce went on. "Even if they are warned of our approach, they cannot have had time to assemble any strength. We shall surround the castle and hope to rush the gates, demanding surrender in King Edward's name. Only if they hold against us need there be bloodshed. Have you anything to add, Sir Nicholas?"

The veteran nodded. "If a woman commands here, we may save ourselves much trouble," he said. "We will take two or three children. Bring them before the castle with ropes round their necks. Threaten to hang them if the castle is not yielded. Hang one, if needs be, as example. No woman will hold out then, I wager."

Bruce frowned. "I do not make war on women and children, sir," he declared, shortly.

"No? It is a woman and her cubs we have to oust from this house, is it not? If they resist, many will die. Which is better — one child or many grown men? And likely other children thereafter? This is war, not a tourney, my lord!"

"Nevertheless, we shall do this *my* way," Bruce said levelly. He did not want to quarrel with the Englishman — was not sure indeed who was truly in command of this expedition. The mass of the men were his, and in theory he was the leader — but he knew that in fact he was little more than a puppet of the English, and Benstead would support this gruff and experienced soldier against him to the hilt. And Benstead, unhappily, stood for Edward Plantagenet in this.

So, when they rode on, the younger man went out of his way to be civil to the knight, to avoid any rupture. They had got on well enough together hitherto — largely thanks to a mutual reaction towards clerks in authority, though essentially they had little in common. Segrave would make a dangerous enemy, Bruce well realised.

Scouts sent ahead reported that Castleton of Douglas, the township clustered round the fine church of St. Bride near the castle demesne, was strangely quiet, with nobody stirring — though no visible sign of alarm.

"It could mean that they have gone. Learned of our coming, and fled," Bruce commented, sounding more hopeful than he knew.

"Or moved into the castle. To hold it against us," the knight countered. "As like the one as the other."

His companion had his own reasons for thinking otherwise, but did not say so. He was the more disappointed then, when, after clattering through the seemingly deserted village — and sending pickets round the back lanes to ensure that no armed men lurked there — they came to Douglas Castle on its mound above the bends and water-meadows of the river, to find the drawbridge raised, all gates closed, and the Douglas banner streaming proudly from its keep.

"I thought as much," Sir Nicholas said grimly. "This lady requires to be taught a lesson."

"Not by hanging bairns, at least," his companion returned.

Douglas Castle, though not so large as Lochmaben, and no fortress like Berwick, was an imposing place, and because of the riverside cliff and the swampy nature of the approach, difficult to reach save by the narrow causeway which led to the drawbridge and gatehouse of the outer bailey. It was a typical stone castle of enceinte, consisting of a lofty stone keep, four-square and massive, having five storeys beneath a battlemented parapet, surrounded by twenty foot high curtain-walls to form a square, with circular flanking-towers at each corner. There were the usual lean-to subsidiary buildings within the curtain-walls, but these scarcely showed from without. Now, men could be seen pacing the parapets that surmounted curtains and towers.

With a trumpeter sounding an imperious summons, Bruce rode forward, Segrave at his side. At the gap of the deep, wide, water-filled ditch, where the drawbridge should have reached, they perforce halted. They were well within arrow-shot of the gatehouse here. The younger man raised his voice.

"I am Robert Bruce, Earl of Carrick, come in the King's name. I request that this bridge be lowered and that I be admitted to speak with whoever holds this castle," he cried.

After a little delay a voice answered from a barred gatehouse window. "This is Douglas's house, and Douglas holds it. Bruce of Carrick is known. But in what king's name does he speak?"

"There is but one king now. King Edward."

"Douglas does not recognise King Edward of England as having any authority in this realm of Scotland, save what he holds with a sword," came back the careful reply. "Does Bruce bring Edward's sword to Douglas Castle?"

The other knew a strange reluctance to admit that he did. "I bring Edward's peace," he said. "And would speak with the Lady of Douglas."

There was something like a hoot from the gatehouse. "We all know of Edward of England's peace! Death's peace is kinder! And does Bruce require half a thousand men, to speak with the Lady Douglas?"

Segrave raised his voice. "Have done," he shouted shortly. "Douglas is traitor and outlaw. Has broken custody. His house and lands are forfeit. Must be yielded to the King. Yield, then. Or suffer!"

"Ha—there speaks an honest voice, at least! Edward Plantagenet's true voice. The Lady of Douglas speaks with none such."

"Then the worse for her, fool...!"

Sir Nicholas bit off the rest of that. With a vicious hissing whine, three arrows came flying past the right ear of each horseman, close enough to fan their cheeks—and to cause each to duck involuntarily, and their beasts to rear and sidle in alarm. Such carefully-placed shots obviously bespoke expert bowmen, and could equally well have been each three inches to the left and in the eye-sockets of the trio.

Segrave, cursing explosively, wheeled his heavy mount around, and went spurring back to the host, shouting that they would hereafter do things *his* way, the trumpeter crouching low in the saddle and nowise behindhand. But Bruce, seeking to quieten his horse, held his ground at the bridgehead. He raised a gauntleted hand—and hoped that any quivering would not be seen from the gatehouse.

"That was Sir Nicholas Segrave, who captains it at Lochmaben," he called urgently. "Hear *me*. Robert Bruce."

There was a pause, short enough no doubt but seeming an eternity to the man who sat there as target for a second flight of arrows. Helmeted and armoured in chain-mail he might be, but these marksmen could wing their bolts to his unprotected face; besides, at that range, a shaft, even if it failed to pierce the mail, could drive the same bodily into a man's heart or lungs.

No arrows hissed meantime, but a woman's voice, high, thin but clear, sounded. "My lord—Eleanor de Louvain, wife to Douglas, speaks. Your father I knew. And his father before him. Edward's men both. What has the son to say to *me*, who would spit in Edward's false face?"

Bruce let his breath go in a sigh of relief—although he was unprepared for the venom in that. This woman was herself English, a widowed heiress that Douglas had carried off without Edward's permission, on the death of his first wife some years before; it appeared that he had made a good Scot of her. "I say that I wish you no ill, lady. You or yours. This house must be yielded to the King—as, by his command, must every stone castle in Scotland. But there need be no bloodshed. Your people may come forth unharmed. Go where they will."

"My people, sir? And my children? And myself?"

Bruce hesitated, as well he might. And as he did so, from behind him sounded the drumming of hooves. Turning, he saw that perhaps a score of riders had detached themselves from the host, and were cantering back towards the village, three quarters of a mile away. One glance sufficed to establish that they were all

English men-at-arms of the Lochmaben garrison. The young man had no least doubt as to their mission.

He turned back, face set. "If you yield the house, no hurt shall befall you, lady. On my knightly word," he cried.

"Why should I trust your word, when you come in Edward's name, my lord?" The high voice was less firm and certain now. "That tyrant cares naught for promises. Have you forgot that my husband was Governor of Berwick?"

"It is *my* word — not Edward's . . ." Bruce was returning, when, like the hissing of a pitful of snakes, a flight of many arrows sliced the air above him. Flinging himself low over his mount's neck, he nevertheless saw three men throw up their arms on the parapet of the gatehouse tower, and one to topple headlong and fall with a splash into the moat.

Uproar followed. Swearingly savagely, amidst angry shouts from both front and rear, the lone horseman dragged his charger's head round, and rode furiously back the two hundred yards or so to his own people.

Segrave's bowmen, dismounted and kneeling, were already fitting second arrows to their strings.

"Hold! Stop, fools!" he yelled. "I commanded no blood-shed . . ."

Segrave gestured with a scornful forward wave of his hand. The second volley of long feathered shafts sped towards the castle.

"I said *no*, man! How dare you . . . !"

"You may command these cattle-thieves and shepherds," the knight said, as Bruce came up, and threw himself down from his saddle, "But even so, only by the King's permission. These *I* command, my lord. And to better effect!"

"Better? You have ruined all, man. They will hold out against us now. Have no faith in our word. And you have soiled my name."

"Then your name is easily soiled! Have I not told you — this is war? We are not here concerned with the honour of high-born lordlings! I have my duty to do . . ."

"You call slaying during a parley duty?"

"Parley! Talk! You win no wars with talk, young man. I know my duty, if you do not." He turned away, ordering his archers to raise their aim to the parapet of the keep itself, targets having all disappeared from closer at hand.

In wrath and frustration Bruce watched — and even in his ire could not withhold his admiration for the magnificent shooting of the English bowmen. That keep's topmost parapet was more than three hundred yards away, yet straight and true the arrows flew to it, zipping between the gaps and crenellations. As he gazed, a scream came thinly to them from that lofty exposed platform. Arrows were shot back at them from the castle, to be sure, but they all fell far short. Archery had never been highly developed or favoured in Scotland. The English long bow, high as a man and shooting a yard-long arrow, made of yew, a tree unknown in Scotland, had fully double the range of the Scots short bows or arbalests. It was also infinitely more accurate. Here, only the odd spent shaft from the castle came anywhere near them.

Quickly the Douglases perceived how ineffectual was their fire. Their shooting ceased, and no more men showed themselves at parapet or loophole. Sir Nicholas called a cease-fire. Bruce left him without another word, and mounting his horse again, rode off in a rageful silence.

He made a circuit of the castle—no easy task amongst the knowes, bogland and river-channels. He noted how thinly spread even six hundred men looked, when extended round a wide perimeter. From a strategic height he surveyed the scene and its possibilities, and thereafter set about regrouping his force. Instead of trying to maintain any unbroken ring, he concentrated his mosstroopers, in parties of fifty or so, where they might best command a comprehensive view of the castle and surroundings. Night-time patrols were going to be difficult.

This took time. When he returned to the main gatehouse front, it was to find Segrave's men hacking and hammering now, erecting a crossbar supported on two uprights, out of the timbers of a nearby cowshed. The bar stretched about ten feet above the ground. Men were being sent in search of ropes.

"Segrave," Bruce announced tensely, at sight of all this, "I tell you, I will not permit the hanging of innocent hostages. Nor even the pretence at it. I have not forgotten my knightly vows, if you have!"

"Permit, my lord? Permit, you say? How think you to permit, or not to permit, what I do? I am King Edward's captain here. What are you?"

"I am the Earl of Carrick, and commander of this host."

"For so long as *I* permit it! You are a name only, man. You no more command here than you command at Lochmaben Castle. King Edward has more trusted servants than you, sir. And needs them, by God!"

"There will be no hanging, Segrave."

"I have my orders."

"From that clerk? From Benstead? I congratulate you!"

Sir Nicholas looked grim but said nothing.

"Very well. We shall see." Bruce rode away again.

Back he went, to the first of the groups of fifty mosstroopers. "Half your men to come with me," he told their leader, and proceeded on round the perimeter.

When he had made the circuit of Douglas Castle for the third time, he had some two hundred rough horsemen at his tail.

As this company rode back towards the causeway area, Bruce could see that there was now some major activity going on beside the completed gallows, with men clustered around in a close circle. Exclaiming, he dug in his spurs.

Faces turned as the newcomers pounded up—including three notably white faces in the midst of it all. Three children, two boys of eight or ten, and a girl somewhat older, were being held on the backs of three horses, their hands tied behind their backs, rough gags in their mouths. Already a rope was around the girl's neck and slung over the cross-bar above her. The same was being done for the boys. The youngsters' terrified eyes made eloquent appeal.

"Sir Nicholas Segrave—cut those children free and let them go," Bruce shouted hoarsely.

There was no response. The English men-at-arms went on with their grim work.

"You heard me, Segrave? I will not have it." Bruce drove his horse forward, into the crowd of watching men, hand on sword-hilt.

"Fool! Young swollen-headed fool!" the knight cried. "Have I not told you? These need suffer no hurt. Unless the Douglas woman is a deal less chicken-hearted than you are! If they hang, it is of her will. Leave men's work to men, if you are so nice of stomach, my lord!"

"I said set them free . . . Englishman!" Deliberately Bruce added that last word.

Segrave did not fail to grasp the significance of it. He glanced around him quickly. "*Your* way, many men will die. Many children will be fatherless. Your own people's children. And these of Douglas likewise. Remember that. My way costs a deal less! Cannot you see it, man?"

"I see shame! Shame that will not be done in my presence. Set them free."

"No."

Bruce's answer was swift, in the thin skirl of steel, as his long two-handed sword was drawn from its sheath. "You have but forty," he jerked. "I have six hundred. You will do as I say."

"You . . . you would not dare! Draw steel against the King's own men? This is rebellion! Treason!"

"Not so—since I command here. Release those bairns."

"No, I say! These men—they are not yours. They are the King's men. All of them. They have sworn allegiance to him. They will do as *I* say, his officer. Not you, fool . . . !"

"Think you so? They are Bruce's men. Bruce of Annandale. We shall see who they obey!" He swung round in his saddle. "Swords, I say!"

Like the screaming of the damned, the savage sound of two hundred blades being wrenched from their scabbards sounded high and shrill above the snarling, menacing growl of angry men.

Sir Nicholas Segrave had not survived decades of warfare by being any sort of a fool. He recognised actualities when he saw them. Narrow-eyed he glared, then shrugged. He turned to his men. "Set them down," he ordered shortly. He strode over to where his horse stood, and mounted.

"You are wise in this, at least," Bruce said evenly.

"And you are not! For this you shall pay. Dearly!" The knight gestured to his trumpeter. "Sound to horse," he commanded.

The man blew a few short blasts, and everywhere the English soldiery turned and made for their mounts.

"What do you intend?" Bruce demanded.

"I leave you. To your treason. Your folly. I go. But I shall be back, my lord. Never fear! With sufficient men to teach you and your treacherous rabble a lesson. You will learn what it costs to set at naught King Edward's authority, I promise you!"

"How may that be? When *I* command. In King Edward's name . . . ?"

Segrave's snort of contempt was converted into a shouted order to his men to follow him, as he reined round and urged his horse to a trot. The men-at-arms fell in behind him, in column, and without a backward glance at the silent ranks of the Scots, rode off south by west.

Robert Bruce stared after them, biting at his lip.

CHAPTER FOUR

His men, save for a few retained with him, back at their positions around Douglas Castle, Bruce paced the turf beside the empty gibbet, cudgelling his brains, and more than his brains. He was under no misapprehensions as to the seriousness of the predicament into which he had got himself. Segrave had been only too accurate when he declared that this would be looked upon as rebellion. Treason might be stretching it to far, but rebellion it would be named. By Edward's administration in Scotland—the Englishmen, Benstead; this Hazelrig, so-called Earl of Clydesdale; Cressingham, the Treasurer, who now was the real ruler of Scotland; Surrey, the viceroy—these would see it as the revolt of a hated and despised Scots lord against the King's authority. So it would be blazoned forth by Benstead and Segrave, and so it would be accepted. As rebellion, Edward himself would hear of it, eventually.

But long before Edward, in Flanders, heard, there would be violent reactions here in Scotland; nothing was more sure. The English would act swiftly; they always did, instead of arguing interminably with each other as was the Scots way. Benstead himself could not find many more men for Segrave than the rest of the Lochmaben garrison, but he would apply to Lanark for them, where the governance of this south-west corner of Scotland was centred. Lanark was no more than ten miles north of Douglas, as the crow flew—and it was strange that Hazelrig himself had not set about the reduction of its castle instead of leaving it to Bruce, from Lochmaben. Except that that had been King Edward's specific instructions. Segrave might even go direct to Lanark from here. Although he was more likely to report to Benstead first, and pick up the rest of his garrison. In two days, or three, then, there would be an English force here at Douglasdale, a heavily-armed, veteran host against which his Annandale men, however gallant, would be like chaff in the wind.

What to do? If he could quickly reduce this castle, of course, and have it occupied and its chatelaine prisoner before such punitive force arrived, he might redeem his reputation with Edward's men. That was. possible, but by no means certain. Segrave and Benstead would consider themselves insulted—and the insulted Englishman was not readily appeased. They would insist on humbling him, demand reparation, reprisals—and none in Scotland in the year 1297 had any doubts as to the style of English reprisals. Edward's example at Berwick was to be a model as well as a warning. Undoubtedly an angry punitive force would do much more than hang two or three children. His gesture here, then, would be nullified, wasted, thrown away. And his reputation, in another sense, with it.

What alternative was there, then? He could bolt. Run. Gather his men and take themselves off, into the empty hills, before the English arrived. Scarcely a noble course, but perhaps wise. Or was it? He would have become a fugitive. For what? Outside Edward's peace, and with nothing to buy himself back into it. Moreover, would these men of his be prepared to turn fugitive with him? Abandon their homes, holdings, womenfolk, to the English ire? For nothing.

But, suppose he could take the Lady of Douglas with him? Persuade the castle to yield, and instead of waiting for the English, take her and her family with him. Into the hills. The great Forest of Ettrick was less than a score of miles to the east. No English would follow them there. Then he would have something to bargain with. Burn the castle and capture its lady—had not these been his orders? If he had achieved them, could Edward's men claim he was in rebellion? The Lady Douglas would make a valuable hostage for him; something to chaffer with. Again less than knightly perhaps—but could he afford knightly sentiments in this pass?

There was always a last resort, of course. He could throw in his lot with the true rebels. With the High Steward and the Bishop of Galloway and their like. Make for Galloway. Accept the man Segrave's charge of revolt, and become a rebel indeed. There were times without number, these last grim months, when he had been brought to the contemplation of it, had toyed with the notion. As would any man of spirit deliberately and consistently humiliated. Even that Elizabeth de Burgh had all but suggested it. What was it she said? That he was loyal to Edward but should be loyal to Scotland. And he had asked her what Scotland was? And rightly so. But . . . these English could go too far. Yet, outright rebellion? It would mean war to the knife, for him. With Edward. The King would never forgive him. And Edward, unforgiving, was a dire thought. It would mean the life of an outlaw, hunted day and night. The forfeiture of all the great Bruce lands. Not only in Scotland but in England. And what hope had these rebels, in fact? Against the power and might of England and the fury of the Plantagenet?

So Robert Bruce paced and harried his wits and his heart and his conscience—and came to no conclusion. Save only this, that it was growing towards dusk and something must be decided before darkness fell—for it would be difficult indeed to ensure that there was no break-out from the castle under cover of night. If his quarry were to steal away in the dark, he would be left without even a bargaining-counter, however poor.

His mind made up thus far at least, Bruce stripped off his handsome heraldic surcoat of linen, and tying it to a lancepoint, like a banner, gave it to one of his men to carry by his side. Hoping this would serve as a flag of truce, he and an extremely doubtful companion paced slowly, on foot, towards the castle ditch once more.

It made an unpleasant walk. But no arrows came at them, no reaction of any sort was evident, no challenging shout was raised.

At the drawbridge-end, Bruce halted and lifted up his voice. "Hear me. Hear me, I say. The Earl of Carrick would speak again with the Lady of Douglas."

He was answered at once. "You are a bold man, Lord of Carrick. Whatever else! Wait you. I send for my lady."

Bruce nodded and waited, seeking to collect his thoughts.

It was some time before the woman's high voice sounded, from a small gatehouse window. "I am here, my Lord Robert. What kindness would your King Edward do me now?"

The young man shrugged. "I speak not for Edward Plantagenet now, lady. But for myself," he said. "I regret what was done. Before. The shooting of arrows. While we talked. It was against my commands. Segrave's Englishry . . ."

"No doubt, sir. It was ill done. But what we might have looked for, from Edward's men. As what they sought to do later. With the children."

"You saw?"

"We saw, yes. They are gone?"

"Aye, gone."

"Your Segrave would have slain those children? Hanged them, before our eyes!"

' I do not know. In the end. Perhaps he would not. Only the threat. To cozen you. I do not know."

"But *I* know. His kind have done the like before. Many times.

68

If I had still refused him, he would have hanged them. And you? You would not have it?"

"No. I would not. Could not."

"I fear you are too tenderhearted to be Edward's man, my lord."

"Sir Nicholas Segrave, I mind, said the same! " Bruce gave back. This shouting was difficult. "I . . . I would speak with you, lady. Not thus. But decently. As becomes our quality."

"I am content to judge your quality from here, my lord! What have you to say?"

Bruce sighed. "Just this. Now that the English are gone, you would do well to open to me. You may trust me, Bruce. You have naught to fear from me."

"Then, my lord, why sit you round Douglas Castle? Go back whence you came. If I have naught to fear from you, I will do very well here!"

"No. Do you not see?" Exasperated, finding this long-range discussion trying in the extreme, he shook his head. "The English will be back. They *must* come back. It is Edward's command. They will come in strength. They will have you. And in ill mood. You must see it? Yield your house to me, now, and I will make a show of spoiling it. Then I will take you away. And your children. Before they come . . ."

"Where? Take me where, my lord?" Clearly he was interrupted.

"To a safe place . . ." There was another interruption, more shouting, but from behind him this time. And Bruce was almost thankful for it, at his wits' end as he was for what he might say to convince and reassure the woman. Some of his men were waving to him, urgently, and pointing. Beside them was a helmeted and leather-jerkined newcomer, obviously an English man-at-arms, and a steaming horse.

"A messenger, lord," the cry came. "Frae Lochmaben. Wi' tidings. Instant tidings, he says . . ."

Bruce hesitated, concerned with how this would look from the castle. Then he called back "Send him to me." Towards the gatehouse he added, "Your pardon, lady."

The courier came forward, far from eagerly, escorted by none. He was clearly as tired as he was doubtful.

"Well, man? You are from Sir Nicholas Segrave? What is your message?"

"Not so, lord. It is Sir Nicholas that I seek. First. To him I was sent. By Master Benstead . . ."

"Eh? Then . . . then you have not seen him? Segrave? Met with him?" Bruce stared. "How came you here?"

"By a great weariness of hills, lord. By Moffat town, see you. And Abington. And Roberton Water." This was a sing-song voiced Welshman, not English, and of some intelligence.

"So! You missed them, then. They would go back as we came —by Lowther. Sir Nicholas returns to Lochmaben. For . . . for more men."

"And is like to need them! But will not find them there, lord. Master Benstead's tidings are of rebellion. War!"

"You mean this Galloway revolt?"

'That, and a deal more. They have broken out of Galloway and marched north, these rebels. They are none so far off, look you—nearing Ayr . . ."

"Ayr, you say?" That was making north, with a vengeance! Nearly fifty miles north of the Galloway border. No more than thirty miles west of this Douglas, indeed. "Then none are opposing them?"

"So it looks, lord. All the country rises to join them. But that is not the worst. The Lord Earl of Clydesdale is dead. Slain."

"Hazelrig? Dead? You mean, in battle? He sought to halt them . . .?"

"No, lord. Not these. Another. He was murdered. Slain in his own town of Lanark. By one Wallace. Some brigand, leading broken men, outlaws. Lanark is now in their hands."

"By the Rude! Lanark fallen? Then these are no broken men! Think you such could take the Sheriff's town of Lanark, and Hazelrig's castle? Stuffed full with Edward's soldiery . . .!"

"Scarce that, lord. It was cunningly, shrewdly done. Most of the Sheriff's force had been sent towards Ayr. To stem the rebels from Galloway. This man Wallace—they say he is the son of some small Renfrew knight, a vassal of the Steward's—struck by night. He is not as the other rebels, led by lords and bishops. A man of no account, a brigand hiding in the hills and forests. By some trick he gained entry to Lanark Castle, and slew the Earl. They say in vengeance for his wife's death. Then turned on the town. The townsfolk aided him. By daylight Lanark was his."

"But, man—this is scarce believable! What were Hazelrig's captains doing? It is the garrison town of the South-West."

"One, Sir Robert Thorn, hangs from the castle's keep, in place of King Edward's banner, they say! The other it was came to Lochmaben with these tidings, looking for men. Sir Hugh le

Despenser. Wounded. Finding no men there, he rode on for Dumfries."

'So-o-o! The South-West is aflame? Edward's iron grip prised loose!"

"Meantime, Lord—meantime, only! But only the South-West. Master Benstead says that there are revolts in the North also. In Ross, wherever that may be. And Argyll, or some such place. But these are afar off. Here is the danger. These sheriffdoms of Lanark, Ayr, Carrick and Galloway—the command of these is vital to the King, Master Benstead says."

"Aye. No doubt he is right. And who *does* command here now, with Hazelrig dead? And Despenser wounded and gone? Who commands in Edward's name, now?"

The courier raised an eloquent hand. "Saving your lordship's presence," he said, diffidently, "*you* do! That was what I was to tell Sir Nicholas, look you. That now he must act in the name of the Earl of Carrick. Meantime. There is none other of earl's rank. My lord Earl of Surrey is at York, they say. Until he appoints other, you command, lord. With . . . with the advice and direction of Master Benstead and Sir Nicholas Segrave, to be sure. I was to say that, mind you . . ."

Robert Bruce's bark of laughter drowned the rest. "*I* command? God save us—*I*! The Earl of Carrick commands now, for King Edward, in the South-West! Here's a jest, by all that's holy!"

"In name, lord. Under direction. Master Benstead was strong on that. You are to gain this castle of Douglas with all speed, and then march for Lanark. Guided by Sir Nicholas. Seek to join with the Lanark force that went to Ayr, to hold the rebels. Threaten Lanark together, but await further orders from Master Benstead . . ."

"*Orders?* To Edward's commander?"

The Welshman coughed. "Instructions, lord. Guidance. Counsel—call it what you will. I am a rough man, lord. No doubt I word it ill. But I was sent, in truth, to Sir Nicholas. He it was was to speak with you . . ."

"You speak full clearly, my friend! And to the point. Never fear. And I thank you for it. Is . . . is that all?"

'Yes, lord. Have I your permission to go? I must still seek Sir Nicholas."

"He will be back at Lochmaben before you are. A shorter road than you came. But go if you will. Tell Master Benstead that I have his message. And his . . . guidance! Now, I must speak with this woman . . .'

As the courier went back towards the others. Bruce, his head in a whirl, faced the gatehouse. Somehow, he must have time to think. All was now changed. In the light of it all, so much called for decision. Instant decision. He must have a little time . . .

"Lady," he called. "My regrets that I have kept you waiting. I have important tidings. Of the utmost importance. To us all. You likewise. But not such as I may shout out to all the world! I must speak with you. Privily. It is essential."

"Very well, my lord," she answered. "Have I your word, as an earl of Scotland, that you will *only* speak? Will make no move to take or harm me?"

"You have. On my oath."

"Then the drawbridge will be lowered. Part-lowered. So that I may walk out on it. None of your people to come near, my lord. Only you. It is understood? And you must wait a little."

He nodded. The longer he might wait, the better. Had ever a man so much to decide in so short a time? Here was a crossroads in his life. Which road he took now might determine all his future.

Sending back his impromptu standard-bearer, Robert Bruce commenced to pace up and down the bank of the moat.

He scarcely heard, presently, the clanking of the portcullis chains or the creaking of the timbering as the massive drawbridge began to come down. His mind, his judgement, his emotions, his whole character and personality, were involved in a turmoil of debate, of contradiction, of conjecture, as never before. And yet, somehow, behind it all, the decision was already made.

With the bridge lowered to within some ten feet of its base, so that it formed only a moderate incline, armed men appeared from the gatehouse arch. And out from among them walked two persons—a woman and a boy.

The Lady of Douglas was younger than Bruce had expected; in her early thirties probably, slightly built but most evidently pregnant, not handsome but not ill favoured, with a proud and confident look. The boy was no more than twelve years old, well-built, sturdy, dark, almost swarthy indeed. He held the woman's hand, and held his head high as they paced out on the echoing timbers.

They came to the lip of the bridge, and so stood, looking down at Bruce. "Well, my lord—what have you to say?" Lady Douglas asked. And, as an afterthought, "This is James Douglas, my husband's heir."

"My sorrow, lady, that we should meet in such case." Bruce was frowning blackly, not at her or the boy but in concentration —however it might seem to them. "Do you know where Sir William Douglas is?"

"If I did, think you I would tell you, sir?"

"I think he may be none so far away. If I agreed to take you to him, would you come with me, madam?"

"Take me . . .? To him?" She stared down at him. "Do you think to mock me now, young man . . .?"

"Not so. Why should I mock you? I do not know for sure, but I think that Sir William may be with the other rebels. Who were in Galloway. His former good-brother, James the Steward, and the Bishop of Galloway."

"Rebels, sir? These are no rebels. How may they be rebels, who rise, in their own land and in the name of their own king, against a foreign tyrant?"

"Aye—it may be so. At any rate, these, I have just learned, are now near to Ayr. Thirty miles, no more. Will you come with me to Ayr, lady?"

"With you? *You?* To Ayr? But . . . but . . ."

"My lord," the boy said tensely but strongly. "if you jest with us now, you are no true knight! This, this lady is in no state for that. For any true knight to make fool of. Did King Edward of England send you to her for that?"

It was bravely said. This boy could not be the Lady Eleanor's son. He must be the child of the first marriage. He was, therefore, nephew of James the Steward—named after him, no doubt.

Bruce inclined his head. "King Edward sent me here to take this lady, and you, to his officers," he told the boy carefully. "But now, I find, *I* am his chiefest officer in these parts! And I have come to think that it might be best to take you to Ayr."

"Why?" the woman demanded. "Or do you seek to trick us? Use us as hostages? Before my husband . . .!"

"No. Give you into your husband's keeping, rather."

"I do not understand. You are Edward's man. My husband is Edward's enemy. What mean you . . .?"

"I am my own man, lady—not Edward's. Bruce supported Edward against the usurper Baliol, yes. But Baliol is no longer here. Nor indeed is Edward! Both across the sea. And Bruce is no puppet to be jerked this way and that . . ."

"You mean, my lord, that you change sides?"

He frowned. "Say that I must choose, in this pass, to do what is best. Wisest. For all. The South-West is aflame, it seems. And Ross and Argyll too, they say. How much else, God knows. Hazelrig is dead, at Lanark. All is changed. From when I was sent to take you . . ."

"Then why not go away, sir? Leave us in peace?" the young James Douglas broke in.

"You would not long thank me for that! Segrave and more English will be back, you may be sure. Douglas Castle would have but a brief respite. And then you would be in more unhappy state. You saw the style of Segrave!"

"So you would go to my husband, and these others, at Ayr? Taking us as, as . . . as sureties? Not hostages but tokens? Tokens, my lord. That they may accept you as honest!" Eleanor Douglas was considering him shrewdly. "I think that I perceive it. They are more like to trust you, if you do not come empty-handed! Bruce, who was Edward's man!"

"You are less than gracious, madam." That was stiff.

"Perhaps." There was a few seconds' pause. She shook her head, in a welter of indecision. "Can *I* trust you, then?"

"Would you rather that I handed you to the English? Or left you to withstand their fury here?"

She sighed. "No. Since I cannot long hold this house against a host. I will come with you. Your reasons for taking me to my husband may be ignoble, sir—but it may best serve my need meantime. I will come with you."

Bruce had flushed a little and knew it, but hoped that it might not be apparent in the half-light. "I do not acclaim your niceness of feeling, madam," he said shortly. "But at least your choice is wise. Will you go, then, and make ready? To ride. Send your folk away, to their own places. Disperse them. That there be no bloodshed when the English come. They may ill-use your house somewhat—but that is small price to pay for lives and freedom. Do not delay, for we ride as soon as we may."

"Ride? Tonight? It is near dark . . . !"

"Yes, tonight. I wish to have you away from here, out of Douglasdale and into my own country of Carrick, by daylight. To delay here now would be folly. And in your state we may not ride overfast." He glanced at her swollen belly. "So, haste you, lady."

She shrugged. "Very well. If so it must be. Come, Jamie . . ."

Bruce turned, blank-faced, and strode back in the gloaming light to his waiting men. Curtly, there, he issued orders that all his host was to be brought back forthwith, abandoning the positions around the castle. All were to assemble.

When his six hundred were gathered before him in the gloom, Bruce had a horn blown for silence, and addressed them.

"My friends," he said, "hear me. This realm is in sore straits, as you all know well. Men know not which way to turn. There has been revolt against the English who lord it here. Lanark is fallen. The High Steward, and a host, is at Ayr. I . . . I have decided to join them."

In the pause there was an absolute silence save for the wary calling of curlews bewailing the night.

"It is that, or marching against Lanark, to seek to recapture it. For the English. Which do you prefer?"

There was a muttering, quickly stilled.

"I think King Edward's cause may no longer be Bruce's cause! And I would not do battle against those who revolt. So I go to Ayr. Who comes with me?"

Again the murmuring arose, this time to continue, to grow loud and prolonged, as men discussed and argued.

After a while, Bruce had the horn blown again. "I could command that you come with me," he said. "But you are my father's vassals. Not my own. He is Lord of Annandale, not I. And my father is King Edward's Governor of Carlisle. If you join me in this, who knows, you may suffer for it. Your homes, your wives and bairns. So I give you choice. It is *my* decision. You make yours."

There was more talk, some of it heated. One voice rose above others, presently.

"Lord—do we fight for this Edward? Or against him? We do not know rightly. You had us to swear an oath. To Edward. Did you no'?"

Bruce drew a deep breath. "An oath, yes. But a commanded oath. An oath given under duress. It is not binding, as is a true oath. So teaches Holy Church. It may be annulled. I, similarly, swore allegiance to Edward. Under duress. But I did not swear to make war against my own people. Not to slay my own folk. No man, I say, holds his own flesh and blood in hatred. I am Earl of Carrick. My own folk of Carrick live yonder." He pointed to the west. "The English would have me lead you, to fight. For them. Against Scots, I cannot, will not, do it. I must join my own people of Carrick. And the nation into which I was born."

He had stopped, at his own last words. He had not known that he was going to say these things. They had come out of him of their own volition, to his surprise. He stood, biting his lip.

Some of his ranked listeners cheered. Some murmured. More stood silent.

Bruce shook his head. "A man must choose his own course," he said slowly, as though to himself. "Aye, a man must choose. Choose *you*, then. You are free to do so. My father's men, not mine. Those who would may turn now. Ride back to Annandale. To their homes. Those who would come with me to Carrick, I welcome. Let each man choose freely." He turned abruptly, and walked away from them.

It was almost an hour later, and quite dark, before the castle drawbridge clanked down again, and, lit by pitch-pine torches, a small party came riding out. Bruce rode to meet them, Lady Douglas, wrapped in a voluminous travelling-cloak, had another child with her now, riding pillion behind young James, a little boy of four or five—Hugh Douglas, her own son. There were also a couple of tiring-women and a few armed servitors.

The Annandale host was now drawn up in two companies— and one was many times larger than the other. Of something under six hundred, only about seventy had elected to go with Bruce into this doubtful adventure—and these were mainly young men, unattached, lacking responsibilities. The rest were for home, discretion and the daily round. Their lord's son was the last to blame them.

There was no further discussion or farewells. Without cere-mony, the two groups parted company, the smaller trotting off south by west up the Douglas Water, the larger turning away eastwards towards the Castleton and the unseen welter of hills beyond.

Behind them, other folk were slipping out of Douglas Castle also now, quietly, singly and in little groups, and disappearing into the night.

.   .   .

Picking their careful way by bridle-paths and cattle-tracks, Bruce's party followed the Douglas Water hour after hour through the spring night, slowly making height as the river shrank and lifted towards its genesis on the lofty flank of mighty Cairntable, where ran the Ayrshire border amongst the long heather hills.

Long before Douglas Water could lead them to its remote birthplace, they had struck off almost due westwards by a drove-road over the high, bleak watershed moorlands where the head-streams of the River Ayr were mothered, and the wastes of Airds Moss stretched in peat-hag and scrub. By dawn they were slanting down out of the wild uplands between Sorn and Ochil-tree, almost twenty weary miles behind them and only a dozen to go to the town of Ayr, and the sea.

Not that it was Ayr, in fact, for which Bruce was making. He was on the edge, now, of his own ancient earldom of Carrick, comprising the nine parishes of South Ayrshire, with Turn-berry Castle, sixteen miles south of Ayr town, its principal seat—and his own birthplace. Turnberry was not for him meantime, however, for its castle had been garrisoned by the English, like Lochmaben, since Comyn had been driven out of it. But May-bole, the largest burgh of Carrick, lay somewhat nearer, and might well supply him with sufficient men to serve his purpose. The English force from Lanark were unlikely to have gone as far south as Maybole.

Tired and travel-worn, they came to the little town in its en-closed green valley, in the early forenoon—to find it in a bustle and stir of excitement. The High Steward's host had passed through it, going north, two days before, and had demanded the adherence of a contingent of the town's menfolk, for the revolt. These had been assembling, with varying degrees of enthusiasm, and were now almost ready to march. The Steward and the Bishop were not at Ayr, but a few miles further north of it, at Irvine. They had passed Ayr by, for there the English contingent from Lanark, said to number about five hundred, had installed themselves; with the place's own garrison, they were considered too strong to assault meantime.

Bruce was well enough pleased with this situation. He had intended to raise a token force, since these were his own vassals, to accompany him to the rebel base. Now they were already assembled for him. As Earl of Carrick, he ordered more to be mustered and to come on later. After rest and refreshment, with an augmented company of about three hundred, he and the

Douglases set out once more, northwards, towards Irvine. The Lady Eleanor was bearing up notably well, even if she remained less than friendly.

They made a wide half-circuit round Ayr, fording Doon and Ayr's own river about three miles inland from the sea. Thereafter, with only occasional glimpses of the town, on their left, they rode through the rolling and populous territory of Kyle until, in late afternoon, they saw the huddle of roofs that was Irvine's royal burgh, dominated by its monastery and Seagate Castle, at the blue sea's edge, with the smoke of an army's cooking-fires rising like a screen around it. Bruce sent forward three emissaries, one of them a magistrate of Maybole brought along for this purpose, to make known his approach and identity.

Presently, while still perhaps half a mile from the town, a fairly large mounted party could be seen coming out towards them. Well out of bowshot-range this company halted, and sent forward two horsemen, one of knightly appearance.

These came cantering up, and Bruce saw that the knight was the same Sir Richard Lundin who had stood before him in the sorry queue to sign the Ragman's Roll at Berwick those months ago. He raised hand in salutation.

"My lord—here is a strange meeting," Lundin called. "I greet you. But my Lord James, the Steward, commands that you leave your company here and come on alone to speak with him."

"As Earl of Carrick, I obey no commands, here in Ayrshire, from the Steward or other, Sir Richard," Bruce returned, but not harshly. "I will, however, come with you of my own goodwill. And gladly. Go you and tell the Lord James so."

Nodding, the knight turned and cantered back whence he had come.

Bruce told his people to wait where they were. But the Lady of Douglas declared that she would come with him.

"Not so, madam," he returned. "You remain here with the others, if you please. Until we see what my reception is."

"So! It is as I thought! You use me as a hostage, sir. You bargain with me. To your shame!"

"Say that I look well to your safety, lady. Until I learn what is to befall. But I will take the lad James. To greet his uncle."

So the young man and the dark boy rode on alone towards the waiting party.

They were within a hundred yards or so when, with a cry, a big burly man, in rusted but once handsome armour, burst out from the Irvine group and came spurring towards them. "Jamie!" he shouted, as he came, "Jamie!"

"Father!" The boy went plunging to meet him.

Bruce watched their reunion, a touching scene, the more unexpected in that Sir William, Lord of Douglas, was known to be a fierce, temperamental and wayward character, as unpredictable as he was ungovernable. Bruce had not met the man but his reputation was known to all. Now he was embracing his son like any more gentle father.

Others rode forward now, foremost amongst them a tall, elderly, cadaverous man, armoured all in black without the usual colourful heraldic surcoat. Tight-lipped, rattrap-jawed, thoughtful of mien, his sour and gloomy features were redeemed by great soulful brown eyes, wildly improbable in such a face — James Stewart, fifth High Steward of Scotland. Bruce knew him, of course; he had been one of the Bruce supporters in his grandfather's claim to the throne.

"My lord of Carrick," this apparition announced in a lisping voice — for his tongue was loose and on the large side for his tight mouth, and he dribbled somewhat, "I had not looked to see *you* here. Do we greet you as friend, or foe? What is your purpose here?"

"The same as is yours, my lord Steward, I would say," Bruce replied. "To help raise the banner of freedom."

"*You* say that? Edward's man!"

"My own man, sir."

"And your father's son!"

"My father will choose for himself. *I* have chosen to come here. Would you have had me choose otherwise?"

"No-o-o." The older man rode closer. "You change sides, then?"

"Sides, my lord? Say that I do not take arms against my own flesh and blood. While that was not required of me, I preferred Edward's train to the man Baliol's. As, I think, did you! Today, all is changed. The sides, not I."

Doubtfully the other was considering that when Douglas came thrusting from his son's side, voice raised.

"My wife, Bruce?" he cried. "You hold her? You dare to lay hands on Douglas's wife! Meddle with me and mine . . . !"

"I brought the Lady of Douglas to you, my lord. For her well-being and safety. She awaits you, there. Unharmed. As is your son . . ."

"Aye, Father," the boy called eagerly. "He is good. The Lord Robert has treated us kindly. Saved us from the English . . ."

Without a word, Sir William wheeled his horse around and set off into a gallop towards the Maybole contingent. After a moment's uncertainty, the boy went hot-foot after him.

The Steward looked from them back to Bruce. "You surprise me, my lord. But the support of Bruce is welcome—so be it is true, sure, honest. Those are men you have brought to our cause?"

"Some seventy from Annandale, two hundred from Maybole. More are to come."

"And we can do with all such. At Ayr—did you have sight of the English?"

"I kept my distance. Saw nothing stirring."

"Aye. Well, come you. We shall go see Wishart, my lord Bishop. Like myself, he stood your grandsire's friend. When Edward Plantagenet chose the wrong king for Scotland . . ."

Chapter Five

That night, in the hall of Eglinton's Seagate Castle at Irvine, Bruce sat at ease, as he had not done for many a day. With him, at the long table, lounged a goodly company—better than he had known or anticipated. As well as the deceptively gentle-seeming and almost diffident Robert Wishart, Bishop of Glasgow, the Steward, and Douglas, were the Steward's brother, Sir John Stewart of Bonkill; Sir Alexander Lindsay, Lord of Crawford; Andrew Moray, Lord of Bothwell, heir of the great de Moravia family of the North; Sir John the Graham, of Dundaff; Sir Robert Boyd of Cunninghame; Thomas Dalton, Bishop of Galloway; and Sir Richard Lundin, as well as other knights and barons of less renown. This revolt, it seemed, was no flicker of a candle-end. The new recruit was comforted, the more so as, after an initial hesitation, almost all had accepted him warmly enough. As the only earl present, of course, though the youngest save for the Graham, he outranked all.

The discussion of future strategy inevitably dominated the evening's talk. Bishop Wishart was for moving on Glasgow, from which bishop's burgh he could assure them of much support; the Steward, whose lands of Renfrew and Bute were in that direction, inclining to agree. Moray of Bothwell, however, declared that this would be a waste of time and strength, at this stage. They should make for the North. All Scotland north of Forth and Clyde could be theirs, with but little effort. That was where the English were weakest. His own uncle had risen, in Ross and Aberdeenshire. And the Comyns, the most powerful house in all Scotland, were there—and hated Edward. They must link up. Graham, whose lands were in Perthshire, supported him; but Douglas declared that they must hold the West March of the Border, above all, and so prevent Edward reinforcing in the west. Then attack across country to Berwick itself, the headquarters of the English dominance. Cut that trunk, and the branches would wither away.

Back and forth went the argument. With the two senior leaders advocating Glasgow, of course, there was most weight in that direction; but on the other hand, Sir William Douglas was the most experienced soldier present, and his views, forcefully given, carried conviction—at least to Bruce, though he could not like the man. Moray's scheme won least backing. It seemed to Bruce a longer-term project—and any talk of linking with his family's enemies, the Comyns, raised his hackles.

He had listened, hitherto, silent save for a brief question or two. Now, he spoke. "You each near convince me that all are right, all best, my lords," he said, with what he hoped would sound like diffidence. "I am young, and little experienced in war. But I would think that our first concern is not Glasgow or the North. Even the Border, though that should take precedence, I think. It is here, on our own doorstep. Ayr. Here we sit, with an English garrison but a dozen miles away. Should we not deal with these, before all else?"

It was Wishart, in his mildly hesitant voice, who answered that. "We have not failed to consider this, and the like questions, my son. But we have decided that the taking of strong castles is not our first task. We must seek to contain such as come in our way, yes. But to use up our strength and precious time òn the slow business of besieging such holds would be unwise. We could waste all our forces, sitting outside a few such castles."

"Aye, my lord Bishop." Having just come from sitting outside Douglas castle, Bruce scarcely required this to be pointed out. "But Ayr is no great fortress. Its old castle was small—one of my mother's father's houses. The English have built a new castle there, I am told. But it is not yet finished and not large. The garrison can be no more than a couple of score. The five hundred men they say are at Ayr are the force from Lanark. Hazelrig's men. They cannot all be cooped up in the castle."

"They built a great barn. A barracks," their host, de Eglinton, told them. "To house the men while the new castle was building. And to hold the Sheriff's stores. The Lanark men lodge in this."

"Is the castle finished?"

"Yes, this month past."

"Nevertheless, they will not crowd five hundred men into it, I wager."

"You know not what you say, Bruce." That was Douglas, harshly. "They do not have to be *in* the castle to defy us, hold us off. Under its walls and within its baileys, five hundred men could laugh at a great army. If it lacks siegery engines. Their archers, close packed along the castle walls, could keep us at a distance— their damned English archers! If *you* do not know them, I do! With longbows on their parapet-walls, we could not get near them."

"By night . . .?"

"By night, man! Think you these English are fools?" Douglas, who gloried in being no respecter of persons, undoubtedly had his reservations about the service Bruce had done him. "They will have beacons blazing on every tower and wallhead. Turning night into day. Had you fought English veterans, you would know better than to talk such havers!"

Frowning darkly, Bruce clenched his fists. "The man Wallace, whoever he is, would seem to think differently from you, sir!" he gave back warmly. "Or he would not have won Lanark!"

At mention of the name, silence fell on that room, sudden, noticeable. Bruce looked round at all the different faces and saw reserve, stiffness, now masking them all.

After a pause, it was the Bishop who spoke. "Your spirit, my lord of Carrick, is praiseworthy. We all welcome it, I am sure. But we must be guided by the voices of experience. Fervour is not sufficient. My lord of Douglas is right. We must not squander our resources. These English at Ayr, though too many to assail, under the protection of their castle, are not of numbers large enough to menace our rear. We shall leave them."

"Aye, by God—but I am right in the other also!" Douglas cried, banging the table with his fist. "That we should turn south. To the Border. Leave your Glasgow and north of Forth. They will wait. Make the West March secure, and then turn on Berwick, I say. That is where we may hit the English where it hurts them most . . ."

"My lord of Douglas has large lands in the West Borders!" Moray interrupted tersely.

"What of it, man? From those lands we shall win many men."

"Sir William would avenge his defeat at Berwick, I swear!" the Graham put in. "But we have more to do than restore his honour! We have all Scotland to win."

"You know not what you say, sir . . . !"

Still they argued, loudly, acrimoniously, with the Bishop and the Steward seeking to calm, soothe and guide. Here were divided counsels, with a vengeance.

Douglas was still holding forth, seeking to carry the day by main force, when the door was thrown open and three newcomers entered. And, strangely, even Douglas's forceful eloquence died on his lips.

Perhaps it was not so strange, for the visitors presented no ordinary sight; or, at least, one of them did not. Quite the largest man that Bruce had ever set eyes upon stood there, a young giant of nearer seven than six feet, of a width of shoulder and length of arm that would have been gross deformity in anyone less tall. Bareheaded, with a wealth of curling auburn hair and a bushy beard, this extraordinary individual had a smiling open face, high complexion and intensely bright blue eyes. He wore a sort of long tunic of rusty and battered ring-mail, with boiled leather guards bound on both arms and legs, making these enormous limbs look even larger. A huge two-handed sword, quite the mightiest weapon Bruce had ever seen, was sheathed down his back so that its great hilt stuck up behind the man's head. He was probably four or five years older than Bruce himself—certainly under thirty. His companions scarcely merited a glance in comparison. One was a ragged priest, half in armour; the other little more than a youth, though armed to the teeth.

"I greet you all, my lords and gentles," the giant said, deep voiced but genial. "It is a fine night. To be up and doing!"

Sir John the Graham alone of the company got to his feet and strode to welcome the newcomers. Douglas raised his voice.

"Who . . . who, a God's name is this?"

"Wallace. Wallace of Elderslie," somebody told him.

Exclamation, comment, remark rose from the company as Wallace clasped the Graham to him affectionately—and beside him that well-built young knight looked a stunted stripling. Bruce turned to his nearest neighbour, the Lord of Crawford, though his eyes remained fixed on the newcomer.

"This man? This Wallace. Who is he?" he asked.

"You do not know, my lord? You have not heard of the Wallace?" Lindsay said, surprised. "When all Scotland rings with his deeds." He corrected himself. "All Scotland of the baser sort, that is!"

"I have heard of Wallace of Riccarton. A small knight, nearby here somewhere. Vassal of my grandsire."

"This is nephew to him. His father, Sir Malcolm, younger brother to Riccarton, got Elderslie, at Renfrew. A mean enough place, of the Steward's. This is the second son. His brother will laird it there now, since their father was slain by the English at Loudoun Hill."

"Ha—slain? And did I not hear that this man's wife was slain, also? At Lanark. For which he slew Hazelrig?"

"Aye. So you are not entirely ignorant of the Wallace, then, my lord!"

"I heard his name only yesterday. For the first time. As an outlaw, a brigand."

"Aye, that is the style of him. A man of no breeding. Of the old native stock. Little better than the Irish." De Lindsay, of good Norman blood, coughed a little, recollecting that Bruce's own mother, and his Carrick earldom, were of the same Celtic origin, however respectable was his father's line. "He impudently belabours the English. They say that he has slain a round hundred of them himself, with that ox-shaft of a sword!"

"He is a skilled warrior, then? A champion?"

"Skilled no! He fights, they say, like a brute-beast. Without regard to the knightly code."

"But you say he is the son and nephew of knights . . .?"

The object of this dialogue had stalked across the hall, to bow briefly in front of the Steward, whose vassal he was. Now he interrupted all talk with his deep rumbling voice.

"My friends, I am new come from the Forest. From Ettrick. With news. From the East March. From Berwick. The English are on the move. Surrey, they tell me, has dispatched an army north, from Newcastle. A great army. Forty thousand foot, no less. Though bare a thousand horse. Under command of Surrey's grandson, Henry Percy. To deal with your rising, my lords."

"Forty thousand . . . !" Bishop Wishart could not keep the quaver out of his voice.

Men stared at each other, appalled.

"Aye. So it is time to be up and doing, is it not, my friends? Not sitting here, at table!" Wallace laughed as he said it, however, and reached out a huge hand to grasp and tear off a foreleg of mutton from a roasted carcase on the table. He bit into it, there and then, standing there.

"Forty thousand foot will move but slowly," Douglas declared heavily. "Ten miles a day, no more. No need to spoil our dinner!"

"Sir Robert de Clifford has three thousand at Berwick. Half cavalry. They will be on their way now. In advance of the greater host."

"You are well-informed, fellow!"

"I make it my business to be, my lord. Since my life could depend on it. Captured, lords are ransomed. *I* would hang!"

"That is true, at least!"

"Certainly these tidings force us to a swift decision," the Steward intervened. "And since this great host comes from the south, it would be folly, with our small numbers, to go meet it. We must move north, then. Seek to raise more men in the North."

"I shall rest happier behind the walls of Glasgow town . . ."

"Rest, my lord Bishop?" Wallace took him up, chuckling. "Rest, I swear, is no word for use this night. With much to do."

"Tonight, man? You would have us go tonight? It is not possible. Such haste would be unseemly. Besides, most of the men will be asleep . . ."

"So, I think, may be the English."

"English? What English? What mean you?"

"The English in Ayr, my lord. But a few miles away. We must smite them. Before it is too late."

"Attack Ayr? Tonight?"

"What folly is this?"

"Is the man mad?"

Everywhere voices were raised in protest.

"That is why I came to Irvine, my friends," the big man asserted, when he could make himself heard. "To take Ayr."

"The more fool you, then!" Douglas cried. "Away with you, and take it, then! If you can. Me, I shall finish my dinner. Douglas does not skulk by night, like some thief or cutpurse!"

"Aye—enough of this. Have done with such talk."

"You will not take a strong castle by night, man." That was Lindsay speaking. "Think you its walls will be unmanned, its bridge down, its gates open? These English are not as they were at Lanark—unawares. These know we are here, and will be on their guard. You will not take another castle by surprise."

"No? That is my lord of Crawford, is it not? Then hear this, Sir Alexander. Last night, from Ettrick, I came by Tweedsmuir and over into upper Clydesdale. By Crawford, indeed. And took your Tower Lindsay, in the by-going! Around midnight. Thirty Englishmen now hang from its parapets. That is all its garrison today. It is your house again, my lord—cleansed of the English who held it. You may possess yourself of it, at will. As I did, last night!"

Not only Lindsay stared at the giant now, speechless.

"So, my lords, let us to Ayr," Wallace said smiling.

Men eyed each other, ill at ease.

"This . . . this was a notable feat, Wallace," the Steward got out, sucking his spittle." And Tower Lindsay is a fine house. But Ayr is quite other. A town. With a great garrison. Five hundred men."

"Nor do we go skulking and creeping in darkness. Like broken men and outlaws," somebody said significantly.

The Bishop coughed. "Besides, my son, it is against our policy. To waste our precious strength on reducing fortresses and castles. These can wait. When the land itself is ours, they will drop off like over-ripe fruit."

"You think so? Then you will give me no men, my lords? For this attempt, I have but fifty of my own band," Wallace said, quietly now.

"Fifty or five hundred—it would make no difference," Douglas snorted.

Bruce was moved to speak. "My lords, I think that we should consider this more. I believe that Ayr should not be left behind us, untouched. It could endanger us. Moreover, its fall, after Lanark, would be great cheer, encouragement, for all Scotland. I do not know about attacking it by night. Here I have no experience. But assault there should be."

The big man was looking at him keenly. "Who speaks so, my friends?" he asked. "I do not know this lord, I think."

"It is the Earl of Carrick, man," the Steward said shortly.

"Carrick! Bruce? The young Lord Robert? Edward's lordling —here?"

There were gasps, murmurs, a snigger or two. Bruce set his jaw but did not answer.

"My lord of Carrick has joined us," Wishart explained. "With three hundred men."

Wallace had not taken his eyes off the younger man. "Scotland's case must be better than I had known, then!" he commented carefully. "But . . ." He shrugged great shoulders. "King Edward, it seems, is a good teacher. In war. *He* would not leave Ayr unassailed. The Lord of Carrick is right in this . . ."

"No!" Douglas roared. "Failure at Ayr would not only tie us down. It would spell the end of this rising. Until we have mustered a great force, we must keep moving . . ."

"Is not that what I urge on you, my lords? To move! Now!" Wallace demanded. "*I* shall move, at least. Here and now. For that I came. Alone if need be. I go to Ayr. Who comes with me?"

Only Graham, who was already standing, nodded his head. There was some shuffling of feet under the table, but no man rose.

"Very well. A good night to you, my lords. God be with you— and God help this poor Scotland!" Wallace threw down the gnawed leg of lamb and strode for the door, his two companions almost running at his heels. Sir John the Graham looked round the company, shrugged, and went after the trio.

After a moment or two, Robert Bruce pushed back his chair. "You will bear with me if I take my leave," he said, to them all. "I think that there may be something to see, tonight. Fifty men against five hundred should show some sport, at the least! I go watch it."

In silence he left the hall. At the door, he found Andrew Moray of Bothwell at his side.

.   .   .

Out in the Seagate of Irvine, by a slender sliver of horned moon they found Wallace's men already mounting their shaggy garrons —and a ruffianly crew they seemed, though heavily armed. At sight of the two noblemen, Wallace, not yet mounted, paused.

"Who is this?" he demanded, peering. "Ha—my lord of Bothwell. And, yes—it is the Bruce! What would you, sirs?"

"I would come with you. To see what fifty men may do,"

Bruce jerked stiffly. "If you will so much trust Edward's lordling!"

"Trust? I trust my eye, my arm and sword, and God's good mercy my lord. Little else. But come if you will."

Bruce and Moray went for their mounts. The horse-lines of the host were down at the main encampment, between the comparatively small Seagate Castle and the river. By the time they got back, Wallace and his band had gone, but left Sir John the Graham behind to bring them on. Wallace was making for Ayr by the coast, he told them. They would have to hurry to catch up —for that one never daundered, however indifferent the quality of his horseflesh.

The three young noblemen—for Moray, the eldest, was no more than twenty-five—skirted the town to the south-west and rode fast, southwards, by the rolling sandy links of Fullarton and Gailes, with the long Atlantic tide sighing along the glimmering strand of Irvine Bay, on their right. It made easy, unobstructed riding, for night-time, with the moon giving just sufficient light to warn them of the few obstacles of the open bents. Nevertheless, better mounted as they were, it was long before, almost at the squat salmon-fishers' huts of Barassie, they perceived the dark mass of the main body ahead of them. They were one-third of the way to Ayr.

Riding hard, talk was difficult. But Bruce did ask of the Graham if he knew why the man Wallace was so set on an attack on Ayr?

"He has debts to pay. At Ayr," the other threw back, in snatches. "His mother's brother, Sir Ronald Crawfurd of Crosbie, was Sheriff of Ayr. Edward made Percy—Henry Percy of Northumberland—Sheriff. In his place. Percy appointed as deputy one Arnulf. Of Southampton. This Arnulf, an evil man. Called a justice-ayres there. Called Sir Ronald. And others. Sir Bryce Blair. Sir Hugh Montgomerie. Others. To advise him, he said. He slew them, when they came. Out of hand. A trap. Hanged them. From the beams of the new barracks. Wallace has sworn vengeance."

"And that we do tonight?"

"We shall see."

With the narrow curving headland of Troon reaching out into the bay, on their right, they at last caught up with Wallace.

After crossing the further links of Monkton and Prestwick, Wallace turned inland, to skirt Ayr town to the east. They forded the river at The Holm, and then circled round through a terrain of knolls and broken pastureland, back towards the sea, south of the town. They climbed a long low ridge of whins and outcrops, startling sleeping cattle, and drew up on its grassy summit.

Sir William Douglas had been right about English precautions at the Castle of Ayr. Down there, flanking the estuary of the river, the town lay spread before them, dark, sleeping. But, a little way apart, nearer, on a mound to this south-east side, the new castle was not dark and gave no aspect of slumber. No fewer than eight bright beacons blazed from its high walls, making the place almost seem to be afire, and casting a red and flickering glow over all the surrounding area. From this ridge it was too far to see men, but there could be little doubt that watchers patrolled those battlements.

"English Arnulf does not sleep without watch-dogs!" Graham commented.

"Even watch-dogs may blink. Or be chained," Wallace returned easily.

Leaving the three nobles, he gathered his band around him, and splitting them up, gave them instructions, pointing this way and that. Bruce could not make much of the snatches he heard, save that somebody called Scrymgeour was to take charge of the castle. It seemed a large order.

In two groups the men rode off downhill, westwards, and were lost in the shadows. Wallace returned with only half a dozen, including the slim youth, whose name was Boyd, and the priest, Master John Blair.

"Come with us, my lords," he called. "If creeping and skulking is not too much for your stomachs!" In the field, he sounded rather less respectful of noble blood than he had done in Seagate Castle.

After a bare half-mile further, nearer the sea, they were directed to dismount and leave their horses, tied up, in a leafy hollow. Then they went forward quietly. Bruce perceived, from the beacons, that they were heading away from the castle vicinity, half-left, towards the coast. A halt was called presently, and Wallace went on alone. When Bruce and Moray exchanged a few wondering words, the priest curtly ordered them to be silent.

Wallace came back after quite an interval, and beckoned them on. Quietly they followed him past a pair of cot-houses, where the smell of smoored peat-fires was strong, and across some tilled land, where they cast long shadows to the left, in the glow of the castle fires, quarter of a mile off. There was rising ground beyond, of no great height, dotted with black shadows—some of which proved to be bullocks, but most whin and broom bushes. At the knobbly crown of this, where there was ample cover amongst the prickly bushes, Wallace, crouching low himself, waved them down on their knees.

"As far as you may come," he said softly. "Wait you here. Do not move from it, see you, if you value your lives. For any man, not of my band, who moves out there tonight, dies!"

"What do you do?" Bruce demanded. "Why bring us here?"

"You will see, my lord—never fear. Just wait."

"Is there nothing that *we* can do, man?" Graham demanded.

"No work for high-born knights!" the other returned, grimly. "But, if I have not come for you before two hours from now, you may do as you will, my lords. For William Wallace will be no more!"

With no further directions for them, the big man slipped away, extraordinarily quiet and agile for so vast a person. The three rejected nobles found that the rest of the party had disappeared also, and they were alone on their whinny knowe.

"He thinks as little of us as he trusts us!" Bruce said, frowning.

"Perhaps he has reason," Graham gave back.

"What mean you by that?"

"He knows us not—and there are many false, these days. Myself he knows a little—I fought with him at the Corheid. A small fray. But that was nothing. And you—you, my lord, yesterday were Edward's man. By repute. Were you not?"

Bruce shrugged. "If I seemed so, it was because I was not *Baliol's* man. I am no more Edward's man than are the many whom he forced to take the oath. The Steward. Your father, Moray. Lindsay. Bishop Dalton. All these swore fealty." He paused, and smiled a little, in the dark, if twistedly. "Although, to be sure, I learned but yesterday that I am now Edward's chiefest commander in the South-West! Now that Hazelrig is dead. In name. Because I am earl. And here I crouch, this night!"

His companions had no comment to make on that.

They seemed to wait a long time, so that they grew stiff and chilled. Once they thought that they heard a suddenly choked-off cry from somewhere fairly near at hand—but it might have been only a night bird. There were unseen rustlings amongst the whin bushes below them, though these again could have been caused by bullocks. Otherwise, the environs of Ayr, that night, might have been as quietly peaceful as was usual and suitable. Time passed heavily for high-spirited young men of high degree.

Then, and this time there was no doubt about it, a high thin scream rang out from no great distance in front of them, its mortal agony raising the hair at the back of the listeners' necks. And quickly thereafter a blaze of flame leapt up, seemingly only about two hundred yards ahead. It grew in size and brightness and was followed by another nearby. Then another. And still another. The crackle of fire sounded, and then muffled clamour, yelling.

Swiftly the fires increased, fanned by the sea breeze. And by their ruddy light, the watchers at last perceived something of what was happening. In front of them, across a dip, was a great building on a low parallel ridge, simple in design but long, bulky, two-storeyed, gabled and obviously timber-constructed. At a guess it might be two hundred feet long and forty wide. And against its many doors and windows, at ground floor level, fires were blazing up—evidently gorse and broom and straw had been piled high at every opening and set alight. Sparking, spluttering, flaring like great torches, this tinderlike and resinous stuff roared devouringly —and dark figures could be seen piling on more and more of the fuel that grew so profusely all around. Already the wooden walls of the place were beginning to burn.

"The Barns!" Graham cried, need for whispering past. "The English barracks. God's Blood—look at that! Wood—it is all of wood. It will burn to ashes."

"It is . . . it is full? Of men . . . ?" Bruce's voice faltered.

"Full, yes. You heard Eglinton. The English, from Lanark, were quartered there. No room in the castle for hundreds. They will be . . . inside there!"

"Saints of Christ—this is a hellish thing!" Moray groaned.

"Aye." Sombrely Bruce nodded. "But did you see Berwick town?".

The muffled shrieks and cries and cursing from within the building were terrible now, rising high above the throbbing roar of the flames. They saw a door crash down, in a great fountain of sparks, and dark frantic figures came rushing out—to be met by slashing, stabbing steel that flashed red in the firelight. A huge leaping shape could be distinguished, silhouetted against the glow, great sword high.

Soon the walls of the barracks were well alight and there was no need for further fuel. The number of waiting figures around increased. Men were jumping, now, from upper windows, in a frenzy, many with hair and clothes ablaze. None could fail to be seen in that lurid fatal light, and none who escaped hot fire escaped cold steel. The sounds that came across the shadow-filled dip from the Barns of Ayr were now blood-curdling, indescribable.

The shrill neighing of a trumpet, from the direction of the castle, drew the three watchers' eyes momentarily. They could not see what went on at that distance, nearly quarter of a mile away —but they could guess.

"They will come out. Lower the drawbridge and sally out. To aid these. And Sandy Scrymgeour and his men will have them," Graham declared excitedly. "They cannot sit within, and watch this!"

"The man is a devil! Wallace! To plan such savagery. Godless! It is unchristian, heathenish!" Moray said. "True men do not fight so."

"Maybe so. But I will tell you one man who would not blink an eye at what is done here tonight," Bruce returned grimly. "Edward Plantagenet! Nor Bishop Anthony Beck, either."

"Aye. It may be that Scotland needs such as this William Wallace, in this pass," Graham nodded. "But . . . it takes a deal of stomaching."

The roof of the barracks was ablaze now, the entire long building a flaming pyre.

Fewer men seemed to be waiting around the doomed barracks, with no sign of Wallace's gigantic figure. No doubt the main scene of operations was shifting to the castle vicinity. The roar of the fire drowned any noises that might be emanating from there.

Restlessly and with very mixed feelings, the trio waited amongst the whins. Their every instinct and urge was to move out, to be active, involved—but Wallace's warning as to possible consequences had been as convincing as it was grim. And nothing that they had since seen inclined them towards disobedience. Though they would not, could not, call it that, of course; obedience was not an attitude that fell to be contemplated by such as these.

They waited where they were, then, in major frustration and impatience, pacing about amongst the bushes to keep warm, since there seemed no further need to hide themselves.

A most unpleasant smell was now reaching them on the sea wind, from the burning building. It was a considerable time since they had seen any men jumping from the upper windows; indeed, no upper windows were now visible, in the unbroken wall of flame.

A scattering of lights showed in the town.

Eventually the priest, Blair, materialised, face streaked with soot, dark eyes glittering in the ruddy light.

"Wallace requires your presence, my lords," he said shortly. "Come with me."

It was eloquent of the effect of the night's experiences on the three that they none of them took active exception to the summons or the ragged cleric's abrupt delivery thereof, but followed him without comment or question.

Turning their backs on the blazing Barns of Ayr, they made for the castle, finding themselves on a roadway between the two buildings.

Soon they were aware of people. Over on their left, a crowd was standing, silent, townsfolk obviously. Dimly seen in the light of the flames, they stood in their hundreds, unmoving, huddled there seemingly rooted, watching, only watching, strangely noncommittal. The priest ignored them entirely.

The walkers came across the first bodies lying sprawled about a hundred yards from the castle's dry ditch. They lay scattered, as though cut down individually, in flight perhaps. Bruce stooped to peer at one or two—for the beacons on the castle ramparts were fading now, untended. These were men-at-arms, all similarly clad, in jacks and small pointed helmets with nose-guards—English obviously. There were perhaps a dozen of them, dotted along the roadway. Then, near the draw-bridge-end, was a dark heap, almost a mound. Here men had died fighting, not running, back to back probably, assailed and surrounded as they issued from the castle. How many there might be there was no knowing. None moved, at any rate. The priest, his hitched-up robe flapping about leather-bound legs, led on without pause or remark—though once he muttered as he slipped on blood, and recovered his balance with difficulty.

Four ruffianly characters, swords in hand, greeted them less than respectfully at the bridge-end, but let them pass. Men were leading out horses from the castle, fine beasts, laden with miscellaneous gear.

They crossed the inner bailey, where more bodies lay. Somewhere a woman was screeching hysterically, and there were groans from nearer at hand.

The castle's interior still smelt of mortar and new wood,

though overlaid now by the smells of blood and burning. Master Blair conducted his charges up the wide turnpike stairway to the hall. There many torches flared, to reveal a dramatic scene. William Wallace stood up on the dais, at the far end, towering over all, with the man Scrymgeour, head bound with a cloth, young Boyd, and one or two others, nearby. Half-way to the door a group of older men stood, white-faced, in some disarray of dress, none armoured, their agitation very evident. Above all, three men hung on ropes from the beams of the high roof, one in armour, one part-clothed, the one in the centre wholly naked. This last was middle-aged, heavily gross, paunchy, his body lardlike and quite hairless, obscene in its nudity. He twitched slightly.

"Ha, my lords!" Wallace called, at sight of the newcomers. "Come, you. Here are the provost and magistrates of this good burgh of Ayr. Some of them. And there," he pointed upwards, "is one Arnulf, who called himself Deputy Sheriff. Also the captain of this castle's garrison, and his lieutenant." To the townsmen he added, "You see before you the Earl of Carrick, the Lord of Bothwell and Sir John the Graham. I ask these lords to receive this town and castle, in the name of John, King of Scots."

Moray looked doubtful, Graham glanced at Bruce, and that young man raised his voice. "*I* will not, sir," he said loudly, clearly. "There is no King of Scots, today. John Baliol was a usurper, and failed the realm. He has vacated the throne. He is now in France. I, for one, can accept nothing in his name."

His companions did not speak.

Wallace looked thoughtfully at them, tugging his beard—which was noticeably singed on one side. "So that is the way of it!" he said. "All men may not hold as you do, my lord."

"That may be so. But I so hold. And state."

"Who, then, may speak in the realm's name? This burgh and castle is taken. In whose name?"

Bruce saw that Wallace was concerned to live down the name of brigand and outlaw that had been pinned upon him, that he sought an aspect of legality for what he did. That was why they had been brought here.

"Who better than the High Steward of Scotland?" he said. "I shall receive Ayr in his name, if so required."

"Aye. Very well. My lord Earl of Carrick, heir of the House of Bruce, receives Ayr burgh and castle, cleansed of the English invader, in the name of James, Lord High Steward of Scotland," the big man intoned impressively. "Is it agreed?"

No one being in any position to say otherwise, the thing was accepted, with nods and shuffles.

Eyeing them all, Wallace smiled thinly. "So be it. My lords, no doubt you will now ride to acquaint the Steward of this matter. Sir John—you could aid me here, if you will. You, my friends of Ayr—get you back to your town. I want every house searched. For Englishmen. Some there may be yet, in hiding. A great grave to be dug. The streets and wynds cleared of folk. All to return to their homes. You have it?" Briskly he issued these orders, and stepped down from the dais. "Now—I have work to do . . ."

Bruce and Moray, finding themselves dismissed as well as redundant, were not long in making their way back to their horses, a little aggrieved perhaps that Graham should have been singled out for employment, and had left them so promptly. They did not go near to the burning barracks. The roof had fallen in now, and some of the walling collapsed.

In thoughtful frame of mind the two young men rode for Irvine again. Some distance on their way, after crossing the Holm ford, they looked back. New fire was rising at Ayr, from the castle now—and it was not the wall beacons rekindled. The keep itself was ablaze.

"I' faith—that man does nothing by the half!" Moray said. "He has ungentle ways. Fears neither God nor man, I swear. But . . . with a few more Wallaces this Scotland would soon be clear of the English, I say."

"You think so? I do not." Bruce shook his head. "Your father, I believe, would not say so. He is hostage in an English prison, is he not? Like I have, he has seen Edward's might. His armies in battle array. His chivalry by the thousand. His archers, longbowmen, by the ten thousand. It is these must be defeated before Scotland is free of Edward Plantagenet. This Wallace can surprise a garrison, capture a castle, slay a few scores, even hundreds. But against the English massed power what could he do? Or a score like him?"

"Then . . . then you believe this vain? Of no avail? Yet you joined us. Left Edward's side for ours."

"Aye. But not to play outlaw. Not to war with dagger and torch and rope! This may serve its turn, give the common folk cause for hope. Rally doubters. But, if Scotland is to gain her freedom, it is not the Wallaces who will win it, I say. It is ourselves, man. Those who can command and lead thousands, not fifties. Mark it—it is not those we have left behind in Ayr who can save Scotland, in the end. But those we ride to Irvine, to tell. And their like."

"And these—these bicker and dispute. And hold their hands!"

"Aye. There you have it. These cannot agree. There is no leader. I know Edward and the English. Divided counsels, pin-pricks, gestures, will not defeat them. Only armed might. And a firm and ruthless hand directing it."

"Wallace has such a hand, at least . . . !"

"Wallace! Think you the lords of Scotland will follow such as Wallace, man?"

The other was silent.

Chapter Six

THE sun was warm, the scent of the yellow gorse flowers was strong, the larks trilled in the blue above, and men relaxed, sat, sprawled, strolled or slept all along the Irvine waterside. For hours they had waited there, at first drawn up in serried ranks, foot in front, cavalry behind, bowmen in knots—pitifully few, these last. But now, in the early afternoon, the ranks were broken, the groups scattered, and men relaxed, all the urgency gone out of the host and the day. Which was no state for any army to be in. Its leaders might have maintained some more suitable spirit—but by and large the leaders were not there, nor had been most of the long day.

The Scots insurgent force had moved out of Irvine, south by east, early in the morning, on word of the English approach. Wallace had sent that word, that Clifford was now no further off than Kilmarnock, a mere six miles away, with Percy coming up from Lochmaben. Even then, the Steward, the Bishop and others, had been for a prompt withdrawal northwards, while there was yet time, making for Glasgow; and only Douglas, this time reinforced by Bruce, Moray and Lindsay, had managed to carry the day in favour of resistance. They had marched out to take up strong defensive positions along the line of the River Irvine and its tribu-tary the Annick Water, facing south and east across what was largely swampland, water-meadows and even a small loch, to slow down any English attack. It was an excellent position—although rather strung-out for their numbers, which still reached only about four thousand. The position was almost too strong in fact, since it produced too great a feeling of security, too defensive an atmosphere altogether.

Bruce and Moray paced a grassy bank above their own lines, ill at ease and short of temper. Since the affair at Ayr, they had drawn together, Andrew Moray's quiet and thoughtful nature making an excellent counter-balance to Bruce's impetuosity. But today even Moray was disgruntled and impatient. They had marshalled their men together, the Annandale and Maybole contingents—the latter now much reinforced—and the Bothwell company from Lanarkshire, totalling in all almost a thousand. They had selected a good position at the right of the long line, not more than a mile from the sea, and holding the Warrix ford. But as the day wore on, and Wallace's scouts were sent back with word that the English were still at Kilmarnock, obviously awaiting the arrival of Percy's force from Lochmaben—where Wallace had in fact boldly attacked them two nights before with indecisve results—Bruce had urged action, a sally. It was crazy, he declared, to let the two English hosts join up, when they might prevent it. A flanking movement with their cavalry could cut off Kilmarnock, north and south. The foot could march the six miles in two hours. Kilmarnock was no strong-point, no citadel or walled town —and the townsfolk would turn against the invaders' rear when they saw the opportunity. Wallace and his men could go in, to rally them.

But there was no convincing the majority of the other lords. It would be folly to desert the strong position here, most said. Others, the most senior, were still advising a retiral northwards. Even Douglas was not for attack meantime.

So it had gone on all day. Wallace himself had sent Sir John the Graham—who was now frequently in his company—to urge the lords to move over to the attack, more or less as Bruce advised. But without avail.

It was in a thwarted and discouraged frame of mind, therefore, that the two young noblemen heard some shouting and commotion from further up the riverside, and, for want of better employment, walked in that direction to see what went on. They discovered Lindsays and Montgomeries, their neighbours in the line, in some consternation and excitement.

"Lundin has ridden off. Deserted to the English!" one of them told the newcomers. "Sir Richard Lundin. He rode off, through our left, there. Over that bit ford. Towards Kilmarnock. With his esquire and three men . . ."

"They say he has had enough. Of folk who dinna ken their ain minds!" another supplemented. "The English aye ken that, at least!"

"This is nonsense!" Bruce declared. "You talk like fools."

"It's true. We saw him, my lord . . ."

"Perhaps he rides as messenger? Courier?" Moray suggested. "To the English?"

"Who else? They would not send him to Wallace. Such as he!"

"Courier for what, then? What have they to say to the English?" Bruce frowned. " 'Fore God—we shall look into this!" He turned, to hurry back for his horse. They rode hastily back to the Mill of Fullarton, where the insurgent leaders were gathered. They heard upraised voices even before they entered the musty-smelling place.

It took some time for them to gather what was in debate—that it was not now whether to attack or not, but in fact whether to stand fast, retire, or make terms. Shocked, the young men demanded what this meant.

Many of the others seemed actually to welcome their arrival, as opportunity to expound their views and seek support. Out of the declamation and persuasion, they learned that a new situation had arisen.

Clifford had sent an envoy from Kilmarnock, a Scot, one Sir Archibald Livingstone. He had brought two messages. One, that the main body of the English foot, allegedly now fifty thousand strong, was less than thirty miles away, having already won through the Mennock Pass. And secondly, that he, Clifford, well understood that what had prompted this revolt of the Scots lords was the command, issued from London, that all Scots nobles, like their English counterparts, should forthwith muster men and, under heads of families or their heirs, bring them to join and assist King Edward in his war against the French. This, the Earl of Surrey, Viceroy for Scotland, recognised to be not only un-popular, but mistaken policy, and bound to provoke serious mis-givings in Scotland, the French war being scarcely more popular in England. He, Clifford, therefore, and Sir Henry Percy, Sheriff of Ayr, had the Viceroy's authority to declare that those Scots lords and knights who had assembled in arms in protest against this policy, if they yielded now, dispersed their forces, and gave certain assurances for their future good and loyal behaviour, would be received back into the King's peace without further penalty. Moreover, the Earl of Surrey undertook to try to persuade King Edward that such commands for Scots levies for the French war should be withdrawn.

All this took some time to be enunciated, by many mouths, with much interpolation, question and refutation.

Douglas's strong voice prevailed over all, eventually. "It is a trick, I tell you!" he cried. "A ruse, to have us yield. Without fighting. This, of going to war in France. Have you heard of it? Have any? He would cozen us."

"Why should he? With his force. With fifty thousand and more, need he trick us?"

"The English, it may be, want no revolt in Scotland, while Edward and his main might is in France," Lindsay declared, "Clifford and Percy have men enough to beat us, to destroy us here. But they would rather have peace. Not have to fight."

"Aye—we cannot win. Not against fifty thousand. I say they are right," Sir John Stewart of Bonkill said.

"It is madness to fight!"

"Better to make for Glasgow, while there is yet time."

"If they would treat with us, we are fools to reject it . . ."

Douglas managed to shout them all down. "Fools, aye! If we yield! We have a strong position. They are not over-eager to attack. The people of the land are for us. Would you surrender without a blow? Could you raise your heads after, if you did?"

"Not only our heads, yes—but our arms, my lord," the Steward intervened thickly. "Do you not see it? At this present we cannot prevail. We may hold off Clifford and Percy, with their horse. But when the fifty thousand foot come up, we are lost. I had been of the opinion that we should hasten northwards, with our force intact. But now, I think we might be better to accept these terms. And fight another day. They are easy terms, are they not?"

"So say I," Lindsay concurred. "These are easy terms, yes. Why they should make them so easy, I know not . . ."

"A trick, I say!" Douglas insisted.

"It may be so. But what are we disadvantaged? They make this excuse for us—this of us rebelling because we do not wish to take our men to France. Which none of us had so much as heard of, by the Mass! This must mean that they do not want a clash. I say we should take advantage of this. Rise again, as the Steward says, when they and their great host are gone south again . . ."

"No!" That was young Andrew Moray, in a burst of hot anger, "This is betrayal! Did we raise the banner of freedom for this? To yield without a blow struck? I, for one, will not do so. My lord of Carrick — will you?"

Bruce cleared his throat. "My Lord Steward," he said, not looking at Moray. "This of hostages? Assurances. What is meant by that? What hostages do they want?"

"That is not certain. So Sir Richard Lundin has gone to Clifford. To discover their mind on this. When we hear . . ."

"What matters it?" Moray interrupted, his normal quietness gone. "Our position, our duty, is clear. We have taken up arms against the invader of our land. We have not been beaten. We stand in our own land, amongst our own folk. I say we cannot yield thus, whatever their terms. I was for attacking, before Percy joined up with Clifford. I was against making any move to the north. Now, I say, better that than this shameful submission."

"Aye! Aye!"

"No! The Steward is right."

"We still would have to face the fifty thousand. At Glasgow. The weaker for moving."

"Fools . . . !"

There was uproar in that mill. In it, Moray turned on his companion, urgently.

"Bruce! Why did you not speak out? You who wanted to attack? Why ask about hostages? You came here to have them fight. Not surrender. Why have you kept silent, man?"

"Because I am using my head, Andrew," the other said. "As others would be wise to do. This needs thinking on. Why do the English act so? It is not like them. I know them better than do you. This is a strange thing — in especial when they have a great army nearby. This finding excuse for us. But . . . Edward himself is far away. And Surrey is a very different man . . ."

"Dear God you would not submit, man? Surrender?"

"Submit! Surrender? These are but words, I tell you. There are times to fight. And times to talk. If the English wish to talk, I say, let us talk. And fight another day, when we are in better case. It may be the Steward and Lindsay are right. Today, I fear, we cannot win. So let us talk."

"This is strange talk," Moray insisted. "From you. Less than honest, I think! There is something in all this, more than you say. You see more in this than these others?"

Bruce took his time to answer. "It could mean so much. Something new. Something that could transform all Scotland's state. Clifford, Percy, Surrey, would not dare to send such message about this of the French war being unpopular unless it was indeed so. Unless they knew that Edward had indeed made a great mistake. Unless, I think, there was near to revolt in England itself. Edward has been long at war. All his reign he has been making war. Against Ireland, Wales, Scotland. Now France. It may be that his own people at last have had enough of their blood shed, their treasure spent. If they are turning, at last—then all could be changed, for Scotland. Do you not see it? We should not fight the English, then—but rather aid them."

Moray shook his head, bewildered. "This is beyond my understanding . . ."

There was more talk, continuing argument, and no decision. Then there was an interruption. Wallace and Graham arrived— and immediately the scene was changed. Decisions crystallised, hardened. Wallace was like that. No half-measures or uncertainties survived his presence.

"My lords, my lords!" he cried, stilling all other voices. "What is this I hear? I spoke with Lundin. On his way to Clifford. Not only will you not attack, he says. But you talk of submission. I cannot believe this is true. Tell me that he has taken leave of his wits, my good lords!"

There was a profound silence—the first Fullarton Mill had known that day. Men glanced at each other, rather than at the clenched-fist giant. Douglas, who normally filled any vacuum with his strong voice and views, would not demean himself to submit answers to such as William Wallace. Others either felt similarly, or dared not meet their inquisitor's hot eye.

Save Bruce, that is. After a few moments, he spoke. "Sir—a new situation has arisen. Did Sir Richard not tell you? Of this matter of a muster for France. And the English offer. This may change all."

"How may it change our struggle for freedom, my lord?"

"It may foreshadow revolt in England. Or, if revolt is too great a word, discontent, resistance. I do not believe they would make such offer to us, this excuse for us, otherwise. If it is so, Surrey may wish to have his fifty thousand back in England!"

"Is that not the more reason to fight? If they are of two minds. Looking back over their shoulders?"

"I say probably not. I say that if the English would indeed

bring their arrogant king to heel, we should aid them in it. Not fight them."

"What the English do with their king is *their* concern, not ours. Or, not mine. Though, to be sure, it may be yours, my lord! I have feared as much."

"What do you mean, sir?"

"I mean that your conversion to our cause was something sudden, my lord of Carrick! You have large lands in England. All knew you one of Edward's men. It may be that you are still more concerned with Edward's case than Scotland's!"

There was a shocked murmur, as Bruce raised a pointing hand. "You doubt my honesty? *You!*"

"I doubt your interests. Your judgement. Where your heart lies. I doubt the judgement of any man who even for a moment considers submission to the English, my lords!" And Wallace stared deliberately round at them all, head high, in reproach and accusation both.

"Curse you . . . !"

"This is not to be borne!"

"How dare the man speak so? To us . . . !"

"My lords—friends," Bishop Wishart cried. "This talk will serve us nothing. Wallace is a man of fierce action. He has wrought mighty deeds. But we must needs take the long view, here. Consider well our course. For the best . . ." The old man's words quavered away.

Wallace obviously took a major grip of himself. "I regret, my lord Bishop, if I spoke ill. But—what does the Earl of Carrick propose? Surrender all our force? Accept this English offer? Make our peace with Edward? If this is so, I say—not Wallace! Never Wallace!"

"Nor Graham either!" the younger man at his side declared.

Bruce was also mastering his hot temper. "I say, since we cannot fight fifty thousand, let us talk with them. Talk at length. Learn what we can. Gain time. And while we talk, send messengers privily to raise the country further. It may be that we will find the English glad to wait. If trouble is brewing in England. I say, let us talk, dissemble, prevaricate, make time."

"We shall make time better, my lord, by remaining free men," Wallace declared, almost contemptuously. "The realm will be freed by war, not talk. Better the sword than the tongue, I say!"

"For *your* sort of war, may be. The surprising of a garrison, here and there. The burning of this castle, or that. The raid by night. This is all we may do with our present support and numbers. It is good—but not good enough, my lords." Bruce was speaking now, earnestly, to them all. "We will not free Scotland of the English so. They are notable fighters, with many times our numbers. They have their bowmen, their chivalry, their hundreds of thousands. Think you we can counter these by night raids, fires and hangings?"

"Is this why you left Edward's camp to join us, my lord of Carrick?" demanded the Graham bitterly. "To tell us that we could not win? To sap our wills and courage?"

"I did not! I came because I must. Because I saw that I must needs choose between Scotland and England. Not John Baliol's Scotland—*my* Scotland! I'd mind you all, my father should be King of Scots today! Let none forget it."

There was silence in that mill, again. Not even Wallace spoke.

"I chose Scotland then. But not to beat with my bare fists against castle walls! More than that is required. Wits, my friends—in this, we must use our wits. We need them, by the saints! Wallace, here, can do the beating at the walls. He does it well. Moreover, I would mind you, *he* cannot talk with the English. They would hang him out of hand! As outlaw and brigand! He knows it." Bruce jabbed a pointing finger at the giant. "We all know it. But it is not so with *us*, my lords. They offer to treat with us. I say treat, then, in this situation. I know Surrey. I know Percy, his nephew. I know Clifford, of Brougham. These are not of Edward's wits, or Edward's ruthlessness. I would not say treat with Edward Plantagenet, God knows! But these are different. Treat. Talk. Discover what is in their minds. What worries them. Something does, I swear. Gain time. This, I counsel you, my lords. And let Wallace go fight his own war. With our blessing!"

An extraordinary change had come over the arguing company. Without warning, as it were, young Robert Bruce had established himself as a leader—not merely the highest in actual rank there, but a man who had come to know his own mind. He had not convinced them all, by any means. It is doubtful, indeed, if many fully understood or accepted what he said. But suddenly he had grown in stature before all. It was as though a new voice had spoken in unhappy Scotland. And more important even than the voice was the manner.

"There is much in what the Earl of Carrick declares," Bishop Wishart said, into the hush. "I believe he has the rights of it."

"I, too," the Steward nodded. "There is wisdom in this. I agree."

"And I do not!" Wallace cried. "I agree with my lord only in this—that the English will hang me if they can! For the rest, I say that you deceive yourselves. Myself, I waste no more time, my lords. There is much to be done. If *you* will not do it, I will. I give you good day—and naught else!"

"I am sorry for that . . ." Bruce began, and paused. The big man, turning on his heel, had halted as the priest, Blair, came hurrying in, to speak a few words in his ear.

Wallace looked back. "You have company it seems! Company *I* would not care to meet. They approach under a flag of truce. I do not congratulate you, my lords. I have no stomach for supping with the devil! I am off."

"And I with you," Sir John the Graham cried.

Moray of Bothwell took a single step as though to follow them, but thought better of it.

There was a stir of excited talk at the word of the English approach. The debate was not now whether to receive them, but who should do so, and on what terms. There was no more agreement on this than on anything else. In the end, the entire company trooped out of the mill—to find the Englishmen, with Sir Richard Lundin of that Ilk, to the number of about thirty, assembled in the yard outside.

The two groups stared at each other, for a little, grimly wordless.

Then a tall, willowy young man, who sat his horse under the proud blue and gold banner of Northumberland, held just slightly higher than the white sheet of truce, dismounted, his magnificent armour agleam in the afternoon sun. Thin-faced, pale of hair and complexion, almost foxy of feature, he scanned the assembled Scots, his manner nervous-seeming. At sight of Bruce his glance flickered. At his back, another man got down, slightly older, dark, solidly-built, heavy-jawed, tough-looking. The rest of the English remained in their saddles. Lundin came round to stand amongst his compatriots.

"I am Percy," the willowy young man said, in a voice as high and reedy as himself. "I come in the name of my uncle, John de Warenne, Earl of Surrey, Viceroy of this Scotland."

None answered him.

"I am Clifford," the darker man declared harshly. "Warden of the West March."

"The *English* West March!" That was Douglas, who himself had been the Scots Warden of that March.

"The West March," the other repeated, flatly.

Sir Henry Percy, Lord of Northumberland, looked quickly away from Douglas. His glance was of the darting sort. Now, insofar as it was directed at any, it flickered around Bruce.

"My Lord Robert," he said, "I regret to see you here." And added, with a little cough, "Kinsman."

Bruce smiled briefly. Their relationship was of the most distant sort, and had not been stressed hitherto. He took it that this mention implied some need felt by the Percy.

"I am nearer to my earldom of Carrick, here, my lord, than you are to your Northumberland!" he returned.

"I am the Sheriff of Ayr," the other said.

"Edward of England's sheriff!" Douglas countered.

"The King's Sheriff. As *I* am the King's Warden!" Clifford jerked.

"England's king. Not Scotland's."

Percy and Bruce both cleared their throats at the same time, and caught each other's eye. Clearly there was as much difference of temperament and approach between the two Englishmen as between Douglas and Bruce. Clifford, son of Isabel de Vieuxpont, of Brougham, one of the greatest heiresses in the North of England, was another plain soldier nevertheless, who spoke his mind. Percy had not come to speak his mind, it seemed. And he took precedence in rank, and as representing Surrey. It was perhaps not Bruce's place to speak, for although he was the only earl amongst the Scots, the Steward was one of the great officers of state, as well as an initiator of this revolt, and the Bishop of Glasgow was senior in years. But neither Steward nor Bishop raised their voices, and much might depend on what was said now. Also how it was said.

"You ride under a flag of truce, my lords," he observed. "I think that you did not bring that to Irvine to discuss offices and positions?"

"No. That is true." Percy nodded, with apparent relief. "We have come to discuss terms. To, to offer you an . . . accommodation."

"Terms? Accommodation? We are not suitors for such, my lord."

"Then the bigger fools are you!" Clifford barked.

"We learn from Sir Richard Lundin that you would know more fully what we propose." Percy went on.

"And what do you propose?"

"That you, who are rebels, surrender on terms. Generous terms, I say." Clifford was making his position very clear.

"Surrender, sir? Without a blow struck? In our own land? To an invader?" Bruce kept his voice almost conversational. "Surely you misjudge, my lords."

"By God, we do not! We could crush you rebellious dogs like that!" Clifford snapped his steel-gauntleted fist shut eloquently.

"But have not yet attempted the feat, sirrah! I would think that the time to talk terms or surrender is when one or other is prostrate in defeat?"

Percy waved a hand. "Sir Robert—*I* will speak. In the name of the Viceroy. If you please." He coughed again. "If we do battle, my lords, *we* must win. We know your numbers. We have many times as many. You are brave men, no doubt, and would fight well. But the end could not be in doubt. Do you wish to die? Is there need for so much bloodshed? Amongst fellow-subjects of King Edward?"

There was a muttered growl at that. Douglas hooted.

"You all have sworn allegiance to Edward," Percy reminded. "Even my lord of Douglas!"

"Under duress, man! How much do you value such swearing, Englishman?"

"Forsworn traitors!" Clifford cried. "What use talking with such? Their word is valueless. They will break faith whenever our backs are turned."

No one attempted to deny it.

But Percy was made of different metal, no less sharp perhaps for being more pliable. "You are all Edward's subjects," he pointed out, and raised his hand, as the murmurs began again. "Hear me, my lords. You are Edward's men all. But free men. Not serfs. In feudal duty, yes. But with your baron's rights. As have I and Sir Robert, here. We are all Edward's men. But we have our rights. And in England, at least, we cherish our rights not a little! We accept that you should do so likewise."

There was quiet now, as all searched that uneasy-eyed, foxy face. Clifford kicked at the earth with his armoured foot.

Percy went on. "We know why you have taken arms against your liege lord. It was foolish—but to be understood. You did this in order that you should not be constrained to fight in the King's foreign wars. You had been better, my friends, to come talk with us. With your fellow-barons. In England. Rather than put hands to your swords."

The Scots eyed each other doubtfully, since none had so much as heard of this obligatory foreign service before that day. Douglas was obviously about to say as much—but Bruce spoke quickly.

"And what would our fellow-barons of England have said?"

Percy licked thin lips. "They would have said, belike, that they were no more eager for the French war than were you, my lords. And that it behoved all His Highness's loyal liegemen, of both realms . . ." The other amended that. ". . . of both nations, to apprise him that this French war was unwise and against the will and judgement of both peoples."

He paused, and this time not even Douglas was for interjection. All the Scots had cause furiously to think—Bruce none the less because he had anticipated something of this.

"So . . . England mislikes Edward's French war?" he said, at length.

"That is so. The land has been overlong at war. We are taxed too dear. This new war is too much . . ."

"Do not tell me that the English have lost their stomach for war!" Douglas interrupted. "That I shall not credit. Here is a trick . . ."

"We are none the less warriors—as you will discover, my lord, soon enough! If you do not listen to reason. But . . . to start a new and long war overseas is folly. We have had twenty years of war, and more. Our coffers are empty. Our fields untilled. Our people weary of it."

"Yet you come against us. In Scotland. With fifty thousand men!" The Steward had found his difficult tongue at last.

"You are in revolt. Rebellion must be put down. We are loyal to our King. It is foreign war that we resist. Make no mistake, my lords—here is no charter for rebels!" Percy's superficial thin hesitancy did not cloak the real man beneath it, there.

"But you would have us, the Scots, with you? In this resistance," Bruce pressed him.

"Yes."

"But . . . does not our revolt serve you well enough, then? Is not revolt in Scotland more apt to bring King Edward home than Scotland in submission?"

"Not so. You know Edward. Revolt will but stiffen his neck. He lives for war, for conflict, for conquest. Revolt will not prevail with him."

"What will, then?"

"A parliament. A united parliament. Of all his lords and barons. Not only of England, but of Scotland also. And Wales. Aye, of Ireland. A parliament that speaks with one voice against these wars."

Bruce drew a long breath. So that was it! At last. The English lords would bring their warlike monarch to heel. It had come to that. No revolt, but a rising of a sort, nevertheless. And if such was contemplated, it was not surprising that Percy and Surrey should be in the forefront. For the grandsire of one and the father-in-law of the other, Richard Percy of Northumberland, had been one of the great barons of England most prominent in forcing the Magna Carta on King John. By the same means. A united display by the nobles. And for such a display, now, not only would the Scots nobles be valuable—for Edward had declared that there was hereafter only one realm and one parliament; but the English nobles must have their men readily available—for their own protection. Edward would listen to their voice only if it was backed by the power he understood. So they wanted no revolt, and no armies of occupation, in Scotland.

Bishop Wishart was speaking. "We may wish you well, my lord. But why should Scotland aid you in this? Edward fighting in France would serve us better than Edward home, and angry!"

"Aye! Aye!"

"Not so. The yoke would be greatly eased for you. Side with us, in this, and we swear you shall gain by it. In earnest of which, my uncle, the Viceroy, will already ease many of your burdens. If you accept his terms."

He had their interest and concern now. Men talked with their neighbours, low-voiced. Douglas was still declaring that it was all a trick, however.

"I say Douglas is right," Andrew Moray asserted, in Bruce's ear. "I do not trust this Percy a yard! And even if it is not a trick, why should the Scots aid the English lords? It is all to their advantage . . ."

"Ours also—if we play it right, Andrew. Besides, nothing is changed in our case, here. We still cannot fight fifty thousand, and win. Here is occasion for talk. Much talk."

"Too much talk! Wallace had the rights of it."

The Steward raised his voice. "These terms, my lord of Northumberland, that you spoke of? What are your terms?"

"The terms are the Viceroy's, my lord. They are light, I think. Such as you can surely accept. To return to the King's peace, only this is necessary. That you disperse your men-at-arms. That you deliver up the murderer Wallace. And that you commit to us certain hostages, as assurance for your continuing loyalty. That is all."

That did not fail to produce animated debate. Looked at from one aspect, these were indeed light terms. Of course the men must disperse—but they could be reassembled, if need be, in a matter of days. As for Wallace, he could look to himself. But what was meant by hostages? That was the question on every lip.

Half a dozen voices asked it, aloud.

Percy's glance flickered like lightning—and this time notably avoided Bruce's. "The hostages need not be many," he said. "But they must be of worth. Substance. Of notable consequence. They must come from the greatest among you. From the Earl of Carrick. From my lord of Douglas. From my Lord Steward. And my lord Bishop of Glasgow. These."

There were caught breaths. Also, undoubtedly, some sighs of relief from the unnamed.

"These you name?" the Steward asked, thickly. "What hostages?"

A cough. "From you, my lord—your son and heir, Walter Stewart. From Douglas, his heir. From the Earl of Carrick, his infant daughter. From the Bishop, all precious relics from the cathedral of Glasgow."

Out of the exclamations, Bruce's voice rasped. "You make war on children and babes, then, my lord!"

"Not so. These hostages will suffer nothing. Indeed they will do very well, better than here in Scotland, I vow! They will lodge with kinsmen, in England. Secure. Honoured guests. Your own daughter, my lord, shall lodge in my own house of Alnwick. Where also now lodges the Lady Elizabeth de Burgh, my cousin— whom you know of! The Steward's son, Walter, may also lodge there—since his mother is likewise a de Burgh. Is it not so, my lord? Sir William of Douglas's wife is the lady Eleanor de Louvain, from Groby, in Northumberland. She may return there, with her children. In the state of Scotland today, will they not all be better so disposed?"

It was specious, but clever. In one respect, all the Percy had said was true. The families of men in revolt were always in danger. If those required to yield the hostages were in fact honest in their acceptance of the terms, the said hostages would indeed be as safe, as well off, so disposed, as at large in unhappy Scotland meantime. And for the four named to refuse this gesture was to reject the whole terms, to deny and fail their colleagues. None failed to see it.

"My daughter is far from here," Bruce jerked. "I cannot yield her to you. She is in my sister's care. At Kildrummy. In Mar. Hundreds of miles north of this."

"You can send for her, my lord. And meantime, these others—the Steward, the Bishop, and, perhaps, my lord of Crawford—will stand surety for her delivery?" Percy almost smiled.

"How now?" Moray murmured, at Bruce's ear. "Are you still for talk with the Englishmen? For terms, man?"

The Steward spoke, with an accession of dignity. "This of the hostages is grievous. We will have to consider your terms. And inform you. But we cannot yield Wallace. He is gone."

"You can bring him back."

"You do not know William Wallace, if you say that! He is his own master. He will come for none here. We can no more deliver up Wallace than fly in the air, sir! You must needs take him for yourself."

"Very well. We shall do so. You wish time to consider these terms?"

"Yes. There is much to consider."

Percy looked at Bruce. "You also, kinsman?"

Set-faced he inclined his head.

The Englishman did likewise. "Then we shall go. And return tomorrow. A good day to you, my lords. And . . . consider well." Nodding to Clifford, he turned for his horse.

"One word, Percy." That was Bruce suddenly. "In all this we have but your word. How do we know that you do not deceive us? As my lord of Douglas feared? That other than yourself would resist Edward."

"Percy's word is sufficient, is it not?" the other returned. "But if you require proof—ask these." He gestured towards those behind him. "They will tell you that two of the greatest earls in England, Norfolk and Hereford, have refused Edward's commands to cross the Channel, with their armies. As contrary to the terms of Magna Carta. Others follow their lead. Is it enough? Or must I name more names?"

"It is enough, yes."

When the Englishmen were gone and the debating began again, it was clear that the great majority of the Scots were for accepting the terms. Even Douglas appeared to be convinced that it was no trick—the news of the resistance of the mighty Earls of Norfolk and Hereford, the Bigods and Bohuns, had stilled even his doubts. He was against the surrender of young James Douglas as hostage, naturally—but otherwise agreed that to challenge the English to battle, at this stage, was not politic. Only Andrew Moray remained obdurate.

"I will not submit. To these terms, or any," he declared, to Bruce. "My people up in Moray and the North are in revolt. I cannot fail them, here. I will go to them. And you, Bruce? You can stand there and consider the yielding up of your own child?"

"They have not got my Marjory yet!" the other returned grimly. "I said to talk, did I not? Talk, rather than fight and be beaten. I still say talk. At length. While the English settle their quarrel with their king."

"Why bide here for it, man? Why not slip away? Go north. Come with me. All Scotland lies open..."

"Not *all* Scotland, Andrew. See you—you and Graham and others may slip away so. Your lands all lie to the north. Even Bothwell is not yet touched. You can raise men and means, from them. But most here, like myself, have their lands in this South-West. Most already overrun by the English. Our sole power comes from our lands and our men. You know that. If we run for it, northwards, we are becoming little more than landless men, outlaws, swords for sale! Is that how we, her great lords, can best fight for Scotland? Resist Edward? I think not. Douglas, the Steward, Crawford, and the rest—they are in the same position. I say talk, then. These terms will keep us talking for long. Go you, if you will..."

.   .   .

Bruce's strategy of talk, and more talk, was more successful, almost crazily so, than he, or anyone, could have hoped. A month later, no less, they were still talking at Irvine.

It was not all merely effective delaying tactics, of course, though that played its part. Events and conditions far from Ayrshire had the greater effect. And the fact that no one really wanted to fight was highly relevant—for Clifford the fire-eater was despatched on the more congenial and active duty of chasing Wallace. Indeed, if

Bruce was the initial designer of what became known, and chuckled over, as the Capitulation of Irvine, the most long-drawn capitulation in Scotland's story, Wallace was the true protractor of it. With Edward Plantagenet's help.

Wallace disappeared from Irvine into the fastnesses of the Ettrick Forest, his favourite refuge and a notorious haunt of broken men. From there, in an extraordinary short time, he emerged again with a tough and highly-mobile cut-throat band of perhaps two hundred. Avoiding embroilment with English garrisons in Lanarkshire, he made a lightning descent upon the town of Glasgow, where Bishop Anthony Beck had gone to collect the cathedral relics and to initiate a campaign for English hegemony over the Scots Church. Taken completely by surprise, the English in Glasgow were overwhelmed, and Beck was forced to flee, a salutary experience for that exponent of the Church Militant.

Wallace well knew that this kind of warfare depended for its success on continual movement and surprise. He did not stay at Glasgow but, reinforced considerably, moved north into the Lennox where the earl aided and abetted him, being no Norman but of the old Celtic stock. Clifford was now tailing him, but far behind. Wallace made a swift and unexpected dash right across Scotland, to Perth, and at Scone managed to surprise Edward's Justiciar of Scotland, William Ormsby, holding harsh courts, who escaped with his life but left behind much valuable booty. Then, by tremendous forced marches across the mountains Wallace descended upon the English-held towns of Brechin, Forfar and Montrose, to wipe out what Edward had done there to John Baliol. All fell. He linked up here with Andrew Moray, who had hastened north to lead his father's people of Moray and the Black Isle, and could now claim the enemy-held castles of Inverness, Urquhart, Elgin and Banff. Together they turned south for Dundee.

This was a brilliant campaign for the summer of 1297. But it was, of course, superficial. Nothing was consolidated behind this guerilla fighting, and it could not be claimed that the so-called rebels held the territory they so vigorously swept through. But it all had an enormous effect, nevertheless, on the Scots people. The name of William Wallace was on every lip. Their lords had failed them, but the common folk saw Wallace as their saviour. Young men flocked to him from far and near, from highlands and lowlands from east and west and north—many of them against the wishes of their own feudal superiors. He had an army now, even though a rag-tag one. And some barons were supporting him, other than Graham and Moray—for word had gone out from the talkers at Irvine, privily, to rouse the land. With this host, Wallace attempted what he had not hitherto risked, the siege of a major fortress and garrison town—Dundee, where he had been educated, and whence came Scrymgeour and many of his band.

If all this had its inevitable effect on Percy's negotiating position, affairs in England had almost more. Edward, with his ally Guy, Count of Flanders, was attacking Philip the Fair, of France, with doubtful success—and at the same time fighting something like a rearguard action with his own recalcitrant barons at home. Many others had joined Norfolk and Hereford in refusing foreign service, some of them of lofty rank indeed. The King could do little against them without coming home, but what he could he did. Many were dismissed their offices by hasty decree—including Surrey, who was demoted from being Viceroy of Scotland, and one Brian Fitz-Alan appointed in his stead. But even royal decrees have their limitations, unless backed by force on the spot, and Surrey was still commander of the northern armies, since they were largely composed of the Northumbrian and Cumbrian levies of the Percies and other North-Country lords. Fitz-Alan, then, required Surrey's co-operation—and got but little.

This bore notably on the spun-out negotiations at Irvine—which, indeed, neither side was now in any hurry to bring to a conclusion. One defeat for Edward in France, and the entire dynastic situation in England would change, and the Scottish position with it. All balanced on a knife's-edge, and men marked time, waiting—save for William Wallace, that is. Percy restored Ayr Castle—which had been only superficially burned—and lodged there, contenting himself with only occasional meetings with the Scots lords at Irvine. Or some of them—for Douglas had soon tired of this, and slipping off to his Nithsdale estates, had gathered together some men and surprised and taken Sanquhar Castle. He had not yielded young James Douglas as hostage, either—and so was now proclaimed outwith the King's peace, outlaw. Bishop Wishart, too, after Wallace's raid on Glasgow and Beck's discomfiture, was declared responsible for his see, and surrendered into English custody at Roxburgh Castle, as a sort of personal hostage for Glasgow. But Bruce, the Steward, Crawford and others continued with the play-acting of negotiation, their men in the main dispersed, looking over their shoulders to north and south. All had English estates as well as Scottish. The fifty thousand foot turned and marched homewards, as far as Berwick.

So passed an extraordinary summer. Bruce's two-year-old daughter Marjory remained safely at Kildrummy Castle, in the care of his sister, Christian, Countess of Mar. And his father, the Lord of Annandale, was dismissed from his position as Governor of Carlisle—by express command from France.

Everywhere men waited.

Bruce received a letter—delivered by Percy himself, no less. It was in feminine writing, and was sealed with the arms of Ulster and de Burgh. It read:

My lord,
   What are you? A loyal man, I understand. A rebel I understand. But what is a man who sits and talks? A clerk? King Edward thought to wed us. Should I thank God for my escape?
                                    Elizabeth de Burgh.

Bruce, in hot anger, crushed the offending paper into a ball, and threw it from him. Later, he retrieved it and spread it smooth again—and once more crumpled it up. He almost burned it, but did not.

CHAPTER SEVEN

As is so often the case, the most carefully thought-out courses, the most masterly inaction and most delicately-balanced fence-sitting, can all be brought to naught in a chaos of violence and unprofitable turmoil – and often by the merest accident or conjunction of otherwise unimportant events. It was so in late August of 1297. Two unconnected incidents, neither in themselves significant, brought about the collapse of so much that had been patiently contrived. And the men who used their wits were overwhelmed in the consequent conflagration just as surely as were the strong-arm realists and fire-eaters.

Edward Plantagenet won a small and insignificant engagement in the north of France, which became magnified by rumour, in England, into a major victory; and an English knight escaped from beleaguered Dundee, by sea to Berwick, with the word that the great fortress-town would have to capitulate to Wallace within a couple of weeks, for lack of provisions.

It so happened that the Earl of Surrey was at Berwick Castle when both tidings arrived, in the process of handing over the civilian duties of Viceroy to Fitz-Alan, Lord of Bedale, in the company of Master Hugo Cressingham, Treasurer and real administrator of Scotland, who made his headquarters at Berwick. It was a humiliating situation for the great Earl of Surrey; moreover he and Cressingham, whom he despised as an upjumped cleric, were on bad terms. Out of this, the entire situation for Scotland suddenly changed. Fitz-Alan, the new broom, wished to prove himself as Viceroy; Cressingham demanded immediate action for the relief of Dundee; and Surrey, with the word from the south that a great victory in France secured, Edward would now come home to set his English house in order, panicked. He had a name and reputation to save. He was still commander-in-chief in the North; and fifty thousand men still lay encamped near Berwick.

So action, crude and vigorous, took the place of dialectics. Blood would flow, not words.

The first indication of this dramatic change reached Ayrshire by urgent courier to Sir Henry Percy, in peremptory terms. The High Steward, Crawford and certain other Scots lords, with the main body of the English forces at Ayr, were to be sent to join Surrey's army forthwith, on its advance on Dundee by Edinburgh and Stirling. But Percy himself was to proceed at once in the other direction, south to Carlisle, taking the Earl of Carrick with him, there to assemble as large a reinforcement army as he could in short time, for the aid of his uncle. Bruce's father, though replaced as Governor of Carlisle by the Bishop thereof, was still detained at that castle. His great lands of Annandale teemed with men, the richest territory in South-West Scotland. The Bruces must provide their thousands from Annandale – on pain of treason.

The velvet gloves were discarded now, with a vengeance.

Percy's cavalry descended upon the unsuspecting Scots, who found themselves under what amounted to arrest, at Irvine. There was no argument or debate now. The Steward and the rest were taken off northwards. Percy and Bruce rode south. The Capitulation of Irvine was over, and the Leopards of England showed their spots again, dark, clear and unchanged.

In the circumstances, Bruce's reunion with his father at Carlisle was less than happy. They had never got on well together, the father finding the son headstrong, independent, and, in especial, extravagant; the younger saw his parent as indecisive, interfering, ineffective, and mean. The son's expensive ways, as compared with his sire's parsimony, had been a stumbling-block between them for long. This was why, as much as because he could not bring himself to make an earl's fealty to his rival John Baliol, the elder Bruce had handed over the old and impoverished Celtic earldom of Carrick, which he had gained by marriage, to his son, and thereafter washed his hands of him—retaining, of course, for himself, the infinitely richer if less lofty-sounding Lordship of Annandale. There was seldom love lost when these two met.

Bruce found his father practically a prisoner in Carlisle Castle—though he did not admit the fact—with the Bishop in command. Percy did not delay in making known his uncle's demands for a large contingent of armed and mounted men from Annandale, his hesitancy of manner now scant cloak for brusque authority – and left father and son to their own company.

"How dare he! How dare that insolent puppy speak me so!" the elder Robert Bruce cried, trembling with outrage. "I, who should be King of Scots!"

"Yet you will bear it, Father—since you must. As must I. For you are *not* King of Scots. And, like me, you are Percy's prisoner in all but name.'

"I am no prisoner, boy! By envy and malice and Edward's spleen. I have been superseded as Governor here—that is all. As though I care for that! If Edward Plantagenet does not know his friends, and trusts instead such as Percy and Surrey, the more fool he! I shall not give them one man from Annandale. They may whistle for their men!"

"Brave words! You did not speak them to Percy!"

"I shall. *You* may lick the boots of such as he. I do not."

"I lick no boots. Nor ever shall. But I recognise facts. Power. The reality of power."

"You! Power? You recognise fine clothes. Jewels. Blood-horses. Women. You recognise those who will pay for your debts! You licked Edward's boots for gold, did you not? *He* paid your debts. Is it Percy, now?"

With a great effort Bruce held in his hot temper. "I lick no man's boots, I tell you," he repeated heavily. And changed the subject, stiffly. "How do you propose, my lord, to assert yourself? Against these commands.'

"I shall go. Leave. I do not remain here, in Carlisle, to be insulted and mistreated, by God!"

"Where shall you go? If they let you. Your lands in England, in Essex and Huntingdon, will scarce offer you protection against Edward! And Annandale, of all the dales of Scotland, lies most open to the English. Its mouth, wide and open to the Border, cannot be defended. Only at its head amongst the hills. And there the English hold Lochmaben."

"I shall not go to Annandale. Nor into England. I go to Norway. To Isabel. I shall seek King Eric's aid. To put me on my throne of Scotland. I shall return with a Norse army."

His son stared, almost unbelievingly. Although, knowing his father, he perhaps should not have been so surprised. Bruce the elder had ever lacked any conspicuous sense of the practical.

"But . . . but this is folly!" he exclaimed. "Eric will not aid you. Not with men, an army. He has his own troubles. Nearer home . . ."

"He is my good-son. To have me King of Scots would greatly strengthen his hand. In his own wars."

The Lord of Annandale had been potent, if not practical, and his countess-wife fertile. They had had five sons and four daughters. And the eldest child, Isabel, had married four years earlier King Eric the Second of Norway, as his second wife, The family had not seen her since—but she was indeed Queen of Norway.

Her brother knew the uselessness of argument with his sire. "They will not let you go," he said. "The English."

"Why should they stop me? I am a free man. I have been put down as Governor—but that is not my doing. It is *your* fault. For your folly, at Irvine. Of turning rebel, at the wrong time! Always you were a fool, Robert! And have cost me dear."

The young man turned away, and strode to the window to gaze out, while he mastered himself. It was a small and undistinguished tower chamber, very different from the fine Governor's apartment which the Bishop now occupied. Without facing his father, he spoke, level-voiced.

"They will not let you go. Unless you seem to aid them. I know these English—if you do not. Though you should, 'fore God! They are merchants. They bargain, always. If they have power, they give nothing for nothing. You can bargain for your freedom with your Annandale men."

"Men! *You* say that? You, the untimely rebel! You would give the English our Annandale men—to fight against our own folk?"

"To fight, no. To assemble and ride, yes."

"What do you mean?"

"I mean that these are your vassals. Bruce's vassals. By the thousand. The English wish them assembled, in arms. Very well. Let them assemble. It is a thing we dared not have done, ourselves. But on Surrey's orders . . .! Then, when we ride north, we shall speak with a different voice! Who, think you, these Bruce levies will obey? Percy? Or Bruce?"

"You mean . . . you mean that you would take them . . . and then change sides? Turn your coat, man?"

"My coat is already turned, is it not? Whatever side I must needs seem to wear! In my need, I cannot afford the luxury of wearing only one side of my coat, my lord!"

"But . . . what of your honour, man? Have you none?"

"Honour? I have been learning what honour means! If Scotland is ever to be free, if Scotland is ever to have its own king again, Bruce or other, we will have to think again on what means honour. Does Edward know the word, I wonder? But . . . enough of this. These men of Annandale, my lord, are your vassals—not mine. Yet. But with your permission, and Percy's aid, I shall make them into an army. To use against our enemies. Your enemies. Those who have so despitefully used you."

The older man chewed at his long upper lip in indecision. "You have your own men. Of Carrick. Use them," he jerked.

"I cannot. Think you Percy would allow that? Carrick, all Ayrshire, is watched, garrisoned, held. Thick with English. A few men I might raise—were I free to do so. But I am not. Here it is different. We would be acting on Surrey's orders. Do you not see it? And do you not see that you have here much to bargain with? Say to Percy that you wish to retire in peace. That your sixty years weigh heavy on you. That you will give me authority to raise your vassals of Annandale. But that you must be allowed to go, in peace. From here. Where you will. Do not say to Norway, I counsel you!"

"Aye." The other had started pacing the floor. "Aye—and when I return from Norway. In the spring. You will have an army waiting for us? To gain my throne?"

His son lifted wide shoulders. "God willing," he said cryptically.

So, for once, father and son were agreed, or seemed to be. Percy, when told, appeared well content. He requested Bruce to proceed forthwith to Annandale—with Sir Harry Beaumont and a contingent of two hundred cavalry to aid and escort him. Other recruiting-agents were sent through Cumberland, Westmorland and Northumberland. Percy himself departed across country eastwards, for a brief visit to his own Alnwick, to raise more men there. One week, and all must be back at Carlisle.

In Annandale, Bruce found all his brothers, in Annan Castle itself, on its mote dominating the straggling red-stone town amongst the green tree-dotted meadows of the deep-running river. Edward, two years younger than Robert, was acting as his father's deputy in this great lordship, a dark, smouldering-eyed, intense young man, despite his name, all Celt; Thomas, just twenty, quiet, slow of speech, but giving the impression of a coiled spring; Nigel, cheerful, irrepressible, wooing half the girls of the town; Alexander, only sixteen, but clever, studious, more diffident than the others. They made a contrasting group, with only a hot temper uniform to them all. Their unmarried sister Mary, a laughing tomboy of a girl of seventeen, acted chatelaine to an undisciplined and lively household in the great gloomy castle.

When Bruce could win free of Sir Henry Beaumont, who clung closer to him than any brother—and whom the Lady Mary was eventually deputed to distract—he took the others into his confidence, and was not long in winning their whole-hearted enthusiasm, Nigel's in especial. All agreed to co-operate in the raising of the men, and all clamoured to accompany the eventual contingent northwards. That would have been folly, but it was agreed that Edward and Nigel should come campaigning.

Thereafter the Bruces rode far and wide through Annandale and lower Eskdale and Nithsdale, which all formed part of the lordship, summoning to the standard the young men of the rich and populous Solway lands. Armed service with their lord was, of course, together with rent in kind, the basis of all land tenure, and able-bodied men between sixteen and sixty could not refuse, from lairds and substantial farmers down to shepherds, foresters and herd-boys. The Lordship of Annandale was particularly highly rated in this respect, being a crown fief of no fewer than twenty-five knights' fees—that is as a condition of the original royal grant to the first Robert de Bruis seven generations before, it had been required to produce, on the king's demand, the equivalent in men, arms and horses, of the followings of twenty-five knightly lairds at, say, fifty men each. Much more than that could be raised now, at a major mobilisation. Bruce reckoned that Annandale could muster three thousand, at a pinch, even in a week; but such was not his intention now, whatever Percy might say. There was no point in denuding and impoverishing the land, in present circumstances. Half that number would be enough.

Five days of recruiting and selecting and mustering saw just over fifteen hundred men assembled at Annan, few enthusiastc, for the presence of Sir Henry's two hundred English horse, in whose close and unremitting escort the Earl of Carrick was very clearly little better than a captive, left few doubts as to which side they would be fighting for. Not that the Annandale men were aggressively Scottish; with their territory wide open to the English border, and great hill masses cutting them off from the rest of Scotland, for generations they had been under southern rather than northern influence. But fighting against their fellow-Scots was another matter—though they had no option, if their lord so commanded.

The sixth day they rode back to Carlisle—rode, for Annandale was a notable place for the breeding of horseflesh, the sturdy, stocky, long-maned garrons which the English mockingly described as ponies but which were in fact full-grown sure-footed horses, though short in the leg. Every man was mounted. This, of course, was one of Surrey's requirements, being short of cavalry. On ahead, Edward and Nigel Bruce flanked their brother, within a tight cohort of Beaumont's men, who were taking no risks with a prisoner who now commanded seven times their own number.

Carlisle was like an ant-hill disturbed, with thousands of the levies of North Country English lords milling around. But the vast majority of these were footmen, it was to be noted—and Bruce sent Nigel back to warn his Annandale host, at the encampment they were allotted beside the Eden, to watch over their horses. There would be many envious glances cast in their direction, that was certain; and Scots might well be looked on as fair game. They should keep out of the town, therefore, or there might be trouble.

A surprise awaited the Bruces at the citadel. Percy was already returned from the east, and he had brought Elizabeth de Burgh with him, for some reason. Unwarned, the young men came face to face with her in the Great Hall—to their distinct unease. She was entirely self-possessed—but betrayed no delight at the meeting. Going on for his interview with Percy, after a somewhat abrupt greeting, Bruce at least was in a turmoil of mixed resentment and speculation.

Percy received the brothers civilly enough, even congratulating them on the numbers of men raised—although he had hoped for perhaps five hundred more, he indicated. He appeared to accept the adherence of the two younger Bruces as no more than appropriate. They would ride north the next day. He mentioned, as an afterthought, that his kinswoman, the Lady Elizabeth de Burgh, had accompanied him to Carlisle, with his wife. His visitors made no comment.

Bruce did not fail to seek a reason for this move. He did not flatter himself that his own presence at Carlisle had itself attracted the young woman across the country. Moreover, the assembling of an army, in a hurry, was no occasion for feminine jaunting. Therefore Percy, who was a cold-blooded fish if ever there was one, and did nothing without a cause, must have brought her for a purpose. She was Edward's god-daughter, the child of the monarch's closest friend—and no doubt it was widely known that the King had once contemplated marrying her to Bruce. Presumably as a precaution, to bind him closer. That could scarcely apply now. But Percy might believe that there was still something between them. He must hope, in some way, to use her to bring pressure to bear. But how? And why?

Bruce, at any rate, did not propose to assist him in whatever was his project. He would avoid the girl. Not that he had any difficulty in this, at first, for Elizabeth appeared to be no more anxious than he for any association. The citadel was swarming with people. The Bruces kept themselves to themselves.

That night, however, the Bishop of Carlisle held a banquet for the leaders of the new army, and the Bruces were summoned. Precedence, for seating, presented an obvious problem, but the Bishop got over the difficulty by providing a special table for the Scots, at the back of the dais. And to Bruce's side here, presently, the prelate brought and seated Elizabeth de Burgh, before all the company, a gesture calculated to attract the maximum of notice, with so few women present and this one the most high-born as well as far and away the most beautiful.

Bruce, although not normally lacking in the powers of speech, on this occasion was practically wordless. Without herself being forthcoming, the young woman was at least civil, but she obtained little response from her right hand neighbour. Fortunately at her other side, the Lord of Annandale saw no reason for either resentment or embarrassment, and finding a courteous listener, launched into anecdotes of the Crusade on which he and Richard de Burgh had accompanied King Edward, in their youth.

Wine, however, had the effect of making Bruce the Elder sleepy, and as the repast proceeded, his talk grew thick and disconnected, and presently died away in puffs and little snores. Elizabeth, although she could not be unaware of the admiring glances cast on her by many, and especially Edward Bruce on his father's left, chose to turn to her heavily silent neighbour on the right.

"So, my lord, you now neither talk nor rebel!" she said, pleasantly.

He frowned. "I keep my own counsel," he jerked, in reply.

"So I perceive. And unpleasing counsel it must be, I think."

"Why think you so?"

"From your face, if naught else! You look uncommon sour, sir! And since the counsel you keep to yourself can scarcely be to your own congratulation."

He began to speak, but thought better of it, and closed his lips tightly.

"You are Edward's man again," she went on, conversationally. "How happy His Majesty!" And when he still did not reply, "You found rebellion unprofitable, did you?"

He answered her questions with another, and abruptly. "Why are you here?" he demanded.

She took a moment or two to answer. "Because I was brought. With the Lady Percy, my cousin."

"Brought, aye. You are not sitting beside the Lady Percy!"

"No doubt she sees sufficient of me. I am living with her, while my father fights with the King in France. Moreover, has she not Sir Robert Clifford to entertain her?"

"So I see. And she is welcome to him! Why were you brought here, then?"

She looked at him thoughtfully. "I do not know," she said. "*You* did not ask Sir Henry to bring me?"

"I did not!" That was vehement.

She smiled faintly. "At least, I see, you are honest in some things, my lord!"

"Are you saying that I am *dis*honest in others, madam?"

"It may be that I used the wrong word, sir. Should I have said frank? Open? Single-minded?"

"You have no very high opinion of me!"

"I do not deny it. Have I reason for it? Am I mistaken about you, my lord? I sent you a letter."

"Aye. I received it. Scarce a letter, it was. An insult, rather!"

"I asked a question then, too. That I might, perhaps, think the better of you. And you did not answer."

"How could I answer such a thing? You asked if I was a man! Or a clerk? And should you thank God to have escaped me!"

"So at least you read my letter."

"More than once. To see if there was any kindness hidden in it. But I found none."

"Kindness? You looked for kindness, then? From me?"

"Women can be kind, can they not? Understanding. There was no understanding, there."

"What did I fail to understand? You could have told me, in answer."

He drew a long breath. It was on the tip of his tongue to speak, to explain something of his position, what he was seeking to do. But he could not, dare not. He shook his head.

"It is of no matter," he said curtly. "What *is* of matter is why you are here. What made Percy bring you? It is concerned with me, for sure. What does he want?"

She sighed a little. "I told you, I do not know. Is it important?"

"It could be. Did he not tell you. Give you some reason? Some task? Perhaps to question me?"

"Think you I am Henry Percy's spy, sir? His informer?"

"You could be. Without intending it. Why bring you? Or his wife? It is a strange time and place to bring women. And to set you here, by me."

"It was the Bishop who did that. But I can leave you, sir, and gladly, if you please?"

He ignored that. "Either he would have you to learn something from me. Or else to sway me. Why?"

"That I should sway *you*, my lord! If he thinks so, he knows little of either of us! And what should I learn from you that he cannot ask himself? That I would tell him?"

"If I knew, I would not be asking. It seems, however, that he does not trust me."

"And is that so strange? Men who change sides so quickly are seldom trusted."

He bit his lip. "Can you not conceive that I may have reasons? That I may be more honest than you think? You, who sit secure in English halls. In Edward's goodwill. When a kingdom is at stake, woman!"

She eyed him closely at that, and said nothing.

Fearing that he had blurted out too much, he frowned, and changed his tack. "Percy himself is perhaps unsure of Edward's goodwill. With reason. If Edward returns quickly from France, heads may fall. You are close to Edward. Could it be that he would use you to gain Edward's favour?"

"I cannot think that King Edward looks on me so warmly. I believe I may have disappointed him."

He weighed that. "But you *are* his god-daughter."

"Is that important? In this matter? Might it not be more important that I am James the Steward's niece? By marriage."

"Ha!" Bruce sat up. "I had forgot. His wife is Egidia de Burgh."

"My father's sister. And, now I think on it, Henry Percy has mentioned the fact to me, of late. More than once."

"This makes more sense. The Steward led this late revolt. I have been close with him. He is now being taken to join Surrey's array, making for Dundee. Where we are going. Now that there is no king in Scotland, and Buchan the Constable lies low in the North, the Steward is the greatest officer of the realm."

"And is he not this William Wallace's lord? Wallace his vassal?"

"So—you know of that also! Aye, Wallace's small lands are held of the Steward."

"Henry Percy said as much."

"I think, then, that we get down to the roots of it now. On how the Steward and myself may make common cause with Surrey, much depends in Scotland. And Surrey's and Percy's reputations with it. And you, my lady, it is thought might weigh heavily with us both."

She shook her corn-coloured head. "It is a weighty edifice to build out of so little!"

"Perhaps. But let us make some test of it. Tomorrow, if we leave you behind here at Carlisle, I will accept that I may have misjudged. But if you are carried with us northwards, into Scotland, then I am like to be right."

"We shall see. But I tell you, my lord, that Elizabeth de Burgh will be pawn in no man's game—Edward's, Percy's . . . or yours! Mind it well!"

Thereafter, for such time as the banquet continued, they got on rather better, able to talk together at least without striking sparks.

The following morning when, amidst much blowing of trumpets and shouting of commands, the various component parts of an army of over eight thousand mustered and moved off over Eden, northwards into Scotland, the Ladies Percy and Elizabeth de Burgh, to the surprise of many, rode with them.

. . .

They marched by Esk to Canonbie, and then up Liddesdale, the horse making no attempt to hold back to the pace of the foot; but even so it was a fairly slow progress. It took the three thousand cavalry two days to cross over the Note o' the Gate pass, to Hawick in Teviotdale. The day following, the leaders were at Selkirk, on the edge of the great Ettrick Forest, when a messenger reached them from Surrey's army, now nearing Stirling, the first crossing of the long Forth estuary which so nearly, with that of the Clyde, cut Scotland in two. The courier came not from Surrey himself, however, but from Cressingham, the Treasurer, in the name of the Viceroy, Fitz-Alan. Percy had sent word ahead, by fast rider, to inform of his coming, his numbers and his route. The reply astonished and incensed him. Cressingham, as Treasurer and cost-conscious, declared that they already had quite sufficient men in arms to deal with such as the scoundrel Wallace and his riff-raff, and consequently the reinforcement army would not be required. It was the Viceroy's wish that Sir Henry returned whence he had come, and disbanded his force.

The thin-lipped, hesitant-seeming Percy's fury was a sight to behold, on receipt of this extraordinary message. He trembled, shivered, looked almost as though he would swoon with rage. He knew well, of course, of the bad blood between Cressingham and his uncle, Surrey. Clearly this was done out of spite, the wretched Treasurer—who indeed had made himself the most hated man in Scotland—prevailing on the new Viceroy to over-ride the authority of the commander-in-chief. But out of a stuttering torrent of white wrath, it became clear that Percy had no intention of obeying. He was a soldier, in arms, and he took his orders from the military commander, not from such a low-born clerk as Master Cressingham. Or even Fitz-Alan. Until detailed commands arrived from Surrey himself, they pressed on.

In this he was supported vigorously by Sir Robert Clifford and most other leaders—indeed by Robert Bruce likewise, whose plans would have been put in much disarray by any turning back now.

Three days later, on the evening of 11th of September, emerging from the Pentland Hills into the West Lothian plain, with the foot now left far behind, the army was again halted by information from the north. But this time it was no mere courier who came to them, but two dishevelled knights, Sir Ralph Basset and Sir John Lutton, with a straggling party of men, some wounded. And their tidings were of disaster.

There had been a great battle, they declared. At Stirling Bridge, over the Forth, twenty-five miles to the north. They had been tricked, betrayed, scattered and ill-led. Surrey's army. It was no more. The man Wallace and an unnumbered great host of rascally Scots had lain in wait for them there. At this bridge. Amongst tidelands and marshes. It had been no fair fight. The work of mean men. Half of the English array across the bridge and on the mile-long causeway beyond. Wallace had attacked, through swamp and bogs. No room to fight. No room to turn. Horses hamstrung, or sinking in the mire. Arrows, spears, knives—no honest chivalry. All in confusion. The Welsh cravens fleeing back, casting away arms and armour. The bridge taken and held behind them. Hundreds drowned trying to swim back. Others still trying to swim across to their aid. Then treachery in the rear, south of the bridge. The damned Scots with Surrey, betraying them. That Steward. The Earl of Lennox. Crawford. Lundin. All turned coat. Attacked the rear. Roused the people of Stirling. To slay and murder. It was a massacre . . .

Appalled, Percy and his companions fired questions at the exhausted men, sought to piece together the picture, to learn the present position. Wallace had been besieging Dundee, fifty miles to the north-east, had he not? Surrey had between fifty and sixty thousand men . . .?

Not any longer! God alone knew how many still lived. Cressingham was dead. The Scots were said to have flayed him, and cut up the skin to send round the country. A hundred and more knights were slain—most without having opportunity to fight as knights should . . .

"And Surrey? And Fitz-Alan?"

Surrey was in full flight for Berwick. Fitz-Alan—none knew where he was. Everywhere men were fleeing, as best they could. Wallace's hordes pursuing, cutting down. And everywhere the common Scots folk were waylaying, slaughtering, from every wood and copse, devils behind every bush. Men and women both. The whole plain of Forth was a shambles. And there was Edinburgh to get through. Before the Border and Berwick. That was why they had come this way, hoping to win through to the West. Before news of the victory turned every hand against them. All over this accursed land the people would be rising.

Hurriedly, distractedly, the leaders of Percy's force conferred. Once their five thousand foot came up, they were a strong force. If they had been but a day or two earlier, they might have saved all. Or, perhaps, been swept away with the rest! If sixty thousand could be so broken, would an extra eight thousand have made the difference? How many, in God's name, had this Wallace managed to muster?

But their foot would take days to catch up with them. They were probably not at Selkirk yet. And had they days to spare? To wait? All Scotland would be rising around them, drunk with the smell of victory, thirsting for bloody vengeance. Wallace would have time to gather together his forces again. It would be sheerest folly to wait. Even Clifford conceded it.

What, then? Would three thousand cavalry, tight-knit and driving forward, turn the tables? While the Scots were yet disorganised? Rallying what was left of Surrey's host. Men eyed each other, and eyed the Bruces, and read doubt in each other's eyes—and knew without saying it that there would be no such thing.

Retire, then? Back, whence they had come? Or to Berwick, to join Surrey? Or west, to Ayr, to hold the South-West, for which Percy was responsible as Sheriff and Governor?

There was some argument about this, complicated by the fact that their foot contingent would still be back amongst the Borderland hills. Eventually it was decided to rejoin the infantry, and then to head east through the hills for Berwick.

Robert Bruce took no part in this discussion, having ample to think about on his own, since the news changed all. Presently he had a few brief words with his brothers, who were hiding their excitement less than successfully. As he was doing so, his glance caught that of Elizabeth de Burgh, who, with Lady Percy, sat her horse a little way apart. It was an eloquent and significant glance.

During these past long days of riding, and nights spent in remote English-held castles, Bruce and the girl had inevitably seen a lot of each other. They had come to a sort of acceptance, a tolerance, of each other's attitude, which could not be called an understanding but which at least enabled them to maintain civility. Awareness had been pronounced between them from the first, however unsympathetic in its outward reactions; now there was a mutual playing down of the friction which seemed to generate spontaneously.

When the hasty and disjointed conference around Percy and the two newcomers had reached a conclusion, and an about-turn was announced, Bruce raised his voice.

"My lord of Northumberland," he said, stiffly formal. "You and yours may make for Berwick. I, and mine, do not."

There was a sudden silence from the leaders' group.

"What do you mean?" Percy asked tensely, after a moment or two.

"I mean that I have not come so far into my own land, to turn back now."

"We have decided otherwise. That King Edward's cause will best be served by turning back to Berwick, for this time."

"It may be so. But I go on. And my host with me."

"Go where, sir? And for what purpose?"

"For good and sufficient purpose."

"There speaks a forsworn traitor and rogue!" Clifford cried. "Have I not always said as much? That he could not be trusted a lance's length?"

"Sir Robert Clifford," Bruce declared quietly, "for these words you shall answer, one day. At lance's length! But . . . here and now, I think, is not the time."

"No," Percy agreed coldly. "More is at stake now. More is required than such barren talk. My lord of Carrick — your men are mustered in King Edward's name. You are here in his service. And under *my* command. I'd mind you of it."

"And may I mind *you* of something, my English friends? You are deep in this Scotland. Part of a beaten, broken army. With a long way to go before you may rest your heads secure. Moreover, half of these men behind you are my father's. Scots. Who, think you, will they obey, in this? Do you wish to put it to the test?"

So it was out, at last, gloves off, the mask down. With a jerk of his head Bruce sent his two brothers spurring back to the main body, their errand clear, obvious.

Even Percy had no words now.

Clifford had. "He came with this intention. To desert us. The treacherous turn-coat! He planned it all. Back in Carlisle. I said we should leave him. Should bring his men, but not Bruce himself. They are all the same, these Scots. I'd trust an adder before any of them! This is treason, by God! Bruce is traitor, for all to see!"

"These are hard words, sir. Perhaps I spoke too soon? That this was not the time to break that lance!" Bruce raised a hand to point at Clifford. "Perhaps Sir Robert had better answer for his words now. After all. Honour demands it . . ."

"Honour! *Your* honour! In flagrant treason, you talk of honour?"

"Has it not entered your head, man, that what would be treason to the English is not treason to the Scots? That we cannot commit treason against a conqueror, a usurper? If the Scots commit treason, it must be against their own realm and king. Only an unthinking fool would say other. And that I name you, Sir Robert—an unthinking fool! Is that sufficient for *your* honour? So—shall we form our respective hosts into lists, my lords? Make a tourney-ground? While Sir Robert and I fight it out, *à l'outrance*. It will be my pleasure . . ."

"No, I say!" Percy intervened, in pale-faced anger. "I forbid any such childish folly! This is war—not tourney-ground posturing. Enough of this."

"If you prefer war to jousting, my lord—let us have it. We are not unevenly matched. We shall have our own battle, here on this hillside, if you will? Scots against English. What could be fairer? Put all to the test. Of war . . ."

"No, by the Mass! It shall not be." Percy's thin voice rose alarmingly. "Think you I do not know what you are at? To keep us here. To delay our retiral. In hope that our presence is discovered. That Wallace's hordes come up with us . . ." His words were lost in the murmuring and muttering of his companions, the two knights from Stirling's debacle loud amongst them. All eyes were turning northwards, as something of the fear of these communicated itself to the others.

"Very well," Bruce said, and had to repeat it, loudly. "Then here we part company, my lord."

"You shall pay dearly for this—that I swear, Bruce!" Clifford shouted, in frustrated fury, and was the first to rein round and ride back towards the host.

As the others followed suit, Bruce waved his hand to his brothers. As they gave their orders for the Annandale men to draw apart and ride on, he urged his mount over to where the two women sat their horses, silent spectators of the scene. He did not speak, but searched Elizabeth's face.

"So you change sides once more, my lord!" she said.

He knew that was what she must say—but had hoped, somehow, that she would not.

"You think it? You think that is what it is?" he demanded.

"What else? That, or you have been acting a lie for long."

He spread his hands. "A lie? What is the lie, and what is the truth? I have not changed in my own mind. I have done what I must. In a storm, a man does not speak of lies and truth, but seeks to keep his bark afloat! To reach its haven."

"And you have a haven in mind?"

"Aye. I have a haven in mind."

Percy had ridden up, frowning. "Come," he commanded the women brusquely.

His wife, a tired-faced and anxious woman with fine eyes, sighed. "This is men's business, my dear," she said. "Leave it to them. Since we can effect nothing." She reached out a hand to the girl's wrist. "Come, yes."

Something of the way she had said that caused Bruce to look keenly from her to Elizabeth, wondering.

The younger woman seemed to ignore them all. "You intended this?" she put to Bruce. "From the beginning? To use this march, these men, for your own ends? Before ever there was the word of this victory. When we talked, at Carlisle that night. Even then, you had conceived it all? And let me name you . . . what I did!"

Wordless at her sudden intensity, he nodded.

"You did not trust *me*, then?" She seemed to be unaware of the Percies at her side.

Still he did not speak.

"If Wallace had not won his victory—what then?" she persisted. "What would you have done?"

He glanced at Percy. "This. The same. Though with bloodshed, perhaps. If we had been withstood."

She let out a long sigh. "Then I am glad," she said simply, and the intensity seemed to go out with her breath.

Percy was looking angry, apprehensive and bewildered, in one. He grasped Elizabeth's bridle, and pulled her beast round after his own.

She did not resist him now. But she turned in her saddle. "Tell my uncle, the Steward, that I wish him well. He and his. And . . . and may God go with you."

Biting his lip, Bruce watched her ride away.

And so the host divided, there on Torphichen heights, in silence, without blows or any other leave-taking. The Scots sat their horses and watched as the English turned and trotted off, file upon file, whence they had come, southwards for the Pentland Hills and the long secret road to the Border.

PART TWO

Chapter Eight

Scotland rejoiced. Abbey and church bells rang day after day, bonfires blazed on the heights for nights on end, folk danced in the streets of towns and on village greens. The English were gone—all save the garrisons of a few impregnable but isolated fortresses, Lochmaben, Roxburgh, Edinburgh and Stirling itself, where the gallant Sir Marmaduke Tweng, who almost alone on the English side had come out of the disaster with untarnished reputation, still held out. But these could achieve nothing, and did little to dampen the enthusiasm, relief and joy of the people. The name of William Wallace was on every lip, prayed for in every kirk, honoured in every burgh and village and hamlet. The Scots, never hero-worshippers until now, acknowledged their saviour, and delighted the more in that he was one of themselves, of the old race, a knight's son admittedly, but of the people. Everywhere the acclaim rang out.

Or, not quite everywhere perhaps. In many a castle and manor of the land there were reservations—even in not a few whose owners had won them back, out of English occupation, thanks to Wallace. The nobles saw a little further than the common folk. They saw the established order endangered. Their men, their own vassals, were everywhere flooding to join this Wallace, quite ignoring their feudal duties and service to their lords, the system on which the entire community was built. Land, enduring, indestructible, viable, calculable land, was the unit on which a realm must be based; not persons, who were ephemeral, unreliable, removable, and who could and did pass away. The land did not die, and the great families who managed the land were not going to pass away either. Yet Wallace held only a miserable few acres of this land, and claimed the people as all-important. And he was not even a Norman, his mother-tongue not French but the Erse gibberish.

Few, of course, even of the most proud, lofty and influential of the lords, denigrated the scale, brilliance or the effect of Wallace's

Stirling Bridge victory. Moreover, although only in a minor capacity and in the later stages, he had been supported in his victory by some of the great ones — the Steward himself, Lennox, Crawford, Macduff, son of the Earl of Fife; and, of course, the Graham. Sir Andrew Moray of Bothwell had been his principal lieutenant, and had indeed fallen, mortally wounded it was said. So Wallace could no longer be called outlaw, brigand, claimed as something like a Highland cateran and guerilla fighter. Even men with legitimate doubts had to recognise realities.

Robert Bruce was one of the doubters, of course, although his concern was rather different from the others — not so much for the land, nor yet the people, but for the kingdom. Wallace's blow had been struck for the people; but it was a blow for the kingdom also, and so must be acclaimed, supported. But Wallace himself did not represent the kingdom's cause; Wallace might indeed endanger the kingdom. He had fought in John Baliol's name.

Bruce, that vital September, did not in fact encounter Wallace. When he arrived at battle-torn Stirling, with his Annandale men, it was to find the Steward and many of the lords assembled there, but Wallace himself gone, pursuing the fleeing English with all his mounted strength. All was falling before him, and he was maintaining the impetus to such an extent that he was said to be actually making for Berwick itself. There was even a suggestion that he intended to drive on, down into England.

This would be folly, all the Scots lords agreed, Bruce included. They sent couriers after Wallace, advising him strongly against any such course. Nothing would be more likely, Bruce pointed out, to reunite the English, at present at sixes and sevens, than an actual invasion of their land.

There was much to do at Stirling, with a whole land, suddenly freed from a fierce and authoritative grip, to be brought under control. The lords and bishops applied themselves to this, under the frowning regard of Stirling's great fortress, still English-held, but impotent, not really besieged even yet, but contained. Buchan, the Constable, had come south with his cousin, John Comyn, Lord of Badenoch; so that there were two great officers of state to represent the highest authority in the land and take charge of the attempts at administration. Again, in the name of King John Baliol.

Bruce protested about this, declaring that Baliol had abdicated and renounced the throne. His deposition and humiliation by

Edward could be overlooked perhaps; but not his renunciation and fleeing the country. He was no longer King, in any sense. To act, here, in his name, was not only wrong but folly.

The matter was complicated. In the past, when the Kingdom of Scotland had been without an effective monarch, for one reason or another, a Guardian had always been appointed to act on behalf of the Crown and bear the supreme authority. Obviously such a Guardian should be appointed now. But who should be the Guardian? Normally it would be one of the great nobles, who should also be a military leader, with powerful forces at his back—since he had to wield the sword of state. The Steward would have been suitable, as to rank and position, but he was no military leader, no leader of any sort, in fact, and his slobbering speech no aid to high dignity. The Earl of Buchan, High Constable, as an earl, could claim seniority in rank, and was indeed a veteran soldier, with large following; but he had played an equivocal part in this rising, had indeed, at Surrey's command, taken the field against Moray's rebels in the north, though half-heartedly and ineffectually. His reputation had suffered, and the common folk of Stirling booed him in the streets, the more so as Moray himself lay dying.

There was another candidate for Guardian, however, Buchan's cousin, the same Sir John Comyn the Red, Lord of Badenoch, who with Bruce had formed part of that unhappy queue to sign the Ragman's Roll at Berwick a year before. He was ambitious, vigorous and an effective soldier—and the Comyns were undoubtedly the most powerful family in the land. Moreover, his mother was John Baliol's sister.

Bruce might have claimed the Guardianship for himself—and undoubtedly would have done had he been less of a realist. For he recognised that he was little more popular with the Scots people than was Buchan. Everyone knew that he had been Edward's man. The Red Comyn even referred to him as Bruce the Englishman. He had taken no actual part in the recent fighting; all had been over when he arrived at Stirling with his little host. His youth was no insuperable difficulty—but he could not claim to be a military leader; though he had been knighted, he had won his spurs at joustings in the tilt-yard. He could not command the confidence necessary for a Guardian, he knew.

But of one thing he was determined—the Red Comyn should not be Guardian. It was not only that he hated the man's arrogant mocking style. John Comyn said openly that if John Baliol had indeed vacated the throne by leaving the country, and taking his young son Edward with him, then he, as his nephew, was next in line to be King.

A more immediate and practical problem than the Guardianship and civil administration, however, quickly made itself evident to the assembled lords—simply that of food. Food for man and beast. The harvest had not been ingathered over much of the land—indeed, because of the English occupation and its harshness, and the removal of wool and grain to England, there had been but little sown, little to reap. Everywhere barns, stackyards and storehouses were empty, and the grim shadow of famine began to grow in war-torn Scotland. No doubt in the more remote parts there was still a sufficiency; but in the areas over which the armies had operated, hunger was growing as the days shortened. By the nature of things, Stirling district was worst hit. The lords could no longer feed their men-at-arms. A general break-up became inevitable.

Bruce's fifteen hundred was the largest single contingent there, and consequently required most food and forage. He was faced with the choice of sending them home to Annandale, to disband; leading them south to join Wallace, who had taken Berwick and was now besieging Roxburgh Castle; or going over to the West with them, to his own area of Carrick, where there was no famine as yet. This last appealed most strongly. A body of fifteen hundred men-in-arms was too useful an asset in the present state of Scotland to disband and throw away, however much of a problem it presented logistically. Wallace was still talking about invading England—now, not only for military and vengeance reasons, but for food; and Bruce had no desire to be involved in any such ill-advsised adventure which would only expedite reprisals.

In mid-October, then, the Bruces left Stirling for Ayrshire, glad to be away. Already there had been clashes with the Comyns in the streets of the town. Andrew Moray had died two days earlier, a good man gone.

It was strange to ride through the countryside, Lanarkshire and Ayrshire, and find the English gone—for here in especial their rule had been most complete, all-embracing, with every town and castle garrisoned. Now, like snow in the smile of the sun, they had quietly withdrawn, disappeared—and in their place many of the tollbooths had small portions of Cressingham's skin nailed to the English gibbets. Bruce was now able to ride, for the first time for years, to his own birthplace, the principal seat of his earldom, Turnberry-in-Carrick, home of his Celtic ancestors for generations. Typically, the English had left it in good order, not burned or destroyed—for they would soon be back, they declared.

But the Bruce brothers had barely disposed themselves in Turnberry Castle, and commenced the process of stocking up with winter fodder for man and beast, than they were rudely jolted. An exhausted messenger came from Annan, via Stirling, from Thomas and Alex Bruce. Annandale was in smoking ruin, sacked, devastated. Sir Robert Clifford had come north, with a great host of Cumberland men, and laid all the Bruce lands waste. Ten townships were destroyed, hundreds slain, Annan itself sacked—though the castle had held out—the harvest all burned and the cattle driven off or slaughtered. Clifford had left again, with his booty—but the lordship was in dire distress.

So Turnberry was abandoned again, and the Bruces spurred southwards in wrath. But some of the wrath, the brothers well knew, was now directed against themselves, as their men contemplated broken homes, ravished women, and widespread ruin to return to—done while they had been held by their young lords kicking their heels in the north. Defiant gestures were all very well for lordlings; but Annandale had ever been too vulnerable to English attack to hazard. The old lord had known that well. But the old lord was gone, apparently, none knew where. And his sons had failed Annandale . . .

Bruce himself was not unaffected by a sense of guilt. He would be the seventh Bruce lord of Annandale, and the first to allow it to be cruelly ravaged. As he rode furiously through the devastated land and saw the burned homesteads, desecrated churches, the corpses of men, women and children choking wells and ditches, hanging from trees, crucified on gates, a great weight of responsibility settled upon him—allied to a cold hatred. It was on his account that these people had suffered. But woe to those who had caused the suffering.

At the douce red-stone town of Annan, blackened and charred now, below the castle that still stood intact on its mote, they learned the full grim details from Thomas, Alex and Mary. Clifford had come raging from Carlisle with thousands, mainly foot —although they had returned to England mounted. It had not been any military campaign but purely a savage punitive onslaught. Indeed Clifford's orders to his men had been every man for himself, no quarter to be given, no prisoners taken, all booty and plunder to remain the property of whoever could take it. The Bishop-Governor of Carlisle had lent him troops for the outrage, offended by Bruce the Elder having bargained Annandale men for his own freedom and then seen them change sides. As a consequence, hell had been let loose on Annandale.

Robert Bruce had now more than enough to keep him busy, without concerning himself overmuch with affairs of state. It was a notably hard winter, setting in early with snow and ice and gales, and folk in no state to cope. The needs of his own people took up all his wrathful energies. He set himself to organise the transfer of grain and cattle from Carrick to Annandale, rehousing and rehabilitation of refugees and homeless, rebuilding and repairing whole townships and villages. He had never applied himself like this in his life, and was glad enough to tire himself out day after day. This he could do, must do. The rest could wait.

Thoughts of Elizabeth de Burgh came to him not infrequently, but she seemed to occupy a different world to his.

Occasionally word of the doings of men outside this South-West reached them. William Wallace had indeed invaded the North of England, and a bitter and harsh retaliatory campaign he appeared to have waged, giving the Northumbrians and Cumbrians precisely the same sort of treatment that had been meted out to the Scots. Tales of savagery, violence and slaughter percolated through to Annandale—and though, in his present mood, Bruce was not inclined to feel squeamish towards the English, part of his mind told him that this must result in a hardening of the enemy's determination, a uniting of fronts, and ultimate fury of attempted reprisals. There were ten times as many English as Scots, and this simple truth was something that they had to live with, to ever take into account. Their every effort, therefore, should be to divide and disunite, not to unify. This campaign, however justified, would have that effect, for certain.

Great convoys of grain and cattle and sheep were said to have been sent back to Scotland. This at least was satisfactory. But the cruel weather triumphed over cruel warfare, and the now distinctly undisciplined Scots army was forced back across the Border before Christmas. Wallace, it was said, had retired to his favourite refuge in Ettrick Forest, and his mixed host had largely dispersed to their homes all over the land.

Then came the first and inevitable counter-attack. Surrey drove north again, on the east side, and retook Berwick and Roxburgh. But the weather was too much for the English likewise. The advance could not penetrate the snow-blocked passes of the hills which guarded most of Scotland's southern counties, and ground to a halt. It was stalemate, meantime, in the worst winter of living memory.

It was late February before the icy grip began to relax—and with it came word from the south that King Edward, from France, had commanded that there be no major invasion of Scotland until he came in person to lead it—ominous tidings. When that would be was not revealed, but rumour said in the late spring. Perhaps spurred by this grim warning, movement stirred again in Scotland. Wallace sallied forth from the Forest, to besiege Roxburgh Castle, and his emissaries were once again going through the land calling men to his standard. None came to Annandale. But in early March a courier arrived from James the Steward, to announce a great assembly of the magnates and community of the realm to be held in Ettrick Forest, at Selkirk, in the middle of the month, and requested the Earl of Carrick's presence thereat.

Bruce considered well. He recognised that important decisions could not be put off for much longer. If Edward was coming, then the ranks had to be closed and vehement steps taken. He himself could not hide away here in Annandale indefinitely. And he might usefully influence the steps that might be taken. The fact that the assembly was being held in the Forest, in Wallace's own chosen haunt, not in Stirling or Edinburgh or at Scone, was surely significant. It meant in large measure an acceptance of Wallace as leader. The lords were to come to him, not he to the lords. Bruce decided that Annandale might now be left to his brothers' care. He would go to Selkirk.

· · ·

It was hills and passes for every mile of the fifty that stretched between Annan and Selkirk, and the snows and floods still blocked much of the way, impeding and delaying Bruce and his small escort more seriously than he had anticipated. He was hours later than intended in reaching the venue of the assembly, in that fair hub of green valleys where Ettrick, Yarrow and Tweed all joined, amongst the oak, ash and pine glades of the greatest forest south of the Highlands. The gathering was being held in the ruins of what had once been the Abbey of Selkirk, a Tyronensian foundation of David the First's, which 170 years before, had been removed twenty miles further down the Tweed, to Kelso, for convenience. The remains, though abandoned, were extensive and picturesque, providing a certain amount of shelter, b.. more of dignity, for a large-scale conclave. As Bru... rode down through the haughs of Yarrow towards it, he saw t.e e.tire wide valley-floor filled with encampments and horselines t. silken pavilions of lords and knights, banners and standards eve ,where, the blue smokes of a hundred cooking-fires rising over all.

It seemed that the actual conference and council was already started, being held partly in the open, in a sort of amphitheatre formed by the broken-down former choir of the abbey, backed by the square of the cloisters and opening on to the neglected sunken gardens and pleasance. Here a great crowd of folk were assembled, of all sorts and conditions, gazing up to where, in the paved approaches to the gaping chancel, the quality and landed men and churchmen stood, or sat on the flanking cloister benches. Up in what was left of the choir stalls certain great ones were seated, in the centre of which was the Steward, who appeared to be presiding. A cleric was holding forth.

". . . all kinds and conditions of men, their treasure, their toil, their very lives," he was declaring, in a richly sonorous voice. "This being so, it is necessary, essential, that due and proper direction be given them. With authority. The Church can do this, in the name of God and His kingdom. But who may speak, with full authority, in the name of this earthly kingdom of Scotland? My Lord Steward—you occupy high office and bear a proud name, of excellent repute. But you cannot speak in the name of the King's realm. My Lord Constable—nor can you. You are one of the great Seven Earls of Scotland, and have authority to raise the realm in the King's cause. But you cannot speak in the realm's name, so that all men must obey. I say that it is entirely necessary for the governance and saving of this kingdom that one be appointed, here and now, lacking the King's royal presence—appointed by the magnates of the realm here assembled, who may take fullest command in all matters, and speak for this ancient people. I do declare that this assembly is entitled to name itself a parliament of the estates of Scotland, and that it should hereby appoint one to be Guardian of the realm."

In the applause and acclaim Bruce, peering over the heads of spectators, asked of a black-robed Dominican friar who it was who spoke.

"That is a great man, Master William Comyn, brother to the Earl of Buchan, sir. They say he will soon be bishop. He is Provost of the Chapel-Royal."

"A Comyn! Then we know what will be coming next!" Bruce began to edge forward through the throng.

The speaker continued. "The Guardian must be strong, else he is useless, my friends. He must dispose of great forces. He must be renowned as a warrior, a man of great repute. Also he must be strong in support of Holy Church. I say to you that such a man stands here amongst us. He is indeed the head of the family of which I am the humblest member. A family which none will deny is the strongest, the greatest, in this land. Which boasts three earls, three bishops, and no less than thirty-three knights. I say to you that none is more fit to be Guardian of Scotland than Sir John Comyn, Lord of Badenoch."

There was considerable acclamation for this nomination, but Bruce noted that it was confined to the quality. Few of the watching throng raised voice—but there was a ground-swell of muttering. Although they were powerful indeed in the North, in the South here the Comyns were not popular. They were too closely identified with the despised Baliol.

Bruce, in his edging forward, had reached a point where he became aware that, behind a massive broken pillar of the former transept, William Wallace stood, towering hugely over a group of his lieutenants—these no longer a ragamuffin crew but now all clad in excellent armour and broadcloth, no doubt captured. Only Wallace himself was dressed exactly as previously in rusty chain-mail and leather guards—perhaps because he could find none amongst his defeated enemies of size sufficient to supply him. He stood listening to the proceedings, hidden from most in his retired position, expressionless.

The Constable was now adding his support to his brother's nomination. It may have cost him dear to do so, for there was said to be little love lost between the two John Comyns, Buchan and Badenoch; but though an older man, more experienced, and outranking his distant cousin, he could not but concede that the other was chief of the name. Their mutual Norman great-great-grandfather had married as his second wife the heiress of the ancient Celtic mormaership and earldom of Buchan; Badenoch was the heir of the first family, himself of the second. And in public, the Comyns always put up a united front.

Earl Malise of Strathearn spoke next. He proposed, as somebody must, in decency, that James, High Steward of Scotland, be appointed Guardian. He was formal, brief.

Men stirred uncomfortably. The Steward was well enough respected as an honest man and a patriot. But as mouthpiece of the nation . . . !

From his presiding seat in the choir, James Stewart raised a thin open hand and waved it back and forth. "I decline. I decline such nomination," he said thickly. "I am old. Of insufficient strength. A younger man is required. I decline." At least, that is probably what he said, though his difficult tongue and slobbers muffled it. But the gesture of his hand was sufficiently clear.

The Abbot of Dunfermline suggested that a bishop of Holy Church might well prove the wise choice, uniting all classes and divisions of the people. He would have proposed their beloved Robert Wishart, Bishop of Glasgow, who had once acted Guardian previously, he said—but unhappily he was a prisoner of the English. The Primate, Bishop Fraser of St. Andrews, had just died, exiled in France. Bishop Crambeth of Dunkeld was also in France, ambassador to the French king. He therefore named Thomas of Dundee, Bishop of Ross.

There was now some applause amongst the commoner folk, for Bishop Thomas was one of Wallace's supporters. But there was no like enthusiasm visible amongst the ranks of the nobility; nor indeed amongst much of the clergy, where Ross was considered to be too junior a see to be thus exalted.

A new voice broke in, musical, with lilting Highland intonation. "My lords and friends," a slight, delicate-seeming but winsomely good-looking youngish man said, "hear me, Gartnait of Mar. I say that if there is one man who should be Guardian of Scotland, it is Robert Bruce of Annandale, who should rightfully be our King. But since he is not within the realm at this present, I say to you that his son should be appointed—the Lord Robert, Earl of Carrick. He is not here, but is expected . . ."

Bruce cursed beneath his breath. His brother-in-law, the Earl of Mar, meant well, no doubt; but this was not the time to advance *his* name. Gartnait, although amiable, had always lacked practicality. He was much troubled by his neighbours, the Comyns, of course, and no doubt was as much concerned to counter their ambitions as to aid Bruce's.

"Bruce *is* here, my lords!" he cried aloud, interrupting Mar, and pushing strongly forward now, through the press, to break out into the open flagged space which had once been the abbey's nave. "I come late—but not too late, I say!"

There was a great stir and exclamation now, on all sides—by no means all of it enthusiastically welcoming, as he strode up to where the Earl of Mar stood, clapped his sister's husband and first wife's brother on the shoulder, and bowed to the Steward.

"You give me leave to speak, my lord?" he said strongly.

James Stewart nodded.

"I have heard what is proposed, my friends," he said. "Not only as regards myself, but others. And I too say that a Guardian of the realm should be appointed. Now. But not myself, who have fought no battles, earned no plaudits, am but untried amongst you. My father, were he here, would himself be no candidate for Guardian—that I swear. If he were to present himself to you, I say, it would be as your rightful King, not Guardian ... !"

A wave of reaction, cheers and dissent mixed, comment and question, greeted that, a new vigour and excitement manifested itself throughout the great gathering.

Bruce held up his hand. "But my father is *not* here. I have heard the names suggested as Guardian, and I say that, good and sound men as these are, they do not, cannot, meet the case, my friends. Only one man can fill Scotland's need today. Only one man will the people follow. Only one man, at this juncture, can speak with the voice that not only the folk but England, Edward Plantagenet, will hear and heed. That man is William Wallace of Elderslie. I name you Wallace as Guardian!"

It was as though a dam had burst, and the emotions of men surged free in clamour. The very surrounding hills seemed to shake to the shout that arose and maintained. Not all of the vociferation was favourable, of course, but the vast mass of it was wildly so. Almost to a man the common folk, the men-at-arms, the lesser lairds and small land-holders, even the bulk of the clergy, roared their approval, hands high or beating each other's shoulders, feet stamping. It was amongst the nobles, needless to say, that the opposition was expressed, but compared with the mighty explosion of applause, it was a small thing that faded where the other went on and on.

It was some time before Bruce could make himself heard again. "I commend ... I say, I commend your judgement!" he shouted. "This man has done what no other could do. He has rid us of the English ..."

Again the uproar.

"Hear me—hear me, my friends. He has rid us of the English, I said. Aye—once! But they will be back. Nothing on God's earth is more sure! They will be back. And so he must needs do it again. I know Edward. Aye, some blame me, they say, that I know him over well! But this I say, that when Edward himself comes chapping at our door again, then we shall need a united realm to withstand him. And more than that, a leader whom all the people will obey and follow. Therefore, I say, William Wallace it must be. None other . . ."

He was interrupted. "And I say this is folly!" It was Sir John Comyn, the Red, himself. "Here is confusion. It is a Guardian of the realm we seek to appoint—not the commander of a host. Wallace has shown that he can do battle, yes. But he is no man for the council-table, no meet representative . . ."

His words were drowned in outcry and protest, angry this time, with an ominous underlying growl. Fists were shaken, even swords were drawn and waved. Everywhere the nobles looked apprehensively around them, at the gesticulating crowds.

The Steward was trying to speak, but Bruce prevailed. He had young and excellent lungs, and no impediments to speech.

"There are sufficient and more for the council-table!" he declared. "Many to advise Wallace. All too many! But the Guardian must carry the people, not just the Council. If Scotland is to withstand Edward of England in his might and wrath. Here is the heart of it. Only the nation in arms will save us, then. And only one man, I declare, can raise this nation in arms, lacking its King . . ."

When the noise again slackened, it was not the Lord of Badenoch but another Comyn, who took up the issue, Master William the churchman.

"What my lord of Carrick says is not in dispute," he claimed, with the careful moderation and reasoned appeal of the practised orator. "None question William Wallace's notable deeds, or his ability to rouse the people. That he must do. But more than this is required of the Guardian. There are decisions of state and policy to make. He must unite more than the common folk—he must unite the lords of this realm. Will Wallace do that? You say, my lord, that he must withstand King Edward. But he must speak with him also, treat, negotiate. Will the proud Plantagenet speak with such as William Wallace . . . ?'

"I say that he will. Edward is proud, yes. But he is a man of deeds, not of words. Because Wallace is of the same kidney, he will respect him where he would not you, sir. Or myself, indeed. Think you he cares for any Scots lord? But the man who defeated Surrey in open battle is altogether different."

The Comyns were not quieted yet. "I know Edward also—to

my cost!" That was Buchan, the Constable. "He does not eat his words. He has named Wallace outlaw, cut-throat, promised to hang him. Think you he will swallow that, and deal with him? Never! Moreover, the Guardian of Scotland speaks in the name of the absent King of Scots. How can this man do that? He is not even a knight! You, my lord, of all men, should know better. The Kingdom cannot be represented by one who is not of the *noblesse*, the men of honour. How shall knights and lords follow and yield their voices to one who is not even of their order . . .?"

"By the Rude—is that what concerns you, my lord?" Bruce cried. "Then we shall see to it!" He swung on his heel, and strode across the moss-grown flagstones, spurs clanking, to where Wallace had stood quietly amongst his own group throughout, a grimly silent spectator of the scene. In front of the giant he halted, and with a screech of steel drew his sword, the short travelling sword that hung from his golden earl's belt. "William Wallace," he declared, voice ringing, "I, Robert Bruce, knight, earl of this realm, do hereby dub you knight. In the name of God and St. Andrew." He brought down the flat of his blade on one great shoulder, then on the other—where it clashed against the long upthrusting handle of the other's own famous and enormous two-handed brand that was said even to sleep with the man. "Earned on the field of battle, if ever knighthood was. Be you faithful, fortunate and bold! Stand, Sir William Wallace!"

There were moments of utter silence, surprise, elation, even consternation. Then, in that green ruin-strewn hollow of the hills, pandemonium broke out, to make feeble and pedestrian even the tumult that had succeeded Bruce's previous proposal of Guardian. In wild emotion, men went all but crazy with jubilation, approbation and a sort of unholy glee. The thing was done, suddenly, dramatically, totally unexpectedly, there before them all —and could nowise be undone. Sir William Wallace!

While undoubtedly there were not a few present who questioned the wisdom, the propriety, even the taste of what Bruce had done, none could doubt his right so to do. In theory, any duly dubbed knight could himself dub another, provided that he had proved his prowess on the field of battle or in single combat, and was accepted as a man of renown; but in practice, only kings, princes, commanders of armies, and very great nobles ever did so, the last but seldom and in special circumstances. Nevertheless, as the holder of one of the ancient Celtic earldoms of Scotland— and knighted most royally by no less than King Edward himself

—none could contest the validity of Bruce's action, even without his claim to being second heir to the throne.

Even the Comyns, therefore, stood dumbfounded, impotent, silenced by their own cherished code. Everywhere the nobility and chivalry of Scotland were in like case.

The Earl of Mar was the first to move. As the din continued, he walked over to Wallace and clapped him on the shoulder, wordless. Words could not have been heard, anyway. The Earl of Lennox came to do the same. These were the only earls present, apart from Carrick, Strathearn and Buchan. Then the Steward stood, and came from his seat to congratulate the new knight. Crawford followed suit, and others, some others, likewise.

As for Wallace himself, for once he seemed quite overcome by events. He stood there, his open features working, his great hands gripped together in front of him, knuckles showing white. He did not speak, had not spoken throughout, appeared all but dazed by his abrupt transition. The last man to be called a respecter of persons, or impressed by mere forms and ceremonies and titles, he was nevertheless very much a man of his age, and only too well aware of what this unlooked-for metamorphosis could do for him. By one brief and simple rite, in that chivalric age, he had been made respectable, transferred to the ranks of the men of honour, given a status that none could take away from him. Knighthood, in 1298, was no empty honour. Much that had been almost inconceivable only a few moments before was now possible. William Wallace was no fool, and however reluctant to be beholden to young Bruce, or any other lord, he would not have rejected this accolade, even if he could.

Bruce was not finished yet. Into the gradually ensuing hush, he spoke. "As Earl of Carrick, and therefore member of the high council of this kingdom, I do now request of that council to declare and appoint Sir William Wallace of Elderslie, Knight, to be Guardian of Scotland, as from this present." He looked first at the Steward, and then nodded to his brother-in-law, Mar.

It was a shrewd thrust, addressing his nomination to the high or privy council. Such body undoubtedly existed, but it had not met formally for long. More important, for his present requirements, it had had no new members appointed to it for years. Therefore, save for one or two elderly men, only those who automatically belonged to it by virtue of their high office or position, could at the moment claim to be members. These were the great officers of state, the senior bishops, and the earls. At one blow,

Bruce had silenced much of the opposition. The Red Comyn, for instance, undoubtedly would have been a privy councillor if that body had been properly appointed; but lacking King or Guardian, no recent additions had been made.

Mar was about to speak, when Lennox forestalled him. As another of the old Celtic nobility, he had no love for the Normans in general and the Comyns in particular.

"I, Malcolm of Lennox, agree," he said. "I say Sir William Wallace for Guardian."

"Aye. As do I," Mar added.

"No!" That was Buchan, gazing round him anxiously. As well he might. Apart from the Earl of Strathearn, and the Steward himself, there was only one other certain privy councillor present, the Bishop of Galloway — and coming from that airt, he was almost bound to be a Bruce supporter. He was.

"I also say for Wallace," the Bishop announced briefly.

"As do I," Malise of Strathearn nodded.

There was a brief pause, and the Steward, licking his lips, spoke. "Does any other . . . of the council . . . say otherwise, my lords?"

"I protest!" Sir John Comyn cried hotly. "At this, of the council. It is a trick, a ruse. Who knows who is of the council? It has not met. These three years and more. Bruce would trick us all. I say all lords and knights may speak. And vote."

There were cries of agreement from not a few, but Bruce shouted through them.

"I declare that the voices of individual lords and knights, however puissant, have no authority in this. Only a parliament duly summoned, or else the council, can appoint a Guardian. This assembly cannot be a parliament — since who had authority to call one? Therefore, the council only may speak for the realm. And there are councillors enough here."

"So . . . so I hold and sustain," the Steward nodded, though obviously uncomfortably. "Can you deny it, my lord Constable?"

Unhappily Buchan eyed his cousin. "In other circumstances . . ." he began, and waved a helpless hand.

"I call the vote," Lennox said.

"Aye." James Stewart acceded. Does any other member of the council speak?"

There was none other to speak.

"I see no need to vote, then. The issue is clear. Five have

spoken for—no, six. One against. If I myself were to vote, nothing would be altered. My lord Constable—will you withdraw your opposition, that all may be more decently done?"

Buchan sighed, and nodded, in one.

"So be it. I declare Sir William Wallace, Knight, to be Guardian of this Scotland—in the name of the famous prince, the Lord John, by God's grace King of Scots."

Strangely, there was comparatively little acclaim and demonstration now. Men seemed to be sobered suddenly by what was done, what the implications were, what this dramatic action foreshadowed. It was as though an irrevocable step had been taken, an assured order all but overturned. All were for the moment abashed. Even Bruce, who should have protested about this being done in the name of Baliol, did not do so.

All looked at Wallace.

That giant appeared to come out of a trance. Almost like a dog shaking itself, he heaved his huge shoulders and raised his auburn head. He gazed round on them all, out of those vivid blue eyes, unspeaking still, a tremendous, vital figure, the very personification of innate strength, vigour and resolve. Then slowly, waving his supporters back, he began to pace forward from his transept.

Not a sound was heard as he stalked up the choir steps and came to stand before the Steward. That man rose, and after a moment, bowed deeply before the other. Then he moved slightly aside, and gestured to Wallace to take the seat he had vacated, the simplest of tokens, but fraught with significance.

Something like a corporate moan rose from the great company. Wallace inclined his head, and moved into the Steward's place. But he did not sit. He turned, to face them all, and raised a hand.

"My friends," he said, and his deep voice shook with emotion. "I thank you. I thank you, with all my heart. For your trust. I swear before Almighty God that it will not be betrayed. God and His saints aiding me, I shall not fail you. Much is needed. I shall demand much of you. But, for myself. I shall give all. This I vow—and you are my witnesses."

The murmur that swept the crowd as like the distant surge and draw of the tide on a long strand.

"And now, my friends, to work." With a flick of his hand Wallace seemed to thrust all that had transpired behind him. Emotion, by-play, ceremony, had had their moment. Typical of the man, all was now decision. "There is much to do, I told you. Most can and must be done hereafter. But it is right that some shall be done here, before you all—and be seen to be done. The council, for one. I know but little of these things—but it is clearly in need of renewing, of enlarging, as my lord of Badenoch says. My first duty, therefore, as Guardian, is to see to this. I now ask Sir John Comyn, Lord of Badenoch, to join it. Also Sir Alexander Lindsay, Lord of Crawford; Sir Alexander Comyn, Lord of Lumphanan; Sir Alexander de Baliol, Lord of Cavers; Sir William Murray, Lord of Tullibardine; and Master William Comyn, Provost of the Chapel-Royal."

Even Bruce gasped at this swift recital, rapped out like the cracking of a whip. At first, like others, he had thought it unsuitable lacking in fitness, for Wallace to plunge so immediately into the exercise of his new authority. But now he saw, as all men of any understanding must see, how astute a move this was. Wallace had been appointed in the face of Comyn opposition; and since they were the most powerful family in the land, he would have them as a burden on his back. But, by this sudden move, he had changed the situation dramatically, and put the Comyns, especially Sir John, into a position of acute difficulty. He had singled out three of them for advancement, in this his first official act. The Red Comyn had himself indicated that the council was in need of new blood. Now, to refuse to sit on it, especially in the company present, was almost unthinkable. Yet it meant that the mighty Comyns were thereby accepting favour at Wallace's hands, the very first to do so, demonstrating to all their acknowledgement of his authority. He had them in a cleft stick.

Bruce almost laughed aloud as, after an agonising moment or two, Sir John inclined his arrogant head, unspeaking. The other surprised nominees murmured varied acceptance.

Apparently satisfied, Wallace went on, "Two other matters. This realm had an ancient alliance with France. The French are now attacked by the same foe as are we—Edward of England. We must see to it that both realms act in common against him. Make a treaty of aid, one with the other. If Edward, as is said, does return from France to lead attack against us again, then the French should attack England in the south. It is our blows, here in Scotland, and into England, that will have brought him back. This must be our enduring policy. King John saw this three years ago, but was forced by Edward to denounce his treaty. We must renew it. I say that we should send envoys at once to King Philip, new envoys. It is in my mind to send Master John Morel, Abbot of Jedburgh. And Sir John Wishart of the Carse, brother to the imprisoned Bishop of Glasgow."

Men stared at each other. The proposal was a sound one, and the envoys named no doubt suitable enough. But none could fail to be astonished at this naming of names. That Wallace should already not only have his road mapped out, but have men in his mind to carry out his designs, could only mean that he had been prepared beforehand for some such eventuality. But his knighting and appointment to the Guardianship had been wholly at Bruce's sudden instigation. How then . . . ?

Bruce himself, listening, came to the conclusion that he had underestimated and misjudged his man. He had thought that, by these actions of his, he had hoisted him into the Guardian's seat; it looked now very much as though Wallace had been prepared to assume it, on his own.

Distinctly chagrined, if not humbled, Bruce listened to a further demonstration of the big man's forethought and sheer ability. He, the former outlaw and small laird, had the effrontery there and then to create a new Bishop of St. Andrews and Primate of all Scotland—or, at least, to take the essential steps therefor. He did it, first by adding Master William Comyn's name as a third envoy to France; then by announcing the senior bishop present, Galloway, as Chancellor of the realm, or first minister of state; and finally proposing one William Lamberton, Wishart's chancellor of Glasgow Cathedral, as Bishop of St. Andrews, in the room of the late Bishop Fraser—adding that, on his necessary visit to Rome to be consecrated, he should also present to the Pope the Scottish realm's entire and leal duty to His Holiness and its request that the Holy See declared its disapproval of Edward of England's invasions and savageries, and threaten him with outlawry from Christendom, anathema and excommunication if he persisted in such wicked warfare.

Quite overwhelmed, the company listened. Never had anyone present heard the like of this, such vehement forcing of the pace, such high-sounding a programme, such confidence of delivery— and all done before a great gathering of the people, not behind the closed doors of the council-chamber.

The Comyns were silenced—for Master William had undoubtedly been hoping for St. Andrews for himself, as a senior member of the chapter and brother of the Constable; Galloway bought off, who might have claimed the Primacy, Wishart being a captive and Crambeth of Dunkeld overseas; and all muffled up and confused by this ambitious bringing in of the Pope as possible ally in the struggle.

—For what? Amongst Wallace's group of immediate supporters, a tall, strong-faced, keen-eyed churchman stood beside the Benedictine friar, John Blair. By the way the others were looking at him, it was evident that this man must be Master William Lamberton. A long sword-hilt peeped from beneath this individual's black robe. Another Benedictine, and a fighting one, apparently. So Wallace was making a bid to control the Church, as well as the state. One of his own band Primate and Galloway Chancellor. And Pope Boniface was a Benedictine also, it was said.

There were murmurs, growls, alarmed looks, amongst the nobility and some of the churchmen, but no vocal or affirmed opposition. That this was not the place, nor the time, any man of discernment would understand. This was Wallace's day, and any who openly opposed him would go down.

Grimly the giant considered them all, waiting. Waiting for the outcry that did not materialise. Then he nodded, and turned.

"My lord Steward," he said, "it is enough. I thank you for your patience, your courtesy. I thank all. Let a feast, a great feeding, be prepared. For many are hungry. There is much food here in the Forest—the famine has not touched it. Many wild cattle, many deer. Sufficient beasts are already slain. All shall eat and drink tonight." And, the King's representative having given his orders to the King's Steward, he bowed briefly and, waving to his own close group to follow, strode by the vestry door out of the ruined chancel.

Later, with the camp-fires lighting up the March evening, and the rich smells of roasting beef and venison filling the night air, a very thoughtful Bruce, in company with the Earl of Mar, pacing the shadowy, broken cloisters of the abbey, was startled by a deep voice speaking close behind them. They swung round, to find Wallace there, with the man Lamberton. Like so many big men, he seemed to have the ability to tread very softly.

"So, my lords," he said, "you commune closely! As well you might! For in this Scotland, I think, the very stones listen and whisper. And there will be much whispering tonight. How long, think you, before word of this days doings reaches Surrey? And Edward?"

The two earls, who had indeed been discussing Wallace, looked a little uncomfortable.

"What mean you, Sir William? By that!" Bruce asked tensely.

"That wise men do well to look over their shoulders—that is all," the other answered lightly. "This is a notable realm for traitors, is it not?"

Was this, could it possibly be, some sort of warning? "I do not take you, sir," Bruce said.

"Then you are less shrewd than I esteemed you, my lord! The House of Comyn may not love Edward Plantagenet. But they may prefer him to William Wallace! Or even Robert Bruce!"

"So-o-o! You fear the Comyns will not accept what is done?"

"Only if they must, I think. And they are very strong. I ask you, my lords, as men of the same noble rank and station as these —should I feel secure, when Edward strikes, with the Comyns in arms at my back?"

Bruce glanced at Mar, and cleared his throat. "I do not know!"

"Nor do I! Master Lamberton, here, believes that I should not."

The tall priest spoke in a crisp voice that smacked of the field rather than the chancel. "I do not name them traitors," he declared. "But I hold that they believe themselves better suited to rule Scotland than is Sir William Wallace! And will not hesitate to stab him in the back, if by so doing they may take over that rule. And esteem themselves to have done Scotland service! To do so, they must be most fully assembled in arms. As they can, in answer to the Guardian's summons to the nation. The Comyns could raise ten thousand men. A sore host to have at your back, in battle!"

"True. But how may this be countered?" Mar demanded. "You cannot keep the Comyns from mustering their men. Nor deny them the right to fight for the realm."

The cleric lowered his voice. "My lord—you control the vast earldom of Mar, a mighty heritage in the North. My lord of Carrick, yours is the Lordship of the Garioch, nearby in Aberdeenshire—half a province. Moreover, Sir Andrew Moray is dead, woe is me—but his brothers are sound for Wallace, and hold the great Moray lordships of Petty, Innes and Duffus. All these abut the Comyn lands. If you, my lords, were to go north and, with the Morays, muster the men of these lordships—as all will be called upon to do by the Guardian—then you have a force assembled on the Comyns' doorstep, do you not? Men so mustered in arms are ever . . . restless. However firm you hold them in, there will be some small spulzie and pillage. Reiving, as we say in the East March of the Border, whence I come. On neighbours' lands. Comyn lands. I swear, so long as they are there, no Comyn host will come south!"

Bruce almost whistled beneath his breath. Here was a crafty, nimble-witted clerk. Could it be that this was where the advice came that was turning Wallace from mere warrior into statesman?

"You would play the realm's nobles one against the other, Sir Priest?" he challenged.

"They need but little encouragement in that, my lord! I but urge that, since all the land must be mustered in arms, it is only wise that sound men muster alongside those who might be led otherwise. I wish for no bloodshed, no fighting. But a due balancing of forces."

"And Bruce *is* sound, in our cause, to be sure!" Wallace put in, smiling into his curling auburn beard. "Since he it was who made me Guardian! With my lord of Mar's aid."

If there was derision in that, it was fairly well covered over. Bruce saw very well that Wallace trusted none of the lords, himself included. He was for sending him north, away from his own great reservoirs of manpower, Carrick and Annandale, to far Garioch, his sister's portion when she married Mar. There to distract Comyn, the Red Comyn in especial, who was his rival in so much.

"How do you know that I will not make common cause with the Comyns?" he demanded.

Wallace actually laughed, apparently having followed the younger man's train of thought accurately. "Because John Comyn is Baliol's man," he said simply. "And you are . . . yourself!"

The acuteness of that silenced Bruce for the moment. Mar spoke.

"If our hosts are up in Moray and Mar, facing Comyn, then we cannot be aiding you here against the English."

"A commander needs more hosts than one, my lord. It is wise not to pit all at one throw. He needs a reserve. Your combined hosts, in the north, will well serve as that."

In other words, Wallace was well content to fight Edward with his own common folk, the masses assembled direct from the nation, holding the great lords' levies at a distance. Bruce saw it, if Mar did not.

"Beware, sir, that you do not estimate Edward Plantagenet too lightly!" he said.

"That I do not," the big man assured. "By God, I do not! But all shall not be won, or lost, in one battle."

There was a mutual silence for a little, as the four men considered each other. Then Bruce shrugged.

"You are Guardian of Scotland," he said.

"Aye. Thanks to you, as I say."

"I wonder!"

"You doubt my thanks, my lord? That is foolish. You did for me, then, what no other could, or would, have done. The knighting. I will not forget it. For that, at least, I do most surely thank you. Your reasons for doing it I do not know. But the deed was good. Of much value. For this, I am in your debt."

"It was merited," Bruce said shortly. "Never was knighthood more so."

"Not all would agree with you! But ... that is no matter. What matters now is the future. How long do you give Scotland? You who know Edward. Before he comes hammering at our gates?"

"Three months. A month to return from France. A month to set his own house in order—to bring the English nobles to heel. A month to raise the men to march north. I give Scotland until June."

"Aye. You have the rights of it, I think. Three months—and so much to be done! So much!"

"You can do it," Lamberton said, in his crisp voice. "You only. For the folk are with you."

"We shall see, my friend. So you, my lords, go north ..."

Chapter Nine

Strangely enough, that spring and early summer of 1298 was one of the happiest periods of Robert Bruce's life—for which he had to thank William Wallace. He was, in fact, essentially a fairly cheerful and light-hearted character—had he not a reputation for extravagance and display? — and the last two years of stress and deep involvement in national tumults had superimposed a gravity and tenseness on his nature which was not normal. Now there was an intermission, a period of enforced detachment—or so he was able to convince himself. His prolonged periods of sham negotiation at Irvine and hard unremitting restoration work in Annandale, had prepared him to embrace the satisfactions of Kildrummy as it were with open arms.

He had not made his way there in unseemly servile haste, of course. He had his dignity to consider. He informed Wallace that he would take over the duties of governor of the South-West, with headquarters at Ayr—and Wallace had acceded with good grace, since it would have been impracticable to appoint anyone else in opposition to him. He had returned from Selkirk to Annan, set affairs there in order, specifically commanding that there was to be no general muster of the Annandale men, save for the lordship's own defence, whatever instructions might come from the Guardian. Then, taking Edward and Nigel with him, he had ridden north to Ayr, where he installed Edward as deputy, to raise the area in arms, including his earldom of Carrick, refortify the castle and keep an eye on Lochmaben—which, being to all intents impregnable, was still in English hands, like Stirling; possibly the insufferable Master Benstead was still there. Then he and Nigel, his favourite brother, had set out on the two hundred mile journey to Aberdeenshire.

Kildrummy Castle, principal seat of the age-old Mar earldom, was a handsome establishment set amongst the uplands of the Don, and guarding the mountain passes to the north-east. A remote secure place, centred in a world of its own, with the most magnificent hunting country for hundreds of square miles around, it was little wonder that its lord seldom chose to leave its fair attractions. Bruce found it much to his taste.

There was more than the place itself to hold him. Here his little daughter Marjory had been brought, when her mother, Mar's sister, died. She was now a laughing, chubby brown-eyed girl of three, and Bruce, who had accepted fatherhood as he had accepted marriage merely as one more normal development in a man's progress, now discovered delight, wonder, pride. This roguish, impulsive, affectionate child was his, all his, in a way that nothing else was his—and he had not realised or appreciated it before. On Isabella's death, at seventeen, soon after the baby was born, he had been anxious only to deposit the unfortunate infant with his sister Christian, take himself off, and forget the whole sorry business, a loveless marriage arranged by his father, an ailing, delicate young woman who cared nothing for the world outside Kildrummy, and then left him at nineteen with a puling, bawling girl-child. But now, here was Marjory Bruce, a poppet.

Christian Bruce, Countess of Mar, was herself good company, the gayest of the family, all vigour, energy and laughter, and twice as much a man as her gentle, slightly melancholy husband. Though womanly enough in all conscience, so that young men were ever round her like a honey-pot; Gartnait of Mar was probably wise enough not to leave home too frequently. She welcomed her brothers with enthusiasm, and proceeded to ensure that time did not hang heavily for them. Nigel himself was a happy-natured, carefree soul, and an excellent companion to take the mind off affairs of state.

Not that all was hunting and jollity, of course. The business of mustering a host went on, with wapinschaws, archery contests, trials of strength, games and races, to keep the men engaged and in training. No doubt the Comyns were doing the same, not so relatively far away—but in this land of vast distances, high mountain ranges, and little sense of involvement with the rest of Scotland, no ominous signs of it disturbed them. Bruce did pay one or two visits to the Bruce lordship of the Garioch, consisting of fifteen parishes, to the east, the rents of which had been Christian's marriage portion. Here he arranged for eight hundred men to assemble at the somewhat tumbledown old castle of Inverurie, and to train for service—Nigel would command these, in due course.

April passed into May, with the snow gone from all but the north-facing corries of the surrounding mountains, whins blazing and cuckoos calling endlessly in all the endless green valleys around Kildrummy. Word percolated through from the outside world occasionally, but seemed to lack urgency up here. Edward had returned from France, and had apparently made a great show of coming to terms with the nobles. He consented to ratify and confirm the terms of Magna Carta and the Charter of Forests, and agreed that the new taxes and tallage should only be levied with the acceptance of the nobility, prelates and knights, and withdrew the edict about compulsory foreign service. But, having done this, he had set up his headquarters at York, even moving the exchequer and law-courts there, as a sign of his displeasure with the south and as convenient for his campaign against Scotland. There was also news that Lamberton had gone to Rome, and that Philip of France had accepted a treaty of mutual aid with Scotland. Wallace had been disciplining his army, hanging not a few who had been pillaging and running wild. The burghs were all raising armed bands, the various crafts vying with each other. Roxburgh and Stirling castles still held out. A Comyn host, said to number six thousand, was assembled in the Laigh of Moray

This last did cast some small shadow at Kildrummy, and Bruce rode north by devious hill passes, further north than he had ever been, to Petty, on the coast east of Inverness, headquarters of the great de Moravia family, of whom Sir Andrew Moray had been the heir—the lord thereof still being Edward's prisoner. Here he found Andrew's two brothers, Alan of Culbin and William of Drumsagard, had already raised fifteen hundred men, while their uncle, Master David, a priest, had gone still further north to raise Avoch and the Black Isle of Cromarty. He also learned that Andrew's widow had given birth to a posthumous son, another Andrew to carry on the line. Giving Wallace's authority, he took the fifteen hundred, with young Alan of Culbin to command them, and rode back to Mar with them, doing a little harmless spoliation and fodder-gathering in outlying Comyn lands *en route*, as per instructions.

Back at Kildrummy, in early June, the news was more grave. Edward had assembled a mighty army at York, and was moving north. He was said to have no fewer than four hundred knights and gentlemen of chivalry, under the Earl Marshal, the Great Constable of England and the Earls of Gloucester, Lincoln, Arundel, Surrey and Warwick, besides the Scottish Earls of Angus and Dunbar. There was also the ominous Bishop Beck, 2,000 heavy cavalry, 2,000 light cavalry and no fewer than 100,000 foot and archers. These figures were almost certainly exaggerated, but clearly Edward was in deadly and determined mood.

There was another piece of news which indicated that however busy Wallace must be in preparing to resist invasion, he was not failing to use his wits in other directions. King Philip of France's signature of the treaty of aid was all very well, but he had not sought to use Edward's return home to implement the bargain by any renewed attack on the English, either on the Flanders borders or by massing for invasion of southern England. So Wallace had sent a new delegation to Paris, to urge military action upon him—and this was headed by John de Strathbogie, Earl of Atholl, and none other than Sir John Comyn, the Red. To have got Comyn out of the way at this juncture was a shrewd move, and might well make the Comyn forces mustered in Moray less dangerous—for the Earl of Buchan was less of a firebrand than his young kinsman.

These tidings were not rumour or hearsay, at any rate, for they had been brought to Kildrummy by the daughters of the Earl of Atholl himself. Strathbogie was the adjoining lordship to Mar on the north-west, and Atholl had married Mar's other sister. Christian Bruce, always a romantic, and a born match-maker, had invited the Ladies Isabel and Mary de Strathbogie to Kildrummy, clearly for the delectation of her brothers. They were pleasant, amiable, uninhibited girls, not beauties but comely enough and high spirited. Nigel was appreciative at least, and was getting on excellently with Isabel. Bruce, however, found some disinclination to live up to his reputation, with Mary — although he was by no means offended by her company, of which his sister saw to it that he had plenty.

A week or so after his return from Petty, riding back from heron-hawking up the Don, Bruce, momentarily alone, was joined by Christian.

"You look thoughtful, Rob," she said, eyeing him keenly. "Indeed, you are much in thought these days. Not as I mind of you. I wonder why?"

"We live in thought-making days, Tina," he returned easily.

"We always did. You are but twenty-four — early to become a greybeard! You used to be otherwise, brother — uncommonly so! Something of a rakehell, even. And a notable wencher! Does that sport no longer rouse you, Rob?"

He shrugged. "Say that I have other matters on my mind, lass."

" I think you have!" She looked at him quickly, and away. "But it is possible to . . . to allow some small distraction, on occasion, is it not? I would not have you turn into another Gartnait!"

It was his turn to look. "Gartnait . . . he does not satisfy you, Tina?"

"No," she admitted, simply.

"I am sorry. He is an honest, kindly man — if scarce a hero! Generous — and not disapproving, I think?"

"True. All true. But it is of *you* we speak, brother — not me! What do you think of Mary Strathbogie?"

He smiled. "She is well enough. Good company. And sits a horse well."

"She might sit a man well, too, Rob!"

"No doubt. Who is eager? She — or you?"

"Not you, it seems!"

"Should I be so?"

"You are still Robert Bruce, are you not? And Mary would make warm trysting. Or better, a good wife. Your Marjory needs a mother. And Mary dotes on the child."

"Insufficient recommendation for a wife, Tina!"

"She has more than that to commend her. She is kind, strong —not like Isabella Mar, a weakling. And she is taken with you, I can see. And mind, Rob—there are not so many women the Earl of Carrick might wed. You could not wed less than an earl's daughter—and there is no routh of such to choose from."

"Even so, I shall wait awhile, lass. My wife, see you, should I marry again, might need even greater qualities than you give Mary Strathbogie."

"You mean . . . you mean . . .? Nigel thinks that you might one day try for the throne. Is that so, Rob?"

"Has any greater right? After our father?"

"Right, no. But is that what matters, Rob? What good would the uneasy crown of Scotland do you? Even if Edward of England let you, or any, have it. You would have to fight long and hard to gain it. And fight as hard to keep it. Does that tempt you? A lifetime of fighting. For what? The empty, barren name of King!"

"Need it be so empty? Barren? Does not this realm require a king? Grievously."

"Need that unfortunate be Robert Bruce?"

He shrugged.

"So . . . you look for a queen, as well as a wife?"

"Did I say I looked for any woman?"

"No. But you are sure that Mary will not serve, it seems. So you have thought of it." Christian leaned forward to scratch her mare between the ears. "Nigel thinks that you are . . . concerned with another. An Irishwoman. The Lady Elizabeth de Burgh. Is it so, Rob?"

"It seems that Nigel thinks too much. Talks too much!"

"So it is true? There is something in this?"

"Nothing," he said shortly.

"Yet you have seen much of this Ulsterwoman? Found her to your taste?"

"Edward once thought to have me wed her. To bind me closer to him, no doubt. But she liked the notion as little as did I!"

"Yet you still see her?"

"Not by our own seeking. She lodged with Percy, while her father was with Edward, in France. Percy sought to use her, to work on me. Not knowing."

"Not knowing what?"

"That we battle together as soon as we see each other. That there is only strife between us."

She considered him thoughtfully. "Strife? Battle? It is thus between you? Then, Nigel has cause for his fears, perhaps!"

"Damn Nigel! He has no more cause to fear than he has to talk. What has he got to fear?"

"An entanglement with one so close to Edward . . .?"

"She approves of rebellion—that is how close to Edward she is! But what of it? I am not like to see her again."

"I wonder! Since you both esteem each other so ill, I think that you will!" Christian smiled a little. "This Elizabeth de Burgh— what is the style of her?"

"She is proud. And lovely. And believes me two-faced," he jerked. "That is all. Enough of this, of a mercy! Where is Nigel?"

"Where do you think? He makes excuse to fall behind. With Isabel. She nothing loth. But *you* leave Mary with Gartnait! You could be more the man than that!"

"Very well. I will go to her. But . . . let her not hope for too much."

Bruce was spared any prolonged skirmishing with the friendly Lady Mary. Two days later the messenger arrived from Wallace. He requested that the Earl of Carrick hasten south, with all the force at his command and at all speed. Edward was moving fast, was in great strength, had already taken Berwick, burned the abbeys of Kelso, Dryburgh and Melrose, and was marching on Edinburgh up Lauderdale. Wallace would require all the help he could muster, to halt him, preferably at Stirling. Once the English were beyond Forth, there would be no holding them, in their present numbers. This message was not to go on to the Comyn host, in Moray. They would hear, no doubt—but, it was hoped, not in time to affect the issue.

The intermission was at an end.

· · ·

Bruce, Nigel and young Alan de Moray of Culbin—Mar stayed at home—led their combined host of about 3,500 southwards as fast as they could. But Mar and Moray were not Annandale, a great horse-breeding area, and the vast mass of their men were not mounted. They had 170 miles and more, to reach Stirling, and though the men were in the main tough, wiry hillmen, their very numbers, and the need to forage for food, precluded any phenomenal rate of travel. Twelve miles a day, over mainly mountain country, was quite as much as they could manage.

Two more of Wallace's messengers reached them during the journey southwards, urging haste. Edward had surprised all by circling Edinburgh, not waiting to take it as expected, contenting himself with taking its port of Leith, as a haven for his anxiously awaited supply ships. Wallace had been falling back before him, deliberately devastating the land in the English path, a land already all but famine-stricken, ordering the folk away with their remaining cattle and destroying all grain, hay and fodder that might remain. Edward's invaders were said to be starving, and his ships delayed, so that there were troubles, the Welsh archers mutinying and eighty had been slain, it was said. Wallace's tactics were to lure the enemy back and back, over devastated land, right to Stirling and the Forth crossing, the most strategic point in all Scotland to hold a great army; but, perceiving it, Edward was pressing after the Scots at whatever the cost, before Wallace could properly clear the land in front. It had become a race for the narrows of the Forth.

Bruce's host had just left Dunblane, between Perth and Stirling, in the early morning of 23rd of July, when Wallace's next courier came up with grim tidings. The Guardian's army could not reach Stirling in time—that was clear. The huge majority of his force was infantry, the common people; and Edward's cavalry, in their vast numbers, were pressing them hard. He would try to hold them somewhere in the Falkirk vicinity, a dozen miles south of Stirling. And though cavalry was what Wallace most required, he had been only doubtful in his welcome to an unlooked for reinforcement which had just arrived, even though led by the High Constable of Scotland. The Earl of Buchan had put in an appearance with some hundreds of Comyn horse; he had evidently heard the news, up in the Laigh of Moray, and leaving behind his great array of foot, had raced south with his horsemen, by the coast route, while Bruce had been so much more slowly marching his combined host through the mountains. Buchan was allegedly hastening to Wallace's rescue; but the latter was uneasy and urged Bruce to do likewise, to leave his foot behind and ride with all haste for Falkirk.

It was about twenty miles from Dunblane, by Stirling Bridge, to Falkirk. Bruce did not delay. He had nearly 700 horse, mounted hillmen on short-legged Highland shelts, in the main. Leaving Alan Moray to bring on the thousands of foot, he and Nigel spurred ahead with this company, unhampered.

At Stirling Bridge they found Wallace's advance party preparing to hold it, if need be. They urged on the northerners anxiously. The English were in greater numbers than anything known before, they said; the plain of Lothian was black with them. Wallace was standing at Callendar Wood, just east of Falkirk — but it was no site to compare with this Stirling. These men were clearly in a state of alarm.

It was afternoon before they rode out from the dark glades of the great Tor Wood above Falkirk, to look down over the swiftly dropping land eastwards towards Lothian, with the grey town nestling below, at the west end of the wooded spine of Callendar Hill. At the other end of that long spine, no doubt, was the battle. But none of the newcomers tested their eyes or wits seeking for signs of it there. They did not have to. For below them, on the wide spread of green braesides between the town and this Tor Wood, was sufficient to take their attention. Scattered all over it were parties of horsemen, in small groups and large, all riding fast and all riding westwards, away from the battle area. Of foot there was no sign — save for the stream of refugees beginning to leave Falkirk, with their pathetic baggage, making uphill, like the cavalry, for the deep recesses of the Tor Wood.

There could be little doubt what it all meant.

Grimly Bruce jutted his jaw. "We are too late, I fear," he said to his brother. "Too late. Cavalry was Wallace's need — and there is his cavalry! Fleeing . . .!"

They hurried on downhill. The first batch of horsemen they came up with, about a dozen, wore the colours of Lennox. Bruce halted them, demanding news.

"All is by wi'," their leader called, scarcely reining in, obviously reluctant to stop. "They were ower many. Armoured knights. A sea of them. And arrows. Like hailstanes! It's all by wi' . . ."

"The battle? All lost? What of Wallace?"

"God kens! He was wi' the foot."

"And they?"

The man shrugged. None of his colleagues, anxious to be elsewhere, amplified. Already they were urging their spume-flecked horses onwards.

"Stay, you!" Bruce cried authoritatively. He pointed. "I see no blood. No single wound amongst you. What sort of battle was this?"

Scowls greeted that, and angry words. Men pointed backwards, in protest, outrage. But they were edging onwards.

"You are Lennox's men, are you not? Where is your lord?" Some shook their heads. Some pointed on, up the hill, some back. Clearly none knew.

Unhappily the Bruces rode on, the seven hundred doubtful behind them.

The next group they encountered wore the blue-and-gold of Stewart, led by a knight in armour.

"You are Stewarts," Bruce challenged him. "Who are you? And where is the Steward?"

"We are of Menteith. I am Sir John Stewart of Cardross. I know not where the Steward is. Or my lord of Menteith. All the lords have gone . . ."

"Gone where, man? Is all over? The battle?"

"God knows! There may be fighting still. The foot. Wallace's rabble. In their schiltroms of spears. Since they cannot flee. But all else is finished."

"You . . . you deserted Wallace and the foot?"

"Deserted! Who are you to talk of deserting? You were not there. They hurled all their strength at us. Between the schiltroms. Their cavalry and bowmen both. Thousands on thousands of them. The Constable's array broke first. In the centre. Then they were in amongst us. Behind us. We had no choice . . ."

"The Constable, you say? The Comyns—they gave way first? But there were no great number of them . . .?"

"The Constable took command of the centre cavalry. As was his right. The English threw all their strength at him . . ."

"Aye. Enough . . ." Without waiting to hear more, Bruce waved on his company.

The long but fairly low and gentle hog's-back of open woodland that was Callendar Hill sank at its east end to the valley of the Westquarter Burn. Where a tributary stream joined this below the south-east face of the hill was an area of marshland surrounding a small reedy loch. On the open slopes above this, Wallace had drawn up his army to make its stand. It was a reasonably good defensive position, the best that the Falkirk vicinity had to offer probably; but it was all on a comparatively small scale, and the water barrier only a minor one. The loch and marsh itself would not take cavalry, but the burn that flowed at either end of it could be splashed through. As an impediment to a vast army, therefore, it was inadequate. And worst of all, the relatively short distances involved meant that the long-range English and Welsh archers could remain drawn up on the east side of the loch and still pour their arrows into the Scots ranks beyond.

Bruce and his people, their formation somewhat broken up by negotiating the woodland and the streams of fleeing wounded, reached the last of the trees. They saw the land across the valley as literally black with men and horses and all the paraphernalia of war, stretching almost as far as eye could see, a dire sight. Though this enormous concourse was not in fact engaged, too great to be marshalled and brought to bear on Wallace's chosen ground. Only the cavalry and the archers were involved, as yet —to the Scots' downfall.

For, of course, it was in these two arms that Wallace was weak. His great mass of spearmen and sworders, however nimble and tough, were of little avail against these. The Guardian had drawn up his host in four great schiltroms, square phalanxes of spearmen, densely packed, facing out in all directions, bristling hedgehogs of pikes and lances and halberds, on which an enemy would throw himself with but little effect. Between these he had set his comparatively few bowmen, backed by the cavalry of the lords. And thus awaited the onslaught.

But unhappily all was within range of the massed thousands of Edward's long-bowmen, who with a methodical, disciplined expertise poured in a continuous stream, a flood, of their deadly yard-long shafts. Against these the Scots were helpless, their own few archers hopelessly outranged, and indeed the first to fall, as primary targets of the enemy. Thereafter the hissing murderous hail had been raised to fall mainly upon the cavalry behind. Here the execution was less lethal, because of breastplates, helmets, chainmail and toughened leather; but even so there was much havoc, especially amongst the horses.

Under cover of this fatal deluge, Edward's pride, his heavy chivalry had swept round the loch and crossed the burns in two horns; the left under Roger de Bigod, Earl of Norfolk, and Humphrey de Bohun, Earl of Hereford; the right under Bishop Beck of Durham and no less than thirty-six senior captains. These both drove uphill, and as the bowmen ceased to shoot at a given signal, bore in in five great prongs of perhaps a thousand each, ignoring the squares of spearmen and concentrating all on the lines of cavalry ranked between the schiltroms. It was then that High Constable Buchan signalled in turn, and at it the Scots nobility broke and turned back. The command was to reform in one mass up the hill, to put in a powerful counter-attack downhill; but this never materialised. The protective shelter of the wood was too great a temptation, and the Comyns' example infectious. The Scots chivalry rode off the field of Falkirk, to fight, perhaps, another day.

This had left Wallace and his foot in four isolated groups, round which Edward's armoured horse eddied and circled unhindered. Not all of the Scots nobility and gentry had bolted with the cavalry of course. Many had gone to join Wallace, on foot. But these found themselves on the outside of the bristling walls of spears, with the grim-visaged angry spearmen in no mood to open and break their tight ranks to let them in. Mostly they died there under the trampling hooves of the English destriers.

By the time that Bruce and his seven hundred arrived on the scene of carnage, all this was a thing of the past. There were only the two schiltroms now, the debris of the others making a trampled bloody chaos of the long slope. These two that were left had lost much of their shape and were tending to coalesce; but they were still fighting, doggedly, their perimeter dead being swiftly and steadily replaced by men from within the squares, to die in their turn as the massed horsemen raged round and round, driving in with lance and sword, battle-axe and heavy mace.

Many of Edward's proud chivalry littered the slopes of Callendar Hill, also, the horses in particular skewered, hamstrung and disembowelled by those deadly spears. The heaps and piles of slain, of both sides, grew thicker and thicker towards the foot of the slope—for this was the way that the battle moved, not uphill towards the wood and escape. The English cavalry were exploiting the advantage of site that should have belonged to their Scots counterparts; downhill. They were thundering in charges time and again down the slope, to overwhelm the schiltroms by sheer weight and impetus, in a trampling, screaming avalanche of horseflesh and armoured humanity. Already the lowermost Scottish spearmen were up to their knees in the mire and water of the valley-floor. Perhaps Wallace was deliberately allowing this to happen, for in the soft ground the heavy cavalry would be unable to come in at them. But then, there was still the serried ranks of the waiting archers, not to mention the vast mass of the so-far uncommitted English foot.

For desperate moments Bruce sat his mount, eyeing that scene. What could he do? Nothing that he might attempt could possibly turn the tide of battle now. To stand still was inglorious, useless. To turn and flee like the others was unthinkable. His men were not armoured. He himself, like Nigel, was in travelling clothes, not full mail. Most of them bestrode Highland shelts. They were the lightest of light horse. Against some of the best heavy chivalry in all Christendom, battle-trained veterans — and outnumbered six or eight to one.

There was only the one condition in their favour, and one thing that they might attempt. The element of surprise would be theirs — for none of the English would look for a return of the Scots horse now. And Wallace himself might yet be saved. They could all see him, unmistakable, in the upper front rank of one of the schiltroms, towering over all, his great brand whirling and slicing. Fighting like a hero, yes — but not like a general.

Bruce made up his mind. He turned to his men of Mar, Garioch and Moray. "My friends — you see it! See it all. We can save Wallace. That is all. Drive down after me. In a wedge. A spearhead. No halting. No fighting. Straight through. If I fall, or my brother, keep on. Drive down through all. To Wallace. Scotland depends on Wallace. Mount him, and as many as you may. Behind you. Then round and back for these woods. Do not wait. Our beasts are lighter, more swift, sure-footed. Come. And shout slogans." He whipped out his sword. "On, then! A Bruce! A Bruce!"

Scarcely enthusiastic as his North-countrymen could have been, they followed, without demur or hesitation.

The Bruce brothers side by side at the apex, they gradually worked themselves into a great arrowhead formation as they thundered down the braeside, yelling. It was not perhaps the most exactly disciplined manoeuvre, but they made a dramatic, effective and fast-moving entry on the scene — and one that it would be very hard to stop.

They had perhaps five hundred yards to cover, the last third strewn with bodies and slippery with mud and blood. The English cavalry down there were in milling, circling thousands, though with many standing back, looking on, unable to push their way in at the surrounded spearmen, ploutering in the deep mire, or just licking their wounds. But many as there were, expecting nothing of this sort, they were not marshalled to resist and break up such an attack, however many times their numbers. Nor, at this stage of the battle, were they under any unified control. Trumpets began to neigh within moments of the attack becoming apparent. But more than that was required to organise and present a coherent front; and the very diversity of trumpet calls bespoke too many commanders. There was no over-all general of the chivalry, on the spot; Edward himself had been kicked by a horse the previous night, while he slept on the ground like any soldier, and was sufficiently incapacitated to be directing this battle from a distance.

Time, here, was all-important. Bruce, at the front of the V, saw that they would, in fact, bore through to the battling Scots almost inevitably, and probably without great difficulty or casualties. It was the turning and getting away again that would be a problem. But he also perceived another inevitability; they could hardly help but ride down the upper front ranks of the Scots themselves, for they dared not rein back and lose their impetus too soon. It made grim recognition.

But it was the littered debris of the fighting that demanded their major attention in this crazy, furious descent, as they drove down through the dead, the dying and the wounded, amongst screaming men and fallen, hoof-lashing horses. Their hill-ponies, the most sure-footed mounts there were, nevertheless had not been trained to battle and blood, and savagely firm mastering was necessary to hold them on through the hell of it, to keep the wedge in shape and straight on course.

A hundred yards or so from the first of the beleaguered Scots, a hastily turned and jostling group of English cavalry barred the way. As he hurtled down on them, Bruce waved his sword round and round above his head, redoubling his shouting, the men behind doing the same, a fearsome sight. It was asking more of flesh and blood than it could take for stationary horsemen to stand there unflinching in the face of such furious downhill onslaught, however armoured. Well before the impact, the Englishmen were reining aside. Some bold spirits actually spurred on to meet the crash in movement at least; but most pushed to one side or the other, turning back, breaking away.

Bruce drove for the point of greatest confusion. Nigel was laughing almost hysterically just half a length on his left.

A red-faced knight in rich armour was suddenly before them, eyes round, mouth open. Bruce, flinging himself aside in his saddle to avoid the wild swinging blow of a gleaming battle-axe, all but cannoned into his brother. Jerking his beast's head back, as he swept by the knight, he felt their legs scrape together. His own sword slashed back-handedly right across the knight's surprised face in red horror. Then he was past.

There was another man directly in front—but he had his back to them, bolting out of the way, as well he might. But he was not nearly quick enough. His blade straight before him, stiff-armed, like a lance, Bruce drove the point in right below the back of the fellow's helmet. The victim pitched forward over his mount's neck, dragging the struck sword right out of its owner's hand. The man's careering mount carried him away to the side, falling.

There were two more in front—but these were decidedly getting out of the way. Swordless, Bruce was shaking a clenched fist at them, when he realised that he was in fact through the press. There were still mounted men between him and the Scots spears, but these were not drawn up, not standing, not going to challenge that mass of yelling riders.

And now, this other problem. How to draw up, not only himself but the close-packed ranks behind him, so as not to crash too terribly into the waiting ranks of spearmen? Those spears in themselves! Would men, seeing themselves about to be ridden down, not be apt almost involuntarily to seek to save themselves? By using their spears? On the riders-down? *He* would.

Dragging desperately at his beast's head with his right hand he raised his left, to make urgent circling signals, half-right, praying that the men behind would in their frenzy perceive what he meant and the need for it. Savagely he dragged and jerked at his horse, and stumbling, its legs sprawling at the suddenness of the change of direction, the brute did manage to swing right. Bruce heard a crash immediately behind him as somebody went down, unable to take the turn. He hoped it was not Nigel.

Still he bore right, so that now he was plunging along the wavering edge of spears, their blood-red tips before his eyes. Some were raised, to allow him passage, but others remained thrust out still, menacing. There were screams at his back now, where some of his Northerners had been unable to bring their beasts round in time and had crashed into their fellow-countrymen. Bruce did not glance round.

His eyes were on Wallace. He stood just behind the kneeling front row of spearmen, a little way along to the south, leaning now on his great sword, head bowed. He had lost his helmet and appeared to be wounded, blood running down his face and into his red bushy beard—though with so much blood splashed everywhere, it need not be his own. Stooping, he nevertheless stood above the press of those around him like a forest tree amongst bushes.

Bruce was seeking to draw up now, with the pressure behind slackened by the turn. He waved and shouted to Wallace.

"Quickly!" he cried. "Come. A chance. To win free. To me, man."

The giant raised his head to stare, but made no other move. He did not answer. He looked dizzy.

"Hurry, I say! Do not stand there," Bruce yelled. "We cannot wait, or all is lost. They will rally. Come."

Wallace shook his head, and gave a single dismissive wave of a huge bloodstained hand.

"Fool!" Bruce was close to him now, shouting and gesticulating over the heads of kneeling men, horse sidling nervously. "Do you not see? You must break out. While you may. Or you are a dead man."

"You . . . you would have me leave these? Abandon my folk? Away with you, Bruce." That was thickly, unevenly cried out. The man was obviously far from clear-headed.

"You can do no good here now. Come away. And fight again . . ."

"No! Run from my friends? Never!"

Others were pleading with him now, arguing, pointing— Scrymgeour his standard-bearer, Blair the priest, Boyd. Bruce saw behind them the drawn and anxious face of James the Steward. And Crawford. All the nobles had not deserted the Guardian.

Desperately Bruce remonstrated, his voice breaking as he heard the battle joining behind him, the English recovering from their surprise and beginning to hurl themselves against the light Scots horse.

"Wallace!" he yelled. "You are the Guardian. Of Scotland. All Scotland. Not just these. If you fall now, Scotland falls. Mind who you are—the Guardian . . ."

Nigel was shouting now, at his side. "These others can break. Into the marsh, and away. Where horse cannot follow. Many will escape. If *you* stay, all will die."

"Aye! Aye!" All around men saw the sense of that, and cried

it. Hands were pushing and pulling Wallace forward, towards the Bruces.

The 700, or what was left of them, now formed a chaotic barrier between the Bruces and the enemy, those towards the rear turned to face outwards and taking the brunt of a so-far disorganised English attack. Others were mounting fellow-Scots behind them.

"Get the Steward," Bruce ordered his brother. He waved to others. "Crawford. Lennox. Scrymgeour. I take Wallace . . ."

A Mar-man pushed up with a riderless horse. "Here—for Wallace."

"Aye . . ."

Eager, desperate hands were propelling the reluctant giant forward, all but lifting him on to the head-tossing, wild-eyed garron. He seemed to be no longer actually resisting.

Hardly waiting for the big man to be astride, Bruce grabbed the other's reins. A swift glance round had shown him that the only possible route of escape was southwards, up the Westquarter Burn. There were English there, yes—but not in the numbers that were behind them, massing everywhere.

"Come!" he commanded. "After me. A wedge again. Keep close." He dug in his spurs.

It was a ragged and much smaller wedge that began to form again behind him, to pound away southwards, along the front of spears. Many of his men had fallen, not a few chose their own route of escape, the rear ranks were too closely engaged to break away with the others. But perhaps two hundred could and did obey his call, and made up a formidable enough phalanx for any but an organised English squadron of cavalry to seek to halt.

They were burdened now, of course, with two men to most horses. They had no longer the advantage of a downward slope. And they were in softer, boggier ground. But this last militated more against the heavier enemy horse than themselves. It was no headlong gallop, but at best a canter. But a determined canter, before which the scattered enemy swerved away, even if thereafter they closed in on the flanks and rear. Indeed, from all sides the English gave chase rather than sought to intercept, but even double-burdened, the nimble hill-ponies were swifter, lighter, than chargers.

Wallace, swaying about alarmingly in the saddle, his long legs positively trailing the ground, was pounding along between Bruce and Nigel, who now had the Steward clinging behind him, heavily-armoured and a great weight. Bruce heard trumpets braying a new and distinctive call, from across the valley. He guessed what that meant, and his heart sank.

The arrows began to come at them in a matter of moments thereafter. They were nearing extreme range, and a moving target —but the bowmen needed only to loose off into the brown mass.

Havoc quickly followed. Nigel's horse was one of the first to fall, pierced through the neck, and throwing both riders. They were all but ridden down immediately. Bruce, reining round violently to the right, more uphill, to increase the range and change of direction of flight, yelled for his brother and the Steward to be picked up—but did not himself slacken pace or leave grip of Wallace's reins. Somehow the pack behind him swung after him, their formation much broken. And still the arrows hissed down on them, amid the screams of men and horses.

Bruce was surprised to find his right ankle gripped, and glanced down to see Nigel leaping along beside him, mud-covered, bare-headed and lacking his sword now also, but apparently unhurt. Bruce reached down a hand and somehow his brother, after three or four attempts, managed to haul himself up behind him, lying stomach down over the beast's broad and heaving rump.

"Steward safe . . . safe," he gasped in Bruce's ear, as he got himself upright.

"Many down?"

"Aye. Curse the bowmen!"

"Not long now. Range. Too far . . ."

The hail of arrows had at least one advantage; they effectively inhibited over-eagerness on the part of the English pursuers. These advisedly left a very clear field for their archer colleagues.

Bruce was now leading almost directly uphill towards the wood but perhaps quarter of a mile further south than where they had come down. This meant, of course, that it was the rear ranks of his party which had to take the main punishment from the bowmen, with only the odd spent shaft falling forward amongst the leaders. Only a heroic dolt would have had it otherwise—and Robert Bruce was not that.

At last, in the blessed shelter of the trees, Bruce pulled up his spume-covered, panting, almost foundered horse. All around him others did likewise. Wallace gripped his saddle-bow and stared blindly ahead of him, wordless. The Steward came up, spitting blood, on a garron from which the owner had fallen. Scrymgeour and Blair came running to Wallace's side.

Bruce looked back, downhill, on chaos and confusion. There was no longer any pattern to the scene, only a hopeless medley of men and horses, heaving and surging this way and that, darting, circling, eddying—or not moving at all. The schiltroms had finally broken up, and most of the spearmen appeared to be seeking escape through the marshland, where the cavalry could not follow, or even in the loch itself, splashing through the shallows, or swimming in deeper water. Some were fleeing uphill towards these woods. Many would escape—but more would die.

Bruce was looking for more than the fleeing foot. Scattered all over the littered slopes, the remnants of his own seven hundred were striving to make their way up here, in ones and twos and small groups, avoiding contests and heroics. Most seemed to be likely to succeed, with the enemy perhaps lacking in enthusiasm for any difficult chase and the battle won; after all, Edward's host was said to be next to starving, horses' fodder as scarce as men's. Bruce was thankful to see that many of his Northerners were winning clear—for no more than one hundred and fifty had managed to follow immediately at his back.

He turned to Wallace. "You are wounded, Sir William? Can you go on? Sit that beast? Or ... shall we make a litter?"

The big man stared downwards. "I ... am ... very well," he said.

"That you are not! But can you ride ...?"

"I am very well," he repeated, heavily. "But others ... are not. Those who looked to me ..."

"Here is folly, man! A battle lost, aye—but others to be fought. And won! What good repining ...?"

"So many dead. Fallen. Pate Boyd. Sim Fraser. Rob Keith. Sir John the Graham. Young MacDuff of Fife, the Earl's son. Sir John Stewart ..."

"Aye, my brother," the Steward broke in thickly. "I saw him shot down. An arrow. And my son ...? Where is Walter?"

"I saw him. Taken up on a horse," someone called. "Riding to the north ..."

"Quiet!" Bruce burst out, cutting the air with his hand. "Here is no time for this talk. Men have fallen, yes. Fighting. They came to fight. And fall, if need be. Time enough for talk, after. But what now? What to do? *Edward* will not wait and talk."

"Aye." Obviously with a great effort, the dazed Wallace pulled himself together. "You are right, my lord. And I thank you. We fight on. But not here. We cannot stand south of the Forth. Even at Stirling. Not now. We must rally again in the hills to the north. And burn the land behind us. Burn Stirling. Burn Dunblane. Burn Perth, if need be. Starve them. Starve England's war host. That is his weakness, now. No more battles, backed by nobles that I cannot trust! I was a fool, to think that I could out-fight Edward Plantagenet, his way. No more! I fight my own way, now. Wallace the outlaw! The brigand . . . !"

"You are still Guardian of this land, man."

"Aye—and I shall fight Edward with the land. What he can ride over but never defeat. Would God I had used my own wits, instead of listening to others. But it is not too late. While Scotland lives, it is never too late! And Scotland will not, cannot, die." The man's great voice shook with a mighty emotion.

Bruce scarcely shared it. "So it is Stirling now?" he demanded impatiently. "Stirling, and beyond. The North?"

"Yes. Take me to Stirling, my lord. But not the North, for you. The lurking in the hills. The raids by night. The burning. The ambuscade. The knife in the back. This is no work for great lords! So back to your West, Bruce—to your own country. And mine. You claimed to be Governor of the South-West, did you not? Go there, then. Hold the South-West. Harry the English West March, if you can. While we starve Edward. Raid into England. Nothing will harass hungry men more than the word that their homes are threatened, endangered. Go west from Stirling, my lord—and such other lords as are not fled! I shall require the West at your hands."

Bruce eyed him levelly for a moment, and then nodded. "Very well, Sir Guardian. Now—Stirling . . ."

CHAPTER TEN

In the selfsame hall of the castle of Ayr where Wallace had hanged Percy's deputy sheriff, Arnulf, and where Percy himself resided during the long farcical negotiations of Irvine, Bruce paced the stone-flagged floor, three weeks after the battle of Falkirk. Only one other man shared the great shadowy apartment with him, its walls still blackened by Wallace's burning, the August evening light slanting in on them through the small high windows. This man sat at the great table, eating and drinking —and doing so in the determined fashion of one hungry, though tired, even if his mind was hardly on what he ate. He was dressed in travel-stained and undistinguished clothing—non-clerical clothing, too, and with dagger still at hip, and a sword laid along the table nearby, strange garb for the Primate of all Scotland. For this was William Lamberton, now duly consecrated and confirmed by the Pope as Bishop of St. Andrews and leader of the Church. A good-looking, strong-featured grave man, youthful-seeming for so high an office, at thirty-five, he nevertheless looked older than his years tonight, weary, stern. But he watched Bruce at his pacing, keen-eyed, nevertheless.

"It would not serve," the younger man declared, shaking his head. "Not with him, of all men. I could not do it. Besides, Wallace is wrong in this. Mistaken. He should not give up the Guardianship. You must persuade him against it, my lord Bishop."

"You do not know William Wallace, if you think that I could! Once he has determined a matter in his mind, nothing will shake him. He is now so decided. He deems himself to have failed the realm, at Falkirk fight. To have forfeited the trust of the people . . ."

"That is folly. The folk all but worship the man! As they do no other."

"Think you that I have not told him so? New back from Rome as I am, I have seen and tested the will of many in this. But he will not hear me. He says that though they still may trust him, he is not fit to be Guardian. That the Guardian must have the support of *all* the realm. And that he has not. The nobles will have none of him . . ."

"*Some*, no. But who will? Show me any man who will receive the support of all!"

"It is not enough. For Wallace. After Falkirk. Fifteen thousand died on that field, and he takes the blame to himself."

"Fifteen thousand . . .? So many?"

"Aye. In a battle which he now says should never have been fought. He takes all the blame—however much others blame the lords who rode off. Says that he should have known better than to front Edward so. Or to trust these others."

"The man must be ill. In his mind. A defeat, by the largest most powerful army ever to invade Scotland, is no disgrace. All commanders must accept defeats. And fight on . . ."

"Wallace will fight on, never fear, my lord. But not as Guardian. Especially as the Comyns threaten to impeach him."

"What! Impeach? The Comyns . . .?"

"Aye. Buchan and the others claim that he mishandled all. Did not send for them. Indeed of intention would have kept them away. From the battle. They claim that he has divided the land . . ."

"God forgive them! This is beyond all. And you would have me to work with these?"

"Wallace would. And, since he will by no means remain Guardian, I deem him right in this, at least. Many other lords and knights follow the Comyns. Would even make Red John the King." Lamberton looked at Bruce shrewdly, there. "John Baliol's nephew. There is only one way to unite the realm, in face of Edward, Wallace says. A joint Guardianship. You, and John Comyn of Badenoch."

"I say it is madness. We can scarce exchange a civil word! How could we rule together?"

"It would be difficult. But not impossible. What is *not* difficult, today? You are not bairns, my lord. So much is at stake. If Bruce and Comyn would agree, the nobility would be united. And Wallace working with you, carrying the common people with him, for he has learned his lesson, he says. And myself, speaking for the Church. The three estates of the realm. As one, for the first time . . ."

"Comyn would never serve with me. He hates me. Besides, he is in France."

"Wallace has sent for him. To come home. With this offer. If you do not accept, I swear Comyn will! And who else is to control him, as joint Guardian? The Steward? Buchan, his own kinsman, another Comyn? Mar? Atholl? Menteith . . .?"

Helplessly Bruce shook his head again. "No—none of these. But . . . John Comyn! Even Buchan himself would be less ill to deal with . . ."

"Buchan led the flight at Falkirk. That will not be forgotten by the people. They would never accept *him* as Guardian. But the Lord of Badenoch was not there. And whatever else, he is a fighter. None doubts *his* courage."

Bruce halted in his pacing, to stare at his visitor. "How many of the Scots folk accept *me*? I am told that they think of me as Edward's man."

"They did, yes. But no longer. You did not fail at Falkirk. You saved Wallace."

There was silence for a little. Then Bruce shrugged. "If I say that I will consider the matter, it must not be taken that I agree," he said, heavily. "That I promise anything. Better to convince Wallace to continue as Guardian."

"He will not. That I promise *you*."

"Where is he now?"

"At Scone. Above Perth. Assembling men. That is where I have come from."

"And Edward? They tell me that he is moving into the West?"

"That is true. He hoped to find food. The English are hungry, my lord. Are not we all? But they are scarce used to it! Edward has heard that the famine has not hit the West so badly. Moreover, he has work to do here! And the West is not yet burned in his face. Wallace burned all before him, right up to Perth. Perth itself. After Falkirk, Edward went to Stirling. There he found all burned black. Save the Dominican Priory. He lay there fifteen days, a sick man. Kicked by a horse they say. But his armies did not lie. He sent them north and east and west. To Perth and Gowrie. To Menteith and Strathearn. To Fothrif and Fife. Seeking food. And harrying, slaying, devastating the country. 'Use all cruelty,' he ordered—Edward Plantagenet! How many thousands they have slain, God knows. Far, far more than on the Falkirk field. Women and children. Especially on the lands of those who supported Wallace—the old Earl of Fife's lands. Menteith's. Strathearn's. Murray of Tullibardine's. And the Church's. Mine. My St. Andrews is now a smoking desert. He spares neither kirk nor monastery, monk nor nun. Dunfermline. Balmerino. Lindores. Dunblane. Inchaffray. All these abbeys and their towns. And many another. No mercy. All to be destroyed. And now he has turned west. To punish Lennox, the Steward, Crawford. And yourself, my lord!"

"Aye." That came out on a long sigh. "Edward, at least, will no longer think me his man! He comes here, you think?"

"He has sworn to punish all whom he says rebelled against his peace! Will he spare Bruce, whom once he held close? But who now holds the South-West against him. *You* should know, if any!"

"He will not. But . . . I cannot hold the South-West against him. Not against this great host. You know that."

"I know it. But you can do what Wallace has done. Deny him food, drink, comfort. Burn the land before him, my lord. Leave him nothing. Burn this castle and town. For, God knows, what you do not burn, *he* will! Alas for this poor Scotland! But only so shall we save her freedom."

"Freedom, yes. And freedom . . .? Is it worth this, my lord Bishop? This cost?"

"Freedom is worth this and more, my friend. Freedom is worth the last breath we draw. Freedom is life. And the life after life. Is there aught greater? Faith, worship, charity, peace—what are these, without freedom to exercise them? Freedom is the soul of the nation. What profit all else if we lose it?"

Long Bruce gazed at the wary man's stern face, deeply moved by his vibrant words. He inclined his head. "Very well. Tell Wallace that I burn the South-West. For freedom. As my brothers even now are burning over the Border. The Lord Nigel I sent to Annandale, then to Galloway, to raid over the West March. But . . . dear God—it is easier to burn other men's lands than your own!"

"I know it, friend. How many men have you assembled here?"

"Four thousand. So few against Edward's hordes."

"Four thousand men can do a deal of burning . . .!"

．　　　．　　　．

So Edward Plantagenet, leaving a blackened smoking desert behind him at Glasgow and the lower Clyde, marched south, up Clyde with his legions—and found only smoking desert before him. Rutherglen, Bothwell, Lanark, he found empty, black, smouldering, and all the land around and ahead billowing unending smoke-clouds in the hazy autumn sunshine. Like an army of Goths and Vandals, grim-faced, their eyes red-rimmed from more than their own smoke, Bruce's men of Carrick, Cunninghame and Kyle, with volunteers from far and near, efficiently, methodically, destroyed the land, their own land, herding the people with roughest kindliness into the hills. Towns and villages were emptied, the thatches pulled off the roofs to burn in the streets, with all stored food and fodder that could not be carted away. Churches and monasteries were denuded of all that made them places of worship, and left vacant shells. Castles and manors were cast down, where possible, rendered untenable, undefendable, and left open, deserted. Farm lands were wasted and despoiled, hay and grain fired, standing corn trampled flat, all beasts and poultry that could not be driven off into the hills slaughtered and tossed on to the blazing barns and byres and cot-houses. Mills, markets, fisheries, harbours, hutments—all were cast down and devastated, in a twenty-mile belt from the sea to the burgeoning purple heather of the wild uplands—now fuller of folk than they had ever been before. From Clydesdale right down into Galloway the pattern was repeated, and the smoke rose over a once-fair land, by day a black rolling pall that darkened the sun, by night a murky red and ominous barrier stretching from horizon to horizon. The folk co-operated, in the main, even did their own burning. There was short shrift for those who objected.

The English, in fuming rage, sought other adversary than fire and smoke, and found none—save odd and pathetic hiders in woods and deans and caves, whom they outraged, tortured and hanged. Day after day they marched south, a blackened snarling host, the fine colourful display of their chivalry dimmed and soiled now, angry, ravenous men; and each day their march grew longer, as their empty bellies forced them on, hoping, hoping for some area undestroyed, some green oasis in the black desert overlooked. But there was none, save in the high fastnesses of the flanking hills, Scotland's ultimate refuge, where Edward dared not let his mutinous men stray—for such as did seldom returned. A great deal of food is necessary to feed over 100,000 men. The leadership was losing control. Great bodies of troops were running amok, fighting with each other, falling sick by the thousand, doing unmentionable things in their terrible hunger. Shaking his fist at the gaunt ruins of the burned-out castle of Ayr, reached on the 27th day of August, Edward, in impotent fury, after giving orders that Bruce must be pursued deep into his Carrick hills, right to the Mull of Galloway if need be, countermanded it all, and ordained the swiftest possible withdrawal to the Border, to English soil. It was as near flight as anything the Plantagenet had ever faced. He left a woeful trail of the weak, the sick and the weary behind him, of men and horses and equipment. And out from the wilderness lairs the folk of the charred land crept by night, knives in hand.

The King, with the view of fair England at last, on 6th September, and much in sight reeking as black as what lay behind them, turned in terrible, savage wrath on Annandale, the last of the Scottish dales, which the younger Bruces had largely spared, after all their building-up from Clifford's raid. Now even that expert, in Edward's train, had to confess himself mastered. If a land can be crucified, the lordship of Annandale was, that September of 1298. When, in the remote tower of Loch Doon, amongst the great heather hills where Carrick and Galloway meet, Nigel brought word of it, Robert Bruce would have wept if he could. Tears were a luxury few Scots could rise to that autumn.

Edward himself was near to tears, at Carlisle, where he halted at last, too tough a nut for the Bruce brothers to have cracked. But they were tears of sheerest choler. For not only had he to bear the humiliations of his undignified scramble back to his own soil, and the frustrations of a campaign abandoned in mid-course, with the benefits of a great victory squandered, and the outrage of mutinous soldiery — now his own lords turned mutineer. And not merely a few disgruntled nonentities, but the greatest of all — Norfolk, the Constable; Hereford; Lincoln; Northumberland. These, and lesser barons, when they heard that Edward was intent only on garnering vast food supplies, re-equipping and disciplining his army, and then marching back into Scotland to complete his task, refused flatly to co-operate. They claimed that this was not only profitless but contrary to the promises that the King had made on his return from France, that he would rule henceforth with the acceptance of his nobility and parliament. In fury the monarch named them treasonable, seditious dogs — and though, on second thoughts, he hastily convened a council, there at Carlisle, and named it a parliament, it was too late. Norfolk, Hereford, and those likeminded, marched off with their followings for the south, leaving an angry sovereign and a make-believe parliament to pass edicts for further ambitious mobilisation, the large-scale provisioning necessary, and the equipping of a great fleet of vessels which would proceed round the Scottish coastline, keeping pace with the armies, and supplying them without fail. This, and the wholesale forfeiture of the lands of all Scots nobles, not only those who had supported Wallace but those who had failed actively to support Edward; and the apportioning of these immense properties to the English lords and knights who remained with the King at Carlisle — though the new owners were faced with the problem of how to take possession. The greatest of these, Guy de Beauchamp, Earl of Warwick, got the Bruce lands, and others, to retain his support.

Then, after a fortnight, Edward marched his somewhat refreshed if still grumbling host north into Scotland once more, but only as a token thrust this time, an indication of what would happen in the spring when campaigning was once again feasible. He moved up Liddesdale, spreading desolation, to Jedburgh, which he sacked and levelled with the ground, wreaking especial vengeance on its great abbey. Contenting himself with this gesture and foretaste, he turned south for Newcastle, Durham, and his winter quarters at York.

Scotland's sigh of relief was grim as it was faint.

* * *

Another sort of relief it was to ride through the green-golden valleys and quiet glades of Ettrick Forest, and see hamlets unburned, churches and shrines intact and cattle grazing peacefully in clearings and water-meadows. To eyes become accustomed to the charred wilderness that was most of Southern Scotland that autumn, this was a bitter-sweet solace. Bruce and his brothers trotted through it all in the mellow October sunshine, in answer to the Guardian's summons, allegedly the last such that would come from Sir William Wallace.

They found Selkirk and its ruined abbey in an even greater stir than on the previous occasion, when Wallace had been knighted and proclaimed Guardian; for this time, more of the nobility and clergy had come, aware of the drama and importance of the proceedings. Their encampments, pavilions and banners were everywhere in the spreading haughlands of the Ettrick, their men-at-arms too many and truculent for peace and comfort. Churchmen were almost as numerous as barons, with their retinues, with no fewer than ten bishops, and abbots, priors and other clerics unnumbered. Lamberton was making his authority felt.

The Bruces found Wallace installed in the old royal castle of Selkirk, a ramshackle, sprawling place built as a hunting lodge for David the First. With him was the Steward, his son Walter, Crawford, Menteith, Lennox and the old Earl of Fife; also, of course, Lamberton and his galaxy of prelates. The Primate was undoubtedly something of a showman, stern though he appeared to be, and there was considerable attempts at dignity and display, including a throne-like chair at the head of the great hall table, for the Guardian, with a huge tressured Rampant Lion standard hung on the wall behind it. The herald King of Arms was present with his minions, and busy establishing precedences and places, superintending the setting up of banners, fussing over details. In view of the appalling devastation that surrounded this green sanctuary of Ettrick Forest, the unburied multitudes, the famine and want and despair, it all seemed as pointless as it was unreal, even ridiculous.

Wallace himself certainly gave the impression that he thought it so, standing about ill at ease and unhappy. Seldom can a man have looked less at one with the surroundings of which he was the central figure. He had changed not a little since Falkirk. He was thinner, more gaunt, older-seeming altogether, and though of course still enormous, of less commanding presence than heretofore, despite the finery which seemed to sit so uncomfortably on his huge frame. His great hands were seldom still, groping about him as though seeking the sword, the dirk, the battle-axe, which were almost extensions of himself, but today were absent. He looked a man at odds with his fate.

He came great-strided to greet Bruce, at least, with an access of animation. "My lord, my lord—you have come! I thank God for it." He gripped the younger man's hand and shoulder. "It is good to see you—for much depends on you hereafter."

Bruce looked doubtful at that, his glance searching past the other for Comyn.

Wallace perceived it. "The Lord of Badenoch is not yet arrived," he said. "But he comes, he comes."

"His coming here, like mine, is the least of it, Sir Guardian! We shall never agree—that I swear."

"Do not say so. If sufficient depends on it, any two men can seem to agree, however ill-matched. Even I have learned that lesson! Think you I have loved all that I have had to deal with, work with, this past year and more? And enough depends, here, on my soul! The future of this realm, no less."

"Scarce so much as that, I think . . ."

"Yes. So much as that. See you, my lord—the magnates of this Scotland are divided. By many things, many feuds, much jealousy, warring interests. But, in the end, all depend on the Crown for their lands and titles. You know that. And the Crown is vacant—or nearly so. I act in the name of King John Baliol, since the Crown must be vested in some name. *De jure*, he is still King. *De facto*, he is not, and the throne empty. One day, if Scotland survives, she will have a king again. That king will be either a Baliol, a Comyn or a Bruce. You know it. John Baliol has a son, Edward—a child. Held, like his father, hostage by the King of England. King John has renounced the throne, for himself and his son, at the demand of King Edward. Renounced and abandoned. Therefore, it is scarce likely that John or his son shall ever reign. So the king shall be your father, the Bruce. Or John Comyn, Baliol's nephew."

Bruce made an impatient gesture, at this rehearsal of facts only too well known to him.

"Aye—you know it. All men know it, my lord. Therefore, since the nobles hold all they have of the Crown, they must take sides. For Comyn or Bruce. In order that they may retain their lands from the winner in this contest. Divided, as I say. And Scotland cannot afford a divided nobility, today, see you, when she fights for her life. So, your father being none knows where, only you, and Comyn, can heal the division. By acting together. Joint Guardians. Nothing else, and no other, will serve."

That was a long speech for Wallace, who was not notably a man of words.

Bruce could not refute the validity of any of it. But it was personality, not validity, that was his trouble.

"John Comyn will not work with me," he said flatly. "We have never agreed on any matter. Nor are like to!"

"But when the matter is the saving of the realm? For whoever may eventually sit on its throne? Can you not, at least, *seem* to agree, my lord? Since neither of you, I vow, would wish the other to be Guardian alone!"

That left the younger man silent.

Lamberton had joined them. "The Comyns have been sighted, my friends," he said. "They are riding down from Tweed. A great company of them. The Constable's banner alongside that of Badenoch, they say. They have come far. From Spey. I do not think that they have come for nothing! John Comyn intends to be Guardian, I swear—whoever else may be!"

Bruce did not fail to take the point.

The Comyns arrived with a deal more circumstance than had the Bruce brothers, in splendid clothing and array, confident, assured, and with an indefinable appearance of prosperity and lack of tension, which contrasted notably with the demeanour of most of those assembled—for, of course, they came from the North, untouched by famine or war. The drawn, guarded, battered look which had become so much part of the others showed in them not at all. They had brought a train of over a score of knights, their own clerics, standard-bearers, pursuivants, trumpeters, entertainers, even a group of Erse-speaking, barbarously-clad West Highland chiefs. There was no doubt that they had come prepared to take over the rule in Scotland.

It was their complete assurance, their unspoken but unmistakable assumption of authority, which almost automatically forced Robert Bruce into a position from which there was no drawing back. At no specific moment did he make his decision. The thing was obvious, no longer to be debated.

John Comyn of Badenoch and he did not actually speak to each other for quite some time, after the arrival, eyeing each other warily, like a pair of stiff-legged dogs considering the same bone, by mutual consent keeping their distance—a metaphysical distance, not an actual one, for inevitably amongst the small circle of the high magnates of the realm, they could not avoid being in the same group frequently. Bruce was apt to find the Red Comyn's brilliant, fleering eyes fixed on him—and realised that his own were drawn equally to the other. But neither went the length of words.

As closely as they watched each other, undoubtedly Wallace watched them both. Lamberton also. All there did, indeed; but these two in especial, and did more than watch. They manoeuvred, they guided, they tempered. And skilfully, their policy to ensure that Bruce and Comyn, or their supporters, did not come into any sort of clash before the thing could be brought to a conclusion. Wallace was less proficient at it than was the Bishop, perhaps.

As soon as it might be done with decency, the King of Arms had them all to sit down to a repast—and all his fussing about precedence was now seen in a new light. As far as the great ones were concerned, everything had been thought out. Normally, in any castle-hall, the dais-table stretched sideways across the head of the chamber, while the main table ran lengthwise down one side of the great apartment, leaving the rest free for the servitors, entertainers and the like. Now, since practically everyone present in Selkirk's castle would have been entitled to sit at the dais-table, this had been brought down to add to the length of the other. Moreover at its head, where the Guardian's great chair was flanked by two others, two further small tables had been placed at right angles, with a couple of seats only at each. At that to the right was placed Buchan the Constable, with Lamberton the Primate at his side; on the left was seated James the Steward, with the herald King. There was no certainty as to which great office of state was senior; but Buchan was an earl and the Steward was not. In the same way, at the main table-head, Bruce was placed on Wallace's immediate right, and Comyn on his left; again there could be no quarrel, since Carrick was an earldom and Badenoch only a lordship. Other nobles found themselves equally heedfully disposed. There were no solid groups of pro-Comyn or pro-Bruce supporters. And everywhere Lamberton's clerics were set between, to act as both catalysts and buffers. The Scots lords, used to jockeying for the best places by initiative or sheer weight, were taken by surprise, and strategically seated where they could cause least trouble.

Bruce and Comyn thus were sitting in isolated prominence—but the mighty figure of Wallace was between them. Moreover, Bruce had Buchan sitting at the little table, next on his right, while Comyn had the Steward to contend with, on his left. Seldom can there have been less general converse at so illustriously attended a meal.

Wallace spoke to each of his immediate companions, and sometimes to them both, seeking to involve them in mutual talk which he might control. But they were a mettlesome pair to drive tandem, and it was a somewhat abortive exercise. The Guardianship issue was not actually mentioned.

"How long have we, think you, before Edward attacks once more?" Wallace asked, presently—a safe subject, surely. "How serious are his troubles with his lords?"

"Do not ask me, Sir Guardian," Comyn returned quickly. "*I* have no dealings with the English. Ask Bruce. He knows Edward passing well. Or his friend Percy may have told him!"

Bruce drew a swift breath. Then he let it out again, slowly and raised his wine goblet to his lips.

"My lord of Carrick has put himself more in Edward's disfavour than has any other in Scotland," Wallace said heavily. "He burned the South-West in Edward's face, forcing him to call off his campaign. Much of the land burned Bruce's own. As for Lord Percy, I think he is scarce likely to call my lord his friend, now!"

"Yet the woman Bruce is like to marry is Percy's kinswoman. And bides with him, at Alnwick, does she not? While her father fights for Edward in France. Against our French allies!"

"Curse you, Comyn! I am not like to marry Elizabeth de Burgh. Edward would have had it once—but now would not, you may be sure!"

"Yet she is a comely wench. And well dowered, I swear! Edward's god-child—a useful go-between . . ."

"I'll thank you to spare the Lady Elizabeth the soiling of your tongue!" Bruce exclaimed, leaning forward to glare round Wallace.

"My lords! My lords—of a mercy!" the big man cried. "Moderate your words, I beg you. Here is no way to speak to each other."

"Have I said aught against the lady? Save that she is Edward's god-daughter. Bruce has a guilty conscience, I think, to be so thin of skin!"

"What knows a Comyn of conscience!"

"My lords—at *my* table, no guest of mine will be insulted. By whomsoever. I ask you to remember it." Wallace brought down his vast fist on the board with a crash to make the platters, flagons and goblets jump—and not a few of the company also. Then pushing back his chair abruptly he rose to his full commanding height. All eyes upon him, he raised his tremendous vibrant voice.

"My lords and friends, fellow subjects of this realm, I, William Wallace, Guardian of Scotland, crave your close heed. I took up that duty and style seven sore months ago. Now the time has come to lay it on other shoulders than mine. They have been ill months for our land. We have survived them only at great cost. But there are as bad, and worse, to come. Let none doubt it. The man, Edward Plantagenet, is set on this. He will make Scotland part of his crown. A lowly servile part. If he can. While breath remains in him. That is sure. And he has ten men for every man of us."

He paused, and though all present were aware of all this, men hung on his careful words.

"I say to you that I know now what I should have known before—that *I* cannot fight Edward the King. I can fight his underlings and minions. I can, I have done, and I will. But not Edward himself. Only Edward's own kind can fight Edward—I see that now. And I am . . . otherwise. Scotland's own king it should be who fights him. But since that is not possible now, it falls to the Guardian. Therefore, I cannot remain Guardian. Falkirk proved that. The Guardianship must be in the hands of Edward's own kind." Deliberately he looked round on them all. "In this realm today there are two men who could, and should, be Guardian. Two men whom all must heed, respect, obey. For what they are, and who they are. They are here at my side. Sir Robert Bruce, Earl of Carrick, grandson of Bruce the Competitor;

and Sir John Comyn, Lord of Badenoch, nephew to the King, King John. On these two, who are both of Edward's kind, I lay my burden. Jointly and together. These two can, and must, unite this realm against the English usurper. These two I charge, in the name of God and of Scotland—fight Edward! Save our land." He pointed. "My lord Bishop of Galloway—the seals."

As men exclaimed, from further down the table, the Chancellor rose, to bring up the two silver caskets that were his charge, and set them before Wallace, opening them to display the Great Seal of Scotland, and the Privy Seal.

The first the big man took out, and raised up—and it required both hands to do it. Not because it was so heavy, but because its bronze was in two parts, two exact halves. He held them high.

"My friends," he cried, "Here is the Great Seal of this realm and nation. I broke it. This day I broke it. For the good of all. Now, before anything may be established and made law, bearing the Seal of Scotland, these two parts must be brought together and set side by side. One, in the name of the Crown, the magnates and the community of this ancient realm, I give to Sir Robert the Bruce, Earl of Carrick. The other to Sir John the Comyn, of Badenoch. I do now declare them both and together to be Joint Guardians of Scotland. To them I hereby pass the rule and governance. Declaring that I, William Wallace, will from now onward be their leal and assured servant. God save them both, I say."

As all men stared, the giant thrust his chair far back, and bowing to Bruce first, then Comyn, turned and strode down the length of that great table, right to its foot, where he gently pushed aside his own standard-bearer, Scrymgeour, modestly seated there, and sat himself down in his place.

Something like uproar filled the hall.

Each holding his half of the Great Seal, Bruce and Comyn gazed at one another before all, wordless.

Gradually the noise abated, and men fell silent, all eyes upon the pair at the head of the table, clutching their half-moons of bronze. All knew that these two hated each other. All knew that they represented mutually antagonistic claims to the throne. Moreover, there could be few indeed who could have accepted Wallace's dramatic gesture in itself as any kind of valid appointment. It was not for the outgoing Guardian to appoint a successor; that was for the barons of the realm to choose, their choice to be confirmed by a parliament. What Wallace had done in itself carried no real authority. Yet, if these two indeed elected to accept it as such, none there were in a position to contravert it, even if they so desired.

The hush was broken by the scrape of Bruce's chair on the rush-strewn flagstones, as he rose. "My lords," he said thickly. "Here is a great matter. Here is the need for decision. I, for myself, do not want this duty, this burden, that Sir William Wallace has laid upon me. I am young, with no experience of the rule of a realm. I have much to see to, without that. My lands are devastated, great numbers of my people homeless, hungry, living in caves and under tree-roots. Winter is coming upon us—a winter that will test us hard. And in the spring, Edward will return. But . . . all this, if it is true for Carrick and Annandale and Galloway, is true also for much of Scotland. Save, perhaps, the North." He glanced down at Comyn. "The land faces trial. Destiny. All the land. The people. The need is great. And in this need, unity is all-important. Only unity can save us from Edward of England. None shall say that Bruce withstood that unity. If you, my lords, will have it so, I accept the office of Guardian. With . . . whomsoever." He sat down abruptly.

There was acclaim. But it was tense, almost breathless, and brief. Every glance was on John Comyn.

That man sat still, toying with the segment of bronze. He seemed to be under no strain, no sense of embarrassment that all waited for him. His sardonically handsome features even bore a twisted smile, as he examined the broken seal in his hand. The seconds passed.

When a voice was raised, it was Bruce's. "Well, man?" he demanded.

"This of the seal was cunning," the other said, almost admiringly amused. He looked up, but not at Bruce. "How think you, my lord Constable?" he asked his fellow-Comyn conversationally.

Buchan huffed and puffed, looking towards his brother, Master William, the cleric, some way down the table. Almost imperceptibly that smooth-faced man nodded.

"Aye. So be it," the earl grunted. "In a storm a man may not always choose the haven he would."

"Ha—neatly put, kinsman!" John Comyn acceded. "No doubt you are right. So there we have it. Joint Guardian—heh? With Bruce! God save us all!"

It was moments before it sank in. That this was acceptance. That Comyn was in fact going to say no more. That, smiling and still lounging in his chair, he was reaching for his goblet, to drink. And that he had pocketed his half of the seal. The thing was done.

As the recognition of this dawned, the company broke forth in excited chatter, comment, speculation. There was no longer any semblance of order. Men rose from their places and went to their friends and fellow-clansmen. Chiefs and lords beckoned their knightly supporters, prelates put their heads together and rubbed their hands. Down at the foot of the table, Wallace sat expressionless.

But after a while, as the noise maintained, the big man signed to the Bishop of Galloway. That cleric raise his hand, called out, and when he could make no impression, banged a flagon on the table for silence.

"My lords—this matter is well resolved. But it falls to be confirmed. To be accepted and duly made lawful. By a parliament, I, therefore, as Chancellor of this realm, for and on behalf of the Guardianship, do call such meeting of parliament tomorrow, at noon, in the former abbey here. To be attended by all and sundry of the three estates of this kingdom. At noon, my lords, gentles and clerks. So be it. God give you a good night."

Bruce rose, and looked down at Comyn. "This means . . . no little . . . accommodation, my lord," he said slowly. "It will tax our patience, I think, ere we are done."

"You think so? Patience is for clerks, and such folk. It is not a quality I aspire to, Bruce!"

"Nevertheless, you will require it, if I am not mistaken! As shall I!"

"If you esteem it so high, then I shall leave it to you! Myself, I see the case calling for quite different virtues. Valour. Daring. Resolution. Spirit. These, and the like."

"Such as the Comyns showed at Falkirk field?" That erupted out of Robert Bruce.

The other was on his feet in an instant, fists clenched. "By the Rude—you dare speak so! To me! You—Edward's . . . lackey!"

"For that, Comyn . . . you shall . . . suffer! As God is my witness!"

For moments they stared eye to eye. Then John Comyn swung about, and stormed from the hall. Few there failed to note it.

There was a deep sigh at Bruce's back, from William Lamberton.

.   .   .

Next day, in the ruined abbey, a tense and anxious company assembled, anticipating trouble naked and undisguised. And they were surprised, relieved, or disappointed, according to their varying dispositions. A night's sleeping on it, second and third thoughts, and the earnest representations of sundry busy mediators — mainly churchmen, and Master William Comyn in especial — had produced a distinct change of atmosphere. Nothing would make Bruce and Comyn love each other, or trust each other; but it was just conceivable that they might sufficiently tolerate each other to work, if not together, at least not openly in opposition.

At any rate, John Comyn arrived at the abbey, with his supporters, apparently in a different frame of mind. He favoured Bruce, even, with a distinct inclination of the head, did not address him directly, but appeared to be prepared to co-operate in some measure with Wallace, Lamberton and the Chancellor. Presently he allowed himself to be escorted to the Guardian's seat by the Steward, while Buchan, stiffly, silently, did the same for Bruce. They sat down, a foot or two apart, not looking at each other but not fighting either. The Primate said a brief prayer over their deliberations, and the Bishop of Galloway, as Chancellor, opened the proceedings by asking if it was the Guardians' will and pleasure to declare this parliament in sitting — even though lacking required 40 days' notice.

Two nods from the chairs established the matter.

There was much routine business to get through, administrative detail which had piled up during Wallace's regime and which required ratification by parliament, most of it of minor importance or uncontentious. There was, in especial, the new French treaty and its ramifications to discuss. John Comyn, who had been sent to take a leading part at its negotiation, now sat silent, allowing his able kinsman, Master William, of the Chapel-Royal, to speak of this — which he did clearly and persuasively. The King of France's promises regarding armed help and intervention were noted and approved — and queries as to how much they were worth were kept to a minimum. Lamberton then gave some account of his negotiations with the Pope, at Rome, on Scotland's behalf, with assurances of Papal sanctions against Edward. Indeed, he had to announce that this, plus France's representations, had already resulted, they had just heard, in Edward releasing King John Baliol and his son from strict ward; they were now more or less free, in the custody of the Pope, at Malmaison in Cambrai.

No cheers greeted this news. Indeed a pregnant silence fell, as men looked at Bruce to see how he took it. He sat motionless, expressionless. In a parliament it was normal for the King to preside, but not to intervene in the actual discussions unless to make some vital and authoritative pronouncement. The Guardians were there as representing the King. Bruce could scarcely express forebodings about John Baliol's limited release.

Then there were a number of appointments recently made by Wallace, which fell to be confirmed, few of any prominence. But one raised eyebrows. Alexander Scrymgeour, of Dundee, his own standard-bearer in all their affrays, had been appointed Standard-Bearer of the Realm, and Constable of Dundee—the former a new office of state.

Buchan was on his feet to question it immediately. "My lord Chancellor," he said, "here is a strange matter. A new office. Is this the time to create new offices of state? Such should be by the King's own appointment. And . . . and if Standard-Bearer there must be, it should be one of the King's nobility. I move against."

There were a number of ayes from the assembly—but some growls also; the first sign of a clash.

"Do you contest the right of the Guardian to create such office, my lord?" the Chancellor asked mildly.

The Constable hesitated. "No," he admitted, after a moment. "But it requires confirmation by this parliament. And by the new Guardians. I move that confirmation be withheld."

"Noted." Galloway looked round. "Does any other wish to speak on this matter?"

"Aye, my lord Chancellor—I do." Wallace, standing in a lowly position but tending to dominate by his very presence, spoke up. "With great respect to my lord Earl, I would say that the creation of this office is no whim or caprice. Nor the filling of it by Alexander Scrymgeour. In this our realm's warfare, none I swear will question who suffers most. The common people. Few will deny who has achieved most in it, as yet. The common people. Even you, my lord Constable, will not gainsay that if the people of Scotland lose heart, or fail in their full support, then the realm is lost. The common folk, then, must see that they are considered. Represented. Given their due place. I say, who are more fitted to bear the Royal Standard of Scotland than one of themselves? And of them, who more fitted than Alexander Scrymgeour, who has fought in every conflict against the English, fought with valour—and stood his ground! I crave, my lords temporal and spiritual, barons of Scotland and gentles all—confirm the office and appointment both."

There was a curious sucking noise as the Steward, rising, sought to control his saliva. "I so move," he got out, and sat down.

This was it, then. So soon. The moment of decision. All eyes were fixed on the two new Guardians who sat side by side looking straight ahead of them, rather than on the Chancellor, Wallace or Buchan.

Galloway, tapping fingers on the stone recumbent effigy of a former abbot, which served him as desk, looked in the same direction as all others. "Before putting this to the vote, I think, the minds of the two Lords Guardian should be known," he said, and for once his confident sonorous voice was uneven.

Promptly Bruce spoke. "I accept the office, and accept and agree to confirm Alexander Scrymgeour as Royal Standard-Bearer of Scotland."

Seconds passed as all waited. Then John Comyn smiled suddenly, that brilliant flashing smile of his which not all found an occasion for joy. "Why, then, we are in happy accord, my friends," he declared easily. "For I too accept and accede. Let the excellent Scrymgeour bear his standard . . . so long as he can!"

The sigh of relief that arose was like a wind sweeping over the Forest outside. Men scarcely noticed the Chancellor's declaration that he thought there was no need for a vote, or Buchan's snorting offence and the angry look he cast at his kinsman. Everywhere the thing was seen as much more than just Scrymgeour's appointment; it was the sought-for sign that these high-born rivals might yet sink their personal preferences for the common good.

But even as the Chancellor, like others, relaxed a little, he was suddenly alert once more. John Comyn was speaking again.

"Since appointments are before us," he said crisply, sitting a little forward in his chair, "here are some that I require. For the better governance of this kingdom. My lord of Buchan to be Justiciar of the North. Sir Alexander Comyn, his brother, to be Sheriff of Aberdeen and keeper of its castle. Sir Walter Comyn to be Sheriff of Banff, and keeper. Sir William Mowat to be Sheriff of Cromarty, and keeper thereof. Sir Robert Comyn to be Sheriff of Inverness. Sir William Baliol to be Sheriff of Forfar. And Master William Comyn, of the Chapel-Royal, to be Lord Privy Seal and elect to the next bishopric to become vacant. All that due rule and governance may be established in the land."

Bruce all but choked, as all around men gasped and exclaimed. Never before had a parliament been presented with such demands from the throne, such an ultimatum. For clearly that is what it was. This, then, was Comyn's price for superficial co-operation. He had come prepared. Already the Comyns possessed enormous power in the North; with these key positions in their hands, they would be in complete control of all the upper half of the kingdom, not only theoretical but actual control.

Bruce bit his lip, as the startled Chancellor groped for words, looking in agitation for guidance, first at Bruce, then at Wallace and Lamberton. Agog, the assembly waited.

Bruce had only brief moments for decision, a decision there was no avoiding. Either he accepted, or refused agreement—and was thereupon branded as the man who broke up the Joint Guardianship, refused to make it work, out of enmity to Comyn. After Comyn had made his gesture of acceptance. The fact that that was on a tiny matter, a mere empty title, while this was a wholesale grab for effective power and dominance, would not help him. That Comyn had chosen to cast down the gauntlet now, before all, had obviously come prepared to do so, was evidence that if he, Bruce, countered him, the Joint Guardianship was finished before it had begun. Nothing was more sure.

Yet, how could it possibly continue, or succeed, on these terms? As good as a knife at his throat. Was there any point in going on with the farce?

There was only one faint glimmer of light that presented itself to Robert Bruce in those agonising moments. All the appointments Comyn had so blatantly demanded were in the North. Apart from the question of the Privy Seal and bishopric, he was at the moment confining his hegemony to the North. Always Scotland had tended to divide into two; the land south of the Forth, and north, echo of the old kingdoms of the Northern and Southern Picts, and their Celtic successors. It might be that Comyn was more or less proposing, not joint guardianship but divided guardianship, one to rule north of Forth, the other south. If this was so, it could change the entire situation. The South was smaller in territory but infinitely more rich and populous. Or had been, before it had burned itself. And it was the South that must bear the brunt of Edward's ire . . .

Lamberton was speaking—and clearly he had been thinking along the same lines as Bruce. ". . . since such appointments undoubtedly would strengthen the rule of the Joint Guardians. In the North. To the internal peace and security of the realm. A similar list of nominations, made by the Earl of Carrick, for the South, would be to the advantage of all. A . . . a balanced responsibility. Of the Joint Guardians. On such joint security the kingdom might rest firm. In this pass." He was looking hard at Bruce —as indeed were all others.

That young man took a deep breath. "Very well," he said, shortly. "I accept these appointments. And shall produce my own, in due course. Proceed."

In the buzz of talk that followed, John Comyn turned in his seat to stare at his companion long and levelly.

After that there was little more than formalities. The main confrontation and decisions had been made, and all knew it. In effect, Scotland would be partitioned into two mighty provinces, North and South. It was the natural, age-old division, and in line with the two great houses' spheres of influence—for though the Comyns held lands in Galloway, and the Bruces in Garioch and Angus, these were very marginal to their main power.

There was, of course, an unspoken corollary, which few failed to perceive. When Edward struck, the South would have to face him first. And it would be wise, then, for Bruce to look back over his shoulder. And if Edward over-ran the South, and could be held again at Stirling, as before, then the North would become all there was of Scotland. In which case, there might well be a new king in the land.

The parliament in the Forest broke up. It was agreed that the Guardians should meet again at Stirling, where North and South joined, in a month's time, to confer, and sign and seal edicts, charters and the like, with their two halves of the Great Seal.

Robert Bruce, with his brothers, rode south again for Annandale, ruler, in name at least, of Scotland south of the Forth.

CHAPTER ELEVEN

So commenced months of trial and frustration as difficult as any Bruce had experienced, with problems multiplying, patience taxed to the limits, and his hatred and distrust of John Comyn gnawing like a canker within him. He felt himself to be hamstrung, almost helpless, ruler in little more than name, able to achieve as little for himself and the Bruce cause as for the country as a whole, a land burned out and a people in dire straits, living in makeshift shelters and ruins, and on the verge of starvation. It was a wet and dismal winter, with little snow but floods making travel difficult—and Bruce seemed to spend his time in wet and uncomfortable travel, constantly on the move, though having little to show for his journeyings. He had nothing that he could feel was home, no real base or headquarters even—for Annandale was too far south for practical use, and his castles of Turnberry and Ayr, like all others, were but burned and blackened shells, and Lochmaben, the all-but-impregnable, was back in English hands. He went to Stirling monthly, for his formal meetings with Comyn—grim and profitless episodes which he loathed—and which only were made bearable by the patient ministrations and devices of the churchmen, especially Lamberton and William Comyn—the last proving himself to be able, shrewd and co-operative, however clearly ambitious. Without these two the Joint Guardianship would not have survived even the first acrimonious encounters.

Lamberton was in fact Bruce's mainstay and prop, without whom he would have thrown up the whole sorry business. More than that, he became a friend as well as guide, a strong, constant, clear-headed man, less stern than he seemed, with a faculty for quiet understanding and even a wintry humour. He was, indeed, if anyone was in these grievous months, the real ruler of Scotland, tireless link between the undamaged North and the devastated South. If Bruce travelled endless uncomfortable miles, then the Primate did double and treble, since not only did he move between the Guardians but he kept in touch with Wallace, who had made Dundee his headquarters for the recruiting of a new people's army—not to mention seeing to the rule of the Church from his own St. Andrews.

Nigel Bruce, too, was a major comfort to his harassed brother, his close companion throughout, a consistently cheerful, extrovert influence and link with happier, carefree days. But Nigel was of little help where guidance and good advice were required, seeing everything in simple blacks and whites.

Bruce's problems, during this period, fell mainly under three heads; to prepare for invasion; to alleviate something of the distress of the people; and to try to get at least the elementary machinery of government working again. All were almost equally difficult, in the prevailing state of the country. He could appoint his nominees to the key sheriffdoms of Lanark, Ayr,

Dumfries, Galloway and the like—his brother Edward in this last position—but these were little more effective than he felt himself to be. Of revenue there was none, so that the sheriffs had only their own pockets, and those of their friends, to call upon, to pay for their efforts—and friends do not long remain so in such circumstances. Had it not been for the whole-hearted support of the Church, little or nothing would have been achieved. The ecclesiastics still had some of the garnered riches of generations hidden away, and now expended them liberally. Moreover, they had great local influence over the minds of the common folk, and could rally and persuade where commands and threats from higher authority were meaningless.

Lamberton gave good reports of Wallace's force, growing in Angus and Fife. But to some extent, this was of little comfort to Bruce. For Wallace made it clear that this was very much a people's army, destined and trained for guerilla warfare, not to be hurled headlong against the English chivalry. Which left Bruce with the task of mustering an anti-invasion army from, as ever, the levies and tenantry of the lords. And since these were needed for the widespread local rehabilitation works, and moreover he had not the wherewithal to feed them, *en masse*, this had to remain very much a paper force, problematical indeed as to numbers and availability.

And all the time, the shadow of the Comyn thousands, and how they would be used, hung over all. Lamberton brought word that John Comyn was assembling great numbers in the North —employing them meantime admittedly to further his sway over the wild Highlands—as perhaps was his right and duty. But their presence, a hundred or so miles to the north of him, was no aid to Bruce's sleep, of a night.

Then, with the long wet winter over at last, and the campaigning season drawing near, a messenger found his way to Bruce at Tor Wood Castle, between Falkirk and Stirling, where he was awaiting Comyn for the April meeting—Stirling Castle still being held by the English, which made the town below its walls unsuitable for the Guardians' conclaves. This was a wandering Dominican friar, who spoke with an English accent. From his leather satchel he brought out a letter, its folds somewhat creased and grubby, but sealed resplendently with the arms of de Burgh of Ulster. The recipient waited carefully until he was alone, even from Nigel's presence, before he broke that seal and read the strong, flowing writing.

My Lord Robert,

I greet you fair and wish you very well. It is long since I spoke with any who has seen you in your person. But I hear of you and of some of your doings from time to time. Although as to how truly, I do not know. For you are scarcely well loved, here at York.

This all men are agreed upon, however, that the Earl of Carrick is now in the rule, with another, of the Scots kingdom. A matter which greatly displeases His Majesty, as you will guess. I must believe it true, and do much wonder at your so high elevation. Not that I deem you unfit, but that I would have doubted your will for it. But if it is so, you have the goodwill of one, at least, in this England.

I cannot conceive that your high office will bring you much of joy, so heavy is Edward's hand against your realm. But this I believe may be to your comfort. The King, although he still makes pretence of marching against Scotland shortly, will not do so. Not for this year. Of this I am assured, and so would have you to know it. For he now does hate the Scots so sorely that he will have no invasion but that he leads himself. He will not so lead, this year. For not only does he have much trouble with his lords, of which you know, the Earls of Norfolk, Hereford and Northumberland in especial, who do say that he has forsworn himself over the Great Charter and the forest laws. But he is to marry again. This same summer. He is to wed the Princess Margaret, sister to King Philip of France, with whom he has lately been at war, in order to make stronger his hold on that country. The lady is said to be even now on her way from France. Edward will make a pilgrimage to St. Albans for blessing for this union, and will marry at Canterbury thereafter. Few know of this as yet, but he told me of it himself yesterday. My father is to go with the King, to St. Albans, and I go to meet the Princess, as one of her ladies. So I hasten to send you word, hoping that the tidings will perhaps something lighten your burden for this year.

I think of you often, my lord. And sorrow that our paths be so wide apart. Although, God knows, we do scarce agree so well when we are close. But I am of a shrewish and haughty disposition. Or so my father and brothers assure me. So that it may be that you are the better off at a distance. Do you not agree? You also are of an awkward mind, as I know. And stubborn. Unlike your brothers, whom I could bend between any two of my fingers, I think. No doubt we shall suit each other best by writing letters. So will you write to me, my lord?

I grieve for Scotland, and the folly and hatred of men. In your fight I wish you God-speed, and confide you to the watchful protection of His saints.

I send my remembrances to your foolish brothers. And, to the ruler of Scotland, all I have of deference.

ELIZABETH DE BURGH, *written from the house of one Uhtred, a clothier, of York.*

ADDENDUM: *The King would now have me to wed Guy de Beauchamp, Earl of Warwick, but I mislike the smell of his breath.*

Bruce rose up, to pace the floor of the little bedchamber which was all that the minor castle of Tor Wood could provide for him. Then he stopped, to read the letter through once more. He was much affected—and oddly enough, even more immediately by that last addendum than by the important news of Edward's forthcoming marriage and consequent postponement of invasion. It was on this, and on the paragraph where the young woman spoke of his brothers, that he concentrated his re-reading.

He was still at it, frowning, when the clatter of hooves and jingle of harness and arms below drew him to the window. Comyn had arrived, with a great company, all resplendent. The man always rode the country as though he were king! Bruce's blood all but boiled at the sight of him, so confident and assured, darkly handsome features twisted in that mocking smile. Lamberton was with him, at least. Lamberton was always present at their meetings now, determined that they should not be alone together. William Comyn, also, smooth as an egg.

Bruce remained in his room, perusing his letter. And even when Nigel came running up the narrow turnpike stair to tell him that Comyn waited below, he curtly dismissed him. He would be damned if he would go hastening to meet the fellow.

Lamberton mounted the stairs, after a while. He looked weary, older, but greeted Bruce with a sort of rueful affection. He glanced quickly at the letter in the younger man's hand, but asked no questions. He contented himself, after the normal civilities, with mentioning that there were a great number of papers for the Guardians' signature and sealing, and that the Lord of Badenoch was in vehement mood, and spoiling for a gesture against the English, claiming to have 20,000 men under arms and ready for a move.

That brought Bruce back to realities, and he went downstairs with the older man in more sober frame of mind.

The hall at Torwood was no more than a moderately-sized room and was already overcrowded with Comyn's entourage. Bruce would have had them all out, for it seemed to him no way to conduct the business of state before all this crew; but he had had this out with Comyn before, and an unseemly argument it had been—worse probably than putting up with the crowd's presence, since this was the way the other wanted it. There were larger measures at issue.

Comyn himself lounged at the table, and did not pause in his eating, although the others all bowed at his co-Guardian's entry.

"Ha, Earl of Carrick," he cried, from a full mouth, "where have you been hiding yourself in this rat's hole? I' faith, I feared I would have to send for you!"

"*Send*, my lord?"

"To apprise you of my presence. And that I have come a long way. And have no desire to spend the night in this rickle o' stanes!"

Their host, Sir John le Forester, Hereditary Keeper of the Forest of the Tor Wood, clenched his fists, but kept silence.

"No doubt Sir John will be relieved to hear it," Bruce returned shortly. "Since we already must bear grievously on his household."

"He will be paid." Comyn shrugged. "I say that it is unsuitable that we should continue to meet in such a place. Like furtive felons. Well enough for Wallace and the like. But not for Comyn. We represent King John, and should meet in King John's palace of Stirling."

"I cannot believe that it has escaped your lordship's notice that Stirling Castle is still in the hands of Englishmen!"

"Aye. After all these months. And not only Stirling. But Edinburgh. Both in Scotland south of the Forth. Not to mention Roxburgh. And your Lochmaben. A poor state of affairs."

"Meaning, sir?"

"Meaning, sir, that *you* are lord of the South. That these strongholds are all in your territory. And that no attempt has been made, I think, to expel Edward's lackeys from any of them."

Bruce strove to keep his voice steady. "My lord, you know very well that these are four of the greatest fortresses in the land. In determined hands, all can withstand siege for months, for years if may be. Well provisioned, and with their own deep wells, they are impregnable. Without great siege engines—of which I have none. Moreover, with a territory in ruins, I have more to do than waste men in idle siegery. Isolated, these fortresses can do us little harm."

"I say there speaks folly. While Edward holds these castles, and denies us the use of our own land, we are still in his occupation. Not free men. They are a reproach and a scorn. I say we cannot make pretence to lead this Scotland while these remain held against us. Stirling and Edinburgh, in especial."

"Then, sir—you reduce them! If you can. You have the men assembled, I hear. Your North is not devastated. And you do not have to watch a hundred miles of Border."

"Will Bruce have Comyn free his castle of Lochmaben for him!"

"Reduce Stirling first, and we shall see!"

"Very well. I shall move against Stirling, forthwith. And when Edward marches, we are the nearer at hand."

Bruce narrowed his eyes, almost spoke, but did not.

"My lords," Lamberton said, "is it wise to waste your strength on these castles? When King Edward crosses the Border it will be in mighty force. We shall not be battling for castles, but for our very lives. Using the land against him again, tiring him, starving him, wearing him down. I see little virtue in seeking to take these castles, which he may be able to retake in but a few months time."

"There speaks a clerk, beat before he so much as draws sword!" Comyn scoffed. "You do not talk of war, my lord Bishop, but of brigandage. Think you I have mustered 20,000 men—and will muster more—to skulk and hide, to pick and peck? We shall face Edward like men—but choosing *our* battlefield, not his. As Wallace did at Falkirk, a mis-fought field if ever there was one. Let Bruce here slink and stab if he will. Comyn will fight to win, not to weary."

"Brave words, my lord," Bruce grated. "And where do you think to hold Edward thus? Where do you choose your battlefield?"

The other grinned. "Why, at Stirling belike! The best place, is it not? In all the land. Even Wallace could win, there. Aye, I shall hold the English again at Stirling. And meantime take Stirling's castle."

"Abandoning all the South to Edward!"

Comyn shrugged. "That is *your* responsibility, is it not? If you would have my counsel, it is that you should retire behind Forth yourself. The Bishop here has admitted that *you* cannot hold Edward in open battle. South of Forth it may be true. Only harass and impede. That is not sufficient. I say give him the South to starve in, then fight at Stirling. Fight to win."

There was a murmur of agreement from his supporters.

"No! Only a man lacking heart would say that. The best of Scotland is in the South. The richest, fairest land. The greatest number of the people . . ."

"And the Bruce lands!"

"You would abandon all this to the invader? I say no."

"How many men have you assembled? To face Edward?"

Bruce cleared his throat. "I do not keep many so assembled. There is over-much for men to do in this stricken land. But in a week I can muster 7,000. In two weeks, four times that."

"Can? *Hope* that you can! Will Edward give you two weeks? I prefer my army as men, not as promises! With *my* men, then, I shall assail Stirling Castle. With your promises, my lord, do what you will!" Comyn rose to his feet, as though he had granted an interview and it was now over. "My Lord Privy Seal—where are the papers to sign? These plaguey papers . . .!"

Bruce was actually trembling with suppressed rage and the effort to restrain his hot temper, the fists gripping his golden earl's sword-belt clenching and unclenching. Lamberton, watching them both closely, intervened.

"It is probably well decided, my lords. One policy to support the other. But not only my Lord of Badenoch will be at Stirling. Holy Church has made shift to muster men from its own lands. No mighty host, but sufficient to achieve much. A balance, shall we say? Four thousand of them, 1,500 horsed. And Wallace has lent us Scrymgeour, the Standard-Bearer, to lead. With Wallace's own host—now 15,000, I am told—my lord of Carrick's rear should be secure."

Both lords looked at the Primate quickly, at that—and Comyn went on looking. Neither commented, though a little of the tension eased out of Bruce.

"The papers for signature, my lords Guardian," Master William Comyn said, setting down a sheaf of documents before them on the table. "The lead for the sealing is heating below . . ."

Later, with the Northerners gone, Bruce, in his own small chamber again, turned to Lamberton.

"It is good to hear of your Church host. A comfort." Bruce took a pace or two about the room. "Wallace . . .?" he said. "You return to St. Andrews, my lord Bishop? Just across Tay from Wallace at Dundee. You will see him? Soon? Good. Then, will you tell him, from me, secretly, that we need not look for Edward's invasion. Not this spring."

"Not . . .? No invasion . . .?"

"No. Not this year, I think. Edward will be otherwise employed. He weds again."

"Dear God! Edward will wed? Soon?"

"Aye. He goes on a pilgrimage to St. Albans. In preparation. Weds at Canterbury. This summer. To the Princess Margaret of France. I fear we risk losing our French allies!"

"Saints cherish us—this is news indeed! You are sure of it? No idle tale?"

"I have it . . . from one I trust. Close to Edward's person."

"So! Then . . . then we have time. We have been given time, precious time. Thank God, I say!" The Bishop paused. "But, my lord—you did not tell him. My lord of Badenoch. You said naught of it . . . !"

"I said naught," the younger man agreed heavily. "Better that he does not know, I think."

"Is that right, my lord? He is your fellow-Guardian."

"Right? I do not know if it is right. But I deem it *wise*. Let Comyn learn it in his own time. Tell Wallace. But others need not know. Yet. I require the time more than does Comyn."

When Lamberton left him, Bruce asked him to have sent up to him paper, a quill and ink. Also a lamp, for the window was small and the light beginning to fade.

It was dark long before the young man finished. Letter-writing did not come easily to him, and in his vehemence he had to send for three more quills before he was finished. He wrote:

My lady,

I do greatly thank you. Your letter came to me this tenth day of April, at the Torwood of Stirling, and I received it with much favour. Your God-speed and goodwill I do treasure. And, I think, do much require. For I am in sorry state here. But the better for your heed for me.

I counsel you to beware of Guy de Beauchamp. He is a man of ill living. Do not consider him. Beware, I say, of any whom Edward would have you to wed. He would but use you, as he uses all, for his own purposes.

The word of his marriage is of great moment and does much aid to my mind's ease. For this I do thank you. Even Edward is scarce like to come warring to Scotland quickly after his wedding.

The more surely in that his wife will be sister to King Philip, with whom we are in treaty of mutual aid. I have no doubt that treaty will be brought to nothing hereafter. But meantime it stands. This gives us time, in Scotland. But God knows, not I, whether I can achieve what is required, in time.

You say well when you conceive that my present state will not bring me joy. Being Joint Guardian of Scotland with this man John Comyn is so ill a fate as to drive me all but from my wits. I think that you know of him, a masterful man of ill tongue, respecting none. But strong, in his own parts, as well as heading the powerfullest house in this realm. We have never agreed, nor ever shall. To act with him in amity is not possible. To bear with him is beyond all supporting. Yet I needs must, on the face of it, if the kingdom is not to fall apart before Edward. Only Comyn and Bruce, it seems to be, can so unite the lords and barons of the land into one, and so oppose England. But the good God alone knows if it is possible, for I do not.

Comyn will be king, if he may. Nothing is more sure. That would be an ill day for Scotland, and I would die first. For it would be the end of Bruce, I think. Anything better than that.

I do not believe that you are a shrew, my lady. Haughty it may be.

I would have news of my father. We are not close, but I am sufficient his son to wish to know how he fares. And he is true heir to Scotland. I fear that Edward may wreak wrath on him because of me. Where he is I do not know. He spoke of proceeding to Norway, to my sister, but I do not think it. He is like to be living on one of his English manors, which you know of, if Edward has not warded him. If you can learn aught and will write it to me, I shall be the more indebted. I think much of you, Lady Elizabeth. I do not believe that we are better thus far parted. I believe I am less stubborn than I was.

The salutations and esteem of ROBERT BRUCE OF CARRICK, GUARDIAN OF SCOTLAND.

Those last three words he scored out, and wrote beneath;

Here is folly, for I am guardian of nothing, scarce even of my own pride and honour. I pray God that He keep you. Also that He holds off Edward until our sown corn may be grown, and reaped, so that we may fight him at least with full bellies.

CHAPTER TWELVE

THE land was fair again, green—better even, turning golden under the August sun, the rigs of corn already yellowing on every valleyside, beasts looking sleek and fat again on the braes. It was a wonder, a transformation, and men rejoiced with an elementary rejoicing at the recurrent bounty of the seasons, a thing which they had not had occasion to consider, in Southern Scotland, for long. Another month. Give them another month, and honest weather, and the harvest would be in. One more month.

But there were ominous signs if not in the landscape. The English, who had withheld all these spring and summer months, were becoming active again. They had reinforced Edinburgh, Dunbar and Roxburgh Castles, and were sending out probing sallies from the latter and Berwick into the East March of the Borderland, even into Ettrick Forest. Why? They would not restart this without orders. King Edward was gone south to his wedding, yes—but he had issued commands for public prayers to be made in all parts of his kingdom for the success of his arms against the rebellious Scots. He had not forgotten, in his newfound felicity—and as a bridegroom of exactly sixty summers, he might well be content with only brief honeymooning. But they would have another month, surely ...

Even Robert Bruce, who these days had developed something of a hunch to his wide shoulders, and a sombre, brooding aspect to his expressionful rugged features, felt the lift and release of it all, of what he saw. The land was no longer black. He had prayed for this, these months, and had been granted them. Nigel sang cheerfully at his side, as they rode, and he almost joined in more than once—unsuitable as this might be for Scotland's Guardian.

Eastwards from Lanark, where Bruce had been conducting an assize of justice, they climbed into the hills out of Clydesdale, by Biggar and Broughton, moving into the unburned land of Ettrick Forest.

This time, Bruce rode at the head of a great company of lords, knights and men-at-arms. He had learned this lesson, at least; that dealing with his fellow-Guardian called for display as well as patience. Moreover, this was not just to be another meeting or council, but with action contemplated. So he had, riding close behind him and his brothers, as well as James the Steward and his son Walter; Gartnait, Earl of Mar; John de Strathbogie, Earl of Atholl; Lindsay, Lord of Crawford; old Robert Wishart, Bishop of Glasgow, out of English hands again; Sir John de Soulis of Liddesdale; and Sir Ingram de Umfraville, brother to the Earl of Angus. As well as many other notables. A thousand and more horsed and armed retainers jingled behind, on long column of march, through the winding valleys.

They made not for Selkirk this time, but for Bishop Lamberton's rich manor of Stobo, on the upper Tweed west of Peebles. This was because of the English raids from Roxburgh, one of which had recently penetrated sufficiently deep into the Forest to burn Selkirk and part of the lower Ettrick and Yarrow valleys, as warning and foretaste. It was as reprisal for this, and in answer to Comyn's taunts regarding military inactivity, that Bruce now rode eastwards.

They came to the wide haugh of Tweed, at Stobo, in the late afternoon, to find its meadows and pastures a great armed camp, out of which the church on its knowe, the Bishop's manor-house and the Dean's little tower, rose like islands. Comyn had arrived first, from his prolonged siege of Stirling Castle, and clearly he had come well supported, as the colourful host of banners flying down there indicated.

It turned out, ominously, that the other Guardian had brought, as well as Buchan, Alexander, Earl of Menteith; William, Earl of Sutherland; Malise, Earl of Strathearn, Alexander MacDougall, Lord of Lorn, his brother-in-law; Sir Robert Keith, the Marischal; Sir David Graham, Lord of Dundaff; and others of similar prominence. It looked as though this was to be a trial of strength with more than the English.

Lamberton, more than aware of all the stresses and strains, was taking his own precautions. Churchmen were everywhere, with all the trappings of religion, relics and the like. Also heralds, with the King of Arms busy with formal pomp and circumstance. Massed trumpets signalised the appearance of Bruce's contingent, and re-echoed from all the round green hills. The Primate was seeking to smother animosities in formality.

The two sides mingled in the wide haughland with a sort of grim wariness, watched over and fussed around by the droves of clerics. There was no clear cut distinction between North and South, for there were Comyn supporters in the South and Bruce supporters in the North; but by and large the division was fairly clear, and none the less because external danger threatened.

John Comyn himself did not come to greet the newcomers, and there was no association until the leaders forgathered in the Bishop's dining-chamber for the evening meal; no real association even then, for Lamberton placed one Guardian at each end of the long table with himself in the middle. The hospitality was lavish, and music, minstrelsy and entertainment went on throughout and continuously, so that there was little opportunity for either co-operation or clash. Wine flowed freely, and it was clear that there would be no serious talking that night with all tired after long riding. A great council was arranged for the following forenoon. It could not be called a parliament, for such required a summons of forty days; but with most of the Privy Council present, it would carry sufficient authority for practical purposes.

The Guardians had not exchanged a single word, directly, by the time that the company broke up to retire to bed, Comyn in the Dean's tower, Bruce in the manor-house itself. The latter and Lamberton, however, talked late into the night.

In the event, it was driving rain in the morning, shrouding the hills, and no conditions for holding a large meeting in the open, as had been intended. The largest room of the Bishop's manor-house was much too small, as was the church. The nearest large chamber was the Hospitium of St. Leonard's, at Peebles, a few miles to the east. There was a castle there also, actually a royal hunting-lodge, but it was a small place.

So to the town of Peebles a great company rode, through the rain, by a Tweed already grown brown and drumly with the hill burns' swift spates. Men forgot their dynastic and clan rivalries for the moment, to look anxiously up at the lowering clouds, and to hope that the good weather was not broken for long and the harvest put in jeopardy.

But in the refectory of the Hospitium at Peebles, even as the Prior welcomed his numerous distinguished guests, all the church-men's efforts at peace-keeping were abruptly brought to naught. Upraised voices in angry altercation drowned the Prior's. All eyes turned.

". . . jumped-up scum! Those lands are mine, I say. And I'll have them back, Wallace or no Wallace!"

The speaker—or shouter, rather—was the Lord of Dundaff, Sir David Graham, younger brother of Wallace's friend, Sir John, who had died heroically on Falkirk field. But brother of a different kidney, a vociferous supporter of Baliol and Comyn. Now he was shaking his fist up in the face of a tall and rather gangling man, largely built but giving the appearance of being but loosely put together, who flinched somewhat at the truculence of the smaller man's outburst.

"The lands are not yours, sir. Never were," this other protested. "They but neighbour yours. And you may covet them. But they were granted to my brother, granted by my lord Guardian . . ."

"Unlawfully granted! Those lands of Strathmartine are ours. Graham's. Always we have claimed them. No upstart bonnet-laird from the West shall have them, I say. The Earl of Carrick had no right to grant them. Any more than he should have knighted such as you . . . !"

"Sirrah!" Bruce rapped out, sharply. "Watch your words."

"It is truth. Strathmartine is Graham land. And you gave it to . . . a felon!"

"Knave!" Stung to fury, the big shambling man dropped his hand to the hilt of his dirk. He was Sir Malcolm, Wallace's brother, recently knighted by Bruce out of respect for his brother's fame. A very different man from the giant Sir William, he was like a blurred, indeterminate and somehow bungled version of the other.

Still more swiftly the Graham's hand dropped, and his dagger was whipped out.

"Fool! Put that away. Are you mad?" Bruce cried.

"This . . . mountebank called me knave! Me, Graham!"

"Sir David! Drawn steel, in the presence of the realm's Guardians, is treason!" That was Lamberton, in his sternest voice. He pushed forward towards the irate knights. "Sheath your dirk, man. I command you. Sir Malcolm—stand back."

"Treason!" Graham cried, beside himself. "*You*, Wallace's creature, to say that! And what of Wallace's own treason? He is bolted. Gone. Fled the country. In time of our need. Without the permission of the Guardians! Here is treason, if ever there was. And you say treason to *me*!"

"You babble, sir. Bairns' havers!" the Primate declared coldly. "Sir William has gone overseas. On a mission to the rulers of nations. To the King of Norway, the Pope, and the King of France. To seek bind them together against Edward of England. How dare you raise your voice against the man who saved this realm! The man your own brother died for!"

"You would have us believe such tales? Is this the time to desert the nation? To go journeying round Christendom? With Edward Plantagenet hammering at our doors! Expected to invade us any day . . ."

"Edward is marrying. In the south. All know it. We had a space for breath. Sir William Wallace was our best ambassador. A man whose name will open all doors . . ."

"I gave no authority for Wallace to leave the country." All faces turned, as this new cold voice intervened, the Red Comyn's voice. If men had been keyed up before, they were more so now.

"You were informed, my lord," the Bishop said.

"I gave no permission, as Guardian."

"*I* gave permission," Bruce declared. "We waited for yours. Requested it, and waited. Time was short. When you sent no answer, my lord, either way, I gave the required permission. As Guardian."

"We are *Joint* Guardians, sir. What Comyn withholds, Bruce cannot grant."

"What the realm's need demands, and when one will not act, the other must needs do so!"

"Ha, you say so? Here is a convenient policy for knavery!"

"I request that you choose your words, my lord. And recollect that Wallace left from Leith, from *my* jurisdiction."

"My lords, my lords!" The Primate, concerned by the broadening of the conflict to include the two Guardians, held up an imploring hand. "Here is no cause for disagreement. Sir William went first to Norway, where my lord of Carrick's sister is Queen. Then to the Pope, at Rome, on a mission from myself as head of Holy Church in this land . . ."

"He went, I say, in the face of the enemy!" That was Graham again, hotly. "He, the warrior! The hero! Who is supposed to lead the people. Edward beat him once — so he scuttles before the Plantagenet comes to finish his work! A craven, as well as a traitor and an upstart! I ask *his* lands, of the Guardians — not that he take mine!"

"As God's my witness — this I'll not stand!" Sir Malcolm cried, and with the rasp of metal his own dagger came out.

"No! No, I say! Put back your steel. Both of you. In the name of Almighty God, in this holy place, I command it!" Lamberton strode forward, hand outstretched.

"Stand back, Sir Priest! Or your wordy wind-bag may be punctured!" the Graham snarled, flickering his dirk in a lightning gesture at the Bishop. "Leave this overgrown mummer to a better man!"

"By God's Blood, this is too much!" Bruce burst out, and flung himself towards the others.

In almost the same instant Comyn and Buchan leapt into action.

Chaos reigned in that normally quiet refectory for the sick and aged.

The Comyns were slightly nearer to the Graham than was Bruce—for he was of their party. Buchan the Constable, a pace or two ahead of his kinsman, reached the angry group first just as Lamberton was stretching out an authoritative and fearless hand to be yielded Graham's weaving steel. Furiously the Earl buffeted the Bishop aside, sending him staggering against Bruce, who came up on the other side.

"How . . . dare . . . you! Comyn!" Bruce shouted, above the hub-bub. "By the Rude—you shall pay . . ."

"Comyn dares more than that!" It was Sir John the Red who answered thus, and coming up, struck Robert Bruce with the back of his hand full across the face.

It was as though a curtain of silence fell suddenly and completely over the raftered hall. With an uncanny abruptness the shouting and noise died away, as all stood appalled, rooted to the spot in horror at what was done, at what that blow stood for. The only sound, in a matter of seconds, was the heavy breathing of the two richly-clad Guardians of Scotland, standing only a foot or so apart, proud flashing eye to eye. Even the Primate and the High Constable were forgotten for the moment.

Bruce, trembling all over almost uncontrollably with the fierceness of his battle with utterly destructive rage, was stark white save for the scarlet hand-mark on his left cheek and jaw. He swayed, as though drunken, in the extremity of his emotion. Comyn himself for once was not smiling. He stood motionless, almost frozen, wary, as though perhaps himself shocked by what he had done; but resiling nothing, giving no hint of regret, of weakening.

It was Nigel Bruce who moved. With an oath, he grabbed at his jewelled dirk, to raise it high. "Dastard!" he whispered. "You . . . struck . . . him!"

Even as the weapon drove down, Bruce seemed to be released

from the straitjacket of his emotion. Like an uncoiling spring he hurled himself against his brother, beating aside the dagger. Comyn had not stirred, even flinched.

"No!" he cried. "No! *My* quarry! Mine. Mine only." Panting, still with one hand on his brother's wrist, he pointed with the other. "Comyn—I should kill you. For that. Now. Before all. But ... but it is not the time. Or the place. Not yet. One day, I will pay that debt. I promise you. As all these, and God and His saints, will be my witness! Till then—wait, you! Wait, and regret!"

"Thank God, my lord—thank God!" Lamberton exclaimed. "For your lenity. Your forbearance. Fortitude." He swung on Comyn. "And you, my lord—shame on you! Here was infamy. Unworthy. Unworthy of any noble knight ..."

"Quiet, priest!" the Red Comyn jerked, from stiff lips. "Enough." He looked at Bruce. "At any time, my lord of Carrick, should you wish to take this matter further, I am at your service. And shall cherish the day!"

"Do so. For it will be your last!" the other said levelly.

Master William Comyn, of the Chapel Royal, laid a hand on the arm of his brother Buchan, who was about to speak, and raised his own mellifluously soothing voice. "My lords and gentles all—we have come here for urgent business. A council. Not for profitless wrangling. Much is at stake. I pray that we may move to that business. If the Lords Guardian will take their seats. At the Prior's table ..."

"Sit!" Bruce swung on him, eyes wide. "Think you that I will sit at any table? With *him*? Now? Do you, man?"

"Here's a mercy, at any rate! I am to be spared that!" Comyn found his smile again.

"My lords, my lords—think! Consider. You are both Guardians and governors of this realm, still." Lamberton supported his fellow-cleric. "The realm's affairs must go forward."

"This joint guardianship is over," Bruce declared shortly.

"On this at least we are agreed." The other bowed elaborately.

"Scotland deserves fairer than that, I think," the Primate said slowly, authoritatively, and with great dignity, looking from one to the other sternly. "Those who take up the realm's direction may not so toss it away, without loss to their honour. I beg your lordships to perceive it. And for your good names' sake recollect your duty."

Those were hard words for such as these. But William Comyn reinforced them, although in his own more suave fashion. "I am sure that my lord of Badenoch, at least, will know his duty. And will well serve the realm, now as always." He eyed his kinsman meaningly.

There was a pause, and then Bruce shrugged. "To business, then," he said. "We will consider this of the guardianship at another time. But—I will not sit there. With that man!"

Comyn was about to speak when Lamberton forestalled him. "Very well," he acceded. "The form of it matters little. Let us proceed, here standing." He pointed. "The clerks may use the table." Without pause he went on. "The matter of Sir William Wallace's mission to the rulers has been dealt with and, I submit, is not profitable for further discussion here and now." And before any might plunge again into those troubled waters, added, "The besiegement of Stirling Castle proceeds. My lord of Badenoch may wish to speak to it?"

Thus invoked, Comyn could scarcely refuse to participate, in his own project. "It goes but slowly," he said, seemingly casual. "My people have assailed it for ten weeks. With little gain, as yet. Save that we constrain the English closely, and have driven them into the inner citadel. But it is strong. The strongest place in Scotland. We shall have it, in time, never fear. And investing it demonstrates to the whole land that at least *some* will draw sword against the invader!" He tossed a glance at Bruce.

"I commend my lord of Badenoch's assault on Stirling," that man commented shortly. "Even if barren of result!"

"The Earl of Carrick might have better fortune were *he* to take up arms against one or other of the less powerful holds the English enjoy in his territories! His own house of Lochmaben, in especial."

None failed to see significance in that; but not all probably perceived the fuller implication. The main object behind holding this meeting here in the Forest was in order, thereafter, to lead a united assault on the great English-held base of Roxburgh, which lay some thirty miles down Tweed, near Kelso and the actual borderline. Bruce, ever chary of becoming bogged down in siege-warfare, had only been persuaded to this by Comyn's threats that he would do it alone, if need be. Such a move undoubtedly would look as though the other Guardian was dragging his feet, in the popular view. Hence the great array of magnates and nobles, of both factions, here assembled. Yet now Comyn was talking about Lochmaben and not mentioning Roxburgh.

"I have not the same itch to take castles as has this lord," Bruce declared, slowly. "Even my own. Which is very strong also. As Sir John Comyn knows—since he assumed possession of it during the short reign of King John Baliol ... !"

"Whom God save and protect!" Comyn rapped out.

In duty bound, many requested the Deity to save the King.

"No doubt," Bruce went on dryly. "But, despite its strength, the English in Lochmaben can do us little harm. They cannot be reinforced without a major invasion."

"I have heard it said," Comyn observed, looking round him, with his hard grin, "that Bruce may be well content to leave the English in Lochmaben. That, should Edward triumph, he may find it a convenient stepping-stone back into the Plantagenet's good graces! Idle havers, no doubt ..."

"Damnation! This is a malicious lie ... !"

"Idle havers, no doubt, as I say!" the other repeated loudly. "But a warning of how men's minds may go. Is it not?"

"My lords," Lamberton intervened again, with a sort of weary urgency, "Lochmaben is of less importance in the realm than are the others. Roxburgh is otherwise ..."

"Aye," the Earl of Mar broke in, "Roxburgh is only a mile or two from the Border. It can be supplied and reinforced with ease by the English ..."

"Which means, my lord, does it not, that it is scarce worth our troubling with?" Comyn asked. "Since, even if we succeed in taking it, as soon as we are gone, the English can retake it. With ease, as you say. If worse does not befall."

"But ... but ... ?"

"They are raiding from there. Becoming devilish bold!" Mar's other brother-in-law, Atholl, supported him. "Did we not come this far to teach them a lesson? At Roxburgh?"

"My information is that they are much reinforced. Their raiding is no more than a ruse to draw us there. Into a trap, with large English strength waiting on their own side of Tweed." Comyn spoke in jerking, unusual fashion, clearly ill at ease on this. But it was equally clear that, whatever the reason for this change of front, his mind was made up. "It would be folly to advance on Roxburgh, in the circumstances."

All men stared at him now, Bruce included. He at least had no doubts as to what this meant. It was highly unlikely that Comyn could have any new information regarding Roxburgh, or that there could be any large English force approached so near without word being brought to Bruce himself. Therefore it was merely an excuse. Comyn, now, would not proceed on any joint action. It was as simple as that. There was to be not even a token co-operation between the Guardians.

Even Buchan was taken by surprise, obviously. He peered at his cousin, and coughed. "A simple blow, John. A show of strength," he suggested. "We need not make a siege of it, if the signs are contrary. But a raid, at least. Into England. Since we are here in force . . ."

"No!" the other snapped. "It would be folly. I march only with my rear secure!"

There was no question what he meant by that. The guardianship was irrevocably, blatantly, split.

As all there contemplated the ruin of it, and perceived the dread shadow of internecine civil war to add to bloody invasion, Lamberton, flat-voiced, sought once more to ease the tension, to salvage something from the wreck, to make time for calmer thinking.

"The Lords Guardian have rejected the suggested raid on Roxburgh, then," he said. "But there is more business. Appointments. First, the Wardenship of the West March. Sir William Douglas, in English hands, has been Warden. While prisoner, his deputy has been Sir Christopher Seton, here present. There are now tidings that the Lord of Douglas has died in the Tower of London. May God rest his soul. Whether he died of Edward's malice, or of bodily ill, we know not. But, my lords, a new Warden is required."

It was skilfully done. The fiery Douglas had been popular, something of a hero, if an awkward one. The announcement of his death, as a prisoner, made a major impact, and set up an angry clamour against the enemy—a healthier demonstration than heretofore. In the stir, it was agreed almost without discussion that Sir Christopher Seton, the deputy, should be raised to full wardenship. He was a sound Bruce supporter.

One or two other appointments were quickly disposed of thereafter, following as far as possible the non-controversial line of Comyn nominees for those in the North, Bruce for the South. Lamberton steered them deftly through that strange, standing assembly, with the curt nods or complete silence of the two hostile Guardians accepted as the ultimate authority of the kingdom. Men stirred, shuffled and fidgeted as the formalities were hurried through.

Undoubtedly all now were anxious for the uncomfortable proceedings to be over. Yet men dreaded what might follow, once the two factions were released from the Primate's dexterous handling and patient but firm authority. That these two men, Comyn and Bruce, could go on ruling Scotland conjointly, for the kingdom's well-being, or their own, was manifestly impossible. But neither was going to resign and leave the other in supreme power. And even if both were to resign, who could effectively replace them? They represented the two great power-divisions of the country, and any other successors would in fact be nothing more than the nominees and puppets of these two. For a land which so desperately needed unity, Scotland was in a sorry state.

As the half-desired, half-dreaded moment arrived, when the proceedings were being closed by William Comyn, the Lord Privy Seal, announcing that the necessary papers and charters were there on the table for the Guardians' signature and sealing, it was a much less smooth and assured clerical voice which at this last moment galvanised the company. Old Robert Wishart, Bishop of Glasgow, had aged noticeably from his spell in an English dungeon. He quavered painfully.

"My lords—we cannot break up so. The government of the realm, in this disarray. It is our bounden duty, before God and the people of Scotland, to take further steps for the better rule of the land. My Lords Guardian, you must see it?"

"I see it." Bruce acceded briefly, but shrugged helplessly.

Comyn showed no reaction.

"The Crown rests in two hands," the old prelate went on, panting a little, "Those two hands may be strong, but they . . . they are scarce in harmony. Why should there not be three hands? If there is joint guardianship, there could likewise be triple guardianship. I commend such to you. I commend to you all my lord Bishop of St. Andrews, Primate and spokesman of Holy Church in this land, as Joint Guardian with the Earl of Carrick and the Lord of Badenoch."

Into the hum of excited comment, James the Steward, Wishart's old colleague, managed to make thick interjection.

"I agree. I say, I agree."

Bruce was about to announce hearty and thankful approval, when Lamberton himself caught his eye and almost imperceptibly shook his head, before looking expectantly at Comyn. Bruce held back, in belated recognition that what he signified approval of, his rival would almost automatically oppose.

Comyn, narrow-eyed, kept them waiting, while he weighed

and calculated. It was his kinsman, the Lord Privy Seal, who, spoke.

"Here is a notable proposal. Which could well serve the realm, I think." Whatever was his reason, Master William was being very co-operative this day.

Ignoring Bruce entirely, Comyn turned to Buchan. "How think you, Cousin? Shall we have the priest?"

Lamberton actually raised a hand involuntarily to restrain the hot flood that rose to Bruce's lips.

The Constable had the grace to flush. "The rule of the realm must go on," he muttered.

"Very well. So be it." The Red Comyn turned away, with a half-shrug, towards the table. "Now—these papers . . . ?"

"My lord . . . !" Robert Wishart gasped. "My lord—the Earl of Carrick! Do *you* agree?"

Strangle-voiced, Bruce got it out. "Aye."

"God be praised!" The old man's voice broke. "Then . . . I declare . . . he is . . . I declare the Bishop of St. Andrews is Guardian of the realm. My lord, my good lord . . . !"

The assembly at last broke up in disorder. But the thing was done. There were now three Guardians in Scotland. And one, men acknowledged with relief, was strong enough and supple enough perhaps for the unenviable task of holding the balance between the other two.

After the signing and sealing there was no pretence at further co-operation between the two great factions. It was clear that despite the rain, Comyn was for heading north again at once. He was going, he declared loudly, back to real work, after his bellyful of clerks, idlers, poltroons and their talk, back to the siege of Stirling. Others could go where they would—to hell, if need be!

Watching the Comyns and their following ride off, Bruce palefaced, fists clenched, found his shoulder gripped by William Lamberton.

"My son, my very good friend—may God reward you for your restraint this day," the Bishop-Guardian said. "It cost you dear, I know. But—it saved the kingdom. Not once, but many times. I thank you, my lord, from the bottom of my heart."

"I feel soiled. Besmirched. The name of Bruce spat upon. Trampled by that . . . that devil! That braggart!"

"I know, I know. But do not fear—no men think Bruce reduced by this day's work. Quite otherwise. You have added to your stature, my good lord. That is certain. But . . . do not name

Comyn braggart, I pray you. Do not delude yourself. Whatever else he is, he is not that. It will pay us to remember it."

"Perhaps. But, whatever he is, he will suffer for today. On that I give you my oath ! Before Almighty God !"

The older man sighed, and shook his head. "Perhaps God will save you from that oath—who knows? But—what do you now? Roxburgh?"

"No. I am none so keen on castle-baiting. Time can be better used. There is much else for me to do."

"Nevertheless, I think it would be well to heed one matter that Comyn said, my friend. Lochmaben. You were wise to lay siege to Lochmaben. What he said, of men's talk, could be true. At least make the gesture of investing your castle."

"You think . . . ? Men do talk so of me? It is not just Comyn's spleen? That I reserve Lochmaben, for Edward's favour?"

"Men are foolish. And uncharitable. I have heard the like talk. Better that you should proclaim it false, by your deeds."

Bruce looked away and away, beyond the rain-shrouded Peebles hills.

Chapter Thirteen

Fires blazed redly against the October blue night sky, on every rounded height that flanked the seven lochs of Lochmaben and were reflected in the prevailing blue-black waters, scores of conflagrations that burned brightly and were being replenished, flames that would be seen from great distances, from all Annandale and Nithsdale and the plain of Solway, even from far Carlisle and the English Cumberland fells behind. And for once they were not burning homes and farmsteads and churches, not even balefires of warning; but bonfires of joy and celebration. For Lochmaben's great castle was in its own people's hands again, after long enemy occupation, the captured garrison imprisoned in the dungeons which had held and seen the last of so many Annandale folk these past years. Now there was no single English-held enclave in all the South-West. Moreover, the harvest was safely in at last, and the weather held. There was cause for rejoicing and bonfires.

Robert Bruce, pacing the timber bretasche, or overhanging parapet-walk of the main central tower of Lochmaben high on the great motehill of earth, and looking out at it all over the surrounding waters, recognised that he had cause for gratification. He it was who had given permission for those beacons to be lit. A success was welcome indeed, after all the months of labour and frustration. The sheer military action itself, the overcome challenge, had been welcome—and the acceptance of Sir Nicholas Segrave's surrender a notable satisfaction—even though the deplorable pantryman, Master Benstead, it seemed, had been withdrawn to England almost a year before. But satisfaction was not really in the man's mind, that night, nevertheless.

None knew better than he how superficial, how temporary, was this celebration. Lochmaben might be his again, meantime—but for how long? *This* harvest was gathered and secured—but would there be another? The basic situation was unchanged. The monstrous shadow of Edward Plantagenet loomed over all divided Scotland still, behind those joyous bonfires, and there was little reason to believe that the future would be any brighter than the past.

Indeed Bruce at least knew the reverse to be likely. He had come up here, to the battlements, to be alone, and to be able to read again the letter which crackled inside his doublet—for beacons blazed here on the topmost parapet also, and would give him light to read, unattended, as was impossible in the crowded castle below. That letter which was itself secret satisfaction and disquiet both. But he was not alone. His brothers Nigel and Edward, and his brother-in-law Gartnait of Mar, had followed him up; and while the former pair knew their brother sufficiently well to perceive the signs that he would be glad of their absence, and had withdrawn round to the other side of the keep's high walk, the latter, an amiable but somewhat stupid man, took no such hint and clung close, talking, talking.

The fact was that the Earl of Mar, who tended to hide himself in his northern fastnesses, was in process of building up the capture of Lochmaben Castle into the adventurous highlight of a not very exciting life. He had committed himself for the first time, against the English, and the venture had been successful. Not that only, but it had been a spectacular and dramatic business, two nights ago, and he had taken an active if minor part. It looked as though the fall of Lochmaben was going to be Gartnait of Mar's theme of conversation for a long time to come.

Admittedly, it had been no ordinary and prolonged siege, than which no military activity could be more dull. It had been Bruce's own conception, for, though he had been born at Turnberry, he had spent a large part of his boyhood here, at his paternal grandfather's favourite castle. It was an old-fashioned place, not one of the new stone castles at all, but a mote-and-bailey stronghold of the sort that had been general for three centuries, built of timber and covered over with hardened clay. If any imagined this to be a frail construction for such a place, they would be mistaken. The artificial mote-hill rose to about fifty feet, and the soil which went to its heightening had been dug from all round in the form of deep encircling ditches, up to thirty feet wide. There were four of these ditches at Lochmaben, each defended by a high wooden palisade, with inner shelf-like parapet-walk and drawbridges. The inner one enclosed a ring-shaped court, around the central mound, in which were the kitchens and domestic quarters, the men-at-arms' barracks, the storehouses and the stables. Also the castle well. Up on the summit of the mote-hill was the great square keep itself, its massive timbers covered in many feet of baked clay plastering, so that it could not be fired from without. Well-provisioned, such a place was well-nigh unconquerable.

But Bruce, sitting down with his host outside it, had had childhood memories which stood him in good stead. That well, in the inner bailey, which permitted prolonged resistance, was nevertheless the place's weakness—though few probably knew it. Deep down it connected not with a spring, which was usual, but with a running underground stream of fair size. A stream that flowed into the Castle Loch some two hundred yards to the south by an inconspicuous exit amongst piled rocks and elder scrub. Bruce had found that exit, playing as a boy, and explored the stream's winding tunnel-like course underground as a boy will, until he had found himself at the foot of the stone-faced well-shaft, with the glimmer of daylight high above. He had never forgotten.

So, on a suitably dark night of cloud and drizzle, he had mounted a sham attack on the outer defences, under Edward, to keep the garrison occupied, and set burning great quantities of cut reeds and brushwood to westwards, to form a blowing smoke-screen to blind the defenders. Then he himself had led three boatloads of men, with muffled oars, from the nearby town, under Nigel and Mar, to the hidden mouth of the stream. The underground course had seemed infinitely smaller, more cramping and alarming than his boyhood recollection; but at length, bruised and coughing with the smoke from the pitch-pine torches, they had reached the well-foot. Its rope and bucket was up at the surface, but the agile Nigel had worked his way up the long shaft, back hard against one side, feet walking up the other, and thereafter quietly let down the rope for the others to follow. The inner bailey had been deserted.

Thereafter a score of desperate men had crept up the steep mote-hill to the central keep, screened by the drifting smoke, to find it standing open and practically empty, all the garrison manning the perimeter palisades, gatehouses and outer defences. Securing the citadel, they had then attacked the bewildered and scattered defenders from the rear, one bailey at a time. Sir Nicholas Segrave, still the castle's Captain, had surrendered his sword at the main gatehouse, like a man betrayed.

Gartnait of Mar had scarcely ceased to talk of it since.

A commotion down in the same inner bailey, over a hundred feet below their lofty stance, with horsemen arriving and torches waving, gave Bruce the excuse he sought. Not every belted earl would run errands, even at the behest of another of the same, but Mar was essentially a modest and gentle man—as his spirited wife complained. His brother-in-law sent him down to find out what was to do.

Alone, Bruce drew out the letter—which he had only had opportunity to skim hitherto—and moved closer to the nearest beacon, for light. It read:

My lord Robert,

I take up my pen again with much concern for you. And some little for myself, should I be discovered thus writing. For King Edward has little mercy on those who counter him, as you do know, even though they be women. Certain ladies here have discovered it to their cost, of late. For this marriage seems to have shortened his temper. So that I fear that I may write but little to-night, for I am much constrained and seldom alone. The Queen is at chapel, for the King has become mighty religious and I have craved excuse over a woman's pains. But she and the others will be back.

Foolish that I am, my lord, to waste precious time and words so. I write from York again, where we are recently returned from London. But not from the house of Uhtred the clothier. I am very grand now, in the Lord Archbishop's palace no less. For I am chief of the Queen's ladies. But we are cramped here mighty tight, nevertheless, and I had more of private space amongst the cloths and wool.

But we do not stay at York. In two days we go north to New-castle where the King assembles another great force against Scotland. He is very wroth about the assault on Stirling and promises dire punishments against his rebellious Scots. He is wroth too with his lords, for many do say that it is too late now in the year for invading Scotland. And that he goes back on his promises to them, in this continuing warfare. God knows they are right. It is a kind of madness with him. He has forbade, by public proclamation, all joustings, tournaments and plays of arms, saying that every knight, esquire and soldier must rather come to do duty against the Scots. I fear then, that by your receipt of this writing, the King will be riding against you, to Stirling.

Your letter did find me at Canterbury and I much esteem it. I am sorry for your state and pray that it may be lightened. The Lord John Comyn I remember and did not like. We did not agree. But nor did I agree with the Lord Robert of Carrick. Is it not so? Even though you do not believe me shrew. Or say that you do not. Perhaps you cozen me. But may the Devil roast John Comyn.

I have heard tidings of your father. He dwells quietly and peaceably on his manor of Hatfield Broadoak in Essex. It is said he has been sickly. The King does not speak of him. He speaks of you, I fear, but less than kindly.

Guy de Beauchamp, of Warwick, is not now in the King's favour, and so I am spared. But he would have me to wed instead Humphrey de Bohun, the new young Earl of Hereford. Do you esteem him the more acceptable, my lord?

From Newcastle when the King marches into Scotland we women are to be left at the Percy's castle of Alnwick where I was beforetime. Near to you in your Border hills although I cannot conceive that we should meet. I do much fear for you and yours, in Edward's wrath. Keep you out of his way my lord Robert.

I hear the Queen returned below.

I know not whom I may obtain to bring this letter to you. Another wandering friar will be safest, it may be. God be with you. I am in haste.

From York, in the night of sixth October, by ELIZABETH DE BURGH.

Humphrey de Bohun, of Hereford! That puppy! Bruce frowned fiercely on the firelit night. A dandified young fool. And

218

shamefully rich. He could no more manage Elizabeth de Burgh than he could fly in the air!

The reader forced his thoughts to the more immediately vital matter of the date. The letter had taken three weeks to come from York, via the Bishop of Galloway—for it was now the end of October. Edward, then, might well have left Newcastle, by now, on his murderous way. Stirling, she said. Making for Stirling, to relieve the siege. Lamberton must be warned. And Comyn, of course. And Wallace was not yet home from across the seas . . .

Mar, panting with the climb, arrived back at the parapet-walk with a young esquire, a stranger, who looked as though he had fallen into more than the one bog on his way to Lochmaben.

"Courier from Seton. Warden of the March," he burst out. "Edward is at Berwick! God save us—Edward is at Berwick, Robert! This . . . here is the Earl of Carrick."

"My lord—my master, Sir Christopher Seton, salutes you," the youth said, his voice declaring his fatigue. "He sends this message. The King of England is at Berwick with a great host. But Sir Christopher learns that he has trouble. His greatest lords have refused to advance into Scotland. Thus late in the year. His first aim was to relieve Stirling Castle. But they will by no means accompany him. There is great upset in the English camp. But . . . Sir Christopher hears that the King comes here. Instead of Stirling . . ."

"Here! You mean—Lochmaben?"

"So says Sir Christopher, my lord. He has spies in the English camp. The word is that the King's wrath is beyond all telling. But his earls are solid against this venture. He has heard of your siege of this castle. Belike he does not know that it is fallen. He swears that he will teach the Earl of Carrick a lesson, at the least. He rides tomorrow for Lochmaben."

"The fiend take him! And these earls? Will they follow him to Lochmaben? But not to Stirling?"

"No, my lord. They and their levies—the main host—move not out of England. But the King has men enough of his own, and hired Welsh archers, with the Cumberland levies of Sir Robert Clifford, to serve for this."

"How many?"

"Sir Christopher says near to ten thousand. Half of them Welsh longbowmen."

"Dear God! And I have less than a third of that. And not two hundred of them archers!"

"Robert! Can you get more? In time?" Mar demanded, in agitation.

"No. Not enough, by half. Not men to face Edward—the greatest soldier in Christendom! Not archers. Or armoured chivalry."

"Then . . . then what? What will you do?"

"Do what I must," Bruce answered grimly. "Go. Retire before him. Give up Lochmaben again. Play the craven! Give Comyn cause for glee! I can do no other. I cannot hold this castle against Edward—even if I would. I cannot fight him in the field, with hope of success. Even survival. So I retire. It is simple as that."

"Where? To Ayr? Lanark? Turnberry?"

"No. Edward could follow to any of these. But we think that he will not go so far as Stirling. There is the best battle-ground of all Scotland. So to Stirling we shall go. Lamberton keeps his Church host watching Stirling. Scrymgeour, with Wallace's people, will come there. Comyn is there. Bruce must needs go also. If a stand is to be made, it should be there. We retire to Stirling."

"Aye. That is best. And quickly."

"Tomorrow. At first light. No sleep for us this night. Nor for the townsfolk. For they must go. Flee again into the hills or Edward will visit his wrath on them. But—by God, we will play Edward's own game, this time! Sir Nicholas Segrave and his captured men go with us. And I leave a letter for the Plantagenet. Any slaughter of my people of Annandale, and Segrave hangs. With his garrison. Every one. Come—we have work to do . . ."

· · ·

The driving late-November rain blattered against the small half-shuttered windows of Torwood Castle, on the high ground above the plain of Forth, and the wind shook the doors and lifted the reeds and rushes strewn on the stone flooring of the draughty hall. Comyn had not so much as thrown off his soaking cloak, and drips from it fell on to the parchment, to the distress of the clerks, as scornfully he added the flourish of his signature to the document.

"Here's a waste of ink and paper!" he declared. "What worth in it? Think you Edward of England will pay heed to such as this? I say he will throw it on his fire!"

"Yet it will have been worth the sending, my lord—even if he does so," Lamberton insisted, stooping to append his own signature. "For it will strengthen our hands with the Holy See, and with the states of Christendom. To have said that we have made the offer of truce. See you, Edward's claim is that we are rebels. *His* lieges in rebellion. This letter makes it clear to all men that we write as the Guardians of an independent realm. After receiving this, though he may spurn it, yet he cannot say that we have accepted his overlordship—we, who act for the King of Scots."

"Bah! Clerkly havers, Sir Bishop! Words written on paper, however fine, will no more affect Edward than a fly on his sleeve. The sword, and a strong arm behind it, alone does he recognise..."

"He recognises the wrath of Almighty God, sir, with the power of Holy Church to display it!" the Primate said sternly. "He recognises His Holiness of Rome, and his spiritual powers. He is much at his devotions these days, my lord of Carrick has heard. And this offer of truce is, in fact, written as much for Pope Boniface as for Edward Plantagenet. The copy which goes to Rome may achieve more than that which goes to England. I work for the threat of excommunication."

Bruce, who had already signed the impressive parchment, spoke—but carefully addressed his words to Lamberton only. "Moreover, my lord Bishop, although Edward would wish to reject this, he may find it convenient. He is much at odds with his lords. He cannot proceed further against us meantime, without their aid. He has already returned to Berwick from Lochmaben. A truce might serve him well enough. Give him the time he needs to come to terms with his earls..."

"Aught that serves Edward well can only serve us ill," Comyn interrupted. "We are not all so concerned to please him!"

Wooden-faced, evenly Bruce went on, still looking only at the Primate. "If he *accepts* this letter, this truce, and acts on it, even to his own advantage, it is more to ours. Not only giving us time also. But it commits him to dealing with us as a sovereign kingdom, not as rebels. Here is its importance. Before all men. We loudly make it known to all Christendom. Copies to all rulers. If Edward accepts the truce, he accepts our right to make it. Yet if he does not, he will *seem* to do so. For he cannot invade us again, with any hope of success, until next spring. And until he has won round his lords. So we have him, by this. Lochmaben was but a gesture. Brief, unimportant, to save his face..."

"Is *Bruce's* face the fairer for that gesture?" Comyn barked.

"To have yielded his own castle, without a blow! To the man who paid his debts . . . !"

"God's mercy—can you see no further than your nose, man? At least I did win my siege of Lochmaben. While you sit still around Stirling!"

"My lords! Such talk is unprofitable and ill becomes you." Now that he was Guardian himself, Lamberton could and did speak with a greater authority. He picked up the parchment. "My lord of Carrick is right. This is carefully worded. Edward would be wise to read it as carefully, before he throws it in his fire!" As device to cool the suddenly risen temperature, he commenced to read the preamble:

To the Lord Edward, by God's grace king of England, by the Guardians and community of the realm of Scotland—greeting. William by divine mercy bishop of St. Andrews, Robert Bruce earl of Carrick and John Comyn the younger, Guardians of the kingdom of Scotland in the name of the famous prince the lord John, by God's grace illustrious King of Scotland, appointed by the community of that realm, together with the community of the realm itself . . .

"A spate of words! Vain puffing words!" Comyn scoffed. "Sound and repetition. To bring me from Stirling, for this!"

"Words, in affairs of state, may speak as loud as a drawn sword, my lord. We declare hereafter that King Philip of France's truce with Edward, signed at the Peace of Paris, required that all prelates, barons, knights, towns, communities and inhabitants of Scotland should be included in the truce, and all hostages given up. We declare that this clause has been broken. We therefore request King Edward to comply with these terms forthwith. To retire from Lochmaben and from Scottish soil. And to enter into a collateral truce with this realm. If he does so we are willing to desist from all aggression of England during the period stipulated." The Primate waved the parchment. "We know that he has, in fact, already withdrawn from Lochmaben Castle, though leaving an English garrison. So now he will seem to have carried out this demand. He is no longer on Scottish soil, nor like to be for six months at least. He has now wed the King of France's sister. Therefore he cannot declare the Peace of Paris void. I say that he may burn this letter—but in the eyes of the world he will seem to have heeded it. Is this not sufficient merit to bring a Guardian of Scotland eight miles from Stirling, my lord?"

Comyn shrugged, for once at a loss. But only for moments. "That is as may be," he jerked. "We shall see how tender is Edward to empty words. But . . . you have your paper and my signature. Let us have it sealed and be done. For I have more important business. At Stirling."

"What do you do at Stirling, these long months?" Bruce asked, as though interested. "Is it not something tedious? Sitting there?"

"Sitting! Who sits? Stirling is not some defenceless, decrepit hold! It is the greatest fortress in Scotland. Or England. A-top a rock four hundred feet high. But . . . I have it in my grasp now. It will not be long. Now that Edward has turned back, they will not survive. No food has reached them for five months. I promise you they will yield before the year's end. Our next meeting, I say, will be held where it ought to be. Not in this rat's-hole but in the palace of Stirling."

Without further leave-taking than that, the Lord of Badenoch stormed out of Tor Wood's hall.

His fellow-Guardians eyed each other.

"I cannot longer bear with this," Bruce said slowly. "You will have to find another Guardian for Scotland, my friend."

"And leave Comyn in power? Over you?"

"I cannot bear with him longer. You must find a way out, my lord Bishop. And quickly. Before one of us slays the other . . . !"

.   .   .

The corporate sigh that swept over the crowded Great Kirk of Rutherglen that sunny May morning of 1300 was eloquent, however disparate were the elements of which it was composed — regret, satisfaction, alarm, I-told-you-so. Men had long seen this coming, in one form or another; indeed had come to this parliament expecting no less. But the significant and ominous implications for Scotland could be lost on none.

The Earl of Carrick, standing in front of the right hand of the three Guardians' chairs set facing the nave, at the chancel steps, raised his hand for quiet. "Therefore, I say that I can no longer, in honest and good faith, serve this kingdom as Guardian. I do hereby lay down that burden and duty, to this parliament. For the better rule and governance of the realm." Turning, he bowed stiffly to Bishop Lamberton beside him, and stepped a little way apart.

The Red Comyn smiled thinly, and played with his jewelled dirk-hilt.

Heavily the Primate spoke, from the central chair. "This decision is to Scotland's loss. My lord's mind is made up, and we must needs accept it. But . . . since the Earl of Carrick remains what he is, head of the greatest house south of Forth, and an aspirant to the throne when it shall become vacant, it is, I say, inconceivable that he should be esteemed of lesser rank than the Guardians. The South-West cannot be governed lacking Bruce's aid and participation. Accordingly I move that my lord retains the style and title of a Guardian, while not actively sustaining the office. This for the benefit of all."

There was no lack of reaction to that, acclaim from the Bruce supporters and the churchmen, dissent and scowls from the opposing faction. Comyn himself did not scowl, but he did look very keenly, thoughtfully, from Lamberton to Bruce, and then flicked a hand.

"Here we are in strange case," he said. "Bruce, it seems, desires to retain the benefits of office, without the cares and responsibilities."

"What benefits?" Bruce jerked.

"Not so," Lamberton declared." It is a matter of seemliness. The Guardianship represents the throne. It is seemly that the Earl of Carrick should remain in name therein. To the greater authority of the office as a whole."

"Words again! Forms! Styles! When what the realm needs are swords. And deeds!"

"Your own party have a new nomination for such form and style, have they not, my lord?"

"Ha!" Comyn said slowly. "You would deal and chaffer, my lord Bishop! Is that it? You offer substance for this shadow? Very well. Accept Sir Ingram de Umfraville as third Joint Guardian, in Bruce's place. And my lord of Carrick may keep such style and title as pleases him!"

"I desire no such empty style," Bruce ground out. "I retire from the Guardianship. And do commend to this parliament Sir John de Soulis, Warden of the Middle March, in my place."

"Wait! Wait, I beg of you," Lamberton said, though his tone held authority rather than begging. "Here is cause for closer consideration than this. We esteem Sir John and Sir Ingram. But the status of the Guardianship is here involved. The name of an earl of Scotland should grace the office still . . ."

"It did not when Wallace was Guardian," somebody pointed out.

"Wallace was sole Guardian. And had to give it up because he lacked sufficient authority."

"My cousin of Buchan is earl, as well as Constable. And would serve suitably," Comyn observed lightly.

"No! Not that," the Lord of Crawford cried. "Two Comyns we can never accept."

There was uproar in the church.

Comyn stood up, to quell it, "I say then," he shouted, glaring menacingly around, "appoint Sir Ingram de Umfraville third Guardian, and allow the Earl of Carrick the style but not the power. And then, a God's name, have done with it! There is more important matter to decide. And to do. Edward has rejected our truce, and musters again at York. Galloway has risen in civil war. And the Earl of Carrick has done little to quell it. There is man's work to be done—not clerkly bickering over titles! Have done, I say." He sat down.

It was cleverly done, the vigorous lead of a practical soldier. Many cheered it. Yet it gave Comyn what he desired, while seeming to go along with Lamberton's suggestion. De Umfraville was a valiant and influential knight, cousin to the Earl of Angus and a kinsman of both Baliol and Comyn. He was firmly of the Comyn faction. Bruce, having word that Umfraville's name was to be put forward, had nominated Sir John de Soulis, an equally renowned warrior, Lord of Liddesdale and one of his own supporters. On a vote, with the churchmen supporting Bruce, de Soulis might have won. Now, in order to have Bruce merely retain the name of Guardian, Lamberton was seemingly bartering away the effective power. Bruce doubted the wisdom of it—although he was only too well aware of the advantages to himself of keeping equal rank with Comyn.

The thing was accepted, since most were prepared to trust Lamberton's judgement. Sir Ingram de Umfraville was appointed Guardian, and came up to the chancel to sit in Bruce's vacated chair. The other remained standing, a little way off.

Comyn was not long in showing his hand. After some formal business, he announced that the internal strife in Galloway must be put down, since it endangered the security of the realm and invited English aggression there. Stirling Castle being now in his hands, and his forces freed from that important task, he would now personally lead a campaign of pacification in Galloway. With de Umfraville, of course. And added, as a cynical afterthought.

". . . where my lord Constable has already preceded me, on a reconnaissance."

That explained the absence of the Earl of Buchan from the parliament.

Bruce stood silent. Comyn intended to take over the South-West, that was clear. Galloway had always been in the Bruce sphere of influence—although Buchan did own land there, the barony of Cruggleton. The man was utterly unscrupulous, ruthless, unrelenting. And cunning. It was not beyond him to have engineered the Galloway disturbances himself, for this very purpose. He implied that Bruce should have put down the trouble himself—when he knew only too well that Bruce's forces were spread right along the eighty miles of the borderline, watching England. And had been for six weeks.

William Lamberton looked understandingly, sympathetically, over towards the younger man, but shook a warning head.

How much could a man take?

The parliament broke up. Men had come to it fearing civil war. That it had not come to this, as yet, was to Bruce's credit. But Comyn was in the ascendant now, for all to see.

Sick at heart Bruce rode south again to rejoin his brothers commanding the long slender line that watched the Border.

Chapter Fourteen

The campaign of 1300 was all fought in Galloway and the South-West. That it reached no further was the measure of the Scots success; but it left that great area in ruins once more. The English invaded from Carlisle, on Midsummer's Day, after a delay which almost certainly was partly accounted for by the Pope's remonstrances on the rejection of the Scots truce offer, reinforced by Wallace's representations at Rome. But Edward's fears of excommunication were at length overborne by his consuming hatred of the Scots, and when he marched, he did so with a magnificent army of over 60,000. Bruce had 8,000, but they were strung along the borderline; Comyn had 15,000 in Galloway, where he had been hanging men by the score, mostly Bruce's adherents; and

Scrymgeour had the absent Wallace's people's army of some 12,000 more waiting in reserve on the north side of Forth.

Edward stormed through lower Annandale for Dumfries. Once again that fair vale became a blackened wilderness, while Bruce dared do no more than harass the English flanks and rear. Then with the early fall of Dumfries and Caerlaverock Castles, the Plantagenet turned west across Nith and entered Galloway. It seemed that he was intent on defeating the Scots in the field rather than on merely gaining territory.

In the past Comyn had talked boldly about the need to confront Edward with the chivalry of Scotland, to gain any lasting success; just as he had talked slightingly of Wallace's guerilla warfare and Bruce's caution about pitched battle, and his scorched earth strategy. But now, faced with four times his own numbers, and the huge preponderance of bowmen, he pursued similar tactics himself, and played them skilfully. He fell back deeper and deeper into Galloway, a difficult country for campaigning, cut up with great estuaries, rivers and hill ranges, extending Edward's lines of communication even further without committing himself to battle. These lines of communication Bruce made it his business to assail.

Once again the strategy paid off, although at terrible cost to the countryside involved. The proud Plantagenet, with his vast and splendid array of armoured and bannered chivalry, and corps of archers unequalled in all the world, found all food and forage burned before him, and his supply lines constantly cut behind him. He ground to a halt at Kirkcudbright. He had, out of past experience, arranged for a shadowing supply fleet to keep his army serviced from the sea; but he had not understood how shelving and shallow were the estuaries of the wide Solway Firth, and at how few points might shipping approach land.

That Edward actually agreed to parley with Comyn and Buchan, at this stage, was indication of his supply embarrassments. But the Scots proposals—the restoration of King John to his throne, a mutual non-aggression treaty, and the right of the Scots-Norman nobles to redeem their English estates from those to whom Edward had granted them—the Plantagenet brusquely brushed aside. He promised mercy, but demanded unconditional surrender.

Comyn, Buchan and Umfraville withdrew, angrily, and against the advice of many, decided to make a stand at the River Cree, near Creetown. Disaster followed, in the first pitched battle since

Falkirk. Although Comyn had chosen the mud-flats of the Cree estuary as battlefield, where Edward's heavy cavalry were at a disadvantage—indeed most knights fought on foot—the terrible host of longbowmen decimated the Scots from afar before ever a single blow was struck. It was the clothyard-shaft once more which won the day, rather than the knightly lance and sword. Themselves horseless, the Scots leaders fled across the quaking tidelands, to escape into the hills—such as did not remain lying in Cree mud.

Edward turned back to deal with Bruce. It was mid-August.

Bruce had no intention of emulating Comyn's recent folly. He drew in his harassing forces and retired before the returning English, laying waste the land as he went—very soon his own land, again. Northwards he turned, from Dumfries, up Nithsdale and through the hill passes to Carrick and the plain of Ayr, Edward pressing hard after him—a most trying retreat, but keeping at arm's length from the enemy advance-guard, burning rather than fighting. And though, at length, Edward's ships were able to supply him at the port of Irvine, it was now late in September and the English army was in a state bordering on mutiny, magnificent no longer. The road back to England lay a smoking menace behind it. Moreover, Scrymgeour had now brought a large guerilla contingent to aid Bruce, and the Church army was standing at Stirling, with Comyn, to hold the vital waist of Scotland.

Edward made a virtue of a necessity. He sent offer to Bruce of a six months' truce. This to enable him to withdraw unmolested over the burned-out terrain to England again, without serious loss from guerilla attack. Lamberton advised acceptance. It had little practical value to the Scots; but it did concede to them the status of combatants with whom the King could deal, instead of the rebels he named them. By the end of October his forces were back in their own land, save for the garrisons in such castles as Lochmaben and Roxburgh. But he swore a great oath, as he crossed the Border, that he would return and lay waste the whole of Scotland from sea to sea, and force its rebellious people into submission or death.

If Edward had little cause for satisfaction from it all, no more had the Scots. The South-West was again devastated. The only real battle fought had been a bad, almost shameful, defeat, and Comyn's military reputation had suffered seriously. If Bruce's had not, he was nevertheless becoming known as a leader who could only burn and destroy his own territories. This situation could not go on and on. And the truce, whatever status it might give them, was only until the next campaigning season.

Morale in Scotland sank low, that winter. If only Wallace would return, men sighed. If only Comyn and Bruce would cut each other's throats, others muttered. If only Lamberton was allowed to run the country unhindered, the churchmen prayed. But none of these things happened.

Lamberton was now an unhappy man, indeed. He obtained no co-operation from the other two Guardians, and most of his proposals were automatically outvoted two to one. Comyn was in his vilest frame of mind, soured by his debacle on the Cree, and for once aware of his unpopularity amongst the people. Umfraville proved to be no statesman, and completely under the younger man's influence. The government of the land sank to new low levels.

It was an open winter, fortunately. The Primate-Guardian besought the Earl of Carrick to come to his manor of Stobo, in the Forest, there to pass Yuletide with him. Bruce was concerned at the appearance of his friend, when he reached Stobo from Turnberry. He had aged grievously in these last months, and there was a strain, tension and brittleness about him unknown previously.

"This cannot continue," he told the younger man, when they were alone before a fire in the Bishop's private sanctum. "To all intents the ship of state is rudderless, drifting helpless. I can do little or nothing. The Comyns would have me out of the Guardianship—and I would thank God to be free of it! But if I go, John Comyn reigns supreme. Now. As he hopes to reign from the throne, one day. I say this would be disaster for Scotland. But ... we can no longer make pretence to work together."

Bruce nodded. "And if *you* cannot, no man can."

The other sighed. "As to that, I do not know. But *this* I know. I cannot longer continue. And even if I could, it would avail nothing. The realm drifts to ruin, calamity. And Edward waits."

"You will not relinquish the Guardianship? To Comyn!"

"I do not know. God help me—I do not know! I do not see which way to turn."

It distressed Bruce to see this man, on whom he had relied so surely, thus broken, at a loss. "The realm needs you. Desperately. There is none other. Of your stature. And Comyn alone as Guardian—for Umfraville is the merest puppet—would be disaster. No man's life would be safe. Is there no way that he may be unseated?"

"I have thought of it, day and night. But he is too powerful. Already he all but controls Scotland. I may seek to steer the ship of state, but Comyn captains it. Because he holds the sword. You should not have resigned, my friend. You must see it, now?"

"I reached my limit, with Comyn. As you now have done, it seems," Bruce said sombrely. "He wears men down as water wears a stone."

"What to do, then? In mercy's name, what to do? He is like a savage animal now. But cunning, too. Smarting from the wounds his pride received at the Cree. Judging men to hate him—as they do. But the more determined. For spirit he does not lack."

"See you—this of the Cree fight. Of his guilt, for that. Of men hating him. This may we not use? A parliament may not only appoint a Guardian—it may unseat one. Could we not so sway a parliament that it would vote Comyn down?"

Lamberton did not answer, gazing deep into the fire.

"My party is sure, in its vote. The Church will vote, in the main, as you direct. The burghs will vote as Scrymgeour, Wallace's lieutenant, says—and he hates Comyn. The Comyn faction is large, yes—but I believe, in this pass, with other men as sour as he is, it could be outvoted."

"And think you Comyn would meekly accept dismissal? Demit office and walk away? When he controls the power of the realm. Without civil war? Which God forbid! And Edward at our doors."

Bruce had risen, to pace the floor. "Not a parliament's vote then—but the *threat* of it! You say he is sore at his unpopularity. He who acts the practised soldier. He would not enjoy a parliament that called for his resignation, named him bungler, at fault at the Cree. Even craven. I say he would sooner resign than face that." ·

The Bishop looked up at him. "You think it? It may be so. Yes, it could be. But . . . he would ensure that Umfraville and another held the Guardianship. Another puppet. With himself behind them. He would never leave me as master. For he mislikes me now, as he mislikes you."

"Scarcely so, my lord, I think—scarcely! But . . . if you offered to resign also? On condition that he did. And with the threat of a vote of parliament against him. A bargain. And Umfraville too. All Guardians resign. Because of the defeat. A new man appointed. One man. Might he not accept that?"

"Aye. But who? Who would be that man? Who would serve any better?"

"De Soulis. Sir John de Soulis. Of Liddesdale. Do you not see it? He is wed to Buchan's sister, and is therefore a kinsman of Comyn's. But he is a true man. Honest, as all do know. He was one of my grandfather's auditors, when he claimed the throne. Is sound in the Bruce cause. Comyn, I think, would accept de Soulis. And I would trust him. Moreover, he is a good soldier. And coming from Liddesdale, has been fighting the English all his days."

"You think he would do it? Accept the task? As sole Guardian. Knowing the ill will, the back-stabbing, the thanklessness of it all?"

"He was prepared to do it, in May, at Rutherglen. If we both besought him . . ."

Lamberton rose. "My friend — you have at least given me hope again. It is possible. Pray God de Soulis will aid us . . ."

. . . .

By early spring John de Soulis was sole active Guardian of Scotland — but with the Guardianship now in scant repute and men looking for power elsewhere. Comyn, like Bruce, and for the same reasons, retained the style and title of Guardian. Lamberton and Umfraville did not.

Comyn, no doubt, believed that he could control de Soulis, a kinsman. But he, and the realm, found the new Guardian, an ageing, stocky, silent man, tougher than seemed probable. He refused to be bullied or frightened. Bruce gave him full support. As did Lamberton and the Church. Wallace's people also. But the Comyn's power was still the major factor in the land. They controlled all Scotland north of the Forth, save the West Highlands and the Isles, which no man could control; and increasingly demonstrated their dominance in the South also — for Comyn's last act as Guardian had been to push through the appointments of his own nominees to most of the southern sheriffdoms. Everywhere unattached and doubtful lords and barons decided that it was wise to side with Comyn. The man was behaving like commander-in-chief, almost like a king, riding the land, holding musters of arms, sitting in at sheriffs' assizes, declaring the size of levies required from each baron and knight, demanding moneys and aid from abbeys and priories. De Soulis might sit in Stirling Castle as nominal and conscientious ruler, refusing to be controlled by Comyn; but he on the other hand could by no means control Comyn, nor attempted to.

Chaos mounted in the land—the land which awaited Edward.

Bruce watched it all with a sort of sullen hopelessness. He had no 8,000 men this year, to string along the Border. His lands of Annandale and Carrick had been so devastated again that his people, as well as being as sullen and demoralised as he was himself, were scattered, huddling where they could, scratching a living for themselves, and with sickness rampant—in no state for military service, willing or unwilling. He had some hundreds under arms, mainly vassals' men from undamaged areas; but these he kept in secret places in Ettrick Forest and the Borderland hills. He had promises of contingents from his supporters, of course, lords like the Steward, Crawford, Mar and Atholl, when invasion actually was imminent. But meantime he could only watch— northwards more sharply, even, than southwards.

Even de Soulis, honest man, worried Bruce in one respect. He did all in the name of King John. The Guardians, hitherto, had issued their edicts and processes of government in their own names, although they claimed nominally to be acting on behalf of the throne. De Soulis seemed to see the position differently. He did all merely as Baliol's deputy, always using a style that gave King John himself the authority, all being signed by the Guardian only in his absence. "These letters patent be valid at our will, this ninth year of our reign, by John de Soulis, knight, Guardian of our kingdom." The new Great Seal was struck, bearing the name and title of King John on the obverse, de Soulis only on the reverse. And Wallace, it was reported from Rome, had succeeded in winning the Pope's full support for a reinstatement of Baliol as ruling monarch.

The Bruce star was far from in the ascendant.

The truce with England expired on the 21st of May—and it was known that all winter Edward had been preparing the new campaign, despite his prolonged correspondence and assurances to the Pope. He marched promptly the day afterwards, and this time brought his son north with him, Edward, Prince of Wales. The English army split into two, in Northumberland, the King heading the main drive to Berwick and the east, while his son and Surrey made for Carlisle and the west. This time the Scots were to fight on two fronts.

Bruce swiftly found himself in trouble, for Edward, after a feint northwards from Berwick, which sent a Scots force hastening to the Lammermuir passes to harry him therein, quickly turned north-westwards up Tweed. Never before had any major invasion taken this mid-country route through the Forest and the hills of the central uplands, where small numbers could so easily hold up large. But nothing could long hold up Edward's scores of thousands, and though Bruce's people contested almost every pass, river-crossing and ambush-site, they were only dealing with the English advance-guard. Edward took his time, pressing inexorably onward. Kelso, Dryburgh and Melrose Abbeys went up in flames, Selkirk fell, and then Peebles. Bruce was driven back and back into the high barren wildernesses of Tweedsmuir, where Clyde and Annan were born as well as Tweed. Then Edward paused and circled skilfully to seal off all the valley-mouths and passes out of that lofty area, turning it from a citadel into something like a vast prison. Individuals could get in and out of it, by lonely hillsides and secret burn-channels; but not large bodies of men.

It was clear that Edward, well served with spies, had set his main strategy, at this stage, against Bruce. And now Bruce, as a fighting force, was largely immobilised.

Meanwhile, the Prince of Wales and Surrey turned into Galloway, with Comyn retiring before them, risking no more pitched battles. De Soulis himself, after deciding the real lines of the English thrusts, positioned himself, with the Church army and Wallace's guerillas, between Lanark and the sea, to deny if he could the Clydesdale access to the north.

Edward seemed to be in no hurry, this time. He consolidated as he went, and once out of the Tweedsmuir hills, struck westwards, to reach the sea at Ayr and Irvine, where his fleet was standing off, with supplies. He had successfully isolated the three Scots forces, Bruce to the east, Comyn to the south and de Soulis to the north. Moreover, this time he had food and forage, arms and siege-equipment readily available from shipping.

He turned north, to besiege Bothwell Castle, the strongest hold in Clydesdale, de Soulis falling back before him. This was a new kind of campaigning for Edward. But as to its effectiveness there could be no question.

That there was something else new about it began to dawn on the Scots as the summer passed into autumn. Despite all the Plantagenet's fierce vows of vengeance earlier, there was little of mass savagery, burnings and sackings. It seemed as though he was seeking, this year, to separate the Scots leadership from the people, trying to antagonise the countryside as little as possible. Moreover, his ships were still unloading supplies in late September, when Bothwell fell, with no signs of a retiral to England. It looked very much as though Edward intended to winter in Scotland.

A new variety of apprehension settled on the land.

Bruce, in his Border hills fretted like a caged eagle. He was not idle, picking away at the English flanks, sallying here and there. But he was held and confined, almost insultingly, and kept out of touch with what went on elsewhere.

When specific news did reach the remote Blackhouse Tower, a Douglas hunting-place deep in Yarrow, which Bruce had made his headquarters, it could hardly have come with more authority — since it came, unexpectedly, by the mouth of the Primate himself. William Lamberton arrived, with only two companions, at dusk of an evening of early October, tired and raggedly-clad as a wandering friar, yet nevertheless looking a good deal less worn and haggard than when last Bruce had seen him. Apparently he found war less of a strain than dealing with John Comyn. Though his information was none the less dire, for that.

"Edward has gone to winter at Linlithgow," he told the younger man. "Aye — he bides in Scotland, to our sorrow. But he is cunning. There have been no burnings, pillagings. He is indeed *paying* for the meat, the grain and the hay he requires! So the land has not risen against him, as before. The folk are weary, helpless, hopeless, to be sure. So, with his armies holding all in check — you here, de Soulis in lower Clydesdale, Umfraville in Galloway, and Lothian and the Merse his own, he sits secure enough in Linlithgow, his ships serving him in the Forth. And in this state he now offers us truce! Of nine months, no less! Edward, magnanimous, offers Scotland truce!"

"By all the saints — truce! He invades, occupies the land, sits down, his feet on our necks — and offers truce?"

"Aye — the Plantagenet tries new tactics. It may be, with more hope of success. The truce is aimed at the Pope, and our doubtful ally the King of France, I swear. It is a gesture. But he loses nothing by it. He is well placed indeed — and this will allow him to remain so, without trouble, through the winter and spring."

"But will de Soulis accept it?"

"What else can he do? He does not know of it yet. It is noteworthy that Edward sent the proposal to *me*. At St. Andrews. As Primate. It is beneath his dignity to treat with a mere knight. He would drive wedges between us, with more than his armies!

This year of our Lord, 1301, the Englishman is being clever! I brought the word straight to you, my friend. To talk of it. Before I tell de Soulis."

"What can I do?" Penned here . . ."

"You can advise me. For, God knows, I do greatly need advice." The Bishop sighed. "De Soulis, I think, will do as I say."

"Perhaps. But Comyn? What will Comyn do? What *does* Comyn? You have not so much as named him."

"Aye—Comyn. There is the rub. Comyn, as ever, plays his own game." Lamberton glanced sidelong at his companion. "Have you heard? What he does?"

"I hear nothing here. Or little that I may trust. He is in Galloway, is he not? Fencing with Edward's son."

"He was. But is no longer. He has left Umfraville to command in Galloway, and with Buchan has slipped north, by unfrequented ways and little-known passes. He is now safe in Stirling Castle, and massing new forces north of Forth."

"Then he is doing more good than I am!"

The other stroked his chin. "That is as may be. But, on his way north, he made pause. To attack Lochmaben. He took much risk, for the Prince of Wales was not far away . . ."

"Attack Lochmaben? Comyn? Besiege the castle . . . ?"

"No siege. He burned the town."

"He burned . . . my town!" That was a whisper. "Dear God!" The other laid a hand on Bruce's arm. "He is a man consumed with hatred."

"So . . . am . . . I!"

"No. Do not say it. Hate, of all man's failings, is the least profitable. Leave hate to Comyn. It will serve him but ill."

"I shall be avenged. For Lochmaben. Nevertheless . . ."

"I think that you have more potent matters to consider than vengeance, my friend. Dealing with Comyn, as we have learned, demands not only patience but a clear head. Burning Lochmaben may have been the spleen of the man. But he threatens your interests more deeply than that."

"What do you mean? He threatens my interests with every breath he draws!"

"Aye. But now in a way we had not thought on. You know how de Soulis has been doing all in the name of King John. Acting as though Baliol still reigned and was only absent. De Soulis has done so as giving him, and the realm, the greater authority against Edward. A king against a king. This I could not contest. But now I have learned that Comyn is behind it. More than that, I have learned *why*. He seeks to have Baliol established as king again, before all. And then for him to abdicate, nominating and securing John Comyn as his successor."

This time the hissing intake of breath was all Bruce produced for reaction, although it was eloquent enough.

"Baliol is now at his family's ancient home, at Bailleul-en-Vimeu, in Picardy. In the care of Philip of France. Comyn has sent to Philip, urging that King John be sent back to Scotland. And with a French army. Forthwith."

"Philip will never do it. Edward is now his brother-in-law."

"Philip may. Wallace has been to him and much affected him. Moreover the Pope is in favour of this. And offers inducements. Wallace has convinced them both that King John should return. Wallace is honest in this. He knows naught of Comyn's plot."

Bruce was striding the small, draughty room now. "This—this then, could be the end of the Bruce claim! To the throne. The end of the Bruces themselves! For Comyn, as king, would not rest while there was one of us left alive to challenge him. This would be utter disaster."

"Disaster for more than Bruce," the Primate agreed sombrely. "Disaster for Scotland. John Comyn on the throne would be the end of more than Bruce."

"What can I do? I would seek him out and slay him with my own hands. But he will be well guarded. He is no fool . . ."

"That is not the way, no." Lamberton leaned forward. "Your father? The Lord of Annandale. He could be the answer. He is the true heir to the throne. *His* father should have been king, not Baliol. If he now would return to Scotland. Proclaim himself king. Before Baliol could come from France. If your father returned, and made such proclamation, Comyn's plot would go agley. Even though he did no more than that. Then it would be for parliament to discuss and decide. Where the Church is strong . . ."

"My father . . . ! He is but a broken reed. I do not believe he would do this."

"If you went to him? Explained. He is proud of his claim. He challenged Edward with it, at Stracathro . . ."

"How could I go to him? Held here. He is in Essex. A sick man. Done. Always he was weak, feckless. We never agreed. Think you, at this ill hour, he would heed me? Bring down Edward's wrath on his grey hairs, by claiming the throne Edward says is his!"

The older man spoke slowly. "Edward will be near as anxious as Bruce to keep Comyn from grasping the Scots throne."

His companion paused in his pacing to look at him. "What do you mean?"

"I believe that Edward, were he to hear of this plot, would be forced to think deeply. He might prefer to have your father *claiming* the throne than Comyn being given it by Baliol. See it as another way of splitting Scotland, of giving him time. He would never admit that the throne was not his own. But he might well make it possible for your father to return and make his claim. Edward would reject it forthwith—but it would keep Baliol, and his nephew Comyn, from any easy victory by such device."

Bruce stared into the flickering fire, biting his lip.

"I could see that Edward learned of it. In these truce negotiations."

"I do not know. I do not know. This is . . . too much . . . for me. To decide. I must consider."

"As must we all. For Scotland's fate is at stake. One way or the other."

"It would mean . . . working with Edward. Against Comyn."

"Put it otherwise. Say *using* Edward to save Scotland. And Bruce. From Comyn."

"You believe it is possible?"

"Who knows? But possible, yes. Perhaps more than possible. And, my good friend—how else can you stop Comyn taking the throne? Bruce's throne?"

The younger man was silent.

"Think of it, then. While I go to de Soulis. With this of the truce. Consider it well, in this hawk's nest of yours. There is a little time. Baliol and the French will not sail in winter's weather. If they sail. But—there would be much to be done before the spring . . ."

Chapter Fifteen

It was, of course, a farce of a truce—all knew it. Little more than a springboard poised for the English to resume their campaign, with maximum advantage, when weather and the state of the land were propitious. But it did offer certain advantages to the

Scots also. Preparations could be made on their side likewise; and although the English armies largely maintained their strategic positions, and sensible men gave them wide berth, people could move fairly freely about the land again.

Bruce was released from his confinement in the high Tweedsmuir section of the Forest at last, and was able not only to go and consider the strategic situation that now ruled, but the state of his properties and lands. It made a sorry prospect. All the lordship of Annandale, the earldom of Carrick and the large Bruce lands in Galloway, had been so fought over, burned and destroyed, by one side or the other, that they made little better than a wilderness. His castles of Turnberry, Annan, Loch Doon and Tibbers were largely demolished, and their towns in ruins; and all the lesser castles and towers likewise cast down. Lochmaben was still garrisoned by the English, and its town, which would have survived, as of use to the invaders, had been burned by Comyn. Bruce found that he had not a single house left fit for his habitation, in all his great domains; and his tenants and vassals were fled, scattered or dead. As a force in the land, he was all but spent.

North of the Forth, Comyn's lands were vast and untouched. He was assembling new and unwearied thousands.

Because, indeed, he had little choice of domicile for his few hundred remaining men-at-arms, Bruce continued to keep them in the Forest; though meantime he made himself a little more comfortable, at the Bishop of St. Andrews' manor of Stobo, than he could do at the remote and windy Blackhouse Tower; even though a large English force lay at Peebles, six miles away. Lamberton himself was not there. After concluding the truce, he had gone straight to France, to try to persuade King Philip not to support Comyn's plot for sending Baliol back to Scotland.

It was from the direction of Peebles that, one grey day in mid-January 1302, with Tweed running thick and brown from melting snows, Bruce's watchers brough him word that a small English party was approaching Stobo; some great man, with esquires, clerks and a score of armed guards, riding with quiet confidence.

The visitor proved to be none other than Sir John de St. John, newly appointed English Warden of Annandale and Galloway, and one of Edward's closest aides. A dignified, handsome, courteous man of middle years, richly dressed, he was almost necessarily soldier as well as courtier, a veteran of the French wars and the man sent by Edward to deputise for the Earl of Fife, whose right it had been to seat John Baliol on the Stone of Destiny at his crowning at Scone, nine years before. Bruce knew him, and liked him better than most of the Plantagenet's entourage—even though he came as usurping master of Bruce's own territories.

St. John made it clear that, for this visit, he would prefer that his nominal position *vis-à-vis* Annandale, Carrick and Galloway, should be ignored.

"I have come, my lord, directly and secretly, from His Majesty," he declared when they were alone. "King Edward sends you greetings and goodwill. Notable goodwill, considering all that has transpired, I may say!"

"Indeed?" his host observed, grimly. "That I will believe when I hear what else you bring, Sir John!"

The other smiled thinly. "You are sceptical. But my master can be generous and far-seeing. I believe that he is being both, in this. He has always esteemed you, as you know well. Even though he has had to move against you, on occasion. And not without cause, you will concede."

"I concede nothing, Sir John. Save that your master is a hard and crafty tyrant, a cruel invader and usurper, who has devastated this land time and again. And *my* lands. Left me nothing but my name. And a modicum of wits. What does he want now?"

"These words are extreme and foolish, my lord. I had hoped, as had the King, that you might have learned to use those wits to guard your tongue. However, as far as I am concerned, they have not been spoken. You have suffered greatly, yes, in a mistaken cause. You have been cheated and cozened and used, yes—but not by His Majesty. The King believes that it is time that you returned to his peace."

"Ha! Edward's peace! Say Edward's maw, his slavery, rather. Is this his generosity?"

St. John was patient. "The King was your friend once. He believes that he could be your friend again. Better, a deal better, than many with whom you have been working. Trusting. The Lord of Badenoch, for instance."

"M'mmm. I have not trusted the Lord of Badenoch for some time!"

"As well! He does not love you. He aspires to the Scots throne. And is willing to do anything to gain it. *Anything*, I say. He cannot do so, of course, since that throne is now united with that of England. But he will try. And since he sees you as an obstacle, you will suffer, my lord."

"You are tender for my interests, sir."

"I am not. But the King is."

"Why?"

"He has not lost all his love for the Earl of Carrick. And he has never loved John Comyn."

"So he would use me to bring down the other? And so preserve for him the stolen throne of Scotland!"

"I say that you judge harshly. And foolishly. Since you have not heard what the King proposes."

"Then tell me."

"The King offers you a return to his peace. With all offences absolved and forgotten. He promises to consider well your advice on all Scottish problems. Indeed to set you over much of his realm here, if so you would have it. He offers compensation for your lands destroyed in war. Maintenance from his privy purse while your fortunes recover. Freedom from disinheritance of any lands which my lord your father may leave you in England. Permission to visit your father . . ."

"Ha! Now why should Edward, in his goodness, offer me that?"

"Your father is ailing. An old and sick man. You would wish to see him. Possibly to bring him back to Scotland. To be under your closer regard."

"Aye. No doubt. His Majesty is . . . thoughtful."

"He offers that if any rights of yours, or your father's be brought in dispute by the Lord of Badenoch, or others, you shall have justice in His Majesty's own courts."

Bruce looked up sharply. "Rights? Which rights, Sir John?"

"The King did not specify which. His words were 'any rights'."

"I would remind you that my father claims rights—indeed sole rights—in the Scots crown!"

"Claims, yes. That fact is known to the King. After all, he judged against your grandsire's claims, nine years past."

"I see. So that is the sort of justice we would get in His Majesty's courts!"

"Justice is justice. A hearing you would receive. Any rights, His Majesty said. And you have others that may be threatened, have you not? Your very earldom of Carrick? The lordship of Annandale? John Comyn would deprive you of these, if he could."

"Perhaps. But might find it difficult!" The younger man

shrugged. "But why does King Edward send you to offer all this. So long a list of graciousness! He must greatly desire me in his peace. Why?"

"I am his servant, my lord—not his confessor. He does not open all of his mind to me. But this is his will. And he thinks kindly of you still."

"I take leave to doubt it . . ."

"Before you do so, here is token of it. He would have you to wed the daughter of his closest friend. The Lady Elizabeth de Burgh."

"God in His heaven! Again?"

"Yes, my lord. And the fair lady herself sends you warm greetings. And hopes that she may see you. Soon."

"See . . . ? She is here? In Scotland?"

"The Queen is come to join the King, at Linlithgow. And the Lady Elizabeth with her."

Bruce turned away, too disturbed to risk speech.

St. John tactfully went to warm his hands at the fire. Over his shoulder, he went on. "One last token of the King's goodwill. He would grant you the wardship and marriage of the young Earl of Mar."

"Eh? Wardship? What do you mean?" Surprised out of his emotion, Bruce looked round. "You have mistaken, sir. Mar is my sister's husband. And is older than I am."

It was the Englishman's turn to show surprise. "*Is*, my lord? Do not tell me that you did not know? Gartnait, Earl of Mar, is dead. Slain in a tussle with Comyns. In his own country."

"By the Mass! Gartnait dead? Slain? And by the Comyns . . . !"

"We believed that you would know of it." St. John coughed. "It is . . . regrettable. But—by granting you the wardship of your nephew, the Earl Donald, my lord, the King gives you in effect another earldom. Mar as well as Carrick. Until the lad is of age. And an earldom in the North. Adjoining Comyn's country! You have a lordship up there, do you not? The Garioch. Mar could serve you notably well."

Bruce required no such reminders. Mar was a great and ancient earldom which Gartnait, gentle man, had never exploited. The wardship of its heir, so long as Edward dominated Scotland, was a potentially powerful weapon.

"Edward must require my services greatly!" he said slowly.

"A mistaken view, my lord. His Majesty can achieve all, master Comyn, and Scotland, without Bruce. But can Bruce now achieve *anything* without King Edward? I urge that you consider it. Consider it well. I return to Peebles. And shall come again tomorrow. For your decision. I hope, my lord, that it will be to conduct you to Linlithgow." St. John paused, clearing his throat. "The Lady Elizabeth said to give you this last word. A wise rebel, she said, knows what to rebel against. That is all. She believed that you would understand. And that she would see you at Linlithgow."

.   .   .

Two days later Robert Bruce, with Sir John de St. John, rode down into the West Lothian plain of the Forth, to the vast armed camp surrounding the red-brown castle on its green hill above the wide loch. He scarcely recognised the place. A whole new wooden city had been erected in régimented lanes and streets to house an army and its followers and horses, through a Scots winter. Great lumber-trains were in constant passage to and from the same Tor Wood, above Falkirk, where Bruce had rescued William Wallace three years before.

St. John had sent word ahead, of their coming, and King Edward had evidently decided to make the most of the occasion. He sent the Scots Earl of March and Dunbar, who all along had sided with the English, along with the Earl of Ulster and Bishop Anthony Beck of Durham, to meet the newcomers and conduct them through the drawn-up lines of much of the army, from which a succession of fanfares of trumpets greeted them. A resplendent corridor of over 200 mounted knights in full armour and heraldic surcoats flanked their climb up the castle-hill; and before the arched courtyard entrance Edward Longshanks himself, despite the inclement weather and threatening rain, stood awaiting them, a massive and magnificent figure, backed by much of his Court. It was a welcome fit for a king.

Edward did not actually open his arms to Bruce, but his greeting was otherwise as for the prodigal son. He hailed him genially, gripped his hand and patted his shoulder.

"Robert, my young friend!" he cried. "Here is a happy day, which has been too long in dawning. I rejoice to see you. To welcome you back into my peace."

The other did not trust himself to speak. He bowed stiffly, and less low than he might have done. The King did not let him withdraw his hand.

"These years I have missed you, boy," Edward declared jovially. "Hard years, and you have suffered. But you have grown a man, I think. Learned your lesson in a hard school. But that is all done with, now."

"I am glad to hear you say it, Sire. Since you were the teacher!"

"Ha! And you will thank me for that teaching. You will see. Sir John—I thank you for your good offices. The Earl of Carrick will have cause to thank you also. Come, now—the Queen would meet you . . ."

Linking arms with the younger man, Edward led him slowly through the bowing ranks of the gaily-dressed crowd, pausing here and there to exchange an affable word with earl, bishop or lord. Bruce went uncomfortably—and not only for the difficulty of matching his pace to that of the extraordinarily long legs of the monarch; his suspicion and wariness was like an armour about him. This was not the Edward Plantagenet he knew.

Linlithgow Castle was a palace rather than a fortress, and now it was thronged as never before. In a lesser hall where two great log fires blazed, Queen Margaret sat with her ladies, at needlework, while a minstrel sang softly to the languid pluckings of a lute, from a deep window-embrasure. Fine tapestries and hangings covered stone walls which undoubtedly had been bare until recently, and the floor was thickly strewn with skins.

Bruce, his arm still in the royal grasp, bowed; but his glance was only momentarily on the Queen's narrow, keen features, before sliding off round the room. He found Elizabeth by a far door, and their eyes met, and held, for seconds. Then, almost imperceptibly, she shook her head and looked towards the Queen. He nodded, as briefly, and bowed again.

"Your Majesty," he said

"So here is the Lord Robert, of whom all speak," Margaret of France exclaimed. "Come to grace our Court at last. You have been long in coming, my lord."

Philip the Fair's sister was less beauteous than her brother, but she was almost certainly a stronger character. A pale, thin, almost gaunt woman in her mid-thirties, over-dressed, she had fine eyes, though darting, shrewd. Edward Plantagenet, in his late years, might have acquired a tartar.

"Had I known of your fair presence, Majesty, I might have come the sooner." It was a long time since Robert Bruce had made that sort of remark.

"La—a flatterer! They did not tell me that you were that. Come, and let me judge if that is all you are!" She held out a slender hand for him to kiss.

"Robert once was one of the gayest of my train, my love," Edward said. "He has a sober look to him, these days. Perhaps we will cure him of it, eh?"

"I scarce think *you* will, Sire. But I may. With a little help . . . from others!" The Queen raised her voice. "Elizabeth! Where are you hiding, girl?"

The idea of Elizabeth de Burgh hiding anywhere was sufficiently bizarre to bring smiles to most faces. She came forward unhurriedly, head held high, a striking, proud beauty, aware of her own potency. Her blue eyes looked directly at none of them.

"You two are old friends, are you not?" the Queen said.

"I have met my lord," Elizabeth acceded, coolly.

The King chuckled. "They were near affianced once. And might be again!"

"In Your Majesty's mind," the girl gave back evenly. "And to other lords, likewise."

Edward's smile faded for a moment, and then returned. "Say that my Majesty's mind is ever heedful for your welfare, lass," he said. "Eh, Dickon?"

Richard, Earl of Ulster, who had followed them in, inclined his handsome head, but did not otherwise commit himself—though he eyed his daughter sidelong.

Queen Margaret's quick eyes were busy all around. "You, my lord?" she said to Bruce. "How goes your flattery now?"

"I flatter none. Your Majesty, or other," he answered, taking his cue from the girl. "I admire the Lady Elizabeth. Who would not? But I would not presume to claim close friendship."

"You are cautious, sir. I am disappointed. I mislike cautious men!"

"I have need to be cautious, Madam. My first meeting with this lady, I tipped her out of her litter. She named me witless dolt. And . . . and masterful ape! I think she has not forgotten. Nor, i' faith, have I!"

"So!" Intrigued, the Queen was all eagerness, looking from one to the other. Bruce perceived that he had probably overdone it. "You did not tell me, Elizabeth. Shame on you! Here is a notable tale! Tipped you from a litter? How long ago? It is years since you have seen him, is it not? And you have thought of it still? And he . . . !"

Bruce had not anticipated being grateful to Edward Plantagenet; but that paladin did not enjoy being in less than the centre of the stage for long, and intervened now.

"You must have mercy on the Lord Robert, my dear. He has ridden far. Sir John will conduct him to his chamber, and refreshment. That he may the better grace our table. We eat, lad, within the hour . . ." The royal gesture to St. John was not to be mistaken.

At the banquet which followed, Bruce was given the place of honour—which did little to calm the turmoil of his mind. He sat between Edward and his son—which at least meant that he was spared close inquisition by the Queen, who sat on the monarch's left. Edward of Carnarvon, Prince of Wales, had grown from boy into young man since last Bruce had seen him and proved to be a secret-faced, diffident youth of eighteen, who all the time kept a wary eye on his father—as well he might. Bruce found little to say to him. He had had no opportunity for a private word with Elizabeth—and now she was seated at some distance, with so many great lords and prelates requiring precedence. Her father was on the Prince's left hand, and Lancaster, holder of five earldoms, on the Queen's right.

Edward remained amiable, almost alarmingly so, pressing food and drink on his guest. So far there had been no hint of reproach, much less condemnation. Nor was there any hint of what was behind this change of front, what the Plantagenet required from him. That it did not all proceed from the essential kindness of his heart, Bruce had little doubt.

At length, when the meal had progressed to the stage of picking, toying and drinking, with entertainment from tumblers, jesters and musicians, the younger man was driven to direct questioning. "Sire," he said "you have brought me here for good purpose, I have no doubt. What do you require of me?"

The other looked at him as though astonished. "Why, Robert —your good company and presence. Your love and leal esteem. What else? Is that so strange?"

"You have been fighting me, hunting me, burning my lands, taking my castles. I see little of love and esteem in that. Why have you changed?"

"Because circumstances have changed, boy. Then we were at war, and you chose to go against me, to my sorrow. Now there is truce. I hold this land, South Scotland, in my hand. And shall soon hold the North. All is changed. You have lost much. No longer is your insurrection any threat to my peace. I may allow my natural affection for you to prevail. Did not Sir John tell you all this? Is it not proven by my tokens of goodwill offered?"

"I conceived there to be something more, Sire. Your Majesty is namely for hard bargaining!"

"You say so? But, that is when I am fighting. When I have won, it is otherwise. Think you I cannot be magnanimous?"

"You believe that you have won, then?"

"Should I not? I sit here in Linlithgow's hall, secure. My armies straddle the land."

"There is a deal of Scotland north of Forth."

"No doubt. But I have conquered it before. And can do again, if need be. It is my hope that I shall not have to."

"The North will not yield tamely. If that is what you hope."

"You think not? But . . . *you* have yielded, have you not?"

"No, Sire. I have not yielded."

"No?" Edward turned in his great chair, to eye the younger man wonderingly. "Do my eyes, my wits, fail me?"

"I came under the safe conduct of an honourable man, Sire. Sir John de St. John. Who vowed, in your royal name, that I could turn and go again, freely, should so I decide. I came, in time of signed truce, to discover your mind. Further to what St. John told me. Is that yielding?"

The King toyed with his goblet, narrow-eyed. "But you came, my young friend—you came!" he said softly.

"I came, yes. But I did not bring my brothers, Sire! If by mischance I am prevented from returning to them, there are four of them still to head the Bruce power!"

"What Bruce power?"

The other took a quick breath, but was silent, biting his lip.

"Let us not misjudge, my young friend," Edward said, then. "Between power and love. Esteem. You have no power. None left. But my esteem and love can raise you again. High. High as you must needs be if you are to counter John Comyn." He paused. "Let us look reality in the face, Robert. It has ever been my custom."

"I have, perhaps, more power left than you believe."

"I think not. I have made shift to discover. Your earldom of Carrick lies shattered and occupied by my forces. Your father's lordship of Annandale is a blackened waste. As are the Bruce lands in Galloway. You have less than three hundred men, hiding like outlaws in Ettrick Forest. That is your strength and power, Robert. A notable heritage squandered."

"Squandered . . . ! You are well informed, Sire. But have you forgot? I have friends, allies, kinsmen. As well as brothers."

"Most in little better state than you are! How many would give what they have left to aid one so weak as the Earl of Carrick? Weak, that is, today. Tomorrow you could be strong again. For you have a better friend than any of these, lad. You have Edward of England for friend."

Bruce said nothing.

"This matter of the earldom of Mar. The late lord was your brother-in-law twice over, was he not? Your sister's husband, and your wife's brother? Control of the heir and his inheritance, until he is of age, could greatly aid you."

"And will. I am my nephew's closest kinsman."

"If I grant you that control. The wardship of all earls who are minors is in the gift of the Crown."

That was true only if Edward was King of Scots. But this was no time to debate that assumption.

The Plantagenet did not give opportunity, anyway. "There are three great royal properties, hunting-forests, bordering on the Mar earldom. Each with strong castles. Kintore, Darnaway and Longmorn. At present keeperless. The man who held those, with Mar and the Garioch, would be a force in the North, indeed. Comyn's country."

Bruce still made no comment.

"I make a progress up to those parts in a few months, sword sheathed or sword drawn. When the weather opens. Think on it, Robert. Think on it." Abruptly the monarch pushed back his great chair, and rose. All men hastily rose after him. "My dear," he said to the Queen, "we retire. You will be tired. Come." He held out his arm. Edward of England had had enough of being pleasant for one evening.

Bruce looked ruefully after the hastening ladies. Elizabeth de Burgh was the only one who was not tripping and scurrying. But even she had had time for only a single significant glance at him, in passing.

* * *

It was fully two hours later, with Bruce preparing for bed in the small tower room which he had been allocated—eloquent of his present prestige, as sole occupant, in the overcrowded palace where great men were sharing rooms—when a tapping at the door announced a slender, pale and pimply youth, a walking clothes-horse of magnificence, who introduced himself as Harry Percy, a page of Her Majesty, and son of Northumberland. He came from the Lady Elizabeth de Burgh, he declared in a dramatic whisper. Would the lord Earl accompany him? But discreetly, very discreetly. And to wear a cloak.

While declining actually to tip-toe after this chinless apparition who was the Lord Henry Percy's son and heir, Bruce did follow him, intrigued. He was led down a winding back stairway, across a cluttered yard where wine-barrels were stacked, through a range of stabling to the outer-bailey, and then by a postern gate, where an armed guard looked the other way, stamping his feet with the cold. Thereafter, down a grassy hillside path of a pleasance garden, they came to the shore of Linlithgow Loch. Here a skiff lay, dipping to the babble of the black water. Harry Percy pointed.

"The island, my lord," he breathed. "You can just see it." And with elaborate caution, like a stealthy crane, he paced back whence he had come.

Bruce seated himself in the boat, and took up the light oars.

The island was nearer and smaller than it had seemed in the darkness, a mere couple of hundred yards from the shore. It was probably no more than an acre in extent, grown with ornamental trees and bushes. There was a little jetty, with rustic steps and rail. Here a dark cloaked figure stood.

"Come, my lord. And haste you. For it is plaguey cold!" Elizabeth greeted him. She held out a hand to aid him ashore.

He said nothing, was in no state for eloquence. But he hung on to that hand.

"This way," she directed, leading him along a narrow path through dripping bushes. "You were sufficiently discreet, I hope?"

"Discreet . . . !" he croaked. "*You* speak of discretion!"

Her tinkle of laughter sounded amused, at least.

A more solid blackness loomed before them, a building of some sort. She drew him inside, and closed the door.

"It is a bower. A summer bower, fashioned like a grotto," she explained. "More comfortable in summer than now, I fear. But at least here we may speak alone. We are safe." She disengaged her hand.

It was Bruce's turn to jerk a short laugh. "I can think of few women who would bring a man to such a place, in the night, and then declare that they were safe!"

"Why, sir—am I mistaken in you?" She did not sound really alarmed.

"That I do not know. But . . . I am a man, you'll mind, Elizabeth!"

"But a cautious man. Did not the Queen say so?"

He sensed the smile behind the words, though he could not see it. He could see only the vague cloaked shape of her—but he was very conscious of her woman's presence, her nearness, in that confined space.

"I would not say that caution has been my guide in life, till this," he told her, a little breathlessly. "Any more than yours, I think."

"I have been sufficiently cautious where *you* have been concerned, at least. Have I not? Until now, perhaps."

"Elizabeth—you have been kind, most kind. Your letters—I do not know how I would have done lacking them. They saved my reason, I think. Apart from the word of Edward's plans, which so greatly aided me. For that, I thank you. But the letters . . . their words, their warm, kind words. I have read them and read them. I carry them always. Indeed I have them here, in my doublet now . . ."

"Then that is very foolish of you, sir! I believed you to have burned them. For my name is on them. If they fell into wrong hands, were shown to the King . . . ! Besides, I would not have thought it of you. Of Bruce, Lord of Carrick, who was Guardian of Scotland. A warrior, a man above such soft toyings. No callow youth—indeed, a married man, with a daughter . . ."

"A man who needs a woman the more, then."

"Ha! A woman? But Bruce can have any woman. Almost! Can he not? Can have many women. Lord of great possessions. Of men—and of women! He needs not to cherish poor paper and ink to his bosom."

"No," he said. His hands reached out to grasp her arms, through the cloak. "No. Not now."

She did not draw away from him; but nor did she come closer. "You have not forgot that I named you witless dolt. And masterful ape!"

"No," he agreed. "Nor ever shall." He pulled her to him, his lips seeking her face in the hooded cloak.

The young woman turned her face away a little, so that his lips met only the damp fur-trimmed broadcloth. "My Lord Robert," she objected, "if a woman you so greatly need, perhaps I might even find one for you. There are many at this Court who would serve you willingly, even hotly, I swear! For myself, I am . . . otherwise."

"What do you mean? Otherwise?"

"I am no . . . serving-woman, sir. I am Elizabeth de Burgh."

"You think I do not know it, woman? Think you I would be thus with any other? It is Elizabeth de Burgh I want, have ached and pined for, have dreamed of, sought and awaited. Aye, and prayed for. All these years. You—your beauty and proud spirit. Your adorable person and comeliness." He had pushed aside her hood now, and was gasping this into her hair and against her ear, her soft turned cheek.

"So it is *my* body you want, my Lord Robert? Not just any woman's. Here is advance . . . !"

"Aye, your body, girl. But your love, also. Your love, your heart . . ."

"Ah, but love is a different matter." She turned to face him again, but held her head well back, almost pushing from him, as though she would search his face there in the darkness. "Love is not just hot desire. Such as I can feel in you. As I have felt in other men. The heart is more than the body . . ."

"Do I not know it! My heart has beat for you, and only you, for long grievous years. My body longed for yours, yes. But the body that holds your heart, my love. I want, desire, need both. My love for you has been eating me up. These many, many months. When I despaired ever to see you again. Yet still loved and hoped. And now—to have you, hold you, here! It is more than flesh and blood can stand . . ."

"Ah, Robert—so it *is* love! Then, my dear, I yield. Sweet God, I yield me!" Suddenly, fiercely, she was pressing forward, against him. "And, save us—I conceive your flesh and blood to be standing very well, my heart . . . !" she got out, before his mouth closed on hers, and their lips and tongues found greater eloquence than in forming foolish words.

The man's hands were almost as busy as his mouth—nor were the girl's totally inactive, either. He shrugged his own cloak to the floor, and hers quickly followed it. Then he was tugging at her gown, while still he all but devoured her with his kissing. Her defter touch came to aid him, and the taffeta fell away from her shoulders. The pale glimmer of her white body was all that he could see, but his urgent fingers groped and stroked and kneaded the smooth, warm, rounded flesh of her, serving him almost better than his eyes, her nobly full, firm breasts filling the ecstatic cups of his hands to overflowing, as they overflowed the cup of his delight.

Suddenly he was down, kneeling, his lips leaving hers to seek those proud, thrusting breasts, the exultant nipples reacting with their own life and vigour. She bent over him, crooning into his hair, her strong arms clasping him to her, rocking.

But their need was a living, growing thing, a progression, and quickly even this bliss was insufficient. He drew her down to him, pulling at the gown's folds which a golden girdle held around her waist; and willingly she came, loosening it. The spread cloaks on the floor received them, and with swift, sure co-operation she disposed herself, guiding his clamant manhood and receiving him into her vital generosity.

The man fought with himself to control the hot tide of his passion, to give her time. Blessedly she required but little, and together their rapturous ardour mounted and soared to the high, unbearable apex of fulfilment. With blinding, blazing release, and a woman's cry of sheer triumph, they yielded themselves in simultaneous surrender into the basic, elemental oneness, a profundity of satisfaction hitherto unknown to either.

So they lay there in the darkness, in blessed quiet and joyful exhaustion.

Presently Elizabeth spoke, murmurously, stroking the man's sweat-damp hair. "To think . . . that I . . . was cold!"

"Cold? You!" His speech was a little slurred. "My adored and adorable. My heart and soul. My joy. My, my woman!"

"Your woman, yes. And my man. *Mine*, Robert Bruce!"

"Aye. Yours. It had to be. From the first. Elizabeth." He turned her name over from slack lips, savouring it. "Elizabeth, my Elizabeth. You gave yourself as you do all else, my Elizabeth. With all your heart. And person. No laggard, sluggard lover!"

"You think me bold? Shameless? Unwomanly?"

"Bold, yes. Shameless, yes. For where is cause for shame? And were you not bold, brave, strong, a woman of your own mind, you would not be Elizabeth de Burgh of Ulster. But unwomanly . . . I' faith, my dear, could there be anything more womanly than this, in all creation? I swear not." And he ran strong, possessive, enquiring hands over all her rich voluptuousness, lingering, pressing, probing. "Woman!" he sighed, burying his face between her breasts.

"This body, yes. Oh, yes—that is woman. But I at times wonder whether I am sufficiently woman in my spirit. My father declares me more man than my brother! Perhaps I think too like a man. Have a man's passions . . ."

He chuckled. "As you have just shown me?"

"Even so, it may be. In that I *joyed* in it, so! Is that not the man's part? Is not the woman said to be the giver? The man the taker? I . . . I take, I fear. As much as I give!"

"Aye, you took me into yourself with a right goodwill, lass, I'll not dispute!" He grinned, kissing and fondling, "As woman. All woman. Taking me, and giving yourself, in most female fashion, by all the powers!"

"There is a difference. Between taking and giving. In this. I cannot take without giving. But—I cannot give without taking. Some women can, must. I cannot. I am taking you, my heart, my man. Mine! I warn you—mine! Elizabeth de Burgh shares with none."

"Jealous, is it? A jealous woman?"

"Aye. Jealous. In some things, I fear. In this. In you."

"So! I must not look at another woman? I am bound hereafter by these fair chains?" He twisted a coil of her yellow hair round his fingers.

"Since you are a man, you will look, yes. Well I know it. You may look. Touch. Play with. Who knows, even lie with. This I could bear. Even laugh at, I think. But—should you ever give your *heart* to another. Take it from me. Then I would not forgive. Or accept. I would leave you. I might . . . I might kill you! So beware, Robert de Bruce! Think well."

"How can I think well, woman? With your nakedness filling my arms! Think any way? You bludgeon my poor wits. These— how may a man think with such as these stirring, pushing, belabouring him?"

"Shall I cover them, then? It grows cold, perhaps. It must be cold, though I feel it not . . ."

"No. Of a mercy—no covering! Not yet. Not yet a long while. The night is young. And we have waited long. So long. At least, I have. You—can it be that you have loved me also? Wished for me? These years?"

"Witless one, indeed! Think you I would be here now, otherwise? Think you I write such letters to *any* man in need? Why think you I resisted all the King's schemes to marry me to others? Worked on my father to oppose him in this . . .?"

"And I did not know it! I believed that you might think a little kindly of me, yes. When you wrote so. And when last we met, and parted. But never this . . ."

"You would not have had me to declare my love, sirrah? Before you did? Bold I maybe, but scarce so brazen. Though, mercy on us, few might agree! If they could see me lying bare as the day I was born, in a man's arms. On this island. Waiting. Waiting for . . ."

"Aye, waiting. For the man to become a man again! As he will, my love—I promise you! You aiding him! You know men, I think? How it is with men. That is clear . . ."

"You mean that I am no shy virgin? Does it trouble you?"

"No. Not so . . ."

"Few girls grow to womanhood in war-rent Ireland and remain virgin. Even de Burgh's daughter. In especial, de Burgh's daughter, it may be! For I was not of the shrinking sort, I fear. And I have managed my father's household since I was fifteen, played the countess since my mother died. But, if I am less than chaste, Robert, I am no harlot. Many men would have me. But I have known none since I saw you that day on the road to Berwick. When you unseated me. Overturned me, in more than my litter . . .!"

"My dear—you shame me. For *I* have been less, less constant. Lacking you. Scarce believing that I should ever have you. I am not so enamoured of virginity. In woman or man. Any mouse, any craven, can be a virgin. You, I would not expect to be. Nor wish. Although, see you, once you are my wife . . .!"

"Wife? Then you would wed me, my lord?" That came a little more quickly than what had gone before.

"What else, woman? Elizabeth de Burgh lies thus, and asks?"

"Elizabeth de Burgh loves. And gives. And takes. But . . . marriage. That is other. That is what King Edward desires. Now. You may not wish to seem to humour him?"

"Aye. Edward would use us, no doubt. We must see that he does not. Or only insofar as it serve *us*."

"That is why I was cool to you. Before the Queen. I would not have you *forced* into marrying me! I have that much pride . . ."

"And a little more, I think. But forced into marrying me you will be! By myself! By you. None other. If you will have me?

For not only do I greatly love you, Elizabeth, my heart. But I need you by my side. Always. Will you wed the ruined Earl of Carrick, Ulster's daughter?"

She ran her fingers lightly over his face. "Perhaps I might. Indeed, I feel wed to you now. This, it may be, is our true marriage. Yes, Elizabeth de Burgh will wed Robert de Bruce. And hold him fast. Till death do them part." She shivered.

He made to draw the cloaks and clothing closer about them.

"It was not cold," she said. "It was a sort of joy."

"Joy?" Suddenly he was sombre, lying there. "I fear that being wife to Robert Bruce will not be all joy. I am scarce the sort of husband to offer you peace and comfort, lass. I was born to trouble, I think. I have lived with it for long. And see scant signs of betterment ahead. Whatever Edward promises . . ."

"Am I one to shirk trouble, think you? Ulster's daughter?"

"No. No, I think not."

"And Ulster's daughter can bring the Earl of Carrick more than her heart and body. My father is the greatest lord in Ireland. He can field more gallowglasses than any man in all Scotland. He is rich, with a score of castles, and manors by the hundred. My dowry will not be scanty. And, allied to Ulster, Bruce will not be weakened."

"Aye. This I have not failed to think on. But . . . Edward must have thought of it also. And your father is his closest friend."

"Close, but not servile. He has opposed the King many times. Is indeed well placed to do so. He is no man's puppet."

"Yet I swear that Edward believes this match to *his* benefit."

"He can make mistakes. He has made many. He misjudges your coming to Linlithgow, does he not?"

"That is my hope. But—who knows? Edward is . . . Edward. He is no fool. I am at a loss to know what he plans for me. Not only in this of the marriage. It is strange. He gets me here, offering great things. Many things. To my advantage. And when I am at my lowest. Least danger to him. Apparently forgiving all my rebellion. Why? It is not like him. He would use me against Comyn, of course . . ."

"Yes. I think that he sees you as the best way of dividing Scotland. So my father believes. If he is to keep Scotland down, without each year having to come campaigning in war, he must keep the Scots divided against themselves . . ."

"Always we are that, by the Rude! Without Edward's aid!"

"Perhaps. But that means that one side must not *win* in this struggle. For if it does, the land will be united behind the winner. At this present, your enemy Comyn grows too strong. Matters have gone his way, while you have suffered and lost ground. So Edward would build you up again. Lest all men flock to Comyn. Who, it is said, would try for the throne. This above all must be stopped. The King would even make you Governor of Scotland, I think. *His* governor. Or so says the Queen. But, get you too strong, in turn; let Comyn be brought low—and he will bring *you* down. It is simple. He has come to know the Scots. How you ever fight amongst yourselves. So he uses you."

"Aye. It could be that. But, offering so much? You, in marriage. Why so much?"

"He is a strange man. I believe that he has a true fondness for you. Of a sort. He would bind you to him if he could. If you would play his game, he would cherish you, I think. But you would wholly have to accept his rule of Scotland."

"That I will never do. I am Bruce."

"He still must believe that he can win you, bribe you, frighten you, hold you. He will work on you, seek to mould you, as a potter moulds his clay. Use you and mould you."

"I am no clay to be moulded. I will watch him always. Like a hawk. And seek to use *him*. Make him win Scotland for me! With your help, my dear."

"So you stay? Here, with Edward. In what he calls his peace?"

"So long as I may. With profit. And you, my wife. Is that not what you would wish? Why you sent the message that I should come? By St. John."

"It is, yes. But—there are dangers in it. For you. Let the King once suspect that you are but waiting to turn against him, and he will be ruthless. Without mercy. However fond he may seem."

"I know it. And you? What of you? If you are my wife?"

"I shall be Elizabeth de Bruce," she said simply.

"Aye, bless you. But it could be to your grievous hurt. What would *you* have me to do?"

"I would have you to be what you are. To do what you must. I do not like puppets. That dance to any man's strings. Or woman's!"

"Or woman's . . .? I think, my love . . . that I am prepared . . . to dance! Now. To your string, again . . .!" His voice had gone thick, husky.

She gurgled willing laughter. Affairs of state and dynastics went down before the assault of still more elemental forces.

*   *   *

They were wed within the month, in the handsome Church of St. Michael, which shared the green hill with Linlithgow Castle, in ceremonial and magnificence seldom seen in Scotland — all at the King's own planning and expense. Edward himself aiding her father to lead the bride to the altar. Old Bishop Wishart of Glasgow officiated, assisted, of all men, by Bishop Beck of Durham — Bruce acceding with a sort of grim forbearance which he was coming to wear like a garment. He would have wished his friend William Lamberton to have married them, but the Primate was still in France; anyway, Edward might not have permitted it in a protégé of Wallace. For, whatever else he might be prepared to wink at meantime, he would not countenance the man Wallace as other than a low-born outlaw. No fewer than fifteen earls attended, and the King may have rubbed his hands that four of them were Scots who had fought against him — Atholl, Lennox, Menteith and Strathearn — this not counting the child Earl of Mar who acted page to his uncle. James the Steward was there, with his lady, Egidia de Burgh, sister of Ulster. Also many of the sore-battered lords of Bruce's party. Of the other faction, needless to say, none came or were invited. It was noticeable that few Scots churchmen graced the occasion; less so that none of Wallace's people came.

Seldom can there have been a marriage so politically contrived, where bride and groom co-operated so satisfactorily.

PART THREE

Chapter Sixteen

Spring came a deal earlier and more kindly to Southern England than it ever did to Scotland, Bruce noted. Already, in March, there was a lightness in the air, a stirring in the woodlands and copses, and a trilling of larks above the rich Essex plain, such as would not be seen in Scotland for a month yet. It was the first spring that he had ever spent in the fair, fat English countryside, despite the presence of Bruce properties here, and he savoured all with a sort of rueful appreciation, all the signs of peace and security, of wealth and ease and genial living that he saw around him. Rueful, for settled and assured as it was, it was all ephemeral, hardly real, for him. This was but an interlude; and though something in his nature responded to it all, he knew that it was not for him, in fact ever, suitably as he and his might appear to blend with the goodly scene, there and then.

For it was not only the rich landscape and air of well-being which affected him, but his own present seeming identity with it all. Surely the condition of few men could have been so radically transformed in one short war? He rode to London, from his father's great manor of Hatfield Broadoak, like any prince, summoned to celebrate the Shrove-tide carnivals with the King. Dressed with a richness to which he had never hitherto aspired even in his most extravagant youth, with his wife as splendid on his right, he rode, magnificently mounted, his brother Nigel brilliant as a peacock at his other side with their cousin Gloucester, married to Edward's daughter. Horsed musicians made melody for them as they went, and half a hundred lords and knights and their ladies trotted behind him, glad to do so. For none was higher in King Edward's apparent regard than the Earl of Carrick, none more smiled upon, more liberally favoured. Where the unpredictable monarch heaped gifts and privileges, much could overflow to others conveniently nearby.

At least there was no danger of all this prosperity going to Bruce's head. Indeed, Elizabeth not infrequently chid him with being unnecessarily wary and foreboding about it. His contention that Edward could, and would, as easily take it all away again, she admitted—but pointed out that by no means all of it was the King's to give or take back. Her own handsome dowry of £10,000 for instance, and the ten manors that went with it. The revenues of the Bruce English estates, which were much larger than either of them had realised, and more wealthy, having an accumulation of receipts scarcely touched for years—with Robert Bruce senior now an ailing shadow of his former self, all but a bed-ridden recluse, spending nothing. Moreover, although the King could remove him from the wardship of the far-away earldom of Mar, in theory, the amassed products of it, thriftily garnered by the careful Gartnait, were already at Bruce's disposal.

He was prepared to concede that all this might be so. But experience had made him chary of good fortune. Though meantime he agreed that it might be wise to spend lavishly—since it all might not be his to spend for much longer. And there was such a thing as making friends with the mammon of unrighteousness while you had it.

The laughing, resounding company made gay progress through London's narrow streets—even though the smells caught at their breaths—but at the Palace of Westminster there was a different atmosphere, decorated for carnival but with no heralds or emissaries sent to greet them, or even welcoming smiles. Sober-faced guards and courtiers indicated that Majesty was in wrathful mood. There was bad news from Scotland.

They found the Great Hall, hung with evergreens and coloured lanterns, and set for feasting, thronged with anxious-looking men and women, who stood in groups and spoke low-voiced. While many turned to bow to Lancaster and Gloucester, it was noticeable that most looked askance at Bruce. They were motioned onwards to the throne-room, where the King was holding a hurriedly-called Council.

A pursuivant slipped in ahead, to inform of their arrival—but it was ominous how long it was, despite the illustriousness of the waiters, before he returned to beckon forward the leaders of the Essex party. Moreover, he signed to the Gloucester Herald not to trumpet the entrance of his lord. Royal Gilbert of Gloucester, Edward's son-in-law as well as Bruce's cousin, looked distinctly chilly at such treatment.

But when they entered the throne-room, Elizabeth holding back a little reluctantly with the other ladies, any petty irritation was quickly lost in sheerest apprehension and alarm. There was absolute silence, save for the sound of heavy breathing from the throne at the far end of the chamber. Right down the long central table men sat stiffly, looking as though they would have risen to their feet, but dared not.

Edward Plantagenet, angry, was a fearsome sight—and worse, emanated a terrifying aura, like a baited bull about to charge. But a cunning, killer-bull that would charge with shrewd deadliness rather than blind fury. He sat hunched forward, purple of face, great head out-thrust, jaw working slowly, rhythmically.

The newcomers bowed—and received no acknowledgement. Gloucester coughed. "My lord Edward—greetings, sire. Had you sent word to us of this Council, we would have attended earlier."

The King ignored him. He was staring at Bruce.

That young man, requiring all his hardihood, held his head high and stared back.

"Perfidious . . . rebellious . . . dogs!" Edward said, at length, enunciating each word as though savouring it. "Base . . . treacherous . . . dastards! Scots!"

Bruce held his tongue if not his peace.

"After my royal patience! My clemency. My forbearance. All wasted. Spurned. Spat upon! By graceless rogues and low-born scum! But, by God's precious blood, they shall suffer! I swear it!"

Bruce did not feel it incumbent upon him to argue.

"Speak, then—curse you!" the King roared suddenly, jabbing a finger towards Bruce, all men jumping. "Speak, man. You—Bruce! These are your friends, your precious countrymen. You are all alike—murderous rebels!"

The other gestured with his hand. "How may I speak, Sire, until Your Majesty informs me what's to do? I know nothing of this."

"Aye—you would say that! Why should I believe you? Are you more to be trusted than the rest? Working against me, despite all I have done for you? There has been bloody rebellion in Scotland. Widespread attack. The slaughter of my servants. It is the ruffian Wallace—I swear it! Behind all. Returned, and spurring on lesser rogues and knaves to murder and treason. It is not to be borne! You knew Wallace had returned, I vow?"

"I had heard so, Sire. But I have been in England with you, since before the truce expired in November. If hostilities have now been resumed . . ."

"Hostilities resumed . . . !" Edward all but choked. "Traitorous revolt and shameful massacre—and you name it hostilities!" The King, crouching, part rose from his throne as though he would launch himself down the chamber at Bruce. But, drawing a deep gulping breath, he swung round instead, to point at a cleric who sat at a side table. "You," he commanded, "tell him."

It was the same Master John Benstead, former royal pantryman who had once lorded it at Lochmaben. Bruce had not noticed him. He stood, a hunched crow of a man, bowing deeply.

"Your gracious Majesty—where do I begin? I do not know how much the Earl of Carrick, and these other lords, may know."

"Begin at the beginning, fool! But be quick about it."

"Yes, Sire. To be sure, Sire." The Pantler turned his chalk-white face in the direction of Bruce. "Since the truce ended there have been small risings all over South Scotland. Attacks on castles, on the King's garrisons. Ambuscades. The work of the man Wallace and his brigands, no doubt. Sir John Lord Segrave, His Highness's Governor, made protest to him they call the Guardian, the Lord of Badenoch, who followed on Sir John de Soulis. You know of this . . .?"

Bruce nodded. De Soulis had relinquished the guardianship in order to go in person to France, with Buchan and de Umfraville, on the return of Wallace and Lamberton, with new proposals about Baliol; and John Comyn had had himself appointed sole Guardian in his place, with the Bruce faction for the time being out of the running.

"The Lord of Badenoch made insolent reply. So His Majesty commanded Governor Segrave—brother to Sir Nicholas, whom you had occasion to know, my lord, at Lochmaben!—to march north from Berwick. With 20,000 men. To punish Wallace's outlaws, who were in the Tor Wood of Stirling. He reached Roslin, in Lothian, in the valley of the Esk, his army in three divisions. And encamped for the night . . ."

"The fool! The thrice-accursed dolt!" Majesty interrupted. "To encamp, apart. In three arrays. In such close valley as the Esk."

"Yes, my lord King. The Scots, under the Lord of Badenoch himself, fell upon Sir John's array, while yet it slept. With great slaughter. In unfair fight. A shameful thing, unworthy of Christian men! Many were slain, some fled, but most were taken prisoner. Sir John himself, and his son. Also Sir Nicholas, his brother. And my own self. Then came the word that our second array was warned, and advancing to our aid, under Master Ralph

Manton, Cofferer to Your Majesty's Wardrobe. The Scots were then beyond all in villainy. Before facing Manton, they slew all the captives. In wanton slaughter. Without mercy. Sir John and Sir Nicholas with the rest. Sixteen other knights, and all their men. Myself and one or two others they spared. Because we were priests. But all others were butchered . . ."

"Wallace's work, Satan roast him, for a surety!" the monarch cried. "The man is no more than a savage beast."

"I think not, Sire," Bruce intervened, greatly daring. "Sir William Wallace fights hard. But he would not slay defenceless prisoners. This I warrant. I know him. The night attack, while they slept—this could be his work. But not the slaying."

"Aye, you know him, my lord. All too well! You had the presumption to dub him knight—this oaf, this savage! A mockery of knighthood. But all men know that he is no true knight."

"If he is not knight, Sire, then nor am I, who knighted him. And *you* knighted me!" Bruce swung on the cleric. "You, Master Benstead—did you see it? With your own eyes, did you see Wallace slay a single captive? Or hear him order it done?"

"Not . . . not of myself, no."

"Who gave the orders, then?"

"The Lord of Badenoch himself, Sir John Comyn."

"Aye. That I can believe! But Wallace—where was he . . .?"

"This is not a court of law, and Bruce the judge!" Edward thundered. "Keep silent, sirrah. Proceed, Clerk."

"Yes, Sire. Ralph the Cofferer's army was ill led. His people fought stoutly, but Comyn had 8,000 horse. They were forced to yield . . ."

"Forced—bah! What forced them to yield? A craven spirit? A clerk leading!"

"Not so, Majesty. I myself saw Master Ralph cut down three before he yielded. But he had ridden into a trap. He tried to retire, in the narrow valley, but could not. He was captured, with much booty—payment for Your Majesty's garrisons." At the monarch's fight for breath, Benstead hurriedly went on. "Scarce was the fighting over when the third division, under Sir Robert de Neville, came up. And again, to free themselves of the prisoners, the Scots slew all. Even Master Ralph himself. I heard him pleading for his life, to Sir Simon Fraser who had captured him, claiming his priestly immunity. But the dastard Scot pointed to his armour and said lewdly that he trusted to this rather than to God's protection, and that the sword he had yielded up was bloody. Then this blasphemer, Fraser, drew his own sword and struck off first the Cofferer's left hand, then his right, and finally, with a single great blow, his head—God's curse on him everlastingly! This I saw."

"Sim Fraser! That renegade, whom once I cherished!" Edward exclaimed. "You see, my lord of Carrick, how much faith is to be placed in the Scots?"

"I see, Sire, men at war, fighting for their lives and land. As Your Majesty has done times amany. May I ask Master Benstead how fared Sir Robert Neville?"

The cleric shrugged. "What chance had he? Unawares he rode to his death. He and his fought well, and long, but without avail. This time there was no quarter, no prisoners taken. Save for a few who escaped by flight, all died."

"Out of 20,000 who left Berwick, how many survived, man? Other than a handful of frocked priests!"

"A few hundreds, perhaps, Highness. No more. I was exchanged. For three Scots knights, held at Berwick . . ."

"Aye—and scarce a good bargain! Enough of this, then. Sit down, man." The King pointed at Bruce. "Now, my Scots lord —what have you to say?"

The younger man looked about him, at the others, and spread his hands. "What is there for me to say? I have accepted Your Majesty's peace. Am I to be responsible for those who have not? I condemn this slaying of prisoners. What else can I say?"

"You can admit that the Scots are of all men the most perfidious and vile! Ingrates. Liars. Assassins. Brute-beasts to be stamped underfoot as I would stamp on an adder! Admit that, sirrah!"

Bruce remained silent, tight-lipped.

"So! You will not? You disobey my royal command—preferring your animal countrymen! So you are one with them. And deserving equally of my righteous retribution. That, if you will not admit, you cannot deny."

"I do deny it, Sire. Since returning to your peace I have kept your peace. What more would you have me to do? By coming to you, I have forfeited any sway that I had in Scotland . . ."

"I will tell you what I would have you do. What you *will* do, Robert. You will end this soft and idle living which I have allowed you here. You will come back to Scotland with me. And aid me in what I should have done long ere this. Aid me in the destruction of that evil land! Hitherto I have been merciful. I will be merciful no longer. And you will be as my right hand, Robert Bruce! You hear?"

The other bowed stiffly, wordless.

Edward sat back. "Here then is my decision. From this day, the armies will assemble. The greatest force that England has fielded. No excuse for service will be accepted from any lord, baron, knight or prelate in all my realms. This Shrove-tide carnival, and all such fancies, are cancelled. The whole nation will march with me. And with the Earl of Carrick! And when we return, Scotland will be but an ill memory. This is my command. My lords—see you to it." The King heaved himself to his feet.

Speechless, men rose, to bow.

As an afterthought, Edward jerked. "The Earl of Carrick to be escorted to his quarters, forthwith. And there guarded. Well guarded."

. . .

The assembly, set for York, took months. It was not only the gathering in of hundreds of thousands of men and horses and equipment from all over England and Wales, even from the English provinces of France; it was the collection of a fleet of ships, in the Tyne and Tees estuaries, and the loading of supplies sufficient to maintain such vast numbers of men in a devastated land for many months. It was early May before the mighty host began to move northwards.

Inevitably it moved slowly. But there was no hurry. Nothing could possibly withstand so enormous a concourse of armed men, nothing even delay it—save only its own ponderous size and weight. Some said that there were 250,000 men; but who could tell, or try to count so many? By its very size and complexity there was little of the atmosphere of war and fighting about the expedition—the more so in that Edward had brought along his Queen and she her ladies. Many of the great lords did the same.

Elizabeth de Burgh, although no longer the Queen's principal lady-in-waiting, was still one of her entourage, and as such accompanied her husband. Bruce was not exactly a prisoner, as had almost been his position in the South; indeed superficially he might have seemed an honoured member of Edward's Court—save that other men now were chary indeed of any association with him. But he was well aware how closely the King watched him, how iron-firm was the hand which gripped as well as sometimes patted his shoulder. For Edward, after his first rage, had behaved with a bewildering inconsistency towards the younger man, affectionate one moment, mocking and spiteful the next, but ever keeping him close as a son—closer indeed than he kept Edward of Carnarvon, Prince of Wales, a young man for whom his father appeared to have little regard. This inconsistency was, however, a surface thing. Bruce, like Scotland, was to be humbled, all men knew.

After a final inspection of shipping at Newcastle, the expeditionary force moving only a few miles a day, came to Morpeth on the 9th of May, there to split up. The Prince of Wales, with Lancaster and Surrey to aid and advise him, was given 100,000 men and sent to chastise Scotland's West. He took, more or less as hostages, Nigel, Edward and Alexander Bruce—the latter two having been for most of the last year at Cambridge University with him, where King Edward, in his gracious period, had sent them at his own expense, ostensibly out of kindness but more practically to keep them out of Scotland. Edward Bruce and the Prince had become friendly at university—but few believed that the association would have scope to ripen.

The monarch, with the main body, held to the east side of the country, crossing the Border and reaching Roxburgh in early June.

As was to be expected, there was no fighting. In fact, they saw Scotland smoking long before they reached it. Wallace's guerillas had had plenty of notice. Methodically they destroyed before the advancing English. There was little for Edward to do—although his outriders ranged far and wide, seeking any unburned territory, any unravaged land or village, savaging, hanging, crucifying any refugees or wretched hiders that they came across. Only the abbeys, monasteries and churches had been left intact—a pointless scruple, since they were more worth harrying than almost any other property. The destruction of arable land was difficult—but river-banks could be broken down, for flooding; dykes, ditches and mill-lades levelled; cornfields systematically trampled; orchards hacked down; wells poisoned. All that would burn was burned. Again there was no hurry; all could be done thoroughly.

At this rate it took the force a full fortnight to reach Edinburgh. Here the fortress had never been relinquished by the English, and the townsfolk, under its shadow, had perforce remained quiet, never rising in revolt. But if they expected therefore to escape Edward's heavy hand, they were much mistaken. With judicial impartiality he hanged one-tenth of the magistracy and leading citizenry, slew one-tenth of the populace by speedier methods, and burned one-tenth of the town—although, owing to the uprising of a summer wind, rather more than the due proportion of the mainly timber buildings happened to catch fire. All this he forced Bruce to watch, even to seem to preside over, with himself, making jocular remarks about John Baliol, or any who thought to be his heirs, scarcely being likely to consider that there was any kingdom left to plot over.

The Plantagenet's treatment of Scotland's notoriously non-rebellious city might give the others something to think about.

While this went on, the majority of the invasion forces were carefully laying waste Lothian and the plain of Forth, again despite its record of acquiescence, driving Wallace's men ever westwards but never actually coming to grips with them. There were signs of Comyn's chivalry being reported, now, but no battles developed. The Guardian was undoubtedly retiring on Stirling Bridge, there to contest the crossing of Forth in the classic fashion.

But Edward had thought of this. He had his shipwrights build three mighty pontoon bridges, at King's Lynn, and these had been towed up by sea. Now he had them placed across the river at a narrowing, five miles downstream from Stirling, and had his light horse swarming across before the Scots knew what was happening. Comyn had hastily to abandon his prepared positions, before he was cut off from the rear, and retired at speed northwards. Wallace and his people were trapped on the wrong side of Forth, and had to take refuge in the far recesses of the Tor Wood where it stretched into the lonely morasses of the Flanders Moss.

And now, as it were on virgin territory, Edward could demonstrate that he had meant what he had sworn in his throne-room at Westminster. Nobody had had time to scorch the good earth of Fife and Fothrif, nor had most of the folk opportunity to flee. The King's peace, therefore, fell to be established in fullest measure.

It was on a late June evening, at Clackmannan, a few miles north of Forth, at the foot of the steep Ochil Hills, that Robert Bruce lay on his couch in the glowing light of his handsome tented pavilion, sprawled but not relaxed. Elizabeth was pressing wine on him, seeking to soothe and ease the tension that now almost permanently had him in its thrall, and that was etching hard lines deep in his rugged features. They were alone, as they so seldom were on this ghastly, endless, death-filled progress, no watchful lords, guards, esquires or servants actually in the tent with them. It had been a long and harrowing day.

"Come—wash the taste of it away with this, my dear," Elizabeth urged. She was strong, understanding, patient, and because of her position and wealth, able to help much. What he would have done without her, these months, he did not know.

He pushed away the proffered goblet. "No. It would make me sick, I swear. My stomach is turned, I tell you! It is too much. I cannot bear with more of this, Elizabeth. That devil has me beaten, destroyed, damned—as much as he has this wretched land! All day and every day he grinds me into the dust of his hatred, even as he smiles and strokes, mocking me. My belly is galled with his insults, poisoned by his spleen. I tell you, many a time I have been near to drawing my dirk and plunging it into his black heart . . . !"

"Hush you, hush you, Robert!" That girl was not easily scared, but she lowered her voice, glancing anxiously around at the golden-glowing silken hangings of the tent, refulgent with the evening sunlight. "These walls are thin. Watch your words, of a mercy!"

"I watch my words the livelong day! While Edward slays me with his! My life is not worth the living. My head rings with words I dare not speak. My nostrils reek with the stench of fire, of burned flesh. My eyes see only savagery decked in smiles and laughter, dead men's eyes reproaching me—aye, and live men's fingers pointing! Pointing at Bruce, as traitor, as turncoat . . . !"

"Not so, my heart. Do not say it. You mistake. It is not at you that men point . . ."

"I say it is. Do you think I do not know? All this day I have been with him at Dollar. Doleur, they say the name once was—and God knows it is meet today! Receiving the submissions and homage of barons and landed men from all this Fothrif. Led in, some at horses' tails, some bound or in chains, some lashed with whips—receiving them in a nunnery with all its orchards and pleasances hung with corpses. Forced to sit beside him, while men were brought to their knees before him. Think you I did not see what their eyes said, whatever their lips muttered? They could not look in Edward's eye—but they could look in *mine!* Sitting there, his hand on my arm . . ."

"It is evil, yes. Grievous. A shameful thing. But you *must* bear it, my love. You must harden your heart. He will break your pride, your spirit. You must not give him the victory."

"There is half of Scotland before me, yet. To see stricken. Crushed. Weeks, months of this venom . . ."

Bruce's voice died away as there was a commotion at the tent door, the armed guard clanking weapons. The entrance-curtain was thrust aside unceremoniously, and two men strode inside unannounced, stooping because both were tall. Both were Plantagenets, though one did not bear the name.

"Ha, Robert! You rest, lad? Plied with refreshment by fair hands, heh? Would I were in your shoes! *My* lady prefers to eat sweetmeats and stitch fool threads!" Edward bowed gallantly to Elizabeth. "But no rest for the King. Despite his years!" At sixty-four, he was heavy, purple of face, but his basic vigour little diminished.

Bruce was slow to rise, striving to school his features. He bowed briefly, unspeaking. Elizabeth had curtsied more promptly.

"News, Robert—tidings," the King went on. "Good, and less good. From France. And from the West. John, here, brings it. From the West. Of folly and knavery. *My* son's folly. And *your* people's knavery! Eh, John?"

The massively tall and sombre-eyed young man with him, so uncannily like the other in build and face, inclined his dark head. Travel stained but richly armoured, he was Sir John de Botetourt, Edward's own bastard, and now Warden of the West March. A man of few words but strong hand, he let his sire do the talking.

"My son—my *other* son—Edward of Carnarvon, lacks much. But wits, most of all! Nor has your friend Lancaster greatly aided him it seems! They have mired themselves in your Galloway and Carrick bogs, a plague on them! A mighty host wasted, in chasing scum! *Your* scum, Robert! Your wretched savages of the West are resisting everywhere. In their accursed hills. It is shameful—not to be borne. My commands, my splendid host, being thwarted by this beggarly rabble. Who act in your name, by the Mass! *Yours*!"

Bruce moistened his lips, but said nothing.

"So you will leave me, Robert, meantime. I must bear to lose your joyous presence! For a space. As must you, my dear. You will go back with John, here, to the West, my friend. You will go and tell your treacherous people to lay down their arms. You will take order with them, hang the leaders, teach them what it means to defy the King of England. You will do more than that. You will muster them to *my* arms! To fight against their rebellious countrymen, not their liege lord. I want a Bruce host in the field, Robert. Fighting by my side. By *our* side! You understand?" Edward was eyeing his victim levelly.

"That I can by no means do, Sire," the younger man declared flatly. "I have no authority in the West, since I have yielded to your peace. My earldom is taken over by others. I have no power and jurisdiction now."

"There you underestimate, Robert. Underestimate my love for you. For you have *my* power. More potent than any earldom of Carrick. To use, lad—to use. Moreover, you shall have authority over more than your former vassals. I want men from more than Carrick, Galloway and Annandale. So you shall be Sheriff of Ayr and Lanark. For the present. Here is sufficient authority to act— even for Robert Bruce!"

The other blinked. "I . . . I do not wish this appointment, Sire."

"But I do, my friend! And it shall be. From this moment, you are Sheriff of Ayr and Lanark, with all the duties thereto belonging! Sir John here, your deputy and companion. Close companion! In token of which I require from your sheriffdom, within the month, 1,000 picked footmen, duly armed. Also a further thousand, half horsed, from your own lands of Carrick and Galloway. These, the first token. Within the month. More to follow. It is clear?"

"But, Sire—you have hundreds of thousands of men! What want you with these? Unwilling . . . !"

"Each one will be worth many of my own, wisely used, lad. You would not begrudge me them? In your loyalty?"

Bruce looked at his wife, helplessly. She nodded, almost imperceptibly.

"I shall go with my lord, to aid him, Sire," she said. "You would not part husband and wife?"

"Alas, my dear—I fear it is necessary. The Queen requires your presence. She greatly leans on you. And this is men's work— mustering forces and hanging rebels. Not such as you may aid in. Moreover, lass—you will but bring Robert back the quicker, will you not? To win back to your side I swear *I* would do all in notable haste! It will be so with him, I vow."

There was silence in that tent for a space.

Then Edward laughed. "But, save us—I have almost forgot the *good* tidings! Eh, John? From France. As you know, my uncouth allies the Flemings surprised and defeated my good brother-in-law of France at Courtrai. Last July. His fortunes have scarce mended since. The foolish fellow has come to blows with His Holiness of Rome! So I have had to act to save him from himself—as kinsman should! Now, at last, he has signed a peace. No truce, but a final peace. After all these years, England and France are at peace. The Holy See also. Is this not excellent?"

Bruce drew a deep breath. "And . . . the terms?"

"Terms? Why, scarce any, Robert. Merely some . . . adjustments. To our mutual advantage. One which will rejoice your heart, I have little doubt. The man Baliol to be held secure in his own house at Bailleul-en-Vimeu. Henceforth. He and his son. Never to return to Scotland. Does this not please you?"

The other knowing Edward Plantagenet, did not commit himself.

"One or two other small matters. We have, as it were, exchanged our allies! Problems, as they were. I relinquish all interest in Flanders and the Flemings—a small loss! And Philip *le Bel* relinquishes all interest in Scotland and the Scots. As is only proper. So an ages-old stumbling block is removed. Is it not satisfactory?"

Hoarsely Bruce spoke. "And the Pope?"

"Why, Pope Boniface also joins in this goodwill. He declares Scotland and Flanders, both, in wicked rebellion. And all who bear arms against me, or Philip, their lawful sovereigns, in danger of hellfire! Were you not wise, my good Robert, to submit to my peace when you did?"

Wordless, Elizabeth moved over, to put her arm in Bruce's, a simple but eloquent gesture which drew a quick frown from the King.

"You seem less joyful than you should, my lord," he grated, suddenly harsh, accusing.

"Should I rejoice, Sire, to see my country utterly betrayed and abandoned? By all. By its most ancient ally. Even by Holy Church?"

"Betrayed, sirrah! *You* to say that? Robert Bruce speaks of betrayal!"

When the younger man answered nothing but looked steadily, directly into the other's choleric eyes, the King thrust out a jabbing, pointing hand.

"We shall see. None betrays Edward, and does not suffer. And Edward is Scotland. Now. Forget it at your peril—you, or any. You will leave at once. Tonight. Ride with Sir John. For Ayr. See you to it." Without any other leave-taking, he turned abruptly and strode from the tent, de Botetourt silent at his heels.

Husband and wife turned to gaze at each other. After a moment, Elizabeth flung herself into the man's arms.

.   .   .

It was many months before Bruce saw his wife again, appalling months for Scotland and grievous for Robert Bruce; months in which Edward stormed his brutally determined way northwards, by Perth and Coupar and Arbroath and Brechin, over the mouth to Aberdeen, and onwards to Banff and Elgin and Kinloss, within sight of the blue mountains of Ross; further than he or any other invader had ever gone, leaving utter desolation behind him in a blackened swathe from the sea to the Highland hills. One by one the Comyn's northern strongholds had fallen until the last remote strength of Lochindorb, on its island in deepest Strathspey, was brought low, and no major strength in all the land, save only Stirling Castle, remained opposed to the conqueror. That is, except for the eyries of Highland chiefs who were interested in neither the one side nor the other.

During those months Bruce in fact sent no thousands of Westcountrymen to increase the King's mighty northern host. It had not been easy to avoid doing so—but after long battling with Edward personally, he found his bastard son de Botetourt rather less hard to get round. Not that Sir John was a lenient guard or mild of temperament—quite the reverse; but he lacked his sire's shrewdness and experience, and Bruce was able to deceive him where he could not have done the King. He managed time and again to put off the required transfer of men, mainly on the grounds that they were more urgently needed there in the West than by the so victorious monarch. He ensured that this was so by secretly fomenting strategically-sited and timed revolts and uprisings in various parts of his domains and sheriffdoms—not too difficult to do here in his own earldom. His newly-mustered vassals and levies were kept busy dashing hither and thither in Galloway and Carrick, ostensibly keeping King Edward's peace. Edward himself would have seen through it and clamped down sternly. De Botetourt may have suspected, but he could prove nothing, and was somewhat beyond his depth in dealing with

Bruce. Moreover he could not deny the need to put down all armed rising in the rear of the Prince of Wales' army, and was much aware of the threat of a link-up with Wallace, who was still active in the central forests and marshes between Clyde and Forth—a danger which Bruce never failed to stress. The Prince, too, was unhappy in his Galloway adventure, finding that vast province a most awkward place to campaign in, as others had done before him. He sent conflicting demands to Botetourt and the Sheriff of Ayr—and Bruce was glad on more than one occasion to despatch south to him parties of men who should have gone north to Edward.

But it was a dire and sorry business, for all that, however great a relief it was to be quit of the monarch's personal presence. His bastard made a sullen and unattractive companion, and Bruce had also to put up with quite a lot of his old foe Clifford, whom the Prince had installed as a sort of governor of Annandale and keeper of Lochmaben. Oddly enough, Clifford had as lieutenants two men who Bruce had thought to be dead—the Lord Segrave, demoted and disgraced but still alive; and Sir Robert Neville, also alleged to have been slain at Roslin. Apparently Master Benstead had not been entirely to be trusted as informant and courier.

It was with mixed feelings, then, that in early October, Bruce received a peremptory summons from Edward, sent from the castle of his own nephew and ward, at Kildrummy in Aberdeenshire, to come north forthwith, still in de Botetourt's care. Presumably the King had come to accept the fact that the West experiment had failed, and that Bruce would be of more value in the North where, for his own interests, he might be expected to desire to keep down any resurgence of the Comyn power. Edward had cancelled his appointments as Sheriff of Ayr and Lanark, making him instead Sheriff of Moray, Nairn and Inverness, and reminding him that he was keeper of the royal forests of Kintore, Darnaway and Longmorn, as well as controller of the earldom of Mar. In name, at any rate. Edward himself was returning south, to winter at Dunfermline in Fife; Bruce was to hold the North, in his name, against any attempt of Comyn. But he would not be left to hold it alone; he would have ample help. Which meant that he still would be a well-guarded prisoner.

So, with the shortening days, Bruce and de Botetourt rode northwards through a ravaged, shattered land. Only the hope that he might find Elizabeth at the end of his journey gave the former any satisfaction.

In this, at least, he was not disappointed. Edward had left behind at Kildrummy, as well as some few thousand Englishmen, both Elizabeth and her father, Richard de Burgh, to ensure Bruce's good behaviour and co-operation in the North.

. . . .

Kildrummy was good for Robert Bruce. As on the previous visit, he was able partly to relax, here amongst the skirts of the great Highland mountains. The air, the people, the entire tempo and tenor of life was different, easier, more genial. The stresses and strains of war and dynastic manoeuvre seemed far away, and even Edward's heavy hand had made but little impression on this mighty land of vast horizons. He had burned a few towns in Aberdeenshire and Moray, yes; but the people hereabouts did not live in towns and villages, being a pastoral folk wide-scattered over a thousand hills and valleys. It was strange that this should be the fierce Comyn's land, for it seemed out of sympathy with all he stood for. Or so mused Bruce that Yuletide, as 1303 gave way to 1304.

He had not, in fact, come to blows with John Comyn as yet, that man having kept his distance. Word of him came intermittently from places wide apart, mainly in the West—Galloway, the Lennox, Argyll, and as near as Lochaber. He was still free, still resisting after a fashion, still sole Guardian of Scotland; but he could effect little, fugitive rather than commander or ruler, and for some reason he avoided the North-East, where Bruce, in name at least, now governed—and where he and Buchan and the other Comyns might between them have raised many thousands more men. Bruce often wondered why—but he was thankful.

Such thoughts were always at the back of his mind—even as he stood this Yuletide night in the hall of Kildrummy, eyeing the pleasantly domestic scene. By the light of two great log fires and many candles, a children's game was in progress, involving Donald, the boy Earl of Mar, Marjory Bruce, and young John de Strathbogie, heir to the Atholl earldom. Assisting were Elizabeth, Christian, Countess of Mar who was taking her widowhood philosophically, and, crawling about on hands and knees, none other than Richard, Earl of Ulster. The last, with a few drinks to aid him, made an excellent charger for Donald, replacing

Bruce, exhausted and sore of knee. The ladies undoubtedly had the best of this game, requiring only to look gracious, curtsy occasionally, and commend the noisy activities of the children. Elizabeth and Christian were already close friends, although so different in temperament. The former was taking her new stepmotherly duties seriously.

Bruce was laughing heartily and heartlessly at his father-in-law, an excellent thing, when a servant came unobtrusively up to him.

"My lord, a friar has come seeking you. A ragged, wandering friar, but asking for your lordship's self. Secretly. He says you will see him if I say he comes from Stowburgh or some such."

"Stowburgh . . .? Ha—Stobo! Stobo, is it?" Bruce glanced over at the others quickly, caught his sister's eye, and shook his head briefly. Then he slipped out, with the servitor.

It was Lamberton, as he had guessed, a weary and dishevelled figure to be Primate of Scotland. This device of dressing as a begging friar might enable him to move about the land with some freedom, but only on foot and with the minimum comfort. The Bishop looked almost an old man, although he was little more than forty. Last time Bruce had seen his friend, he had been disguised thus. It was two years ago.

Stiffly formal until they could be alone in a private room, the two men then gripped each other with some emotion.

"God be praised for the sight of you!" Lamberton said unsteadily. "It is long, long. I have feared if ever I would see you again. Feared that I was a done and broken man. Priest of a done and broken land. And you lost to both of us . . ."

"Not that, my friend—not that. I am not lost. Yet! Although at times I know not where I go. Which way. Whether indeed there is anywhere to go. Save into the Plantagenet's bloody arms! Where most men think me already, I swear!"

They looked at each other.

"Were we wrong, then? In error?" the Bishop asked. "In what we put our hands to?"

"God knows. But we have achieved little. Or, *I* have. Save sorrow and affliction, the land destroyed. Everywhere, save in Galloway, Edward supreme. Myself a watched puppet, forced to dance to this tune. You, head of the Holy Church, a furtive skulker, forced to creep and crawl, hungry . . .!"

"The land is not destroyed. Not yet. Nor, pray God, ever will be. Sore stricken, yes. But not beat, not destroyed." He paused for a moment. "And something is achieved, at least. What I came chiefly to tell you. Comyn will yield. He is seeking terms from Edward."

"So-o-o! Comyn! *He* is beat, then?"

"Aye. Or, shall we say, forced to a new course. There has been great talking, great debate, great wrath. John Comyn sees no hope of success in this warfare. He will yield if Edward accepts him to what he calls his peace. And restores him to these his Comyn lands."

"His lands! Aye, his lands. Now that the North, his lands, are in Edward's hands, the man is less bold a campaigner! While it was the South, it mattered not! His lands are his price, then!"

"Part of it. And I think that Edward knew it, always. He is shrewd, cunning. That is why *you* are here, my friend. Edward knew that you, sitting supreme in the Comyns' lands, was more than the man could stomach. If it had been just the English, he might have lain low, left them and hoped for better days. But Bruce . . . ! So he yields to Edward. On terms. And your removal from the North, his sheriffdoms back again—these are his terms. As Edward foresaw from the first, I do swear!"

"Dear God! Plantagenet . . . and Comyn! Curse them both— they are the bane of my life! They stand between me and all that is worth having . . ."

Lamberton looked at him steadily. "At least the throne is safe from him, now. Him and Baliol both. This of France and the Pope. Ill as it is, it means Baliol will never return to Scotland. So . . . the throne stands vacant. As never before."

Bruce drew a long quivering breath. Then abruptly he changed the subject. "Comyn would yield, then. But what of the others? There is more than John Comyn opposing Edward."

"All see it as Comyn does—save one. All will yield. Save William Wallace."

"Ha—Wallace! Aye, Wallace will not yield. Ever. And who supports Wallace?"

"None. Save his own band. And William Lamberton!"

"Save us—so it has come to that? We are back to where we started!"

"Not quite, friend. Not quite. There is an evil here you may not have thought on. When Comyn yields, it will be as Guardian of Scotland. This Edward requires, and this Comyn will agree. So he yields Scotland, not just John Comyn. And yielding Scotland to Edward's peace, leaves Wallace, who will not yield, an undoubted and disavowed rebel and outlaw. And those who aid him."

"But that would be betrayal! Throwing him to the wolves!"

"Will Comyn care for that? He has ever hated and despised the man. Though, see you, we must give Comyn his due. He has fought bravely and ably. Moreover, there is more to the terms he seeks than just his own weal. In surrendering Scotland he asks that our laws and liberties be protected. And that there should be no disinheritance of other lords' lands as well as his own. But he will not speak for Wallace."

"What are we to do, then? What *can* we do?"

"Nothing, I fear. I tried to sway Comyn, but to no avail. Wallace will have to look to himself. Edward will never treat with *him*. But the people will aid him. He has their love . . ."

"Aye. And what guidance do you have for *me*? In my present state?" Bruce asked.

"That you endure, Robert—that is all. Endure. Seem to go along with Edward, where you may with any honour. Your time, if it comes, will only come out of patient endurance. As will Scotland's."

Bruce's sigh of acceptance of that was almost a groan.

Lamberton would not, dare not, stay at Kildrummy, tired as he was. At any time someone might recognise the Primate. Given food and money for his further journeying, he was not long in taking leave of his friend, commending him to God's care, and then slipping out into the cold and windy dark, quietly as he had come. He was going to Wallace, somewhere in the Tor Wood, a hundred miles to the south.

·   ·   ·

A month later, in early February, the anticipated summons had come from Dunfermline. The Earl of Carrick, no longer it seemed Sheriff of Moray, Nairn and Inverness, was to be brought south without delay, by order of the King's Majesty. As bald and unvarnished as that.

The Kildrummy party found a changed atmosphere prevailing when they reached the ancient grey town on the north side of Forth, from which Malcolm Canmore had ruled Scotland. The smoke of war had dispersed, superseded by the smell of triumph. The Scots had finally surrendered—or all of them that were worth acknowledging. Comyn, the so-called Guardian, was due to yield himself two days hence, at Strathord near Perth, and

Edward was in expansive mood. He welcomed them all affably, publicly commended Bruce for his alleged notable aid in bringing the rebels to heel in the North, and announced more or less unlimited wassail and celebration to mark the establishment of peace, Edward's final and distinctive brand of peace. A parliament would be held to formalise matters—an English parliament, of course, but with some suitable Scots taking their places. Bygones would be bygones.

The first large-scale demonstration of the new genial dispensation was not the parliament but an elaborate reception, at Dunfermline, of the surrendered Scots leadership. Edward had a fondness for defeated opponents in clanking chains, wearing sackcloth and ashes, and otherwise emphasising the evident; but on this occasion it was to be different. The victor would be magnanimous, and the vanquished made aware of how mistaken and foolish, as well as wicked, they had been.

The ceremony was held in the Abbey itself, since the English earlier had burned down the Great Hall of the palace, one of the finest buildings in the land. It was packed, for the occasion, with half the nobility of England, and all foreign ambassadors.

Bruce found himself very much part of the proceedings, to his discomfiture. The King and Queen had thrones set up within the chancel, with the Prince of Wales seated a little to one side. Bruce was commanded to come and stand directly at Edward's left hand, with Ulster at the right, Elizabeth being required to take up a similar position beside the Queen, with her aunt, the Steward's wife, at the right. Not only so, but the Bruce brothers, with the exception of Alexander, who was still at Cambridge, had been summoned to Dunfermline also, and were now placed behind the thrones. None looked any more happy than their elder brother; but there was no doubt that the impression given was that the Bruce family was the principal support of the King as far as Scotland was concerned.

When all was in readiness, a fanfare of trumpets sounded, and the great church doors were thrown open. Then, as musicians played a funereal dirge, the Scots filed in.

Edward evidently had been concerned to make this a very different affair from the somewhat similar occasion eight years before, at Stracathro parish church, when John Baliol had made his submission. Now the iron fist was to be hidden in the velvet glove. There was no armour, little steel, and certainly no warhorses in sight. The King and his whole Court were in a glittering splendour of gold, silver and jewellery, velvets, satins and silks. The Scots had also been told to eschew all armour and warlike garb—and a sorry, ragged, threadbare crew they looked in consequence, patched and out-at-elbows. For these were men surrendered only after long and unsuccessful campaigning in the field, living rough and in the saddle. Their armour, however rusty and battered, would have had some dignity; but denied it they had come to court little better than a band of scarecrows. They held their heads the higher therefore, of course—but it was difficult to maintain any martial carriage shuffling forward to the slow strains of a dirge.

Three gorgeously-apparelled English heralds led, setting the desperately slow pace. Then, alone, paced John Comyn, the Guardian. Bruce, watching, was almost sorry for his enemy. Not that the man looked humbled, or other than a proud fighter forced to take part in folly; but unkempt, unshaven, shabbily-clad and obviously weary, he represented defeat, a grievous state for the Lord of Badenoch. He did not hang his head, however, but, avoiding looking at the King, stared levelly at Bruce as he walked.

Behind him came Lamberton, the Steward, Buchan the Constable and the Earls of Lennox and Strathearn. The Steward was better dressed than the others; perhaps his wife had managed to smuggle clothing to him. The Primate was not in his wandering friar's rags, but not a great deal finer. Buchan was limping from a leg wound. Lamberton exchanged a quick glance with Bruce, and then gazed straight ahead.

There followed the main body of the Scots lords, temporal and spiritual, led by de Umfraville, the former Guardian, the Lord of Crawford, the Bishops of Glasgow and Galloway, Master William Comyn. De Soulis was still in France, Wallace's enormous figure notably absent.

The sight of them all stirred a great wave of emotion in Bruce. These grim years he had sought to steel himself against emotion, a weakness he could not afford. But in the face of his former associates and comrades in arms, thin, war-ravaged, humiliated, he groaned a little—though he did not know it. He saw himself as they must see him, and swallowed.

Edward, smiling genially and tossing comments and identities to his wife loudly, waited until no more of the surrendered Scots could be crammed into the great church. Even after a trumpet had stilled the mournful music and a herald demanded silence for the King's Majesty, he chatted on, apparently casual, to the Queen, to Ulster, to Bruce—however unforthcoming the latter. Then, as the ranks before him fidgeted, stirred, he gestured to them.

"Welcome, friends, to my peace," he exclaimed. "You come belatedly to my Court and presence. But now here, you are welcome."

None attempted answer to that.

"So many faces well known to me," the King went on, jovially. "Some less ruddy, it may be, than when last I saw them! So many who swore fealty to me at Berwick, that day—eh, Robert my friend? You were there assisting!"

"Scarce assisting, Sire. Then. Any more than today." That was level, almost expressionless, from stiff lips.

Edward ignored it. "Friends of yours. Friends of my own—or so they swore! Absent friends—so long absent. Now wisely returned to my peace. But . . . less wise than you, Robert. Better that they had followed your lead the sooner?"

Biting his lip, Bruce forced himself to meet Comyn's baleful stare.

Edward actually turned in his throne, to grin at the younger man. "You are silent, lad? Does the sight of these your friends distress you? On my oath, it should not! For you greatly aided in bringing them here, did you not?"

"You credit me with too much, Sire," Bruce got out. "I have done nothing. Towards this."

"Ha—you were not always so modest, Robert! How say you, my lord of Badenoch? Are not you—is not all this Scotland—beholden to my lord of Carrick for leading the way into my peace? And then labouring valiantly to establish it."

Comyn bowed, wordless.

"Another modest man!" Edward's smile was wearing thin. "Yet you both set yourselves up to rule this realm of mine. In *my* place. And that is treason is it not, my lords?"

Into the quivering quiet which greeted the enunciation of that dread word, it was William Lamberton who spoke. "My lord King," he said clearly, firmly, "the Lord of Badenoch, as Guardian of Scotland, has surrendered on terms. We with him. To which terms Your Majesty has assented. We are here to claim those terms. There was not, and could not be, treason. From Scots, to the King of England. But even had there been, you annulled it. By treating. This is established usage, known by all. Which none can contest."

"God's eyes—you are bold, Sir Priest! You will be the clerk, Lamberton? Whom the outlaw Wallace raised up."

"I am William Lamberton, appointed to the see of St. Andrews by the Guardian and Council of Scotland, and consecrated Bishop thereof by His Holiness of Rome."

"The Crown appoints to bishoprics, sirrah! And *I* am the Crown!" Edward thundered. "Hereafter keep silent. No man speaks in my presence save by my invitation."

Bruce flashed a glance of acknowledgement at his friend, who had so evidently sought to divert the Plantagenet from his strategy of seeming to establish Bruce as largely responsible for the downfall of his fellow-countrymen, and so still more deeply dividing Scotland.

Edward turned back to Comyn. "You, my lord—if you still have a tongue in your head! Did you or did you not swear fealty to me at Berwick, eight years ago? Do you deny your signature on that Ragman's Roll?"

"I do not, Sire," the other admitted. "But an oath taken under duress is not binding."

"So that is how you keep your word! Why, then, should you expect me to keep mine now? As to these so-called terms."

"Your Majesty assented to the terms under no duress. You could have rejected them. *We* could not have rejected your oath, at Berwick, and saved our heads."

"You have a nice sense of honour, sirrah! As well for you that Edward of England is otherwise. For, by the Mass, the heads of every one of you should fall this day! As forsworn rebels and traitors. But . . . I honour my word. Even to such as you. The terms stand. Your lives are spared, your lands are not forfeit. And the laws, customs and liberties of this part of my realm shall remain unchanged. Some of you I shall require to go into exile furth of Scotland, at my pleasure. For the better peace of this my realm. In exchange for these mercies, I accept your fullest surrender. Yours, and that of all who have risen in arms against me. Save one—the base murderer Wallace! Him I will nowise accept to my peace. Now or ever. It is understood?"

Lamberton seemed about to speak again, despite the King's warning, but Bruce's quick head-shaking halted him.

Edward leaned forward, pointing that imperious finger at Comyn. "My lord, where is he? I do not see the man Wallace.

Yet I commanded that you bring him with you. To me. Bound. Where is he?"

"Wallace is not a man easily bound. Or brought. Or found. Of this Your Majesty is well aware. Your servants have sought him often enough . . ."

"Where is he, man? Do not bandy words with me!"

"I do not know, Sire. Wallace . . . is Wallace. A man apart. He heeds no man's voice . . ."

"He shall heed mine, by God's wounds! And you also. All of you. See you, Comyn—I want Wallace and shall have him. I give you command to find him. To deliver him. And I do not give you overlong. Wallace was at that devilish massacre at Roslin. When you slew, as prisoners, better men than yourselves. You commanded there, my lord of Badenoch. With Sir Simon Fraser, Sir Alexander Lindsay of Crawford and Sir David Graham of Dundaff. I require Wallace of you all. I will do most favour to whosoever shall capture him, in expiation of that vile deed. And let the others beware!"

"Sire—this was no part of the terms . . ."

"Silence! You have heard me. See you to it." As so often happened, Edward Plantagenet tired suddenly of the scene he had himself prepared. Without warning he stood up. "It is enough. This audience is over. Away with them." He reached over and almost lifted the Queen out of her chair, and turning his back on the entire alarmed assembly, strode with her up the chancel, to the vestry-door, and out.

Belatedly the trumpeters grabbed their instruments and blew a notably ragged and uneven fanfare.

The eyes of Bruce and Comyn met in a long hard glare, before the heralds pushed the latter round and hustled him off.

Few there contemplated the festivities to follow with any delight.

CHAPTER SEVENTEEN

HEAVILY, even tripping a little with weariness on the worn stone steps, Robert Bruce climbed the narrow turnpike stair of the Sea Tower of St. Andrews Castle—well named, with the spray from the surging waves below actually coming in at him through the arrow slit windows as he mounted, and the chill March wind off the North Sea flapping his long mud-stained travelling-cloak. The single smoking pitch-pine torch-flame, flickering and waving wildly in the draughts, did little to light his footsteps. He cursed as he stumbled for the third time, sword clanking, spurs scraping —but his cursing was spiritless, automatic, and not only with physical weariness. It seemed a long time since he had even cursed with spirit and enthusiasm.

The door on the third-floor landing was thrown open before even he reached it, and Elizabeth held out welcoming hands to him. "My dear," she said, "I prayed that it might be you. Thank God that you are back!"

He took her in his arms, and she clung to him, wet as he was. "Bless you, lass! You are the first sight to gladden my eyes in three weeks." He kissed her hungrily, and then held her away at arm's-length. "Dear God—you are bonny! Fairer, more beautiful, than ever, I swear! You are the saving of me, and that is plain truth."

"Has it been so bad, Robert?"

"Bad? Worse than bad. I have been mocked and trodden under by these English like any condemned felon. Day in, day out. To send me to hunt Wallace was ill enough. But to place me under Clifford, who has ever hated me, and who lords it over my Annandale! And Segrave, a man soured with disgrace. And that bastard Botetourt. This was beyond all bearing. Yet, God forgive me, I had to bear it! A round score of days and nights of it. Of Clifford's and Segrave's spleen. Safe to bait me as they would. By Edward's permission!"

"One day you will repay them, my heart. But . . . Wallace? Did you catch him?"

"No. For that, thank all the saints! A fine dance he led us. All over the Forest, in foulest weather. But never once were we within reach of him. Fraser we almost caught, twice. At Peebles and at Tweedsmuir. But Wallace, never. He was always an hour gone from every hiding-place we flushed—though we quartered Ettrick Forest for him. More than once, mind, I was able to lead those devils the wrong road—for none of them knew the Forest as I did . . ."

"Oh, I am glad! Glad." Elizabeth was aiding him off with his soaking and mud-stained outer wear, before the blazing fire in the little tower chamber which was all that even Lamberton could provide for the Bruces in his over-crowded Castle of St. Andrews, where Edward was holding his parliament.

"Aye. Had we indeed captured Wallace, I scarce know how I would have done. That Edward should send *me* on such errand, and in such company . . . ! But he will be beside himself now. Beyond all in fury. For if he hates me, tramples me, it is as nothing to his hatred of Wallace."

"He has, I think, more to dwell on tonight than your failure to bring him Wallace," the young woman interrupted. "The King is ill, Robert."

"Ill? Edward ill? Sick?"

"Yes. It was at today's parliament. He was speaking. Very angry that Stirling Castle still holds out against him. When he was seized. A great choking and gasping, that felled him. I was with the Queen, watching. His face was blue, like to burst with blood! Always he has had too much blood. We feared him dead . . ."

"Feared! By the Rude—why fear?" Bruce cried, eyes alight as they had not been for long. "Edward dead might mean life for many. For us. For this Scotland. But . . . he is not dead? Only ill, you say."

"Ill, yes. And making recovery, they say. I am not long back from the Queen's chamber. She is much upset. They are bleeding him. The fever abates. But it is a warning. To be heeded . . ."

"Heeded, yes. Pray God he does *not* heed it!"

She shook her fair head. "Do not say it, Robert. He can be hard, cruel. But he can be kind, too. I have known much kindness from him. He is my father's friend. He is a king, and kings are not to be judged as other men."

"They need not become monsters! As he has done. I esteemed Edward once. But he has forfeited all esteem."

"And yet, he still has esteem for *you*. In some measure. Today, before the parliament broke up, he appointed you, with Wishart, Bishop of Glasgow, and Sir John de Moubray, to take rule in Scotland. Until his nephew, the Lord John of Brittany, can come to be Governor . . ."

"A trap, I vow! Another trick. An empty title, with his underlings firm in control. Have you forgot that he made me Sheriff of Ayr and Lanark? Aye, then Moray. With no more power than a babe at the breast! Wishart is an old done man. And Moubray is a creature of the Comyn's. So much for Edward's esteem! He would but use me again."

"It may be so. But at least he *seems* to honour you. And more. You three are empowered to work out a new policy for Scotland. The new Scotland as he names it. What he called a constitution.

To be presented before a great parliament at Westminster in the autumn of the year . . ."

"What is this? A constitution? A new constitution for a new Scotland! For a beaten, humbled vassal Scotland, in thrall to the Plantagenet. A province of England, ruled from Westminster. This he would have me to make up—Robert Bruce!"

"It might give you opportunity to serve Scotland well," she pointed out. "Better that you make up such a constitution than some others, is it not?"

"I' faith, no! Think you Edward will accept anything that does not give him all he wants? And then can use my name, and Wishart's to take the blame for it, when the bite hurts. Bruce, the traitor, contrived this! Do you not know Edward yet, my dear?"

"You cannot concede him any good, Robert? Anything?"

"The only good thing I will concede to Edward Longshanks is that he desired me to marry *you*, my dearest! For that, and that only, I am his debtor."

She smiled. "You still believe yourself favoured in that? Still find me to your taste?"

"To my taste? Save us, girl—I'll show you how much to my taste you are! Here is simple proving. As I have been desiring to prove since I entered this room! Why waste we time talking!" And he advanced on her, weariness apparently quite forgotten.

"No, no!" Laughing, she backed away. "That is not what I asked. You rise too fast, my lord! I but questioned whether you still find me a good and dutiful wife . . . ?"

"And that is what you yourself will prove, young woman. Here and now!" he declared. It was not a large apartment, and her backing away soon was halted.

"Foolish fool! Here's no time. Besides . . . you will be hungry. I have food and drink . . ."

"Hungry, yes! Well you may say it. But they have not starved me of *food*, see you!" He had her now, urgent, knowledgeable hands pressing, moulding, caressing. Her protests were vocal only, and easily stopped with kisses; and her person made no resistance—indeed her hands were soon aiding his with her gown. In glorious disorder he picked her up bodily in his arms and, no light weight as she was, strode with her to the couch.

Elizabeth de Burgh was all woman, and no passive partner in love-making. In mutual fervour and uninhibited passion they took and received each other, mounting swiftly, joyfully, to tremendous cataclysmic fulfilment.

As well they were so swift. Scarcely were they lying back, in murmurous relaxation, than they heard footsteps on the stairway, and voices. They waited, for there were two more storeys above; but when a knocking sounded at their door, Bruce sat up, cursing again—although this time the spirit and vigour had returned.

"Wait you," he called, out of it.

In haste they drew on and rearranged their clothing—though even so there was a quiet calm and dignity about that young woman's movements that seemed to be part of her very nature.

They were only approximately restored to respectability when Elizabeth went to open the door. Bishop Lamberton stood there, with another man who louted low respectfully. If the Primate noted anything amiss, in heightened colour and dishevelment, he did not remark on it.

"Your pardon, my friends, for this intrusion," he said. "I would not trouble you, with my lord so newly returned. But I believed that you would wish to hear this man's tidings, without delay. He comes from England. From Essex, Robert."

"My lord, I come from Hatfield Broadoak. Sent by the steward of the manor. Your father, my lord—he is dead. I have ridden day and night to bring you word."

Bruce drew a long breath.

"I am sorry," Lamberton said. "But he had retired from this world for long, Robert. He would not be loth to go, I think."

Elizabeth turned to her husband. "A father is a father," she said.

"Aye. God rest his soul." Bruce nodded. "I was no good son for him. We never agreed, all my days. I do not weep for him, in death—when I scarce thought of him in life. That would be folly. But at least I acknowledge that, as son, I failed him."

There was silence in that little fire-lit room. Then Bruce asked the courier for details. He rewarded him generously, and dismissed him to find food and rest. Lamberton remained.

"So we have a new situation, Robert," the Bishop said, when they were alone. "You are now Scotland's heir. Rightful king of this unhappy realm. Its only hope."

"Hope!" Bruce barked the word. "What hope am I? What hope is there in me, or for me? Or for Scotland? I have long ceased to hope, my friend. Or . . . or had. Until . . . until . . ."

"Until you heard of Edward's sickness? Aye, there could be hope there. We must not wish his death. But if he is stricken in body, the man might think more of his latter end and less of imposing his will on Scotland. For this we may lawfully pray.

Though, they tell me that he is already much bettered. So that he may not yet heed God's warning."

"I do not think he will. Edward is too old to change now. His hatred the strongest part of him! My hope is not that he will change, but . . . !" He left the rest unsaid.

"You have reason for bitterness, my friend. Who in Scotland has not?" the Primate commented. "But if Scotland is to survive, *you* must survive. To be its king. You are no longer your own man, my lord. Nor even this lady's. You are Scotland's man now. And Scotland never more greatly needed a man, strong, wise, constant, patient . . ."

"God help me—I am none of these!"

"I think that you are. Or can be. *Must* be. Great things are demanded of Robert Bruce, now. But a great reward, a great heritage awaits you. In all true men's eyes you are now the only possible aspirant to the throne. You, or one of your young brothers after you. Comyn based his claim on being Baliol's nephew. Baliol, a wrong choice from the first, is now totally discredited and debarred, his name a hindrance and no aid. Moreover, Comyn, in surrendering not only himself but the whole kingdom to Edward, has forfeited any personal support. . . ."

"I also yielded, you will mind! On your advice."

"But not in the same degree. Or on the same conditions. It was Comyn's misfortune to surrender as Guardian and commander. He has thrown away any claim to the throne."

"But what can I do? The throne of Scotland! What is it? Even if I could reach it."

"It is the symbol and surety of the continuance of this ancient realm and people. Lacking it, we are nothing. Supporting it and supported by it, we are a kingdom, a community of men, small, poor perhaps, but proud, independent, masters under God of our land and destiny. It is our grievous weakness that we are so prone to disunity. To this end, if no other, we need a king, an undoubted monarch, to rule and unite us. That monarch should be, must be, Robert Bruce."

"Should be, perhaps. But what is possible? While Edward lives?" That was Elizabeth.

"Only patient waiting. Readiness. Quiet preparation. Resolution. Only these are possible meantime. And notable caution. For when Edward hears of the Lord of Annandale's death, he will the more closely watch his son. Knowing that he holds the throne which should be that son's."

"He could watch me no closer than he does!"

"He might seek to hold you in ward. A prisoner, in truth."

"Would that be any worse than what he does? Shame me? Mock me? Send me to capture Wallace . . . ?"

"Ah yes, Robert—yes!" the young woman cried. "To be held. Shut up. Lodged in a cell. Taken from me . . . !"

"It would be more grievous, friend. Assuredly. And you did not, indeed, catch Wallace. I did not think you would!"

"It was grievous enough. If Wallace had been taken, and *I* had had hand in it . . . !"

"That would have been bad. For more than Wallace. But I believe he will never be taken. Unless he is betrayed. But he has the love of the people. Could any man sell Wallace?"

"I do not know. I do not know. Even Comyn would not do that. But some lost, damned soul, eaten with gall, there might be."

"Pray that you are wrong. And pray that none betray him and bring him before *you*, as one of Edward's three governors. You have heard of this? That with Moubray and my lord of Glasgow, you are appointed to the rule. Until John of Brittany comes."

"I shall refuse to rule Edward's Scotland."

"Are you sure, Robert? Think you. It is *your* Scotland—not Edward's. You might do much to soften the worst of an English harshness. And, one day, when you are King, your people will know that you are also their friend."

"When I am King." The younger man shook his head, looking away and away.

Elizabeth came to slip her arm in his.

Chapter Eighteen

The stink of fire and stale burning still clung to the Great Hall of Stirling Castle—really the parliament-hall of the kingdom, and the most splendid apartment in Scotland—emanating from the charred timbers of the fine lofty hammerbeam roofing, set alight by Edward's own ballistas and siege-engines, with their flaming missiles, a year before. The place was draughty too, that early November afternoon, from the gaps in the masonry made by the English mangonels, trebuchets and battering rams in the long siege, and as yet inadequately patched. It was not, in fact, a suitable venue for such a meeting, and the group of a dozen or so who sat at one end of the vast table built to seat hundreds, looked somewhat lost and uncomfortable in all this decayed and battered magnificence. But John of Brittany, Earl of Richmond, King's Lieutenant of Scotland, was a stiffly formal, dignified man, an upholder of ceremonial and etiquette, markedly unlike his puissant uncle, and he insisted on holding his council-meeting herein.

The assembled councillors were uncomfortable in more than their surroundings. Added to their normal resentment at having thus to obey the summons of an alien governor, and their mutual suspicions and hostilities, but little healed by general adversity, they were more sorely divided today than usual. Wallace had been captured three weeks before; and this, the successor of the Privy Council of Scotland, was split into three over the business—those who were sadly depressed thereby, those who were not, and those who cared little for the fact of it but reserved the right to cast disapproving glances at the man whose lot it had been to deliver up the national hero to English Edward.

Sir John Stewart of Menteith was only too well aware of his unhappy position, and showed it. He sat a little way apart from all others, a young man, dark, almost swarthy, with tight secretive features and a slight, tense body. Younger son of Walter, the late Earl of Menteith, and uncle of the present young Earl, although he had fought well against the English, he had recently caught the eye of Edward and been appointed Sheriff of Dumbarton and Keeper of its great castle. It was as holder of that position that he was present at this council.

There was a diversion as an English herald threw open a door and announced the entry of the three advisers of His Majesty's Lieutenant and Governor. These were old Bishop Wishart, Sir John de Moubray and Robert Bruce—now that John of Brittany was here in person, demoted from ruling triumvirate to special advisers. Those already assembled greeted them variously, nodding or scowling according to taste.

As the newcomers moved to take their seats near the head of the vast table, John Comyn of Badenoch spoke.

"Come, come, Menteith," he called loudly. "Give place. The Earl of Carrick, friend of Wallace, will not wish to sit beside the man who gave Wallace over to the English! Even though he is such good friend to King Edward also!"

Men drew quick breaths. Comyn was the more embittered since the general surrender, and none expected his attitude to Bruce to mellow; but this casting down of the gauntlet immediately on his enemy's appearance was hardly anticipated. This was the first meeting of the newly-constituted Lieutenant's Council.

As Bruce paused on his way to his chair, Menteith jumped to his feet, flushing hotly.

"My lord of Badenoch is again Sheriff of Moray," he declared. "Had the man Wallace been found and captured in *his* sheriffdom, would he have done other than I did? As I *had* to do?"

"The question scarce arises, sir. Being a modest man, I would have seen to it that whoever gained the glory of taking this notable outlaw, it would not have been me! I would have conceived my duty to lie . . . elsewhere! At the time. Besides, my lord of Carrick would not wish to sit beside me, in any case. Nor I him!"

"My lords! My lords!" Robert Wishart's frail voice quavered. "Peace, I pray you."

But Menteith, who had been simmering in frustrated silence for too long, was determined to exculpate himself, caring nothing for the quarrel between Bruce and Comyn.

"I did neither more nor less than my duty," he cried. "Ralph de Haliburton came to me at Dumbarton. Said that he believed Wallace to be hiding at Robroyston. He demanded that I apprehend him. Declared that he had been sent by King Edward, from England, for this very purpose. In the train of this Sir John de Moubray." And Menteith pointed a finger at Bruce's and Wishart's companion.

Moubray, a kinsman of Comyn's, shrugged. "Haliburton came north with my company, yes. From Westminster. I knew naught of the business. He had been a prisoner. Had fought bravely. One of the defenders of this castle of Stirling. When it fell, he was carried captive to England. He had gained his release—how I knew not—and joined my train, to return home. That is all I knew of him."

"We know now, then, how he bought his release!" Crawford growled. "The dastard!"

"But how did *he* know?" That was James the Steward, looking now but a shadow of his former self. "Know where Wallace was? How to come to him. For years others have sought Wallace, and failed to find him. How did this man do it?"

"He had a brother in Wallace's band. He is brother to Sir Henry de Haliburton," Menteith told them. "He must have made shift to find his brother. And so found Wallace. They would not suspect him, for those one hundred and twenty, at Stirling, had held all Edward's might at bay for many months. Heroes. None would doubt one of that company."

"And you? You played this felon's game, sir? And yielded up Wallace!" Bruce said.

"What else could I do, my lord? *You* went seeking Wallace yourself one time, did you not? In duty, since you could do no other. Haliburton asked servants from me. To seek him. Then brought him to me, bound. As sheriff. How he laid hands on the man, I know not. But having him, I could not let him go. I had no choice but to hand him over to the King's Lieutenant."

"Some might have used their wits to find another course, man."

"Is this Edward's friend that speaks? Or Wallace's?" Comyn asked, grinning wickedly. "The Lieutenant's adviser!"

Bruce sought to ignore him. He sat down, even though it was beside Menteith. Lamberton came to sit at his other side. But Comyn was not to be silenced thus.

"My lord says that some might better have used their wits, to get round Edward's commands," he went on. "As, it may be, did Bruce himself when Edward asked for his siege-engines to aid batter down this Stirling!"

"Not mine. His own siege-engines," Bruce gave back. "Left in my castles of Lochmaben and Turnberry."

"But he thanked you for them, nevertheless. Most graciously, if I mind aright!"

"Aye. And for the same reason that *you* speak of the matter now! For the further dividing of this realm against itself! Let us have no doubts as to that, my lords. While blame is being laid."

There was a murmur of agreement from not a few of those present. Lamberton spoke up.

"My lord of Carrick has the rights of it. This endless fighting amongst ourselves but aids our English masters. We are here for Scotland's good, not its ill. Soon this Richmond will come. A stiff and difficult man, but honest, I think. Something lacking in wits, himself, it may be—but with cunning hard minions, as we have reason to know. De Bevercotes and de Sandale are men who will guide him towards harshness, to the hurt of this realm. It must be our task to counter them, to move this nephew of Edward to gentler, better rule. It will demand all *our* wits. All our wisdom and patience."

The Steward, and one or two others, applauded.

"What will they be wanting from us?" the Earl of Atholl asked. "What will be the main business they put before us?"

"We understand it to be the carrying out of certain provisions passed by the Westminster parliament," Bruce answered. "Certain have already been implemented. Others have not. These others, it seems, are difficult. Grievous it may be. It seems that the English require our assistance in carrying them forward. Whether we can give it remains to be decided. But some here may tell us more. Before the English come. As you know we were required to send ten Commissioners to the Westminster parliament. Under the new constitution. Four of them are here present. If they would inform us further . . ."

He was interrupted by a stamping, clanking bodyguard of English men-at-arms, and the herald announcing, in noticeably more deferential tones, the arrival of the most noble and puissant Earl of Richmond, Lieutenant of Scotland of the high and mighty King Edward of England, whom God preserve. All men to stand.

Most of the Scots made but a poor business of getting to their feet, some barely raising their posteriors from their seats.

John of Brittany paced slowly in, flanked by two richly-dressed older men, and followed by a cohort of clerks and officers. For a man only a year or two senior to Bruce himself, Richmond seemed almost elderly. Tall, thin, sombre-featured, prematurely grey, he gave a notable impression of years, gloom, disillusionment, and possibly indigestion, with little of the Plantagenet about him. With his stiff gait, balding head and down-turned mouth, he seemed as unlikely a ruler of turbulent Scotland as nephew of Edward Longshanks.

His two companions redressed the balance somewhat. Both had the hard-bitten look of experienced administrators, self-made and ruthless, although one was a plump cleric and the other a square, stocky soldier. Master William de Bevercotes was Edward's Chancellor in Scotland, and Sir John de Sandale, Chamberlain.

When these three had seated themselves, amidst much fussing of clerks and arranging of papers, Richmond looked gravely, heavily, down the ranks of his Scots councillors, scrutinising each face and seeming almost to count them as he did so. It was a slow process, and the Breton evidently in no hurry. At last he broke the uncomfortable silence.

"Seventeen," he said, almost querulously. "Seventeen. I named twenty-two for my Council."

Comyn snorted eloquently, others coughed, and Lamberton spoke.

"Yes, my lord Lieutenant. All were apprised. The Earl of Dunbar and March is still with King Edward in London. The Bishop of Moray is indisposed. The young Earl of Menteith is represented by his uncle, Sir John Stewart of Menteith. As to the others, I know not."

Richmond took his time to digest that. Almost he chewed on it, underhung jaw working—and did not look as though he liked the taste.

"Fullest attendance is required," Master Bevercotes said, thinly for such a well-fleshed man. "Obligatory."

The Scots looked at each other. Bruce spoke, evenly.

"My lord, you have here seventeen of the greatest lords in Scotland, spiritual and temporal. Enough, surely, to advise you?"

The Lieutenant eyed him thoughtfully, but did not commit himself. Then he seemed to begin a recount, just to make sure.

John Comyn was not the man to accept much of this treatment. "I have come a long and hard road to attend this Council," he said. "I move to business."

De Sandale rapped out an oath. "Insolent!" he said.

"Sir!"

"My lord Lieutenant," Lamberton intervened hurriedly. "We are very ready to lend such aid and counsel as you may require. All here are men of weight and responsibility. Four indeed have been Guardians of this realm . . ."

"This *former* realm!" Richmond corrected. He could think and speak quickly enough when he so desired, apparently.

None commented on his amendment.

"Do you desire me to proceed, my lord?" the Chancellor asked.

That required consideration also. At length, Richmond answered. "First to the matter of Wallace."

"Yes, my lord. Exactly, my lord." Bevercotes beamed approval. "The man Wallace, by all means." He shuffled his papers. "My lord Lieutenant has word this day. From His Majesty in London. The man Wallace is dead."

Consternation greeted his statement.

"Taken, examined, tried, condemned and executed. For treason. On . . . where is it? Yes—on the 23rd day of the month of October. Ten days past this day."

"Treason . . . !" Bruce got out. "Treason against whom?"

"Treason, sir, against his liege lord. And yours! King Edward of this realm."

"But . . ." A jolt to his knee beneath the table, from Lamberton, gave Bruce pause.

"May we hear more of this trial? If your lordship pleases," the Primate said.

Richmond nodded, and the Chancellor read from his paper.

"The prisoner Wallace, after being lodged within the house of one William de Leyre, alderman, in Fenchurch Street, was brought by the mayor, aldermen and magistrates of the said city of London, to trial at Westminster Hall. By order of His Majesty. Before the King's Justice, Sir Peter Mallorie. The outlaw Wallace was thereupon impeached as traitor to the King's royal person and authority, in that he did notoriously and shamefully slay the King's lieges, burn his abbeys, towns and villages, storm his castles, imprudently call parliaments in that part of the King's realm called Scotland, and set at naught the royal commands. In especial that he did slay and murder the duly appointed Sheriff of Lanark and many other officers, in particular at the King's castle of Ayr. After burning many to the death . . ."

"That was war, not treason!" Bruce protested. "The two realms were in a state of war. How could it be treason?"

"My lord of Carrick—may I remind you of my presence!" Richmond said sternly.

"The prisoner admitted all," the Chancellor read on. "He but made claim that since he had not sworn fealty to the King's name and person, he was no subject of King Edward, and so his acts were not treasonable. Justice Mallorie made observation that if only those who had sworn the oath of fealty could be guilty of treason, then most of the King's subjects could turn traitor with impunity . . ."

"My lord," Bishop Wishart broke in, frail voice cracking. "Does King Edward distinguish nothing between his English subjects and the Scots?"

"Nothing, my lord of Glasgow. As *you* should know right well. Scotland is part of the realm of England, and its people subjects of His Majesty."

"So says Edward now. But it was not so when Sir William Wallace so acted," Bruce countered. "He was in lawful arms against invaders."

"He was a rebel!" de Sandale declared harshly. "As were you all. All rebels. Worthy of death. But His Majesty was merciful. Too merciful, it seems! He took you back into his peace. But when surrender was made, Wallace refused the King's peace,

Wilfully. With war over, he remained at war. An outlaw. He had no rights, therefore. No call on mercy."

"No call on mercy!" Lamberton repeated heavily. "He was a brave man. If he should have received mercy, he did not plead for it—that I swear!"

"He received his deserts, my lord Bishop," Master Bevercotes declared primly. He consulted his papers. "Found guilty by the Court, the traitor Wallace was tied, naked and in chains, at the tails of horses, and dragged four miles through the streets of the city, to the much acclamation of the loyal populace. At Smithfield, he was part-hanged in his chains, and cut down while yet alive. Thereupon he was disembowelled, and his entrails burned before his eyes." The Chancellor moistened his lips, and raised his voice to overspeak the snarling growl which was arising round that table. "Thereafter the prisoner's head was cut from his body. Then the limbs. The said head was affixed to a pole to be set on London Bridge. And the said limbs thus distributed—the right arm sent to Newcastle-upon-the-Tyne; the left arm to Berwick-upon-the-Tweed; the right leg to St. John's Town of Perth; and the left leg to Aberdeen. By order of the King's Majesty."

The tension in that draughty hall was tight as a bow-string, as men sat, scarcely breathing. Yet John of Brittany appeared to be completely impervious to it, or unaware of it. He was rustling amongst other papers.

"Yes," he said, after an unbearable moment or two. "Thank you, Master Chancellor. That is the matter of Wallace. For your information, my lords. Now we proceed to more urgent business. I think, first, this of the failure of much of the Church in this land to pay its share of the costs of the late war. My lord of St. Andrews . . . ?"

The crash of Bruce's chair falling over backwards as he thrust it from him, rising to his feet, brought Richmond to a sudden stop.

"My lord Lieutenant," he said, thick-voiced. "I pray to be excused from further attendance at this Council."

Outraged, the other stared up at him. "My lord—do I hear you aright? Excused . . . ? Or are you taken sick . . . ?"

"Aye, sick! Well you say it. Sick at the evil that has been done. I, for one, will have no further part in working with such monstrous rule and governance. You are Edward of England's Lieutenant and representative. I can no longer act on your Council."

"Robert! My lord . . . !" Lamberton's warning, beseeching hand came up to grasp Bruce's arm—and was roughly shaken off.

"Sir—this is beyond all!" Richmond declared. "Have you lost your wits? Sit down, my lord . . ."

"No. I leave the loss of wits to you and yours! To your master and kinsman, in especial! To have turned ravening savage and brute-beast . . . !"

"Silence, sir!" De Sandale the Chamberlain was on his feet now, pointing. "To so asperse His Majesty's name! And in the presence of His Majesty's Lieutenant! How dare you . . . !"

Bruce did not so much as glance at him. "Wallace was a noble man. Not noble as we here are noble, perhaps—but nobler than any here by his deeds! A man all here should have been proud to call friend. And did not, to our shame! In him was the true spirit of this Scotland. And Edward Plantagenet dealt with him as he would not a dog!" Furiously he shouted down the protesting English. "Wallace was no traitor. How could he be? To an English king, when he fought only for the Crown of Scotland? Which Crown . . . which Crown . . ." He faltered, as well he might, even wincing at the vice-like urgency of the Primate's grip on his arm. But he went on, a little differently. "A traitor is traitor only to his country, or his friends, or to those that trust in him. Was Wallace ever traitor to his country? Was Edward ever his friend? Did Edward ever trust him? Some here might, by others, be named traitor. *I* have been! But not Wallace. And yet, he is treated worse than any murdering scullion!"

"You have run mad, my lord of Carrick!" Richmond said, as Bruce paused for breath. "What you say is stark treason."

"Mad? The madness is not mine, but Edward's. Madness indeed. Do you not see it? The folly of it, as well as the sin? The people of Scotland loved William Wallace. Better than any man who ever lived in this kingdom. As they do not love any here. Edward, by this evil, will set every heart in Scotland ablaze against him. As all his burnings and slayings and conquests have not done. They are a strong, hard people, as Edward has learned. This will turn them to steel. Against himself. Against his rule. The blood shamefully shed at your Smithfield is but the first of a flood, I tell you! It will make ill ruling of this land, my lord of Richmond, that is certain. And I—I will not aid you to do it." He made a final gesture with his hand. "I have asked your permission to withdraw, my lord. Now I go."

"Aye, go! Go, Earl of Carrick. Before I have my officers take you. As I ought. Throw you into close ward . . . !"

Bruce did not answer, being already on his way to the door,

with uncertain officers and clerks hesitating. It was John Comyn who interrupted.

"You must needs take Comyn also, then, my friend!" he said, rising. "For once, Robert Bruce has the rights of it! I never conceived this Council of worth. I will no more serve on it, now, than he. I, nor mine." He looked down at the Earl of Buchan. The Constable, puffing and grunting, rose to his feet.

Despite Richmond's protests, amidst a great scraping of chairs, the Council broke up in disorder.

Bruce found Comyn at his shoulder, in the passage outside. "I did not think it was in you to do it!" the latter said. "Edward will not like it."

"I do not do only what Edward likes."

"You do *much* that Edward likes!"

Bruce swung on the man. "You think so? Why then does Edward hate me? Tell me that, Comyn. He hates me almost as much as he hated Wallace. Why, if I do his will?"

The other looked at him searchingly. "And you? You hate Edward?"

"Aye. I hate Edward. And all that he stands for."

Lamberton was there, now. "My lord—less loud! Those words could be a rope round your neck! If another such was needed! I advise that you put distance between yourself and this Stirling. And as swiftly as you may."

"Aye—do that, Bruce." Comyn laughed. "Hide, you! And if your South will not sufficiently hide you from Edward Plantagenet, come North! Come to Badenoch! Can I offer you fairer ...?"

. . .

But despite all the good advice, Bruce was still in Stirling town that night—and, oddly enough, at Lamberton's urging. Indeed the Primate was his sole companion as they hurried through the dark, narrow streets, heads down against the smirr of chill November rain.

Comyn was lodged in the Blackfriars' Monastery, where one of his clan was Prior. Lamberton summoned the Prior to his own door, and required a private room and the Lord of Badenoch privily informed.

Comyn came presently. Although not actually the worse for liquor, clearly he had been drinking. He stood with his back to the door of the small sparsely-furnished chamber, eyeing his visitors curiously in the mellow lamplight.

"So soon!" he commented. "Bruce takes refuge with Comyn already? From Edward's wrath!"

"We have come for a word in your private ear, my lord," the Bishop said. "Believing that you will heed. And come to some agreement with us."

That was not strictly true. Lamberton may have believed it, but Bruce was highly doubtful. He had come only at his friend's strong persuasion and almost against his own better judgement. The Primate had argued that, for the first time, Comyn had that day acted, if not in co-operation with Bruce, at least in parallel. Had even commended Bruce's step before all. Here was opportunity not to be missed, therefore.

"Agreement?" Comyn repeated. "You grow ambitious, my lords!"

"Perhaps. For Scotland. It is time, I think, that we grew ambitious for this unhappy realm. All of us. For her freedom. For her very survival."

"Scotland's? Or your own? Bruce's? Which?" The words were a little slurred, but the challenge was swift enough.

"The survival of us all. As other than slaves. Wallace's fate may be our last warning. His dying cries our final awakening. Then, at least, he will not have suffered in vain."

"Fine words, Sir Bishop. But what do they mean?"

"They mean, Comyn," Bruce interposed bluntly, "that if Scotland is to be saved, then first and foremost you and I must come to agreement. The realm cannot afford your faction fighting mine. Either we come to terms, or the Kingdom of Scotland can be forgotten. Become but a memory. And Wallace has given his life for nothing."

"Terms?" the other said. "And what are Bruce's terms? To Comyn."

"Scotland needs a king. Only an acknowledged monarch will now rally her. To take up arms against the conqueror. Baliol's arrow is shot. None will fight for him now. Not even you, I think. He does not desire the crown. I say the crown should be mine. You say otherwise . . ."

"An old story, Bruce. These terms?"

"One of us must be the King of Scots. Mine is the direct claim. Through the old line of our kings. Yours only through the discredited Baliol. But . . . I offer terms, that this impasse may be resolved. Withdraw your claim and support mine, and I will hand over to you all the Bruce lands in Scotland—save only some small properties for my brothers. Or . . ." He took a deep breath. ". . . or hand over to me all the Comyn lands, and I will stand down in your favour as King."

The other stared, moving a step or two forward from the door. "You *are* in your right mind, man?" he demanded.

"I am." Bruce jerked his head. "My lord Bishop will confirm what I say."

"That I do," Lamberton nodded. "My lord of Carrick's offer is a true one. Made on my own advising. For the sake of the realm. His the crown and yours the lands. Or yours the crown and his the lands. If the Scots people will accept you as King. Which would you?"

"But . . . this is scarce believable! To offer up the Bruce lands. The greatest in Scotland . . . !"

The other two exchanged quick glances. It was significant that it was the broad acres that Comyn thought of first, rather than the empty crown.

Swiftly the Primate took him up. "Aye, the greatest in Scotland. A notable offer, such as never has been made before. Especially since *your* claim to the throne is now weakened. This would make you a greater lord and earl than ever Scotland has known."

"And, if my claim is so weak, why make this offer?"

"Because, weak or no, there can be no true decision as to the kingdom while you hold to it. Without dividing the land. Internal strife. If we are to unite against the English, at last, one of us must stand down. So I offer all that I have to offer." That was Robert Bruce.

It was not often that John Comyn appeared at a loss. In fact never had Bruce seen him irresolute, before this night. He paced the small chamber, biting his lip. He stopped, presently.

"If this is a trick . . . !" he said.

"No trick," Lamberton assured. "In the name of Saint Andrew of Scotland. I swear it. And will do, before any company you name."

"Save that it must be kept secret," Bruce put in. "This, coming to Edward's ears, would be my death-warrant!"

Comyn looked at him, long and hard.

"Which do you choose, my lord?" Bruce challenged him.

"It . . . it would require to be written. And sealed," the other declared. "I would so require."

"So would we!" Lamberton agreed grimly. He reached inside his damp travelling-cloak and brought out a leather satchel, from which he took four folded papers, a pen, a horn of ink, and a block of wax. Also flint and tinder. "All is in readiness, my lord. Four indentures. Two promising the throne to my lord of Carrick, and his lands to you; and two the other way. Sign which you will. My lord here will sign its neighbour. And the other two we shall burn. Each will keep a copy. Secretly. Yours is the choice. For the realm's fair sake."

Only Comyn's heavy breathing sounded as he took the papers closer to the lamp, reading closely. He took an unconscionable time about it, seeming to weigh each word of all four indentures. But, at length, he laid them down on the table.

"The pen," he said.

Wordless, Lamberton handed over the quill and opened inkhorn.

John Comyn looked up into Bruce's eyes for a long moment, then stooped and dashed off his bold signature, quill spluttering. It was on one of the papers that conceded the crown to Bruce, and the Bruce lands to himself.

His rival emitted a long sigh, and picked up the pen Comyn had thrown down. Without comment he signed the companion document.

"I sign as witness to both," Lamberton declared. "Have you your seals to hand, my lords?"

And so the thing was done. As the heated wax, with the two seals impressed thereon, cooled, and the last black fragments of burned paper fluttered to the floor, the three men looked at each other.

"When do I get your lands?" Comyn asked.

"On the day I am crowned King."

"Will that day ever dawn?"

"We must see that it does. Between us."

"With the aid of Holy Church," Lamberton added.

"Why should you . . . why should *we* be able to achieve now what we could not do before?"

"Because we are fighting, in the main, one man. Edward. And Edward is not the man he was. Edward's sickness could be Scotland's saving."

"He recovered well."

"Aye. But once the heart gives such warning, no man is ever the same. The finger of God is on him," Lamberton said. "And we have heard that since he returned to London he has had another slight seizure. A sign to him. And to us. To be ready."

"It could be years, even so."

"It could be, yes. But at least we can be prepared. To move. Not to await his death. To act when Edward himself cannot lead his hosts northwards. For that day we wait." Bruce spoke urgently. "So secrecy is all-important. You will see it. I charge you, Comyn, tell no man of this night's work. If it got to Edward's ears, all would be lost. My life not worth a snap of the fingers!"

"And my lord of Badenoch's life also, I would point out!" the Bishop added, significantly. "Edward would feel little more kindly to the one than the other. Both would be taking from him the Scots crown which he usurps." He picked up the two sealed papers, assured that the wax was firm, and handed each man that with the other's signature.

Almost reluctantly now they took the fateful documents, wordless. Abruptly Comyn turned to open the door, and held it wide for his visitors.

They parted no better friends than heretofore.

Chapter Nineteen

WITH much trepidation, however much he tried to hide it, Robert Bruce waited amongst the gaily-dressed and glittering throng, his wife at his side. He had been against bringing her, first to England at all, and then to this Palace of Westminster. But she had insisted on both, declaring that she would not let him come without her. Not that he himself had been anxious to come; very much the reverse. But what could he do? Edward's summons, although courteous, even friendly, had been a command not a request, for the attendance of his well-loved Lord Robert at the celebration of the royal birthday, his sixty-seventh. To have refused would have been a declaration of war, premature and foolhardy; yet this acceptance was putting his head into the lion's mouth, with a vengeance. It was Elizabeth's belief that her presence with her husband could do no harm, and might possibly do good.

The pair from Scotland were interested, and to some extent encouraged, by the attitude and bearing of the courtiers who thronged around them, waiting for the royal entrance to this great reception and entertainment. All were respectful, attentive, and at least as friendly as they were ever likely to be. Which presumably meant that if Edward had sent for Bruce to rend him, he had let no hint of it escape to those close to him—for nothing was more certain than that if he had, it would have been reflected in the quality of the Bruces' reception by his Court. Not only this night but in the four days they had been in London. That the King had not sent for them for personal audience during that time, admittedly could be interpreted either way; but at least it implied that the Plantagenet was not in any fury of haste to explode his anger on them. Edward was unpredictable, of course.

The new Gloucester, Ralph de Monthermer, who had succeeded Bruce's late cousin Gilbert de Clare, as husband to King Edward's daughter—and bore the title by courtesy while the child was a minor—stood beside them with his somewhat horse-faced countess. Gloucester gave no impression of wrath to come. A friendly, modest man, he could not keep his eyes off Elizabeth—who was tonight looking at her loveliest.

"The King's health?" Bruce asked—by no means the first such enquiry he had made since coming south. He hoped always to hear some inkling, some clue as to the true condition of the royal heart.

"Eh? Ah, yes. The King." With difficulty Ralph of Gloucester partially withdrew from contemplation of more pleasing subjects. "His health, yes. It is improved. Indubitably much improved."

"Excellent," Bruce commented heavily. "After that last small seizure. In the autumn, was it? Nothing more?"

"Nothing. He is himself again. For which God be praised. For Edward of Carnarvon is little fit for the throne. Not yet."

"He lacks his father's fire, yes."

"More than that. He chooses ill friends. Prefers the company of singers, mummers and mimers, players. Priests of the baser sort. He does not play the man."

"I would have thought that England might have had enough of warrior kings!"

"We would esteem a few years of peace, yes. But now that Scotland is subdued; Wales and Ireland also; and we are in treaty with France and the Pope, peace there is. It must be preserved, you will agree, Cousin. And a weak king, you must admit, is a sure road to war and rebellion."

"Edward has never been a man of peace. Think you he will be content with peace now? Or is this sickness like to affect him? Prevent him from leading more campaigns? In person?"

"Who knows? Queen Margaret will keep him from that. If she may . . ."

A fanfare cut short this exchange. Everyone bowed as a herald announced the resounding titles of Edward, by God's grace King of England, Lord of Scotland, Ireland and Wales, Duke of Normandy and Aquitaine.

It was not only the reference to Scotland which made Bruce's brow darken as he bowed with the rest, but the manner of the King's arrival. He positively swept into the great chamber, no more like an ailing man than Bruce was, smiling, jovial, dragging his pregnant wife along by the hand, high-coloured and heavy but as full of energy as of goodwill. It was a sore disappointment.

But disappointment was quickly overlaid by a more urgent emotion—apprehension. The royal summons to Bruce had been for no mere social celebration—that was not in Edward's character. Richmond, or more likely Bevercotes, would have sent a full account of the proceedings at Stirling in November last. There had been no repercussions in the meantime. Bruce had been left alone to manage his own affairs, on his estates, and had taken no further part in the rule of Scotland. Now he must look for a reckoning. Elizabeth came close, and slipped her hand within his arm.

To the soft strains of the musicians, the King made unhurried progress towards the twin thrones at the head of the hall, having a gracious word with lords and ladies in passing. Quite quickly Queen Margaret espied Elizabeth, and began to draw her husband towards her former favourite lady-in-waiting.

"A good sign," Elizabeth murmured. "The Queen at least suspects no clash, I think."

"Edward may not have revealed his mind. Even to her. He is a law unto himself."

The King did not allow his consort to hurry him unduly, certainly. The royal progress was agonisingly slow for the pair from Scotland.

At last the two couples were face to face, with the Queen reaching out to embrace the curtsying Elizabeth, and Bruce bowing again.

"Ha, Robert—do I see you well?" Edward demanded genially. "I vow I can scarce discern you, so dazzled are my old eyes by your lady's beauty!" And he in turn bowed gallantly.

"I am well, Sire, yes. And you?"

"Never better, lad. Never better. You will rejoice to hear!" And the older man eyed him directly.

Bruce swallowed. "All Your Majesty's subjects must rejoice at that," he said.

"They should, lad—they should!" Edward agreed. "As you will see, my wife has no reason to complain of my . . . inadequacy!—Yours has less to thank you for, by the looks of her!"

The other inclined his head slightly. "There is time and to spare, I hope."

Edward's smile faded for a moment. "Who knows!" he gave back, shortly. He turned to Elizabeth. "My dear, you gladden as well as dazzle our eyes," he said. "We have missed you."

"Ah, yes," the Queen agreed. "So much. So very much. There is none like my Elizabeth."

"Your Majesties are too kind."

"This lord of yours," the King said. "He tells me that he is well. Yet he has been hiding himself away. In Annandale and Galloway, I am told. Neglecting the rule of my Scotland."

"There has been much to do, Sire, in the Bruce lands. Much to put to rights. After these past years. And you have servants in plenty to rule Scotland," Elizabeth pointed out.

"None so many when my Scots lords withdraw their aid and duty!"

"My lord of Richmond is well able to govern Scotland, Sire," Bruce claimed. "He has . . ."

"My lord of Richmond is a fool! But I am not, Robert—I am not!"

"Yet Richmond's troubles in Scotland stem from the slaying of Wallace here in London. And the manner of the slaying," Bruce said, through tight lips.

"To be sure. Your notions on Wallace were reported to me!" That was coldly enunciated. "Do you wish to add to them now?"

"No, Sire. That would be to no purpose. I but remark that your nephew's present difficulties arise from the people's anger at Wallace's cruel death."

"And you will not aid him in those difficulties? At my command?"

"Your Majesty's command I must obey," the younger man said woodenly. "If my lord of Richmond seeks my aid, in your name, then I must needs give it."

"I am glad that you perceive that fact, Robert."

"Edward—my legs!" the Queen broke in. "I am weary of standing. With this great belly of mine! Let us sit, of a mercy!"

"To be sure, my love. Come. Elizabeth—you also." He glanced back at Bruce. "We shall talk of this later, my lord." With curt dismissal, the King moved on.

Elizabeth looked unhappily at her husband, but could not refuse to obey the royal command, especially when the Queen's hand was on her arm. Bruce was left standing alone.

And he remained alone. For now the watchful courtiers, practised in discerning favour and disfavour, perceived the difference of treatment as between man and wife, and shunned him. Even Gloucester, though he did not ignore him entirely, tended to keep his distance.

A programme of music, dancing, miming, tumbling and the like followed, during all of which the Scot remained isolated, separated from Elizabeth and avoided by almost all the company. Too proud to approach those who looked away, Bruce fumed what seemed endless hours away in ill-suppressed rage. He could not take himself off, as he would have wished, and leave Elizabeth behind; moreover, Edward had cunningly said that they would talk more later—which was as good as a command to stay.

Once, while meats and drink were being brought in by a host of servants, Elizabeth did manage to slip away, temporarily, from the Queen's side, for a word with her husband.

"I am sorry, my heart," she murmured. "This is hard to bear. But . . . it is perhaps less ill than might have been. The King is teaching you one of his lessons."

"And I must needs stand here and suffer it! Before all. Like a corrected child! I cannot come up to you, at the thrones, without being invited. I cannot leave. And all these know I am now frowned on, and frown in turn . . ."

"I grieve for you. But we did fear worse, Robert. After what you said and did at Stirling. At least this chastening hurts only your pride. And he cannot intend more dire punishment, or he would not act thus. With the hour growing late . . ."

"With Edward, who can tell? The devil could be hatching greater evil!"

"Not at this hour. Not tonight. And the Queen grows very weary. The child is heavy in her. She will soon seek to retire. Then we should see an end to this . . ."

The Queen's weariness, however, took a long time to affect her husband's enjoyment of the evening. And when Edward did finally rise, to escort her out, amidst genuflection from all present, he in fact led her down the opposite side of the room from Bruce's position, and without a glance thitherward. The younger man did not know whether to be relieved or further infuriated—although Elizabeth, released and rejoining him, was in no doubts.

They were too soon in debating the issue. A court official came hurrying back through the throng to the Bruces.

"My lord, His Majesty requires your attendance. At once. Follow me," he said briefly.

Exchanging glances, they moved after him, though without haste.

The King was talking to Gloucester just outside in the vestibule, the Queen looking very pale and near to tears. He broke off.

"My lord," he said, as the Bruces came up, unsmiling now, "I had intended to speak you further. On another matter of grave import. But Her Majesty is fatigued. The matter must keep. But not for long. You will attend on me, at my privy quarters in this house, tomorrow. At noon. You understand?"

"At noon. Yes, Sire. As you command."

"Aye, as I command. And see you, my friend—come well versed in explanation! As to your . . . ambitions! You may have a queen for sister, Robert—but that is as near the royal estate as you' will ever win! Noon, tomorrow. Come, my dear."

Monarchy moved off.

Eyeing the Plantagenet's massive back, Bruce murmured, setfaced. "So now we come to it! Tomorrow noon I will hear the real reason for my summons to London!"

· · ·

Back at their lodging they were still discussing the King's intentions, fearing that he might have heard some rumour of the bond with Comyn, when knocking sounded at the street door. Elizabeth's alarm was immediate, and out of character; but Bruce pointed out that the knocking was discreet rather than peremptory. He had lived long enough on the edge of danger to sense the difference.

One of his servants brought in a cloaked figure wearing no insignia, colours or livery. This man waited silent until the servitor had gone. Then, assuring himself that nobody listened outside the door, he brought out from beneath his cloak a pair of spurs. In the other hand he held out a silver shilling.

"From my lord of Gloucester," he said quietly, cryptically.

Bruce looked from the man to Elizabeth. "Aye," he said heavily. He took both the spurs and the coin.

The visitor reached out, wordless, and turned over the shilling, so that the likeness of King Edward's head was uppermost.

Bruce nodded. "I perceive the message," he said. "You will

thank your lord. Here—take this." He handed him back the silver coin.

"I thank *you*, my lord." The man bowed briefly to the wide-eyed Elizabeth, and turned away.

"My friend," Bruce said to his back, "I do not wish further to endanger you. But, as a citizen of this London, can you tell me if all the city gates are kept locked of a night?"

"All," the other nodded. "But I have heard it said that the watch will open any, if commanded in the King's name."

"I see. For this also I thank you."

Without another word the visitor departed.

Two hours later the small Bruce party, of no more than a dozen men-at-arms and servitors, with Elizabeth muffled and cloaked to look like a youthful page, rode quietly through the narrow sleeping streets of the February night, to Eastgate. At the walls and gatehouse there Bruce reluctantly, and with a deal more confidence of voice than he felt, shouted authoritatively.

"Watch! Watch, I say! Waken, fools! Dolts—awake! Open, in the King's name."

There was some small delay, nerve-racking but inevitable. No argument, however, or enquiry. Bruce's imperious second demand, with some realistic cursing, was followed by the rattle of chains and the creaking of the great double doors, as they swung wide.

The Scots clattered through the cobbled pend, and took the dark Essex road beyond, and heard the gates clang to behind.

A mile or so on, they turned due north, something under four hundred miles of hard riding before them. It was nearly 3 a.m. They could probably reckon on a start of anything from five to nine hours. As well that Elizabeth was strong and an excellent horse-woman.

•   •   •

It was a desperately tired and bedraggled company—though three short, two servants and a man-at-arms having fallen out—which, four days and three nights later avoiding Carlisle, crossed the Border near Kirkandrews. Whether they had been pursued they did not know. After fording the Esk, they came within a mile or so to the lesser Glenzier Water, which they must also cross before turning westwards through the low green hills for Annandale.

It was as they were approaching this second ford that they perceived two horsemen already splashing across, but from the other direction. There was little for comment in this, perhaps—save that anyone taking this route could only be making to cross the Border, and by the inconspicuous road that avoided the English garrison-town of Carlisle. But Bruce, however weary, may have been hypersensitive to certain colours. He reined up, pointing.

"Do my eyes deceive me, or are those men wearing the Comyn colours of blue and gold?" he demanded.

Elizabeth narrowed heavy, red-rimmed eyes. "Yes," she nodded. "Blue and gold. Is it of any matter?"

"They are a long way from home, for Comyns. And heading south."

"John Comyn has lands in Dumfriesshire, has he not? And Galloway?"

"Yes. But these are riding away from them. For England. And avoiding Carlisle. As we have done. Why?" With a toss of his shoulders, he seemed to shake off his fatigue. "Come."

He reined his all-but foundered horse around—the fourth he had ridden since leaving London—and led his silently protesting party back the way they had come for a little distance, to a thicket of scrub oak and thorn in a marshy hollow, which they had passed through a minute or two before. Into this he turned his people, right and left, to hide amongst the trees.

The two horsemen appeared presently, trotting unconcernedly. One was young, well-dressed, an esquire presumably; the other a bearded man-at-arms riding slightly behind. Bruce allowed them to come nearly up to his hiding-place, then spurred forward into their path.

"Wait you, friend," he called. "One moment. How come you to ride this road to England, this day?"

The young man had drawn up, startled, hand dropping to sword-hilt. Behind, the soldier was quicker, his whinger whipped out with a scrape of metal. Looking round, the former was in time to see four of Bruce's own men-at-arms emerging from the thickets at the other side of the road.

"What is this, sirrah?" he demanded hotly. "How dare you!"

"I but asked your business, sir. The Border is but a mile away, and no place between. It concerns me who crosses that Border."

"Why should it? I am on lord's business. A great lord, Comyn, Lord of Badenoch's business. Do you dare, sir, to question?"

"I do," Bruce answered, mildly enough. "And with cause. For I am Sheriff of Dumfries. And was Scots Warden of this March ... when Scots wardens meant anything."

"Sheriff ... !" the other repeated falteringly. He looked round again, and saw that he and his man were now quite surrounded. "Who are you, sir?"

"The name is Bruce. You may have heard of it? You are a long way from Comyn country, friend."

"Bruce? The . . . the earl!"

"The same. You do not look, friend, as though you had ridden from Badenoch and the Spey?"

"No, my lord. Only from Dalswinton. From my lord's house near to Dumfries . . ."

"Comyn is there? At Dalswinton?"

"Yes. The Justiciary Court meets this week at Dumfries. My lord attends."

"And you? Your business, sir?"

"My lord's business. Not mine. Nor yours, my lord!"

"Mine, yes. If you are for crossing this Border. And on this road you can be going nowhere other. But . . . see you, your lord and I are in bond to each other. You have naught to fear."

The other was silent.

"I am waiting, sir. And tired! Your business in England?"

"I am not at liberty to tell, my lord."

"You will not long be at liberty to refuse!" Bruce commented grimly. "Do you carry letters?"

Nibbling his lip, the younger man shook his head.

"I think that you do. Tell me who they are for, and if you know their purpose. If you do, I may not require to do more than look at the superscription and seal."

"I will not, cannot, do it."

"Fool! Who knows, the letter may be for me! I have been in England. Comyn could well be writing to me. A warning, perhaps."

"The letter is not for you, Earl of Carrick."

"Then, a God's name, who is it? You have admitted you have a letter. As Sheriff of this shire I require you to let me see."

The unhappy courier shook his head stubbornly. Bruce jerked a brief command to his men. They kneed their mounts close. One drew sword, to point at the esquire's throat. Two pinioned each an arm. Two more engaged the guard behind, who only put up token resistance. A sixth reached out to fumble in the victim's bulging saddle-bags.

It took a little while, amidst some shouting and protest, for the horses sidled and pranced. But at length this last man brought out a sealed paper package. He handed it over to Bruce.

Apart from the seal, which showed the Comyn arms of three golden wheatsheafs on a blue ground, the package was entirely plain, without superscription. Unhesitantly Bruce opened it. Inside was another sealed package. But this one had a superscription. It read:

TO HIS HIENES EDWARD KING OF INGLAND, AT WESTMINSTER

"Ha!" Bruce leaned over, to show this to Elizabeth. "See where John Comyn's letter goes!" He swung back to the courier. "You knew this. You were taking this to King Edward, in London. You must have known. But—do you know what is in it?"

White-faced now, the other shook his head.

"Tell me. Or I shall open it."

"I do not know. My lord said that it was most secret. That . . . that I guard it with my life!" The young man's voice broke.

"Aye." With a swift gesture Bruce broke open the second seal, and unfolded the stiff paper.

The inner side was written upon. But enclosed in it was another folded paper. And this bore another seal. But not Comyn's. This was Bruce's own. With his signature likewise. Witnessed by William Lamberton.

"Christ . . . in . . . His . . . heaven!" he whispered.

"Robert! What is it?"

"What is it?" he got out, thickly. "It is death! It is my neck! My head—sent to Edward! For execution! By the living God— our bond! I did not believe . . . that any man . . . could sink so low! My death-warrant. And Lamberton's. Here is infamy beyond all telling!"

She reached over and took Comyn's copy of the crown-and-lands agreement, which Bruce had signed that November night in the Blackfriars Monastery at Stirling.

With fingers that trembled now with emotion her husband smoothed out the folds of the enclosing letter. It was notably brief:

Hienes,

Since you require proof of the matter wch I wrote to you before. Here is proof. I desire to receive it back by bearer. Also that yr Hienes seems not to have seen it. For it is mch value and dangerous. Bruce has the other like, wth my name and seal. If yr Hienes takes him you will win it for yr proof and purpose.

I remain yr Hienes servant,

JNO COMYN OF BADENOCH

"The forsworn dastard! For this John Comyn shall die! I swear it, by all the saints!"

Anxiously, Elizabeth looked at her husband. She had never seen him like this, so black of brow, so savage of expression.

"It is vile treachery, yes. Thank God that we won out of London when we did! This was what Edward was meaning. He knew of this, all the time."

"Aye. Comyn had written him, betraying all. Edward demanded proof. For my trial! Had we not bolted when we did, I would never have left London alive. Gloucester saved my head!"

"What will you do, Robert? Now?"

"Do? I will do what needs to be done. What I should have done long since. Make a reckoning with John Comyn! I will . . ." He paused, looking at the anxious courier. "Here is not the time and place to talk of that. Nor are these two the men to hear it. They must remain silenced. Close warded. Until the matter is resolved. We will take them with us, to Lochmaben."

"My lord—here is no fault of mine . . ." the esquire faltered.

"None. Save to own a dastard lord! You will suffer nothing, so long as you cause no further trouble. Do as you are bidden. But I cannot let you go free, until I have come to a conclusion with your master. That is certain."

They rode on northwards for Lochmaben, and the shadow of evil was like a threatening cloud about them.

Chapter Twenty

The red-stone town of Dumfries was busy that frosty February morning, with Edward's English justices in session at the castle, and half the lords and lairds of the South-West summoned to be present, either to speak to complaints, seek redress, support charged feudal vassals, or give account for their heritable jurisdictions. Soldiers and men-at-arms were everywhere, English and Scots. The citizenry, well aware of the potential explosiveness of this mixture, tended to keep indoors and out of sight.

Bruce had been heedful about the numbers of his own men he brought into town from Lochmaben. Too many would arouse comment, might seem like a challenge, and provoke trouble with the English. On the other hand, that he might well require a substantial force of men went without saying. On the principle that a great lord was entitled, in most circumstances, to a train of from fifty to a hundred, just to maintain his dignity, he had brought about seventy-five selected horsemen. But, as well, he had arranged that certain of his more important local vassals and supporters should make independent entry to the town, with their own smaller followings. With these, he reckoned that he could call upon a couple of hundred men, at short notice, if the need arose.

His information that Comyn would be in town today was quickly confirmed. He learned that his enemy, who was much involved in this bout of litigation, had installed himself at the small monastery of the Franciscan or Grey Friars, founded by the Lady Devorgilla, Baliol's mother, in the Castle Wynd, conveniently close to the castle itself. Here Bruce sought him—to learn that his quarry was at present attending the court nearby, but would be back. Bruce declared grimly that he would wait.

He had with him his brothers Nigel and Thomas, and his new brother-in-law Sir Christopher Seton, whom Christian of Mar had recently married. As Bruce anticipated, the news that he was back in Scotland and in fact here in Dumfries, very speedily was conveyed to Comyn in the castle, who promptly found his business there insufficiently vital to detain him from coming to verify the matter.

With a party of relatives and supporters he arrived at the monastery, and even though warned, the sight of Bruce sitting waiting for him before the fire of the refectory undoubtedly perturbed him. He stared.

"I had not looked to see you, my lord. Back. Here in Scotland," he jerked. "So soon."

"No? I warrant you did not! But I am here. Safe and in order." Bruce's voice may have sounded steady enough, but only iron control hid the quivering tension that had been part of the man since the fact of Comyn's treachery had struck him four days before.

"You come from London? From Edward?"

"From Edward, yes. That surprises you?"

"Only that you are not long gone. To return so soon . . ." Comyn shrugged. "You saw the King? Spoke with him?"

"I did."

The other obviously was nonplussed. "He treated you . . . kindly?"

"Not kindly, no. Edward is seldom kind to Scots."

"Did he speak . . . of me?"

"What he said is for your privy ear, my lord."

"Ah, yes. To be sure." Comyn looked around him at all the interested throng of his own supporters and Bruce's, filling the small refectory. He beckoned to the Prior, who fussed about, in a flutter with all this splendid company. "Where may I speak alone with my lord of Carrick?" he demanded.

"My poor house is full, my good lord. With all this of the assize. I can clear a chamber for your lordships, if you will. But . . . if you would but talk together, for a short time, the chapel is nigh. And empty."

"The chapel, yes. That will serve. Take us there."

The Prior led them out of a side-door and down a cloister-walk. At a short distance behind them Bruce's brothers and Sir Christopher Seton followed on, as did Comyn's uncle, Sir Robert, and his kinsman Master William.

Their guide opened another door at the end of the cloister, which proved to be the vestry entrance to the little church, leading directly into the choir.

Gesturing to the others to stay at the door, Comyn beckoned Bruce forward to just before the altar itself. "We may speak safely here," he said.

"A strange place for what falls to pass between you and me!" the other commented.

"As well as another. What have you to tell me, Bruce?"

"Sufficient to prove you a viler scoundrel than I knew defiled the face of this Scotland!"

"Christ God! You dare to speak so!"

"Aye, and more! And speak with good cause. Dastard! Judas!"

Comyn's hand dropped to the jewelled hilt of his dirk. "You will unsay that, Bruce!" he whispered. "No man speaks so to John Comyn, and lives!"

"Unsay it? I will prove it!"

The other's dagger was half-out of its sheath before he realised that Bruce's hand was reaching into a pocket, not for his own dirk.

"What say you to this?" Bruce held out his signed bond, and the enclosing letter to Edward.

Comyn's swiftly indrawn breath was as eloquent as any words. He stared at the out-thrust offering.

"I am waiting?"

His opponent moistened his lips. "Where . . . did you . . . get that?" he got out.

"What matters it? Since I have it now."

"I have been betrayed, then . . ."

"Betrayed! *You* to speak of betrayal! You, who made this compact with me. To be your King! And then betrayed me to Edward—to a certain death! Lamberton also—since he signed witness."

"Faugh! To betray traitors is no fault!"

"Traitors! You name me traitor? Is it possible . . . that this forsworn wretch . . . should so name Bruce?" And his hand rose, to point a quivering finger at the other.

Swift as thought Comyn smashed down the accusing hand with his own clenched fist—his left, since his right was still clutching the dagger-haft.

"Aye—traitor, as I have ever known you! Sold to Edward, always. Sold, for his favour. And his Ulsterwoman, de Burgh . . .!"

Whether at the snarling mention of Elizabeth's name, or at the physical blow to his arm, the second such that Comyn had struck him, something snapped in Bruce's overwrought brain as surely as a breaking bowstring, releasing a scalding red tide which rose swiftly to engulf him. The tingling downstruck hand went straight to his dagger. Scarcely knowing what he did, certainly not hearing the cries from the doorway, he whipped out the weapon and, beating aside the still upraised hand that had struck him, drove the steel deep into John Comyn's breast.

With a choking, bubbling groan, the other collapsed sideways against the altar, handsome features contorted, limbs writhing, and slid to the stone floor.

Dazed, unseeing, Robert Bruce stood, panting for breath.

The horrified shouting of the watchers by the door changed to action. Sir Robert Comyn, nearest, came running forward, drawing his sword. Nigel Bruce sprang after him, but the two clerics threw themselves in his way; while young Thomas stood appalled, paralysed. Not so Seton. A veteran soldier, he knocked Master William to the ground with a single blow, and leaping over him, raced after Sir Robert.

Comyn's uncle, cursing in fury, rushed on Bruce, who stood unmoving, as though stunned by what he had done. He did not attempt to parry or even dodge the blow which the older man aimed at him.

The other's sword-thrust was rageful rather than shrewd. And Bruce, unlike his fallen enemy, had anticipated that this might be a day in which armour would be a wise precaution, and was clad in a jerkin of light chain-mail. The slashing angry swipe drove him staggering backwards against the altar, in turn, but the steel did not penetrate the mail.

With a great roar, Seton hurled himself upon Sir Robert, his own blade high. Down it crashed, not in any wild swiping but in sheerest expert killing, on the unprotected neck of the older man. Head all but severed by that one stroke, Robert Comyn fell, spouting fountains of blood, over the body of his nephew.

Nigel came running to his brother now. "Robert!" he cried. "You are hurt? Stricken? Curse him! Robert speak! God's mercy —are you sore hurt?"

Bruce did not answer, did not so much as shake his head.

"Rob—answer me!" Nigel was running over his brother's steel-girt torso with urgent hands.

"He is but dazed, man," Seton panted. "His harness would save him . . ."

"Quick!" Thomas Bruce exclaimed, hurrying to them, and pointing backwards. "They have gone. The churchmen. To tell the others. The Comyns. They will be back. Seeking blood! Let us away from here."

"Aye," Seton agreed grimly. "That is sense, at least. Come. Take his arm. An arm each. He will be well enough. The other door. To the street. Haste you!"

So, without a glance at the fallen Comyns, a brother supporting him on either side, the silent, glazed-eyed Bruce was led, hustled indeed, down the nave to the little church's main door, Sir Christopher striding ahead, reddened sword still in his hand.

They emerged into the cold, frost-gleaming Castle Wynd. The alleys and entries of the climbing street were filled with chilled, waiting Bruce supporters. Nigel yelled for horses.

Men came starting out, at sight of their lord's party and the bloody sword. Shouts filled the crisp air.

Two knights came running, drawing their own swords—Sir Roger Kirkpatrick of Closeburn, nearby, and Sir John Lindsay, a kinsman of Crawford's. Nigel was still demanding horses, but Kirkpatrick came right up to his feudal master.

"What's to do?" he demanded. "My lord—are you hurt? What is this?"

Bruce shook his head.

"Get our men assembled," Seton cried. "There will be trouble."

"They are near. On the green. And on the castle hill. And

behind yonder church. A trumpet blast will summon them. But
. . . what's to do? That blood? Whose is it?" Kirkpatrick, a big,
rough, fierce man, was not to be put off.

At last Bruce spoke. "I doubt . . . I have slain . . . the Comyn,"
he said, slowly, distinctly.

"God's eyes! Comyn? Himself? Where?"

"God pity me—at the altar. In the church." That came out as
a groan.

"In the church? Praises be—where better? For that snake!
And you doubt it? Doubt he's slain? Then, by the Mass—I'll
make sure of it!" Kirkpatrick thrust past them, on the word,
and into the church doorway, followed by Sir John Lindsay, Sir
Robert Fleming and a few other men.

"Watch you!" Nigel shouted after them. "They will be there.
The rest of them. By now. Take heed, man!"

Neither Kirkpatrick nor any of the others so much as looked
back.

Rapping out an oath, Seton turned and hurried after them.

Whether with the cold, or just the passage of time, Bruce's
trance-like shock was beginning to wear off. He was still shaken
and not himself, but he became increasingly aware at least of the
dangers inherent in the situation. He shook off his brothers'
hands.

"My trumpeter," he jerked. "Get him. Quickly. To me. Up at
the castle-yard. You, Tom. Nigel—gather some men. Find and
take the Comyn horses. Away with them. Then join me up at the
castle. See to it."

"You are well enough . . .?"

"Yes. Go. Quickly. There is no time to lose."

Left alone for the moment, Bruce stared bleakly, unseeing,
before him. Then he looked down at his hand. It was splashed
with blood. Hastily he sought to wipe it away, his breath catching.
Then he desisted. No amount of rubbing would wipe away this
day's work. He might as well accept that. The deed was done,
and there could be no turning back. What lay ahead he could not
tell—save that nothing would ever be the same again for him. He
had slain a man. Not in honest battle, but in blind anger. Committed murder. Done the unforgivable thing. Taken another
man's life with his own hand. And in God's house, before His
very altar. The unholy upon the unforgivable . . .

Even that was not all. He had murdered the most powerful
man in Scotland. With a following great enough to turn the land

upside-down. Moreover he was completely lost with King Edward. Nothing could repair that break now. Suddenly all his ropes were cut. He was a bark adrift in a rising storm.

Or not quite adrift, perhaps. Alone, yes. For ever alone now. Anchors and warps gone. Sore beset. But still he had a rudder. And a purpose. Made simpler now. Wholly simplified indeed, since it was now all or nothing. There was nothing left to him now but to fight. Fight to the death. Fight to win, or to lose. No alternative course, any more.

To the fight, then! With a new enemy to face, instead of John Comyn. His own conscience.

He set off, heavy-strided, up the cobbled climbing street.

• • • •

The shrilling trumpet brought men streaming up on to the grassy hillock on which Dumfries Castle was built—no major fortress this but rather an administrative centre in a provincial walled town. All sorts of men came to that imperious summons, by no means all Bruce levies; many were, if not neutral, at least little involved, some were Comyn supporters, and not a few were English men-at-arms. But Bruce's people were there as a disciplined body, under the personal command of their lord. Moreover they all were mounted. They displayed all the difference between men of purpose and authority, and mere onlookers.

Nigel was one of the last to join his brother on the seething castle hill, where an air of strange and heady excitement prevailed, with rumours flying thick and fast.

"The Comyn horses are driven off," he reported. "The leaders' beasts, that is. And many others. Little trouble."

"Yes. And Christopher? Kirkpatrick?"

"I have not seen them. Do you think . . .?"

"I think if any can look to themselves, these can."

"What do you do now?"

"Take Dumfries. I have no choice."

"What . . .?" Astounded, Nigel stared at him.

"I have crossed my river, now," his brother said evenly, almost sternly. "There is no turning back. I can only go forward. Whatever the cost. But that is for myself. You—you need not go where I go. You, or any. For it will be a sore road. There is time, still, to turn back. For you. If you will."

Nigel looked across at his younger brother, brows raised. "You are not wandering? In the head? That blow . . ."

"Look," Thomas pointed. "Christopher. And the others."

Seton, Kirkpatrick and Lindsay, with some small following, were hastening up the rise towards them. They had the look of victorious men. Others made way for them automatically.

"Well?" Bruce, the new Bruce, barked the single word.

"You were right, my lord," Kirkpatrick shouted back, grinning. "A botched blow! He was still alive. I finished your work. The Red Comyn is dead. And others with him. Not a few! And this world the sweeter!"

A long shuddering sigh broke from the listening crowd.

Bruce looked at the newcomers long and levelly. Then he spoke, tonelessly. "Very well. I thank you for completing my work." He took a deep breath, and turned. "And now, there is more work to do, my friends. Much more. This castle, for a start." He pointed upwards, to where the Leopards of England flew above the highest tower. "That banner. I'll have it down, see you."

There was a corporate gasp from the company, a gasp that developed and changed into a rumbling roar as men perceived something of the significance of this declaration. Englishmen in the crowd began suddenly to look alarmed.

There were a number of men-at-arms at the castle gateway, but these were a ceremonial guard for the justices rather than any sort of garrison. Already, from the sitting in the hall, the chief magistrate, Sir John Kingston, had sent officers to enquire the reason for the trumpeting and noise outside, and to demand respectful quiet. As Bruce led his mounted cohort directly for the gateway, these turned and hurried away.

If the captain of the guard-house was of heroic stuff he wisely decided, in the face of a force ten times the size of his own, that this was not the occasion to demonstrate it. He and his men exchanged eloquent glances and promptly took themselves off after the officers.

There was no moat and drawbridge here, and Bruce led his men through the gatehouse pend and into the courtyard, without hindrance. There he halted, sitting his horse, while he gave his lieutenants orders to secure all gates and strongpoints, to man the parapets, and to bring him that banner. To Nigel he gave special instructions.

"My compliments to King Edward's justices," he said, "Inform them that their duties here are now over. And that I will provide them with safe-conduct over the Border. Forthwith."

His brother laughed aloud, and without dismounting, he or his men, rode indoors.

Soon he was back. "They have locked themselves into the hall," he reported. "I shouted your commands. But they said they will have no dealings with rebels. And that you are to disperse your force at once. Or all will be arraigned for treason."

"For judges, they much lack judgement!" Bruce declared grimly. "Have woodwork chopped down. And brushwood from outside. Those whins on the braeside will burn well. Pile all against doors and windows, and set alight. See how they judge *that*!"

Nigel's chuckling was stilled by the steely expression on his brother's face. He hurried off to do as he was told.

A warning shout from high above was followed by a muffled clatter that set Bruce's horse sidling. The Leopard standard of Plantagenet, wrapped round an English guard's helmet, and cast down from the parapet aloft, lay there on the flagstones.

A hoarse cheer rose from all who saw. Bruce had the thing handed up to him.

It was not long before, without the incendiaries waiting for brushwood, smoke was billowing along the corridors and vaulted passages of Dumfries Castle. And swiftly if belatedly the judicial qualities of those within asserted themselves. A messenger emerged from the smoke-enshrouded hall to request passage for His Majesty's judges.

Bruce ordered the pile of burning woodwork at the main hall-door to be cleared a little to one side—but only a little. The justices, clerks, officers, litigants, prisoners and soldiers alike, in consequence, had to hop and skip nimbly through as they emerged.

Sir John Kingston would have made suitable and dignified protest, out in the courtyard, but Bruce curtly cut him short.

"Enough, sir. Spare us this. We in Scotland have seen enough of English justice. More than enough to have any respect for its practitioners. Have you forgot the justice Sir William Wallace received?"

The angry growling from the onlookers was enough to convince Sir John that the moment was inopportune.

"You will be escorted to the Border, at Carlisle. You will be roped together, until then." And when shocked heads were raised, Bruce added, "And you may praise God that the ropes are not used to hang you!"

Without further exchange, Edward's representatives were

marched off, under guard, the summons-bell rope of the castle, used symbolically, a loop round each neck, to link them together. The roar of derision and unholy joy from the waiting throng outside, as these feared and hated dignitaries passed out from the gatehouse, could have been heard all over Dumfries.

So was struck the first blow of the second War of Independence suddenly, without warning, almost by accident.

When Bruce himself rode out from the castle, it was to find the crowd vastly increased, the citizenry now obviously present in large numbers. Bruce's appearance was greeted with loud and prolonged cheering. If there were not a few nominal Comyn vassals and supporters there, they did not proclaim the fact. Confused and leaderless, yet caught up in the vital sense of occasion and excitement, for the moment they went with the tide.

With his people marshalled into a great semi-circle behind him, Bruce faced the throng, and had his trumpeter blow for silence.

He spoke slowly, almost broodingly, with nothing of triumph and drama, however dramatic might be his actual words. "My friends—this day, the tenth of February, of our Lord the thirteenth hundred and sixth year, we commence to cleanse our land. We have commenced here at Dumfries. Sir John Comyn, Lord of Badenoch, turned traitor and is dead."

There was an uneasy stirring amongst the crowd, but no outcry.

"Cleansed, yes," Bruce went on steadily. "We have also cleansed this castle. The English are gone from it, with scarce a blow struck." He picked up the Leopard standard from his saddle-bow, and shook out its handsome folds. "Here is the usurper's banner, from the tower." He crumpled it up in his fist, and tossed it to the ground, contemptuously. "It will serve for a shroud for Comyn. He has well earned it!"

There was reaction now, but no shouting, no clamour. Something in the manner, voice and expression of the young man who sat his horse and spoke so sombrely, precluded that. Men whispered, shuffled, stared at each other. And waited.

Bruce held up his hand. "This castle is but the first of many which we must take and cleanse. Till all the land is cleared. And that will take long. Long. Let none doubt it. Edward of England will come for his banner—nothing more sure. We shall have to fight. Fight as we have never fought before. But not for so long, I think. For Edward is grown old. And sick. This is in our favour." He paused, and looked round. "Sir Roger Kirkpatrick, you will be captain of this Castle of Dumfries. To hold it secure. You will hoist another and better banner on that tower. And see that it flies there, against all comers."

"To be sure, my lord," Kirkpatrick cried, loudly. "Trust me for that. Bruce's banner will not fall like that rag, there!"

"Who said Bruce's banner?" Very slightly Bruce raised his voice. "Find you our royal standard of Scotland, my friend. The tressured Lion Rampant, red on gold. And raise that, see you. For all to see. In my name. For this day, I, Robert, do claim, take and assume my rightful and true heritage, the throne of Scotland. I stand before you now as your liege lord, Robert, King of Scots!"

For endless breathless moments there was complete and astonished silence. Men and women questioned their own ears. Only the slow ringing of the Greyfriars Monastery bell, tolling for the dead, broke the hush.

It was the Yorkshireman, Sir Christopher Seton, who first recovered himself. Wrenching out his sword for the second time that day, he held it high. "God save King Robert!" he cried. "God save the King! The King!"

It was as though a damned-up flood had been abruptly released. Pandemonium broke loose. The entire company went almost crazy in a frenzy of excitement and emotion. Men shouted, laughed, capered, threw their bonnets in the air, shook hands, even embraced each other. Women skirled, sang, wept, fell on their knees and prayed. Hardened knights and veterans of the wars kissed the cross-hilts of their swords and blinked away weak tears. The least demonstrative just grinned foolishly.

Nigel and Thomas Bruce, as amazed and dumbfounded as anybody else, were too overwhelmed to do more than gabble and stammer and stroke their brother's arms.

Of all that great gathering only the central figure himself remained apparently unaffected. Bruce sat unmoved and unmoving amongst the wild tumult, stiff and upright in his saddle as though carved there in stone. Never had he looked less pleased, less jubilant or exultant. And never more determined.

Out of the joyous confusion a pattern developed. Again it was the Englishman, Seton, who initiated it. He jumped down from his horse, casting away his sword with a clang. He came to Bruce's side. Half-bending on one armoured knee, he held up two hands, open and a little apart.

"Majesty," he exclaimed hoarsely, "I would be first to swear my oath of fealty. Give me your royal hand."

"Not Majesty, friend," Bruce told him. "In this Scotland we leave majesty to such as Edward Plantagenet! Grace, we say. By God's grace. Majesty I do not aspire to. But if ever a man required God's grace, I do!" He gave his brother-in-law his hand nevertheless.

"Aye, Sire." Taking the hand flat between his own two palms, Seton kissed it, then so holding it, said, "I, Christopher Seton, swear before Almighty God and all His saints, to be Your Grace's true man, in fealty and homage, in life and in death. I hereby declare Robert, King of Scots, to be my liege lord, and no other. Amen!"

This brought every other mounted man of gentle blood off his horse and into a clamorous queue, Kirkpatrick foremost. It was Seton himself who held them off, belatedly insisting that the King's brothers must have precedence. So Nigel and Thomas each took Robert's hand within their own, stumbling and stuttering in their near-distraction—yet even so somehow looking askance at their brother's set, stern features.

Before the rest of the eager columns of aspirants took the oath, Bruce raised the much-kissed hand for quiet.

"My friends all," he said. "I warn you. My service will be a hard one. It cannot be otherwise. English Edward will not smile on those who kiss this hand, this day. Think well before you do so. For me there can be no turning back now. I win this realm of Scotland's freedom, or die. But for you the die is not yet cast. Think well, I say."

Whatever brief stouns at the heart those ominous words may have aroused amongst his hearers, not one of the queue left place. Indeed more urgent was the clamour to reach his hand.

Bruce suffered the long oath-taking ceremonial with a grim patience. But as soon as it was finished, he commanded silence again.

"I cherish your loyalty, value your trust," he declared. "But now we have work to do. Only one castle, one town, and a few hundred of men, at this moment acknowledge the King of Scots. All must be brought to do so, willingly or unwillingly. I go back to Lochmaben, and command that all leal men rally to my standard there. But on the way I must take Dalswinton Castle, Comyn's house—for we can afford to let no enemies hold it. Likewise we must take Tibbers, which, though mine, is English-held. It commands the Nith pass into Ayrshire. Sir Christopher—I charge you to take it. And hold it. I give it to you. Sir John Lindsay—Caerlaverock must be secured. In these Solway marshes. The passage from Carlisle. See you to it. Surprise will be our most potent weapon. To strike before any look for war. This will serve us. Go now—enough of talk. And if I could, I would say God go with you! To work."

"God save the King's Grace!" somebody shouted. "God bless King Robert!" Immediately the cry was taken up by the entire gathering in a ringing and repeated chant, amidst cheers. To its resounding echoes, Robert Bruce rode downhill from Dumfries Castle, into the town, making for the north gate.

.   .   .

Elizabeth and Christian Bruce were sitting before the fire in the February dusk, stitching tapestries and watching the children play, when the brothers got back to Lochmaben. Bruce stood in the doorway eyeing this pleasantly domestic scene almost guiltily, before venturing in.

Elizabeth looked up, a little anxiously for her. She was well aware, of course, that her husband had gone to Dumfries that day specifically to confront Comyn with his treachery. However cosy the scene seemed now, she had been on edge all day. But she did not question him, waiting for the man to speak.

Not so Christian of Mar, now the Lady Seton. She seldom waited for anyone to speak first. "So, my brave brothers," she greeted them, "are you struck dumb by our beauty? Or has that reptile Comyn escaped you?"

"No," Bruce said briefly.

"No? What does no mean? Have you settled with the man?"

"I have, yes."

"Then I vow you are precious dull about it, Robert! And what have you done with my great ox of a husband? Do not tell me you let Comyn master *him*!"

"No. Christopher is well enough. He is gone on an errand for me. To Tibbers."

"Tibbers? And why, a mercy's sake? Why go to Tibbers? The English hold it, do they not?"

"It is my hope that they will not, for much longer."

"So! You send my foolish Yorkshireman to ask his fellow-Englishmen to give you back your Tibbers! You are become mighty bold, my Lord Robert, of a truth ...!"

Elizabeth raised a hand to quell her irrepressible sister-in-law. "Let him tell it at his own pace," she urged.

But Nigel could contain himself no longer. "Quiet, you, by all the saints, Christie!" he burst out. "Your tongue is like a bell in the wind! And show something more of respect, I charge you. Call your brother Grace, now—not Lord!"

"Grace . . .? What folly is this?"

Elizabeth did not speak, but her hand went up to the white column of her throat.

"He is the King!" Thomas exclaimed excitedly. "He has taken the kingdom."

Bruce looked at his wife, not his sister. "Scarce that!" he said. "The kingdom will require a deal of taking, I fear!"

"Robert, You . . . you . . . what have you done?"

"Well may you ask, my dear. What can I say . . .?"

"*I'll* tell you what he has done," Nigel declared. "He has slain the Comyn and assumed the crown. Here is Robert, King of Scots!"

The two women stared, even Christian silenced. They both rose to their feet.

Bruce, still in his armour, strode forward to take his wife's hand. "My heart," he said, "What can I say to you? I have done what is beyond telling, this day. I come to you with hands stained with blood. I slew Comyn, yes. But not in fair fight. I dirked him, with this hand. And in church. Before God's altar! I come to you, a murderer . . .!"

"No!" Nigel insisted. "It is not so. He struck him down, yes. But not to the death. Kirkpatrick it was that killed him. Later."

"Besides, Comyn called him traitor! And struck him with his hand. I saw it, heard it." Thomas told them, voice breaking with emotion.

"I murdered him," Bruce repeated evenly. "Whoever finished my work. Drew on him, when his hands were empty . . ."

"In a church, you say?" Elizabeth faltered. "An altar . . .?"

"Aye—God pity me! He fell . . . against the altar."

"So long as he fell!" Christian commented briefly. "That man is better dead."

Elizabeth bit her lip. "I am sorry, Robert."

"Yes. It was ill done. I lost my wits. A kind of madness. I scarce knew what I had done. Until too late . . ."

"God in His heaven!" Nigel cried exasperatedly. "All this talk of what is of no matter anyway! The death of a proven traitor—who had to die. And naught said of what matters everything! That now you are King of Scots. And you, Elizabeth, are Queen." He ran forward, to half-bend one knee, as far as his armour would let him, and took her hand. "Highness!" he said, kissing it. "Your most faithful subject and servant." His younger brother hastened to follow suit.

Elizabeth shook her head. "It is less simple than that, I fear," she said sadly.

"Aye. Nigel speaks in innocence," Bruce agreed grimly. "Would that innocence were mine! Apart from the guilt on me, do you not see what this must cost? I am no true King until my coronation. And for that I require the aid of Holy Church. Think you Holy Church will smile on a murderer?"

"Why must you call it murder . . .?"

"Because that is what it was. Moreover, it is what my enemies will call it."

"But the chief churchmen are your friends, not your enemies. Lamberton, Wishart, and the rest."

"Not all. Cheyne, of Aberdeen. Andrew, of Argyll. Both Comyn men. And have you forgot Master William, cleverer than any? Who saw the deed done. The Comyns have many churchmen. The Pope is now no friend to Scotland. These will petition him for my excommunication—nothing surer. And if they do not, Edward will! And an excommunicated man could not be anointed King!"

There was silence for a little. Then Christian spoke. "It is a long way to Rome," she observed.

"Aye. There lies my one hope. A swift coronation, before my enemies' emissaries can reach the Pope and bring back his edict. Without the Pope's authority, only the Primate could excommunicate, I believe. And Lamberton will not do that, I think. All, then, depends on haste."

"All . . .?" Elizabeth echoed. "You do not fear the excommunication itself?"

"I fear the righteous wrath of God," he told her levelly. "I know well that I have grievously incurred it. In itself, I have no reason to fear any man's lesser condemnation." Bruce took her hand. "My heart—what I have done was a great sin. But that done, the rest had to follow. You will see it? The kingship. I had to act. Forthwith. There could be no delay. All then fell to be won, or lost. You understand?"

"I understand *that*, yes."

"I endanger you, by it. Endanger all here. I know it well. I have told these two. I tell you. The decision was mine. Others need not suffer for it. *You*—you are free to choose."

"I am your wife."

"To be sure. But this is a desperate venture. A new life that, short or long, will never again be the same. And liker to be short than long, I fear!"

"I married Robert Bruce for better or for worse. I knew when we were wed that this day might dawn. Would almost certainly dawn. I did not think to see it happen this way, Robert — but what of that? I am your wedded wife — whatever you have done. And now, it seems, your queen."

"That, see you, Edward will never forgive."

"Edward is no longer my king. You are, my dear."

He raised the hand he held to his lips. "I thank you, lass."

"So what now?" the impatient Christian asked.

"Now I send letters. I inform Edward — as one monarch to another." Almost he smiled. "Who knows — the news might even serve our cause enough to stop his heart! More urgent, to William Lamberton. This very night. Nigel — you had best go. He is at Berwick still, I think — summoned there by Richmond, as adviser. He must be told all, with nothing hidden. I will ask him to arrange an immediate coronation. If he will . . ."

"Lamberton will do it," Nigel asserted. "He has been your friend always. You have a bond with him, have you not?"

"A bond cannot tie a man's conscience. In especial, a churchman's. I can only hope. And you — you can pray!"

Elizabeth looked at him long and searchingly. "My love," she said gently, "I think that you should come with me. A little quiet refreshment. Write your letters later."

He drew a hand over his brow. "Later. Later, yes."

"When last did you eat?" she asked.

"Eat? I . . . I do not know."

"I thought as much. And even kings must eat! Come . . . Sire!"

Chapter Twenty-one

HURRIEDLY assembled though it was, the train that set out northwards from Lochmaben that bright and breezy March morning was a splendid one — the King of Scots on his way to Scone for his coronation. Whatever the dark uncertainties of the future, and all the thronging problems of the present and the guilt of the past, Bruce had sought to lay all aside for this great and significant event. His coffers had been drastically raided, scraped indeed, his feudal vassals summoned from far and near, his womenfolk charged to prepare a magnificence of raiment and gaiety of colour and spectacle not seen in Scotland for half a century. Five hundred rode on this leisurely, seemingly joyful, 100-mile pilgrimage, a third of that number ladies, with scarcely a suit of armour or shirt of mail in sight — although, not in sight but far out on either flank, powerful armed contingents rode a parallel course, to ensure against any surprise attack from Richmond's occupying forces, Comyn sympathisers, or other enemies. A company of mounted instrumentalists and minstrels led the procession, dispensing sweet music; banners fluttered by the score; gorgeously-caparisoned horses, heraldically-emblazoned litters, silks, satins, velvets and jewellery, dazzled the eye. Bruce himself wore a cloth-of-gold tabard, with the Lion of Scotland embroidered in red front and rear, picked out in rubies; and his queen was in royal purple velvet, tight of bodice and long flowing of skirt, high-standing collar and cuffs trimmed with seed pearls. Marjory, now a delicately lovely child of eleven, and making her first public appearance, was dressed wholly in white taffeta. Christian, with her sisters Mary and young Matilda, the baby of the family, her son Donald of Mar, and the four Bruce brothers, were little less fine.

But perhaps Bruce's greatest satisfaction, in all this display, was in what was immediately in front of him and behind the musicians, where rode three churchmen — the Dean of Glasgow, the Abbot of Inchaffray and the Vicar of Dumfries. They carried a gold and jewelled pectoral cross, a great banner with the arms of the See of Glasgow, and a precious relic, allegedly a bone of Saint Kentigern. But more important than what they carried was what they represented — the support and blessing of Holy Church, proved by a parchment in Bruce's own possession, signed by Robert Wishart, Bishop of Glasgow, the diocese in which the deed was committed, granting him full absolution for the death of John Comyn, on grounds of personal and national necessity. Bruce's conscience may have been little the lighter for this document, but his wits indeed were.

And, despite all this brilliance of circumstance and colour, he required every scrap of encouragement which he could muster. For, although it was nearly six weeks since the day when he had stabbed Comyn and proclaimed himself King, the fact was that so far no large proportion of the nation had rallied to his standard. Here in the South-West, his own domains, the response had been good; but elsewhere it had been patchy indeed. He had issued a twenty-four hour warning for mobilisation, to the whole realm—but what response there might be to it, who could tell? The common people, who had followed Wallace, had greeted the claiming of the crown with enthusiasm, in the main. But these had little to lose, and at this stage not a great deal to contribute. It was the landed men, the nobles, lairds and knights, whom he must have, able to provide armed men, horses, money. And these held back. They were scarcely to be blamed, perhaps—even Bruce did not condemn them too fiercely. The land was in English occupation, and though Richmond's forces were limited, anyone coming out in Bruce's support was a marked man for the inevitable day when Edward sent his legions north again to wipe out this affront. By then, that Bruce would be in any position to withstand, or to protect his supporters, was highly questionable. Ten years of bitter warfare had borne too heavily on such as these to leave many starry-eyed enthusiasts.

It was, therefore, with roused feelings that, riding down towards the grey town of Lanark, Bruce saw a tight and strong well-mounted company of about a hundred come spurring over a grassy ridge from the east, to meet the royal cavalcade at a tangent, lances glinting under a large blue-and-white banner. There were not a few Scots families which flew blue-and-white colours—but here in Lanarkshire the chances were that it was Douglas.

A young man, slender, swarthy, dark-eyed, graceful of carriage, led this squadron on a magnificent stallion. He drew rein a little way in front and to the side of the advancing column, and leapt down, to stand, waiting.

Bruce had his trumpeter sound the halt, and sitting his horse, beckoned the young man forward.

"Who are you, my friend?" he asked. "And would you ride with me to Scone, this day?"

The other bowed deeply. "I would ride with you farther than to Scone, my lord King," he said impulsively, clear-voiced. "I am James Douglas. Whom once you took out of Douglas Castle. To Irvine, and my father."

"Ha! James Douglas? Sir William's son. To be sure. I mind you now. Save us—you make me feel old! A boy then, a man now."

"Your man, Sire." He took the outstretched hand between his own. "Four days ago, only, I was of age. For long years I have waited for this. To come to you. Even when you were not King.

With my strength. As Lord of Douglas. Before, I could not. Others held me back. Now they can do so no more. And now I am come. In time for your Grace's crowning! God be praised!" All this was jerked out with a breathless urgency.

Bruce looked down into the eager dark eyes, and found an unaccountable lump in his throat. "Aye, lad," he said. "And I am glad. But . . . why? What did I ever do for you? Save escort you and your step-mother to your father? Whose soul rest in peace. All those years ago."

"Nine years, Sire. I have well counted them. Five of them in France. Think you I could forget what you did that day? Outside the walls of Douglas. How you saved the children from hanging. By Segrave. How you defied King Edward's commands. How you came to us in courtesy, offered us rescue, conducted us to safety. Then threw in your lot with the rebels. You, who were named Edward's chief commander in the South-West! I vowed then that when I was a man, I would seek to be a man like the Earl of Carrick!" James Douglas paused, and swallowed. "Your Grace's pardon. I . . . I forgot myself!"

"Would God more in this realm would forget themselves, my lord of Douglas!" Suddenly Bruce rose in his stirrups, and dismounted. Hastily everywhere men jumped down, not to remain seated when the monarch stood. "Give me that sword, lad," he said.

Wonderingly the younger man drew, and handed over the handsome weapon.

"Now, kneel." He tapped each bent shoulder with the flat of the blade. "I dub thee knight. Be thou a good and faithful knight until thy life's end. Arise, Sir James!"

Quite stunned with the suddenness and proportions of the honour done him, Douglas stood at a loss.

Leaning a little in her saddle, Elizabeth, who had watched and listened interestedly, held out her hand, well aware of what this all meant to her husband. "My felicities, Sir James. For the first knight of my lord's creating."

"Not the first," Bruce said sombrely. "I knighted Wallace. May you, sir, be more fortunate than he!"

"That is in God's hands, Sire. But if I can strive to be one half so true a knight, I shall rejoice. I thank you, with all my heart, Your Grace." Douglas took the Queen's hand. "Highness, I am yours, and the King's, to command. Always. To the death."

"This is too joyous a day to talk of death," she told him. "*Live* for us." And she smiled down on the lively, eager, almost worshipping face.

"That too, Madam . . ."

"Aye, my friend—so be it," Bruce said. "This day we ride my realm without swords and lances and armour. For once! So take you these fine Douglas blades of yours, and find Sir Christopher Seton. He rides some way to the west, holding our flank secure. Leave them with him. He will use them well. Then come back to our side, my lord of Douglas. You shall be our good augury and fortune, on the way to Scone . . ."

.   .   .

The Abbey of Scone, a few miles North of Perth, above the cattle-dotted meadows of the silver Tay, was a fair place in a lovely setting. Admittedly it was not so fair as once it had been, for Edward had been here in 1296, and part-destroyed the Abbey when he took away its precious Stone, the symbol of Scotland's sovereignty. And sent another punitive raid two years later. But there had been considerable rebuilding since then, much renewing of burned woodlands and a ravaged countryside in this the ancient Pictish capital and most hallowed spot in Scotland, where rose the Moot-hill that had been the centre of rule and the coronation-place of the most ancient kingdom of all Christendom. For this day, at least, all traces of ruin and devastation were covered up and hidden. All was colour, flourish and acclaim.

A tented city had been set up, on the flats by the river, below the twelve acres of abbey buildings and the Moot-hill, furnished with the gorgeous silken pavilions of lords and bishops, the bowers of ladies, the lodges of lesser men, the canopied shrines of religious orders and holy relics, the booths of merchants and craftsmen, the enclosures for entertainers, tumblers, musicians and the like, the tourney-grounds, race-courses and playing-fields, stretching to the vast horse-lines and cattle-pens. Every sort of standard, flag, banner and pennon flew, ecclesiastical, heraldic, burghal, guild and purely decorative. Late March, it was scarcely the time of the year for such outdoor activities; but the weather was kind, and though a stiff breeze blew, the sun shone.

Robert Bruce had reason for some satisfaction. It was no feeble or humiliating affair, such as might have been. None could point the finger of scorn and claim that this was only a shameful pretence at a coronation. There were three earls present—four if young Donald of Mar was counted; John de Strathbogie, of

Atholl; Malcolm of Lennox; and Alan of Menteith—although he had been more or less dragooned, and his uncle, Sir John Stewart of Menteith not only was not present but had refused to yield up Dumbarton Castle to Bruce. There were three bishops—the Primate, Glasgow and Moray—with a number of mitred abbots and priors. Of lords, apart from Douglas, there were Hay of Erroll and his brother; Lindsay of Crawford; Somerville of Carnwath; Campbell of Lochawe; and Fleming of Cumbernauld. James the Steward, aged and sick, had sent his surviving son Walter. And there were a great many barons, knights and lairds, the most prominent of whom were Sir Hugh, brother of the heroic Sir Simon Fraser of Oliver; Sir John Lindsay; Sir Robert Boyd, who had just captured Rothesay and Dunaverty Castles for Bruce; Sir David de Inchmartin and Sir Alexander Menzies. Alexander Scrymgeour, Wallace's lieutenant, the Standard-Bearer, was there. The Bruce family itself made an impressive phalanx, with Seton and Sir Thomas Randolph, a nephew.

But, though all this was well enough, it was scarcely possible not to reflect on who was *not* present. Two-thirds of the earls and bishops and three-quarters of the lords had found it necessary or expedient to be elsewhere—although all had been summoned. There was no overlooking this fact. Most significant, perhaps, for a coronation, was the absence of the young MacDuff, Earl of Fife, whose duty and privilege it was to place the new monarch on the fabled Stone of Destiny and to crown him thereafter. Some whispered indeed, with head-shakings, that without the magic symbol of the Stone, and lacking the MacDuff presence, it could be no true crowning.

William Lamberton arrived at Scone within hours of the royal party's coming, and it was Bruce who quickly thereafter sought the Bishop, in the Abbot's quarters, not *vice versa*.

"My lord King!" the older man protested, as the other was shown into his chamber. "This should not be! You should have let me seek audience. I was but preparing myself first, after my journeying . . ."

"Tush, man! Seek audience—you?" Bruce interrupted. "Has it come to this, between us?"

"Conditions have changed, Sire," the Primate said. "Notably."

"Changed, yes. But how much? Between us, my old friend? That is what I came to discover. And at once."

"They cannot be the same ever again, Sire, I fear. Since we are now master and subject."

"Master and subject! That is for the ruck. Say what you mean, man."

"Mean, Your Grace? I do not understand . . . ?"

"Have done, my lord Bishop! You know well what is between us. Blood! Murder! Say it."

"If it is John Comyn you speak of, his blood does not lie between you and me. You have absolution, have you not?"

"Absolution, yes. And why granted? Because you so ordained? That I might not be debarred the throne? Before the Pope in Rome excommunicates me!"

"In part true, Sire. But only in part. Your slaying of Comyn was a sin, yes. The manner of it. I do not gainsay it. But a sin meet for absolution. Given repentance. Since the man was evil. Had plotted your own death. And would have done so again. It was Comyn, or Bruce! If ever a man ensured his own death, that man was John Comyn."

"So . . . you are still my friend?"

"If Your Grace will still consent to name me so."

"Thank God! This, I think, I feared most of all." Bruce reached out to take the other's hand. "The excommunication I could have tholed. God's judgement hereafter I must await. But *your* estrangement would have been beyond all bearing."

Much moved, the Bishop for once could find no words. He gripped the younger man's hand for long moments before he raised it to his lips.

"This of the kingship," Bruce went on, after a while. "Having defied and fled from Edward, and slain Comyn, I had to move. To take the throne, without delay. Before Edward could have the Pope excommunicate me. From a coronation. It was oversoon, for our plans, for Scotland. But my hand was forced."

"Think you I do not know it? It had to be. Over-soon, yes. But better that than over-late. Now, we must set the crown on your brow, for all to see, in fashion that none can question. And to that end, Sire, I would have you speak with the Abbot here. Abbot Henry."

"I have already met the good Abbot."

"Yes. But he asks for this further audience. He says that he has something to show to Your Grace . . ."

"A mercy, friend! While we are alone, must you so grace and sire me? I was Robert before. And to you, would be Robert still."

"Very well, Robert my friend—if it is your royal wish..."

"It is. Now—what would this abbot show me?"

"That he must declare himself. So he assured me..."

So King and Primate went in search of the Abbot of Scone, and presently found that busy man superintending the decoration of the great semi-ruined church for the next day's ceremonies. Master Henry was an old man, but bore his years and trials lightly. Small, grizzled, eager, he was almost monkey-like, the negation of the pompous cleric, quick and agile, but shrewd. He chuckled and laughed and rubbed his hands much of the time, and would abide no doleful monks in his establishment, declaring that there was more amusement and hearty joy to be won from religion than from any other subject, that God was the prime humorist and that the major sin against the Holy Ghost was a sour and gloomy piety.

When Lamberton beckoned him to the King, he came grinning, and making a most sketchy obeisance, led them aside, to announce, in a stage whisper, that he had something to disclose. Then almost on tip-toe, he conducted them through a side-door and down a winding stair. On the ledge of the last slit-window was a lantern, which he lit with a flint, and led on downwards into the dark honeycomb of crypts beneath the main church.

"Save us—is it a corpse you have for us, man?" Bruce asked.

"Wait you," the little man advised.

Amongst the damp and dripping vaults, stone and lead coffins and rusted iron yetts of that shadowy, chill place, the Abbot selected one massive door, and opened it with one of the keys hanging from his girdle. Stepping inside a small vaulted cell, he held the lantern high.

The two visitors stared. The place was empty save for a solid block of stone that gleamed black and polished in the lamplight.

"By all the Saints!" Lamberton murmured. "The Stone! The true Stone..."

"The Stone...?" Bruce demanded. "You cannot mean the Stone of Destiny? The Stone of Scone? Itself!"

Master Henry skirled laughter that echoed in all the vaults. "I do that, my lord King. None other." He rubbed his hands. "Yon's the right Stone. Your Coronation Stone, *My* Stone."

"So-o-o! I heard that Edward took a false Stone to London. Or so some said. But... how did you do it, man?"

"Did you expect me to let the accursed Southron have Scotland's most precious talisman?" the little man demanded. "I am

Abbot of Scone. Custodian of Scotland's Stone. It belongs here at Scone. And there it is."

"But how, man? How?"

Lamberton was kneeling beside the thing, running his hands over it. The block was about twenty-four inches high and twenty-eight long by twenty wide, a heavy, shiny black cube, its top dipped slightly in a hollow, the whole curiously wrought and carved with Celtic designs. It had two great rolls, or volutes, like handles, sculptured on either side, to carry it by—but when the Bishop sought to raise it, he could not do so much as move it an inch.

"Aye—this is it. The true Stone," he exclaimed. "I saw it. At Baliol's coronation. This . . . this is next to a miracle!"

"No miracle," the Abbot chuckled. "Just cozening. I cozened Edward Longshanks—that is all."

"Out with it," Bruce commanded, impatiently.

"Och, well—see you, it was not that difficult, Sire. King Edward had sworn, yon time, to destroy Scotland. To bring down its throne, to burn this abbey, to take away its Stone. Sworn before all. The Stone was in my care. Was I to allow that? I could scarce prevent him from burning my abbey. But I could try to save the Stone. He had warned me. Three days warning I had. So I had it taken from its place hard by the altar. By night. Secretly. Eight stark men bore it, in a covered litter. They bore it down Tay, four miles. To Boat of Moncrieffe. And ferried it across. Then they carried it up Moncrieffe Hill, and hid it in the cave where Wallace sheltered one time, Sir John Moncrieffe of that Ilk aiding them." The old man licked grinning lips. "And myself, I had the masons cut a great skelb of stone out of the quarry here. A rude block enough, but stout and heavy. And this I set before the altar. For Edward of England!"

"And . . . he took it. Your lump from the quarry. Knowing no better? It is scarce believable."

"As to that, Sire—who knows? Yon Edward is a man with the pride of Lucifer. He had sworn he would carry Scotland's Stone back to London. He may have jaloused that this was false. But there was none other—and a stone he must take. It would serve as well as the other, for most! It *has* served, has it no'?"

"By the Rude—here is a wonder!" Bruce cried. "Perhaps that is why he was so angry, that time at Berwick? Knowing it false. Man—I have never heard the like!" He stepped forward to touch

Scotland's famed talisman with reverent hand. "The Stone of Destiny. For my crowning. Here is good augury, indeed."

"Here is the work of a leal and stout-hearted man," Lamberton said, deep-voiced.

"You are right. My lord Abbot—for this I owe you more than I can say. All Scotland is hereby in your debt. I thank you. The Stone could scarce have had a better custodian."

"My simple duty, Your Grace. And my pleasure." The little man performed almost a skip of glee. "Nights I lie awake, and think of Edward Plantagenet with his lump of Scone sandstone! It is my prayer that he was not deceived. That he knows it false. I think it so. For, two years after he took it, he sent an ill band of Englishry back here, to wreak their fury on this place again. They came only here, from Stirling. They smashed and raged and defaced, in fury. They broke down everything that had been left and that we had set up again—the doors of this church, the refectory, dormitories, cloisters. Laid axes to every cupboard, chest, casket and plenishing. It was hate, naught else. I think Edward knows well that he was cozened—and does not like it. But dares not confess it, lest all men conceive him fooled! So the English are saddled with their stolen false Stone, and can scarce come back for this one. Is it not a joy?"

Shaking their heads, the other two considered the diminutive cleric—and Bruce found a smile, even if Lamberton did not.

Next day, therefore, the King of Scots at least was enthroned on the Stone of Destiny, even if there was no MacDuff to place him thereon. To the deafening clamour of trumpet fanfares the new monarch strode alone up through the crowded church to the high altar, and there seated himself upon the ancient Stone, which legend claimed to have been Jacob's pillow in the wilderness, brought to Ireland by Scota, Pharaoh's daughter, from whom the Scots took their name; but which was more likely to have been the portable altar of a travelling saint, possibly Columba himself, fashioned out of a meteorite. There Bruce sat while Abbot Henry brought up his Queen to sit on a throne opposite him, and the Primate, leading the Bishops Wishart and David of Moray, paced out of the vestry, themselves gorgeously attired, bearing magnificent robes of purple and gold in which to deck the King. These were canonicals, saved and hidden by Wishart at the sack of Glasgow, and now produced for this momentous occasion. The trumpets silenced, a great choir of singing boys chanted sweet music, while the bishops and abbot robed Robert Bruce ceremonially, and acolytes filled the air with the fragrance of their swinging censers.

The service that followed was impressive, if inevitably lengthy, conducted by the Abbot and the Primate, the sonorous Latinities of the Mass rolling richly, the anthems resounding, the silent pauses dramatic. Then to the high, pure liquid notes of a single singer reciting the *Gloria in Excelsis*, William Lamberton took the ampulla, and consecrating it at the altar, turned to anoint the King with oil.

Bruce, stern-faced as Lamberton himself, gazed across the chancel, hearing and seeing little, aware more vividly of that other high altar and the blood-stained figure collapsing against it, a picture which would haunt him until his dying day.

While the people still shivered to the aching beauty of that lone singing, conjoined with the dread significance of the holy anointing, they were rudely roused, to the extent of almost gasping with fright, by the sudden, unheralded, furious clashing of cymbals, that went on and on, as old Robert Wishart hobbled to the altar to take up the crown. It was in fact no true crown— Edward had seen to that—being but a simple gold circlet, taken from some saint's image; but no more valid diadem survived in all Scotland, and this must serve. To the shattering clangour of the cymbals, the aged prelate placed the slender symbol over the Bruce's brow.

"God save the King! God save the King! God save the King!" Drowning even the clashing brass, the great cry arose and continued, every man and woman in the crowded church on their feet and shouting—save only Bruce himself and Elizabeth. On and on went the refrain, like an ocean's tide crashing on a shingle beach, as all gave rein to their pent-up emotions. Looking across at her husband, the Queen perceived his lips to be moving, in turn.

"God save me! God save me, indeed!" he was whispering.

She would have run to him then, if she might.

At length the trumpets triumphed, and to their imperious ululation the Bishop of Moray brought Bruce the sceptre for his right hand, from the altar, while Abbot Henry brought him the Book of the Laws. Then, from the front of the nave, the Earl of Atholl came forward with the great two-handed sword of state. He knelt before Bruce and proffered it for the monarch to touch. Then, holding it up before him, he took his stance behind the Stone.

The Earls of Lennox and Menteith brought up the spurs and the ring, respectively, and Scrymgeour the Standard-Bearer stalked forward with the great Lion Rampant banner of the King, dipped it over Bruce's head, and then laid it on the altar.

The main coronation procedure completed, Lamberton stepped across, to bow before the Queen and place another golden circlet over her corn-coloured hair. Kissing her hand, he raised her, and led her across the chancel to the King's side, where she curtsied low, and took her husband's hand between both her own, the first to do him homage. Her throne carried over by acolytes, she seated herself at his right hand.

There remained but the ceremony of homage-giving, when all landed men and prelates might come up to take the King's hand and swear fealty, their names and styles called out by the King of Arms, a lengthy process but not to be scamped.

At last it was all over, and the royal couple could go outside to show themselves to the common folk who had gathered in their thousands to acclaim them.

The remainder of the day, and the day following, were given over to feasting, jousting, games and entertainments for all classes and tastes, with music and dancing late into the night. Bruce made a number of celebratory appointments to his household and to offices of state, granted charters and decrees, and created knights. There was only one flaw in the colourful tapestry. A courier arrived from the South-West, to inform the King that Sir Aymer de Valence, Earl of Pembroke, had been appointed commander in Scotland, to succeed the somewhat feeble John of Brittany, and had arrived at Carlisle to assemble a great army. De Valence was no puppet, but a fierce and able soldier, a second cousin of Edward's and, significantly, brother-in-law to the dead Comyn. Moreover Edward had sent the Prince of Wales on after Pembroke, gathering a second army; and he himself was preparing to come north.

It had had to come to this, sooner or later.

Two forenoons later, when Bruce was in conference with his lords, he was brought new and more surprising tidings. There was a latecomer to the coronation scene—none other than Isabel, Countess of Buchan. It was perhaps strange that the King should immediately interrupt his Council and go in person to greet this lady, the young wife of one of his most consistent enemies. But Isabel of Buchan had been Isabel MacDuff before her marriage, sister of the Earl of Fife.

He found the Countess with Elizabeth and Christian, little more than a girl, but a sonsy, high-coloured, laughing girl, strange wife for the dour, elderly High Constable of Scotland. She sank low before him.

"My lord King," she said, "I am desolated. That I am come too late. I have ridden for twelve days. Four hundred miles. Ever since I heard. For Your Grace's coronation. And come too late by two days. It is a sore sorrow."

"Why, lady—here's a woeful mischance," Bruce said, raising her. "Had we but known. To come so far. You must, then, have been in England?"

"At my lord's manor of Fishwick, in Leicestershire. He has made his peace with Edward. Since . . . since . . ."

"Aye—I understand. And you left my lord behind?"

"Yes, Sire. He . . . he knew not that I came."

"So! A leal subject, indeed—if less leal a wife!"

"I am, first, MacDuff of Fife's daughter! When I learned, to my sorrow, that my brother, the Earl Duncan, preferred to bide at Edward's Court in London than play his rightful part in the crowning of his King, I made haste to come myself. That there should be a MacDuff, if only a woman, to place the crown on your head. Lacking the Stone of Scone, this at least I could do. I took my husband's best horses. And now—now it is all too late . . .!" Her eager voice broke.

Bruce thrust out a hand to clasp her bent shoulder. "Not so, lass—not so. Would you had been here two days ago, yes. But today is also a day. I do greatly esteem the presence of a MacDuff —especially so fair a one! In order that you should do what only MacDuff can rightfully do. You shall crown me again, forthwith. And seat me on the true Stone of Destiny also. For it is here, despite all. The Stone of Scone. The Abbot Henry saved it. Edward has a false boulder, a worthless lump of building-stone, to cherish at his Westminster! We shall have a second crowning. And none shall say that Robert Bruce is not truly King of Scots!"

The girl burst into tears, there and then.

So, that afternoon, in another brief but joyful ceremony, the Countess of Buchan led her sovereign to the Stone, and there placed the gold circlet over his brow, to the lusty cheers of the concourse. And, as lustily, Bruce kissed her for her services, declaring that he felt a King indeed.

CHAPTER TWENTY-TWO

ALTHOUGH Bruce ordained that the festivities continue at Scone for some days longer, the very next morning he himself, with Elizabeth and a small Court—including the Countess of Buchan whom the Queen appointed her principal lady-in-waiting—set off on a progress through the land. Admittedly it was partly a recruiting drive, with Aymer de Valence's invasion threat bearing heavily on his mind—but it was advisable, necessary, that the King should show himself to as large a number of his people as was possible.

Meanwhile emissaries, including his brothers Thomas and Alexander, and the Bishops of Glasgow and Moray, rode south, east and west, to raise troops and rouse the country—especially south-west, where lay the greatest opportunity to harry and distract Pembroke.

The King chose to travel northwards, for it was there that the Comyn influence was strongest and must be countered. His progress was not entirely formal and processional, for he took the English-held royal castles of Forfar and Kincardine on the way. But most of the time was spent visiting towns and abbeys and communities, receiving tokens of loyalty, dispensing largesse and requiring the fealties of local barons—including the reluctant Malise, Earl of Strathearn, whom he more or less kidnapped. All the while, however, he had, as it were, one eye turned backwards, one ear listening for tidings of Pembroke and the English.

The royal company had left Aberdeen for Inverness, and were in fact at the Mar castle of Kildrummy when the vital word reached them. Pembroke had moved—and in no uncertain fashion. Presumably perceiving that every day's delay was likely to strengthen Bruce's hand, he had left his main body of foot at Carlisle, to await the arrival of the Prince of Wales, who had now reached Lancaster with another large army, and had spurred onwards with some three thousand picked horse. Refusing to be distracted either right or left after crossing the Border, he was driving due north at an impressive pace, avoiding all entanglements and leaving any opposition to be looked after by the slower-moving main body. Fairly clearly Edward's particular orders were to close with Bruce at all costs and bring him to immediate battle.

His general orders to all ranks were, however, to slay, burn and raise dragon—that is, to show the dreaded dragon banner which proclaimed that no mercy was to be granted.

In the Council that followed the King was offered varied advice, but most urged that he withdrew promptly into the deeper fastnesses of the Highlands, where the English could not follow, leaving Pembroke to his own devices, and living to fight another day when he had suitable forces assembled. Bruce himself was the principal objector to this superficially wise and reasonable course. It was not that he was rash, unthinking or over-sanguine. But he was the new-crowned monarch, he pointed out. To start his reign by disappearing into the safety of the trackless mountains, abandoning his people to the unchecked fury of the baulked invaders, was not to be considered. If he was to maintain any credit with his subjects, he must challenge Pembroke somehow, and be seen to do so. He might fail the first test, but he must not seem to shirk it.

Somewhat reluctantly those of most experience conceded that.

Bruce's reasoning and judgement might be sound, but how to implement it was another matter. There was not more than 600 fighting-men with the King at this juncture, and though many more could be raised, from comparatively near at hand, within a day or so, and thousands in a week or two, Pembroke's swift advance denied them the time they required.

Lamberton, whom Bruce had appointed Chancellor meantime, seizing on this need for time, declared that they must use cunning. Valour for all to see was all very well for the monarch, but his ministers could afford to be more devious. He proposed that while the King was ready to meet Pembroke in the field, he himself should hasten south and seek a parley with the English civil authorities, make moves towards entering into negotiations. As Chancellor. This might blunt the edge of Pembroke's drive and effect a delay—especially as it was requested that such negotiations should await King Edward's own arrival. Doubt and delay —those could be valuable weapons in the circumstances, and every weapon must be used.

Bruce demurred. Hints at such early surrender, even though they had no base in fact, were repugnant. Also it would put Lamberton himself in a position of extreme danger, when the deceit was discovered—as in due course it must be. If the Chancellor was available for negotiations, he would equally be available for capture.

The other shook his head. It was a risk that fell to be taken. They all were adventuring all. Danger was their lot, every one, from henceforth until the kingdom was won and secure.

So it was accepted, and thereafter the royal party turned its face south again, the King calling on all leal men to rally to his standard. But Lamberton hastened ahead, making for Edinburgh where the English civil administration had its base. None doubted that he was putting his head into the lion's mouth.

By mid-June Bruce was at the Abbey of Coupar, at the west end of Strathmore, with 4,000 men, a quarter of them cavalry, when he learned that Pembroke was at Stirling and had halted. Whether this was on account of Lamberton's gesture at opening negotiations, they could not tell. But it gave the King a little more time to wait for his hoped-for reinforcements.

Only a few had come in, a day or two later, when the next courier arrived from the south. Pembroke had not been wasting his time. He had been sending out detachments to take loyalist castles, and amongst others had captured old Bishop Wishart at Cuper Castle in Fife. Worse, the Earl of Buchan had come north from England, and had called to arms the whole force of Comyn against Bruce. Now he was marching to join Pembroke, who was on his way to Perth.

Grimly Bruce abandoned his waiting game. Time, it seemed, was no longer in his favour. He gave the word to break camp and march. Elizabeth and the ladies he left behind in the care of his brother Nigel.

On the 18th of June the King of Scots approached the walled city of Perth, so close to Scone where three months earlier he had been enthroned. In the city, Aymer de Valence, Earl of Pembroke, lay, with reputedly 6,000 chivalry, 1,500 more than Bruce's total force, and with Sir Henry Percy and Sir Robert Clifford as lieutenants. Taking up a position with the wide Tay on his left hand and the marshes of the incoming Almond on his right, the King sent forward a colourful party of heralds and trumpeters, under the King of Arms, to declare that the King of Scots wished to know the business of the Earl of Pembroke in his city of Perth. Let him come forth and give an account of himself.

De Valence announced in reply that he could not have dealings with traitors to his King Edward. And he was very comfortable where he was.

Bruce had to weigh the pros and cons of this. Pembroke was a proved and veteran fighter and no craven; moreover he had the larger force. And it was against his honour and reputation to hold back thus in the face of the enemy. He must have good reason for waiting, therefore. Was he expecting reinforcements? Or was this the result of Lamberton's activities? Had he been ordered to hold his hand while the Primate's peace feelers were investigated?

Would delay benefit Bruce more than the invaders? The Prince of Wales was held up in Galloway, fulfilling his father's injunctions anent savagery. Edward himself, by his physicians' orders, was having to travel very slowly, and was said to be no further north than York. Bruce himself was hoping for adherents from all over his kingdom. He would wait, therefore—and seek to cut off the English supply routes into Perth. The word of their new King already besieging the English invaders ought to be a fillip to the morale of the Scots people.

But before adopting such programme, Bruce sent a further and more explicit challenge to de Valence, that all should be plainly established for the folk to see. He urged Pembroke, or Percy, or Clifford, to come out and put their differences to the test in knightly fashion, by single combat with himself, by chosen champions, by set battle, or in whatever fashion they would. To which Pembroke answered that he should be patient; the day was too far spent—but he might fight with him next day.

So Bruce, shrugging, sent out detachments to control all the roads leading to Perth, and foraging parties to collect supplies for his host—which had been on the march long enough to have a very depleted commissariat. And, as evening fell, moved his main force some three miles westwards, to set up camp on the long, low, tree-dotted ridge of Methven that flanked the River Almond to the south, a reasonably strong position, with the land falling away to north and south, yet with opportunity for retiral and escape, by wooded lands to the west, towards the Highland hills. They would see if Pembroke had intention, or stomach, for fight the next day—the Feast of St. Gervase.

There was some talk of the King spending the night in the small castle of Methven. But Bruce preferred to camp with his men. Besides, the laird, Sir Roger de Moubray, had been a Baliol supporter, and might well still be pro-Comyn.

It was the first night that Bruce had been parted from Elizabeth since the coronation. It was chilly, with intermittent showers, and he slept fully clad beneath his cloak, amongst a grove of hawthorns.

As well that he did. In the early hours of the morning he, and all others, were aroused by the urgent shouts of sentinels. The enemy was upon them, the cries rang out. To arms! To arms!

It is never actually dark in Scotland, of a June night, but the cloud and overcast greatly hindered vision, especially amongst the scattered woodlands of Methven ridge. Starting up and staring around, Bruce could make out nothing distinct or detailed, save only the sleepy confusion of his own men. Dragging on his jerkin of chain-mail, he shouted for Sir Neil Campbell, who was acting guard-commander. But of that stout fighter there was no sign. Young Sir James Douglas, who was never now far from the King, declared that men said that Campbell had ridden off eastwards just before the first shouted alarm had rung out.

Bruce ordered his trumpeters to sound the rally, as precaution.

Barely had the high neighing notes died away than they were answered, and from no great distance to the eastwards. A somewhat ragged and breathless rendering it was—but there was no doubting its tenor and significance. It was the advance, English version.

Shouting for his own mount, Bruce ordered to horse to be sounded. Even as he cried it, he heard, felt indeed beneath his feet, the thunder of drumming hooves, thousands of hooves.

There was no time for any thinking out of tactics. Commanding that three main groups be formed, under his brother Edward on the right, the Earl of Lennox on the left and himself in the centre, and indicating that they so face the foe, there was no opportunity for even this limited manoeuvre to be completed before the dark mass of charging cavalry loomed out of the shadowy gloom before them, seeming to spread right across the ridge in solid menace.

To stand and wait, stationary, for such a charge, was as good as to seek annihilation. Bruce was ordering the advance, when diagonally across their front a single rider spurred, from the north-east. It was Sir Neil Campbell of Lochawe, guard-commander.

"Sire!" he yelled, "they attack from the north. Two assaults. They circle to the north. Out of the valley. To take us in rear. A large force. Rode down my few guards. Shouting A Comyn! A Comyn!"

Cursing, the King directed Lennox and the left to swing off, to seek to deal with this threat, and waved on his main body.

It was hopeless of course. Taken by surprise, short in numbers —for the foragers were still absent, as were the detachments to close the Perth roads—scattered, bemused and lacking the impetus successfully to meet a massive charge, the royal force was beaten before ever it met the enemy. It was not so much a defeat as a rout. Valour, leadership, experience—these might affect the issue for individuals and small groups, but on the outcome of the day they were irrelevant. Pembroke and his disciplined English cohorts smashed through and overwhelmed the Scots in a single furious onslaught, hardly slackening the pace of their charge. In a few brief moments the King's force was reduced to no more than chaos, and a number of desperately struggling groups of individuals.

In the forefront, Bruce himself was unhorsed and thrown to the ground in the first headlong clash. Only James Douglas, first, and then Sir Gilbert Hay, leaping down and flailing their swords above the fallen monarch, saved him from being trampled to death. Others sought to make a ring round them, with Alexander Scrymgeour and the royal standard proclaiming the King's position.

It proclaimed it to the English likewise, of course, and swiftly the greater pressure was swung on Bruce. In the mêlée of a cavalry fight no great degree of coherence is possible; but Pembroke was an experienced commander and was swift in seeking to control his force. He was already swinging round his flanks, right and left, to ensure that the Scots had no opportunity to rally and reform.

A riderless horse was found for the staggering Bruce—there were all too many of them to choose from—and he was aided into the saddle. Seton spurred close.

"We must cut our way out, Sire," he cried. "Onwards. East. Quickly. Behind them."

The King peered around him, dazedly. "The others . . .?"

"Not possible. All is lost here. Cut up. No rallying . . ."

"He is right, Sire," Hay agreed, "All we can save is you! And must!"

"Edward . . .? Over on the right . . .?"

"God knows!"

"That way, then . . ."

In a tight phalanx the little group drew even closer around the King and drove forward, others joining themselves to it. But quickly the opposition solidified. A large body of knights materialised against them, and with shouts that here was the Bruce, made furious onslaught.

The King, recovering from his shake, dealt effectively enough with the first assailant to reach him. Swerving in the saddle to avoid a jabbing sword-point at the throat, like a lance-thrust, and standing in his stirrups he thereafter swung round his own great two-handed blade in a sideways swipe that struck the knight on the back of his neck and pitched him forward over his mount's head helmet spinning. But there were another two attackers immediately at his back, and the King was their chosen target. Part unbalanced by his own slashing stroke he was the more vulnerable to the double assault.

The man on the right wielded a windmilling sword, but he on the left bore an upraised mace. In the instant of decision Bruce chose the latter—for though the sword was menace enough, one blow from a heavy mace could end all there and then. Ducking low, he dragged his horse round, to drive it straight at the mace-wielder, and thrust up his lion-painted shield to take the smashing blow. It beat down and numbed his left arm, all but jerking it out of its socket. But the attacker was left, for the moment thereafter, almost defenceless. Hay was on the King's left side, and having disarmed his previous assailant, now swung on the maceman, and felled him with a single blow.

But Bruce paid the price of his swift decision. He flung himself round to face the swordsman on his right too late by seconds. The great blade struck him a downward hacking buffet on the shoulder and, sideways in the saddle as he was, toppled him headlong. The chain-mail turned the edge of it, but the pain was stouning. He crashed to the ground, only part-conscious.

Once again the ring formed around the fallen monarch, and men died there to save him. Eager hands raised him, while steel clashed on every side.

"God's curse on him—the dastard traitor!" Hay gasped. "Did you see who struck him down? Moubray! Philip Moubray."

"What? Roger of Methven's son?"

"Aye. The felon! He has brought them down on us . . ."

"Quick—hold him up. He swoons again. His horse . . ."

Somehow they got Bruce hoisted into the saddle again, where he slumped, swaying. But before Hay and Douglas could themselves remount, the Scots ring was broken by a new assault, again aimed determinedly at the King. Bruce, his sword lost, his head swimming, was in no state to defend himself. His previous assailant, young Sir Philip Moubray, led again. He drove right up alongside the reeling monarch, and seeing him disarmed, grabbed his shoulder.

"I have him!" he yelled. "I have the Bruce! Yield, Earl of Carrick!"

That cry of triumph and the fierce pain of the damaged shoulder, convulsed Bruce. Cringing, and seeking to strike out blindly at the same time, he jerked round—and the movement and agony was too much for his precarious equilibrium. He overbalanced quite, and fell to the ground for the third time that grim midsummer morning.

Almost crazed that he might lose a prize which King Edward would reward surely with an earldom at least, Moubray leapt down to straddle his fallen victim, shouting to his colleagues to close in around him. But before they could do so, Sir Christopher Seton, with a roar of fury, thrust in, completely overturning one horse and rider in the excess of his rage, and, reaching Moubray first, towering above him, felled him with a mighty blow.

Then the big Yorkshireman performed a feat which was to be forever afterwards remembered of him. Leaping down and tossing away his sword, he picked up his half-stunned brother-in-law almost as though he had been a child, and lifted him high on to his own horse in an access of next to superhuman strength. Then, as the others spurred to protect him, he clambered up behind the King.

Without any more delay, searching for Edward Bruce or anyone else, the tight knot of the King's closest friends set about the business of beating their way, swords flailing right and left rhythmically, monotonously, out of that shambles, eastwards. In the face of their savagely dedicated determination few remained long in their path.

So, ingloriously, the new King of Scots left his first battlefield, only semi-conscious.

His escort won through the rear of the English array, and swinging away southwards in a wide arc through the marshlands of Methven Moss, were able to turn back westwards. The Highland hills, a black barrier ahead, beckoned like a blessed haven in a storm.

CHAPTER TWENTY-THREE

THE larks trilled joyously high in the blue, the cuckoos called hauntingly from the lower birch-woods, and the myriad bees hummed lazy contentment from the rich purple carpet of the bell heather and the blazing gold of the whins which crackled in the early July sunshine; while the tumbling, spouting, peat-stained Dochart shouted its laughter up from its rocky bed, all in praise of as fine a noontide as that lovely land of the mountains could proffer. But the man who sat alone on the heathery knoll, chin cupped in hand, elbow on knee, and stared eastwards towards Ben Lawers and Loch Tay, heard and saw and felt none of it. His brow was dark, his jaw set, his thoughts bitter. And it was not the pain of a broken shoulder that troubled him; he scarcely felt that in his present state.

He sat alone only because he would have it so; for down in the camp by the riverside there were friends enough who felt for him, who often gazed up towards him, most of whom indeed had already shed blood for him. But the King, in his deep hurt, wanted none of them. He was sick, sick not so much of pain and the body but of the heart, the mind, the spirit; and was by no means to be comforted.

None denied that he had cause for bitterness, for hurt; but few accepted his self-censure, his burning sense of personal blame—which can be the sorest burden a man can carry.

Robert Bruce was not unduly introspective, self-centred or guilt-conscious as a rule. As a youth and younger man he had not been noted for a sense of responsibility indeed. But he had undoubtedly changed, of late. His brothers, and those closest to him, averred that the change dated substantially from the murder of Comyn. Guilt was now seldom far from his mind. And the fact that the Pope had indeed now pronounced the dread sentence of excommunication upon him, however much it might be politic to make light of it, was like a leaden weight on his soul. He felt that the hand of God was against him—and deservedly so. Moreover, equally daunting was his awareness that so many others must pay the price for his fault.

This last assumption was hard to gainsay, at least. It was two weeks since Methven, two weeks of flight, of skulking and hiding in the mountains of Strathyre and Breadalbane, while survivors, refugees and broken men joined him, singly and in little parties, bringing with them the grim details necessary to build up a true picture of what that shameful debacle had cost. A glance at the camp below, by the Dochart, revealed the broad outline. Barely 500 men were there—all that was left of the King's army. His brother Edward was there; and Christopher Seton. But Thomas Randolph, his nephew, was captured. The tight group which had carried him off the field—and whom he now blamed for that very thing—James Douglas, Gilbert Hay, Robert Boyd and Robert Fleming, were present, though nearly all wounded to a greater or lesser degree. Also the Earl of Atholl, the Bishop of Moray and Sir Neil Campbell. But that was all.

The long list of the dead was like a knell tolling in the King's mind; for the vast majority of those surprised at Methven were now dead. Fortunate indeed were those who had fallen cleanly in the heat of battle for, true to his master's orders, Pembroke had carried the dragon flag, and the wounded and captured had been slain out of hand. Only a few of the highest ranks had been taken prisoner. And these, with the exception of Thomas Randolph— saved not out of mercy, but that he might be used against his uncle—had all been summarily hanged, drawn and quartered; Sir Alexander Fraser, Sir Simon's brother; Sir Hugh Hay, brother to Gilbert of Erroll; Sir John Somerville, Lord of Carnwath; Sir David Barclay of Cairns; Sir David de Inchmartin; and Alexander Scrymgeour, the Standard-Bearer, dying the same death as his master Wallace. All had paid the price for supporting Bruce. The Earl of Lennox was wounded and missing, the Earl of Mentieth captured and none knew whether alive or dead. Even the Earl of Strathearn, forced almost at the sword-point to the coronation at Scone, and not present at Methven, was taken and sent south in chains.

Nor was that all. Lamberton himself, the King had just heard, had been apprehended at his cathedral of St. Andrews, and with Bishop Wishart, in irons both, sent with every indignity to London.

As for the people, the common people, *his* subjects, they died in their thousands, in a reign of terror that was going to leave little for Edward himself to do when eventually he reached unhappy Scotland.

So Robert Bruce sat and called himself accursed, a man who brought death, destruction and horror upon all. He was not far from breaking-point.

It was almost with dread, then, that he presently glimpsed the flash of sunlight on steel, and the colours of banners and gaily-canopied litters, approaching from the direction of Killin and Loch Tay—which he had come up here to look for. He had sent a message to Blair-in-Atholl, where Nigel had been guarding the Queen's party, to join them here, a two-days' march westwards. Now he wondered how he could face Elizabeth.

That he did not go down to meet her was the measure of his depression and despair.

Eventually Nigel brought her up the hillock, but at a sign from her, left Elizabeth some little way from his brother's position. The Queen came on alone.

"Robert!" she said, going to him, hands out. "At last. Together again. I have prayed for this. How I have prayed!"

"Prayed? For *this*?"

Three words could scarcely have been more eloquent. Closely, concernedly, she eyed him, reaching to take one of his hands. Her splendid fairness was heart-breaking, this fine noonday. He looked steadily away from her.

"Prayed, my dear. That I might at least see you again. See you, touch you, hold you—and alive! Was it so ill a prayer? At least it has been granted."

He did not answer.

"But you are hurt. Your shoulder . . ."

"*I* am hurt? Who talks such folly, when all is lost and better men die by the hundred, the thousand!"

"Such better men are not my husband," she answered simply. "Let me see it. Your shoulder, Robert."

"Leave it," he jerked. "It is less than nothing."

"My dear," she said quietly, sitting down beside him. "Tell me."

"Tell! What is there to tell? Save evil. God's hand turned against a lost and condemned sinner. Punishment. Retribution. Poured out. Not on the sinner, but on those who aided and supported him. His friends. Hugh Hay. Alexander Fraser. Somerville. Barclay. Inchmartin. Scrymgeour. And others by the score. Dead—all dead. Tortured and shamefully slain. Thomas Randolph a prisoner. Lamberton in chains. And Wishart . . ."

It all poured out, the pent-up pain and remorse and sorrow, in a searing, passionate flood, all the disappointment, the frustration, the disillusionment, the desperation.

She listened quietly, with no word spoken.

At length the spate wore itself out. Elizabeth touched his sweating brow.

"It is grievous, my heart. All grievous. I am sorry," she said. "But why torture yourself with it? The fault is not yours."

"Not mine? Then whose is it, before God?" he demanded. "Did other than I slay Comyn? Did other than I declare himself King? All stems from that."

"Comyn deserved to die. More, he *had* to die. Had you not slain him, another must. And this your kingdom requires a king."

"Not a king who leads to disaster."

"Any king can lose a battle."

"It was not a battle. It was a massacre. We were taken unawares. Asleep. Because of my fault. I had challenged Pembroke to fight, that afternoon. Twice. He refused, and said that he might fight the next day. Like a fool, I took him at his word. It did not cross my mind that he would steal out on me by night, six miles, to Methven. Betrayed by Philip Moubray. We were taken by surprise. But the fault was mine."

"In any fight, Robert, *one* must lose . . ."

"But I—I was carried off the field. To safety. While others, thousands, fell. Or, lacking leader, yielded. And were then slaughtered like dumb cattle!"

"That shame was not yours, but Edward's. And it was right that you should be saved. Necessary. You are the King. The King lost, and all is lost."

"Scotland, I swear, were better without this King! For he is lost, even so. Lost and damned!"

"No! No, I say!" Suddenly Elizabeth de Burgh changed. She sat up straight, her eyes blazing, and turning to him gripped his undamaged arm—but not tenderly. "You speak like a child. A child sorrowing for itself! This is not the Robert Bruce I wed. I married a man—not a brooding, puling bairn!"

He recoiled from her, almost as though she had struck him. "Woman—you do not know what you say . . .!"

"I know full well. Hear *me* speak—since you, Robert speak folly! I would liefer have the man for husband who slew Comyn and defied all Edward's fury, than . . . than this weakling!"

He groaned. "You say this? You, also? God pity me . . .!" That was a whisper.

"Aye, God pity you, Robert Bruce! And me, wed to you! And this land, with a faint-heart for King! A broken sceptre, indeed!"

He stiffened. "You are finished?" he asked.

"No, I am not. You *took* that sceptre. None thrust it upon you. You *are* the King, now. Crowned and anointed. There is no undoing it, no turning back. So—if you are the King, for God's good sake *be* the King! A weak king is the greatest curse upon a nation."

He stared at her, biting his lip.

"What was it that we did at Scone?" she demanded, her beauty only heightened by her passion. "Was it only a show? Play-acting? Or was it the truth? God's work? Did Abbot Henry save the Stone for nothing? That oil on your brow—what was it? A priest's mummery? Or the blessed anointing of God's Holy Spirit upon you? *You*, only. Which? For if it was truth, then it gave you authority. Above all men. Whatever you have done, you are now God's Anointed. Take that authority. Use it. Wield your sword of state. You have many loyal men still. A whole people still looks to you, in hope. Fight on. Avenge Methven. Be Robert the King!" Abruptly her voice broke, and her fiercely upright carriage seemed to crumble. "Oh, Robert, Robert—be Elizabeth de Burgh's man!"

Slowly he rose to his feet, looking from her down to the camp, and then away and away.

"Say that you will do it, my dear," she pleaded now.

"For you . . . I think . . . I would do anything. Anything!"

"Thank God! Do it for me, then. If for naught else . . ."

There was an interruption. A strange-looking figure was climbing the knowe towards them, one or two of the King's people trailing rather doubtfully behind. The man was elderly, enormous but frail and stooping, bearded to the waist, and clad apparently and wholly in a great tartan plaid, stained and torn, draped about his person in voluminous folds and peculiar fashion, and belted, oddly, with a girdle of pure gold links, in a Celtic design of entwined snakes. He was aiding himself up the hill with a long staff having a hook-shaped head, like a shepherd's crook.

Nigel Bruce had waited, some way back from the royal couple. Now he stepped forward to halt this apparition. But the old man waved him aside peremptorily—and when this had no effect, raised his staff on high and shook it threateningly, screeching a flood of Gaelic invective of such vehemence and power as to give even Nigel pause in some alarm.

The ancient gold-girdled ragbag came trudging on, right up to the monarch. He said something less fierce, in the Gaelic.

Bruce, whose mother had been a Celtic countess in her own right, knew something of the ancient tongue; but not sufficient to understand this swift flow, liquid and hurrying as a Highland river, and strangely musical to be coming from so uncouth a character.

· "I am sorry, friend," he said, when there was a pause. "I do not know what you say."

The other looked him up and down disapprovingly, then shrugged the bent tartan-draped shoulders. "You are Robert son of Mariot, daughter of Niall, son of Duncan, son of Gilbert, son of Fergus, son of Fergus?" he demanded, and added, "*Ard Righ*," almost grudgingly.

Bruce at least knew those last two words, which meant High King. He nodded. "I am he."

"And I—I am the Dewar of the Coigreach," the other said dramatically and waved his staff.

Bruce dredged in his bemused mind for what this might signify. And then recollected. The *Coigreach*, of course. It was the lengendary pastoral staff of Saint Fillan, one of the most celebrated of all the ancient Celtic saints, a prince of the royal Dalriadic house, out of which the united kingdom of the Picts and Scots had come, and Abbot of the long defunct Culdee Abbey of Glendochart—and a leper, it was said. A precious relic since the eighth century, this crozier was handed down in a long line of hereditary custodians, known as Dewars or Diors, who were venerated all over the Celtic Highlands and islands as holy men.

"I greet you, Dewar of the Coigreach," he acknowledged. "How can I serve you?"

The other snorted. "*I* came to serve you!" he corrected. "I have come to bless you. Who is this woman?"

"She is the Queen. My wife."

The Dewar sniffed, and shrugged. But he raised the crozier, with its curious, elaborately-wrought bronze head, and extending it over the royal couple, launched into a stream, a flood, of Gaelic. When he at length lowered the staff, he added factually, "You are now blessed with the Blessing of Saint Fillan."

"I thank you," Bruce said, level-voiced. "But I would remind you that I have been excommunicated by the Pope. His Holiness of Rome."

"The Pope? Who is the Pope?" the Dewar asked haughtily. "And where is Rome? It is not in Ireland, the Cradle of the Church. Do you question the authority of Saint Fillan?"

"No." Bruce swallowed. "No, I do not."

"As well." The ancient scratched amongst his rags, eyed Elizabeth balefully, and then, without any leave-taking, even so much as a nod, turned and went stumping off down the hill, as independent as he had come.

Bruce, from looking after him, stared at his wife.

Elizabeth's eyes were shining. "Robert! Robert!" she cried. "It is a miracle! God be praised! See you, the Old Church has come to the rescue of its prince. The Romish Church may excommunicate you—but this is a Church older than Rome. And it blesses you! Takes you for its own." Her laughter was high-pitched, tinged almost with hysteria, but with its own joy. "Here is a lesson, as well as a blessing. For the King. To remember whence he came. It was a Celtic kingdom, not a Norman one. And you are half a Celt. I am less so—but I have some Celtic blood. And, and I do come from Ireland! The Cradle of the Church, no less! It is a sign, my dear. Come most timely."

"A sign, yes." He nodded, a new light in his eye. "I believe that it is. A sign. Perhaps I have been *led* to Saint Fillan's land. To this Glen Dochart where his abbey was. He was, you might say, a forebear. In some degree. Since King Malcolm Canmore, my ancestor, was of his line." He raised one shoulder. "And Malcolm's Romish wife, Margaret, it was who brought down the Celtic Church! An old story. Another Queen stronger than her husband . . . !" He looked at her.

"I am not that." Elizabeth shook her head. "In much I am weak, foolish. But in my love for you, Robert, I am strong. Strong with *your* strength. It was your strength that first drew me to you. You are strong still—only weary. In pain. Mourning your friends. And alone. As only a king may be alone. But now I am with you again. To restore part of your strength. That I had borrowed—in exchange for my heart!"

He drew her to him, there on the hillock in sight of all. "Quiet, you," he said gently. "You have said enough. Done enough. Done it all. I will be strong, yes. Strong, now. Until one day I give you a whole realm to cherish. Instead of one stumbling man, Elizabeth de Burgh."

"To that I will hold you, Robert Bruce," she agreed, glad-eyed. "I . . . and Saint Fillan!"

Hand in hand they turned, to face downhill.

AUTHOR'S NOTE

ROBERT BRUCE, after the Battle of Methven in 1306, was at the parting of the ways indeed. He had made his desperate throw, and lost. He had put his extravagant, almost irresponsible youth behind him; become involved, less than willingly, in the national cause; suffered the devilish ire of King Edward, and the almost insupportable spleen of John Comyn; accepted humiliation on humiliation; forfeited a great inheritance; committed an unpardonable sin; grasped at an empty throne.

Now he was a king without a kingdom, an army, even a court. He had in fact nothing left, save a wife, a daughter and a tiny band of faithful friends—but these were only further hostages to a fortune that had forsaken him. He had but these, and the character which, from the hammering and forging of these ten grim years, was now almost incandescent, molten, ready either to liquefy into complete collapse or to firm and harden into adamantine, unshakeable strength.

The second book of this trilogy, *The Path of the Hero King*, will portray something of the stature and quality of the very human mortal whose name, for almost seven centuries, has spelt courage, constancy and indomitable determination, wherever the spirit of man is acclaimed.

N.T.